Malice

By

Kerry Barnes

Copyright

Malice by Kerry Barnes

This is a work of fiction. Names, characters, places, and incidents either are the product of the author's imagination or are used fictitiously. Any resemblance to actual persons, living or dead, events, or locales is entirely coincidental.

ISBN 978-1-7393019-1-0

Copyright © 2023 Kerry Barnes

Malice by Kerry Barnes

All rights reserved. No part of this book may be reproduced or used in any manner without written permission of the copyright owner except for the use of quotations in a book review.

Once Upon A Book

Note - This book is written in British English.

Dedication

I dedicate this book to Christine Wood – a very kind, patient, and understanding lady, who has put up with me for years now. Thank you so much. X

Acknowledgements

Once again, I must acknowledge my editor Robert Wood for all his hard work and dedication. I probably don't tell him enough how much I appreciate his loyalty and devotion, and without him, I wouldn't be able to have a polished version of my work. This is now book twenty and he is still with me, encouraging me and teaching me. So I haven't managed to scare him off – yet.

Deryl Easton and the NotRights Book Club for their endless support.

To all the readers for their kindness and for spreading the word – forever grateful.

PROLOGUE

Feeling part of a gang at only fourteen, Joseph eagerly took the pill from Bacca Lardon, who he assumed was probably the eldest member of the crew. They had all kept their names a secret, and he was sure that Bacca was a nickname. They'd even chosen one for him to make him feel part of it – Curly, on account that he had curly hair.

He had only been hanging around with the gang for a few days before the leader, Bacca Lardon, invited him to share a few joints. Feeling grown up, he'd accepted the offer. After taking a deep drag, as he had seen the others do, he coughed up his lungs, dry-heaved, and then laughed to save face. Within minutes, he realised he was experiencing a dreamy feeling that instantly washed his worries away.

***

For a few weeks now, he had met up looking forward to a puff, but tonight was a big deal for him. It was his 'initiation' into becoming a fully-fledged member of the 'get high gang'. He wanted to belong to something bigger than himself. His life was simple and boring, and the popular kids at school picked on him for being the geek. Worse, he didn't even have flash designer clothes or trainers, like the other lads, which made him an even bigger target for the butt of their jokes.

He often wished he had older brothers to lean on. But bumping into this gang who, when he first met them, he assumed would pick on him – even though they didn't – was a blessing.

They brought him into their fold. Of course, he couldn't tell them that he lived at home with his mum and grandfather. So he came up with his own story. He was homeless, his own person, no family, no one.

He hoped this gang could be the next best thing to having big brothers because, clearly, he was the youngest. As far as he could tell, they were hard, yet cool, with their labelled tracksuits and expensive trainers, which he begged his mum to buy for him.

***

As soon as the drug took effect, Joseph spoke a million miles an hour, gaining in confidence to be heard.

'Bacco, I fancy a pair of trainers like yours. How can I get a pair?'

Bacco tapped the side of his nose. 'Listen, Curly, my little pal, you do well tonight, and I'll make sure you have a pair of trainers. What size are you? Thirty-six, thirty-seven?'

Joseph nodded. 'Yeah, thirty-six. How did you guess?'

''Cos you're so small, mate. Anyway, let's get you initiated, but I warn you, you have to have a blindfold on. The place we are going to is for us members only, so it's a secret.'

Joseph was hopping about in excitement.

'Here, Curly, how about another tablet to boost your mood?'

Joseph nodded and opened his mouth, sticking out his tongue. Not clocking that the second pill was a different colour, naïvely, he trusted Bacca.

A car pulled over and the back door opened.

'Is this for us?' asked Joseph, admiring the flash-looking car with the blacked-out windows.

Bacca tapped Joseph's shoulder. 'That, my friend, is your carriage. Now, first things first. As I said, you need to put on this blindfold.'

Joseph looked nervously at Bacca, whose smile caused creases in his cheeks. 'Are you coming?'

Bacca pulled a blindfold from his back pocket and placed it over Joseph's eyes. 'Yeah, yeah, mate. See you there.'

As soon as the blindfold was over his eyes, he heard another voice, a deep manly voice, say 'Your sister will have a package waiting for you. Good lad. Well done.'

Joseph felt Bacca guiding him into the back of the car, and before he knew it, the car pulled away.

As much as the first tablet gave Joseph a real rush and a feeling of euphoria, he was now feeling strange – very woozy and dreamy. He tried to pull the blindfold away from his face, but his hands were heavy, and someone beside him was stopping him from doing so. When he tried to speak, no words came out; even his tongue felt as though it was choking him. His whole body suddenly became a dead weight. His muscles were like mush, and even though he was struck by terror, he couldn't scream.

He knew he was being dragged out of the car and inside a building, but everything appeared in slow motion, and voices seemed distant and echoing. He had no idea who, but someone forced his hands behind his back. And then the voices became somewhat more real, but they weren't the voices of teenagers; these were older men who cackled and snorted like grunting pigs.

While pulling him around, the blindfold came off long enough for him to get a glimpse at the man who dominated the room. He had a very distinctive voice and it appeared he was in charge.

Moments later, someone shoved a mask over his mouth and nose and administered gas. Before he even resisted and put up a fight, he was unconscious.

When he came to, Joseph found himself on a chair and his blindfold was off. The men were still in the room. They were standing by a small bar area laughing and talking, while he was smarting in excruciating pain.

His hands had been tied behind his back, which made him panic. Were they going to kill him? What would they do next? Everything seemed surreal; he wasn't in an old derelict building but in an exquisite drawing room with heavy drapes, huge gilt-edged mirrors, and dark oak furnishings. This was a grand house, and the way the men spoke in such a lardy-dardy way, he guessed they were men of power. They could have been judges or lords, for all he knew.

The smell of cigar smoke and whisky on the breath of those immediately around him permeated the room, and he held back his feeling of nausea, knowing that eventually he would end up vomiting.

However, the men weren't looking at him. They were talking among themselves with slurred speech and in a drunken sway.

Joseph slowly moved his feet, ensuring he could feel his legs, and then he felt how tight the rope binding his hands was. A small sense of elation that the rope was not tight enough to hold him there gave him some hope he might be able to escape.

He closed his eyes, in case any of the men noticed he was conscious. But before he did, he clocked a window, partially opened to the side of him. He figured he could escape through the window, his advantage being that he was small enough. And he also thought that if he could get away, he doubted whether these men with their beer bellies would be able to catch him.

As soon as he got his hands free, he opened his eyes, leaped up from the chair, and dived headfirst out of the window onto the grass below. Once he had himself back on his feet, he then ran for his life.

Tears streamed down his face as he hurtled through the streets, running through gardens and over fences, until he finally recognised where he was and paused in the safety of the shadows. With his hands on his knees, he gasped for breath; the fear of being captured had knocked the air clean out of him. Sweat soaked every inch of his skin, and the vomit he'd held back finally shot out of his mouth and coated his feet. Only then did he realise his trainers were back at the classy house with the stinking rapists.

Finally, he reached home. He wanted to tell his mother and grandfather, but how could he? He crept in the back door and snuck upstairs, ditching his tracksuit bottoms, which were covered in blood, and climbed into the soft flannelette pyjamas he wore when he felt poorly. Gripping his pillow, he silently sobbed, ashamed, frightened, and in absolute agony.

CHAPTER ONE

Detective Sergeant Rajesh Raj knew the instant he opened his mouth, he couldn't take back those words that tumbled out. Telling Georgie her husband had been murdered was bad enough, but why did he have to elaborate and say 'We believe it was a revenge killing'? He could feel all eyes on him and hear Detective Constable Petra Holland, his partner, breathing uneasily beside him.

Henry suddenly leaped up from his chair, almost spilling the contents of his tea, and helped Georgie to her seat before glaring at the detective.

'All right, mate, did you have to put it like that? Fuck me, you need to go back to school and learn to be a little more tactful.'

Banger Billy rushed from his chair and swiftly shut the café door before swivelling the sign around to 'closed'. Only then did he realise that there was a woman sitting in the corner nursing a cup of tea.

She had been there for an hour before he and Kirby had even arrived for their tea. In fact, she had been in the café on a few occasions lately, although she had merely blended into the coloured tiles on the back wall.

Kirby, who remained seated, was speechless as he stared in disbelief at the detective. He couldn't comprehend what Raj was saying because he'd only left Dixie a few hours ago to finish off a job.

'What do you mean *a revenge killing*? Are you sure it's my Dixie?' asked Georgie, her face as white as a sheet.

Raj looked at the three men. Henry, the café owner, Banger Billy, the owner of the scaffolding company, who himself had served time inside for armed robbery, and Kirby Fodder, who had evaded prison a few times because his enemies had been too scared to grass. But he respected the men. They were hard workers, and their past was their business.

Resting his eyes on Georgie, he couldn't imagine what the poor woman was going through.

As he understood it, Dixie Deacon had been declared dead over eighteen years ago as a result of a bomb explosion while he was on tour in Afghanistan. However, he hadn't died at all. He had been holding his fellow soldier's dog tag before the explosion occurred, leaving him with amnesia and burns covering a considerable portion of his body.

Raj remembered how surprised he felt when he met Dixie; considering what the man had been through, it was a miracle he was pretty well mentally together. And now Georgie was facing his death all over again. What were the odds of that happening to someone?

'It's a shock, Georgie, I know but . . .' He paused. 'You are a straight-talking woman, and I know you aren't up for me pussyfooting around.' He looked back at Henry, trying to instil a message that said he knew Georgie well enough.

'Who did it, Raj?'

Raj shook his head. 'We don't know, Georgie.'

'So how do you know it was a revenge killing?' snapped Kirby, who had now found his tongue and disliked anyone involved in the law except his solicitor. He liked him.

Holland stepped forward. Her hair was long and tied back in a plait. She wore a grey suit a size too big because she hadn't bothered to shop for new clothes since she had lost weight. She was now a perfect size ten. 'He was alone in the alley beside the village hall and the church.'

'Yeah, so! He was removing the scaffolding 'cos the church roof repairs are now complete, but that doesn't explain why you seem to think it was a revenge killing.'

Holland sighed heavily. 'He was shot dead.'

'No!' gasped Georgie. '*Shot?*'

'Hang on, how is that a revenge killing? It could have been a mistaken identity. I mean he ain't no fucking gang member. He's a scaffolder,' said Billy.

Raj stared at Georgie, biting his lip.

'Spit it out, Raj. What ain't you telling me?'

'Okay, your husband was shot at fairly close range, and the perpetrator carved a cross into his head.'

Georgie threw her hands over her eyes.

Henry sat beside her and rubbed her back. 'I'm so sorry, Georgie,' he whispered.

Suddenly, she jumped up and wiped her face. 'Oh my God, where's Dixie-Lee? If there is a nutter planning on taking revenge, he may hurt my daughter.' With trembling hands, she searched the apron pocket for her phone and dialled her daughter's number. 'Pick up, pick up!'

The phone rang for what seemed like ages until it went over to voicemail.

'Where is she supposed to be, Georgie?' Raj asked.

'At Bromley College.'

Raj immediately radioed through to have a police officer track her down and bring her to the café. By the look on Georgie's face, he knew she was like a volcano ready to erupt. She wasn't prepared to grieve, or maybe she had done that for so many years she didn't have enough grief left. However, that expression was like a riot going off in her eyes.

'Georgie, please don't take the matter into your own hands.' Raj paused and looked at the TV screen.

The newscaster read out highlights of the latest news. Lieutenant Marston-Smith's body was found today by a beachcomber. His head was barely attached to his body.

Raj pulled his attention away and back to Georgie. *Marston-Smith could wait*, he thought. He had more pressing issues to deal with. With Dixie Deacon being shot dead in the Bromley area, the press would have a field day; no doubt they would rake up the Marx murders all over again.

'We will find out who did this.'

'Oh yeah? What, like you found out who hurt my daughter?'

'I know we messed up, but she is safe and well, and—'

'Is she, Raj? How the fuck would you know, eh? My Dixie-Lee is still suffering. She may have her speech back, but she walks with a limp. Her doctor has put it down to trauma. And she has nightmares because the poor little thing had to murder someone to save her father, her grandmother, and herself. Major Ashby was prepared to torture and kill her, and none of you fucking believed me, so please, Raj, don't tell me you will find out who did this to my husband because I don't hold out much hope of that. Now, if you'll excuse me, I have a daughter to find.'

Raj stepped back, shocked that Georgie wasn't in floods of tears but instead hellbent on ensuring her daughter was okay. He shouldn't have been surprised because the few times he had spent with Georgie, it was evident she wasn't all about sentiment.

A lot of that had to do with the fact that she had spent eight torrid years in the Army. And at the end of that period, the regiment had had to do some soul-searching itself over alleged rape incidents by officers on female personnel and acts of revenge by one Georgie Deacon.

And then, when she returned to civilian life, Georgie had been accused herself of murdering two of the Marx family that led to a short spell on remand at HM Prison Bronzefield before she was released on account of inconclusive evidence against her.

Raj couldn't help but smile inwardly as he observed Georgie's demeanour. Every crisis in her personal life was like water off a duck's back to her. Hard as nails came to mind as well as being devious and extremely clever. He was the only one who knew that, though, as well as knowing her secrets.

At forty-three, Georgie's quick and precise movements were like those of a twenty-year-old. Raj secretly admired her because she was smart but also very attractive if she ever cracked a smile, which wasn't often. Her features were hard, yet her face was pretty – in a Julia Roberts kind of way.

When the door slammed shut behind her, all Raj could do was glance back at Henry, who glared at him. 'Don't you have a kid to find and a bit bleedin' well sharpish, if you ask me?'

Billy got up from his seat, placed his napkin on the table, and flicked his fingers at Kirby. 'Come on, mate. Let's find Dixie-Lee before Georgie turns The Crays up on their arse.'

'Oh, for fuck's sake.' Raj realised that if an officer wasn't guarding Georgie's daughter by the time Georgie reached the college, there would be hell to pay.

As soon as everyone had left, Henry clocked the only customer remaining in the café. A woman was sitting in the corner nursing a cup of tea. 'Sorry, love. I'm gonna have to shut up the café.'

'I heard what that detective said, so who d'ya reckon shot this geezer?'

Henry didn't know the woman. Although, it occurred to him now, she'd recently been coming in around teatime, the same time as Billy and his workmates. Henry didn't go a bundle on people using his café for refuge unless they were locals and they held a polite conversation with him. However, this woman was obviously an 'outsider'. And she had a sneer about her. Her smile stretched thin, her eyes were like ferrets, and she stank of piss and disappointment. *What a shame*, he thought, *for a woman, possibly in her late thirties, to be so clearly ravaged by drugs and spirits.* When he looked at her dirty fingernails and rotten teeth, he knew he would be throwing another perfectly good piece of cutlery into the bin. Retrieving the cup, he could smell the spirits she'd poured into it, but worse, he imagined the germs crawling all over it. He had a thing about cleanliness. Then his eyes rested on the side pocket of her overcoat and the bottle of whisky poking out of it.

'Listen, love, I don't appreciate people coming in here using my café as a place to drink their booze. There's a Wetherspoons up the road. Go there.'

'Fecking nice, I must say,' she replied, looking daggers at him.

Henry felt guilty. It was clear that the woman was down on her luck. Although her jeans and jumper looked clean and her coat was reasonably tidy looking, that was as far as it went. Her dark hair was greasy, and her face looked as though it had spent a few weeks dodging a bar of soap. Yet even though he could smell the alcohol, she didn't seem drunk. There was definitely something very odd about her, but he couldn't put his finger on what it was.

She rose from her chair and strolled towards the door before she glanced back at Henry and laughed like she had something over him. She didn't slam the door behind her as he would have expected. Instead, she gently closed it and stared through the window with a cocksure grin and a purposeful nod.

Henry locked the door and walked over to the till where he'd left his phone on charge. He checked to see if there were any missed calls, but there were none. He'd text Georgie in an hour, and, hopefully, she would have her Dixie-Lee home safe and sound. His mind returned to Dixie. He'd only known him for six months and he had been so shocked to discover that the homeless guy who had regularly dropped the money off in a brown envelope for Georgie as a tip was actually her husband. Life seemed to be full of surprises and not all good ones either. He shook his head. 'Poor Georgie,' he mumbled, under his breath.

As he looked up and out through the window, he saw the woman; she was now standing across the street. She was smoking but staring at him with a crooked grin this time. *What was going on?* he wondered.

Her presence distracted him from something far more sinister going on. Seconds later, though, he detected a telltale smell that was now becoming increasingly overpowering. He spun around to see where it was coming from, but it wasn't until he crept into the back area of the café, where he prepared and cooked the food and baked his bread and made his famous desserts, that the odour was more potent. A trickling sound coming from the back door jolted his senses. He saw the petrol. It was pouring in through a hose poked through the letterbox. And it was now soaking the floor. A rush of blood pounded in his head as panic rose to a pitch. He had to get out before the café went up in flames. But he momentarily froze. His body turned to ice when he heard a deep chuckle from the other side of the door.

Before he put one foot in front of the other, he heard the letterbox slam shut and the sound of a metal lighter hitting the floor. He knew that Clipper lighter sound. He owned one himself. Instantly, the room was engulfed in a bright orange light. Unforgiving flames tore up the walls, licking their way up to the ceiling. The whooshing sound came at him just like a fast train racing through a railway station. Seconds later, Henry felt the flames grab his clothes. He ran towards the front of the café where he threw himself onto the floor, now desperate to stop the terrible feeling of a million bee stings as the flames engulfed his shirt and glued it to his back. Rolling around, he frantically tried to extinguish the fire. But, suddenly, there was an almighty bang. The refrigerated cabinet flew across the room and smashed down on top of him. Then the window exploded, and a huge monstrous flame tore out of the back room, flicking its powerful tendrils, as if it was searching for the next flammable obstacle to grow its inferno.

Henry lay there unable to move. With his head turned to the side staring out of the window, he once again saw the strange woman. She was cruelly grinning at him before she walked away.

***

Georgie drove her bright-red Audi A1, a gift from her mother-in-law, well over the speed limit, frantic to find her daughter. She didn't have time to process the fact that her husband was now dead.

But as she sped along the streets, her brain began to work overtime. So many thoughts were tumbling around in her mind. She had tried to make a go of it with her husband. Really tried. And she had wanted the three of them to be a normal family, particularly for her daughter's sake. And that had been the case. At first. The affection and the sex were just like when they'd first ever dated. And the passion and the hunger for love had definitely been there. However, it had all been short-lived. In reality, how could everything ever be the same again? The conversation wasn't, that was for sure. She thought she could do the talking for both of them. Even smile twice as much. But she wasn't a natural smiler. It was always Dixie-Lee who brought a smile to them both. Seriousness had crept into Dixie's bones, and she could never work out if it was guilt, shame, or depression that was responsible. Nevertheless, it amounted to the same thing: For the past six months, she had been flogging a dead horse.

It had always only ever been her and her daughter. Having him sitting in her living room silently watching the TV and eating his dinner wasn't her idea of a good relationship. And when he wanted to go for a long walk, sometimes for hours, he would never ask her to go with him. He always said he needed to think, or he needed space, or he needed time alone. It always seemed to be what *he* needed. He didn't exactly ignore her, but his one-word answers were enough to cause a silence between them, and not a comfortable one either. It was as if he didn't want her to know him or anything about his past. Those years were kept a secret from her. She had thought that maybe one day he would tell her about them, but, in her heart, she had known he wouldn't. But, as if that wasn't bad enough, what really concerned her was why he was hiding his past? *Was there something dark lurking there?*

She had thought about Dixie's brother Rohan, and dare she admit it, she thought about him when she was making love with her husband.

A car in front paused at the junction of Crown Lane and Bromley Common. Georgie could see the entrance to Rookery Lane and the enormous imposing building of the new Bromley College, now called London South East Colleges. All she wanted to do was to get inside and find her child. She glanced at her phone in the footwell and while the driver in front idled their car, hesitant to pull out, she retrieved her phone and redialled her daughter's number, but there was no response. Nothing. Her throat felt tight, like someone was strangling her. 'Please be in a lesson.'

Finally, the driver pulled away, and Georgie followed, putting her foot down before she spun into Rookery Lane. The barriers to the college were down, and so knowing she would have to park in the lane, she glared frustratedly at the cars all parked like a caterpillar, bumper to bumper. In a blind panic, she drove her car onto the double yellow lines right beside the entrance. And the second she got out of her car, she could see a security guard waving his hands as he headed her way. She wasn't in the mood for an argument. She had to find Dixie-Lee. However, just as she was about to storm past him and march through the opened gates, her eyes widened, and she paused momentarily.

Just inside the entrance gates, partially hidden by a brick pillar, was someone she recognised. A flash of anger, mixed with a tremor of anxiety, filled her chest, causing her to take deep breaths. It was one of the remaining Marx brothers, the youngest one, the village idiot, except he didn't look so daft as before. His hair had grown; it was covering his ridiculous tattoo that stated his own name, RILEY.

As soon as he spotted her and their eyes met, he turned away, clearly hoping she hadn't recognised him. However, her eyesight was good, and so despite the fact he was wearing smart black trousers, black shoes, and a wool coat and showing off a new haircut, he wasn't able to mask his distinctive almond-shaped beady eyes that all the Marxes seemed to possess.

He was out of place. Why was he at this college? Georgie's thirst for answers overpowered her sense of reason, and in a split second, she was off, sprinting towards him. As he turned around, she was on to him. She grabbed the collar of his expensive-looking coat, pulling his face close to hers. 'What the fuck are you doing here?'

He grabbed her wrists. 'Get off me!'

She shook him. 'What are you doing here?' Her voice went up a notch, her eyes blazing.

'Nothing. I was going to my classes. Now, please, get off. You're hurting me.'

'Liar!' she screamed, as spittle left her mouth. 'Liar! Now, why are you here? If you so much as lay a finger on my girl, I'll fucking annihilate you.'

'Oi, madam, that's enough!' came the deep voice of a man from behind her. 'Leave him alone. You are parked on double yellow lines, and now I'm asking you to leave the premises before I call the police.'

Georgie let go of Riley. 'If anything has happened to my girl, believe me, I will fucking chop your head off.' As soon as those words left her mouth, she realised what she'd just said. *Had Riley worked out the significance of 'chop your head off'?* she wondered. But it appeared he hadn't. Riley was looking down, his face filled with sadness. She had half expected him to launch himself at her, or, at the very least, give her verbal abuse. After all, the family still believed she had killed Todd and Eve Marx.

'I said, that's enough, madam.'

Georgie spun around and sneered. 'Don't worry. The police, if they ain't already here, are on their way.'

Riley didn't hang around. She saw him running out of the gates and down Rookery Lane. *So he must have parked his car down there*, she thought, *or he would have turned right and onto Bromley Common to catch a bus, if, of course, he still lived in St Mary Cray.*

'Would you like to tell me exactly what is going on?' asked the six-foot gangly security guard, who was one tooth short of a perfect set.

'No, I'll leave that to the police. I need to find my daughter.'

As soon as she said those words, a police car drove through the gates and stopped in front of the barrier. The driver nodded to the guard to let them in. Without hesitation, the guard skipped over, waved his fob, and the barrier opened.

Georgie was fuming. She had arrived before the police, and right now, she had no interest in them or how they could help. Their way of handling a bad situation had left a nasty taste in her mouth. So she would have to deal with this herself.

CHAPTER TWO

Raj had the most disturbing call before he even reached Bromley College. It came through his radio stating that Henry's café had been set on fire, and the firefighters were at the scene trying to put out the blaze.

Raj had to make sure they found Dixie-Lee because he had no doubt in his mind that the Marx family were behind these attacks. Georgie's husband was murdered, and her place of work had suffered an arson attack. His mind was awash with dark thoughts. He wondered if the Marx family had planned to hurt Georgie by slowly destroying her life before they destroyed her. Maybe they wanted to exact revenge, but in a cruel, almost unthinkable way, by hurting the people she loved the most.

'Raj, are you okay?' Holland asked, noticing how his skin had turned a chalky-white colour.

'Fuck. Petra, there is no way that Georgie's husband's murder and Henry's café aren't connected.'

'Don't jump to conclusions. The fire could easily be an accident. It's a café with gas ovens for cooking. You know what I mean. I've set my own kitchen alight before now. It's easily done, Raj.'

Raj shook his head. 'I don't believe in coincidences. If I did, I probably wouldn't be a detective.'

'Ah, cheers for that, Raj. You've just made me feel like shit now.'

With one hand on the wheel, he slid the other across and patted her knee. 'Sorry, Petra. Look, you are a good detective. I'm not implying otherwise. But I feel very anxious regarding Georgie Deacon. There is so much more to her, probably a shedload of shit that we may not even get to know. And Henry's café on fire, I guarantee, is linked to Georgie, like the death of her husband probably is too.'

'Talking of which, I got a text, Raj, saying that they have already removed Dixie Deacon. He is being transported to the postmortem labs.'

'Shit, what a fucking mess. Hang on, that's a bit bloody quick. Did forensics even have a chance to do their job?' He sighed. 'I bet the Deacon brothers will be back.'

'Yeah, no doubt. Er . . . Raj, what do they actually do as a profession?'

Raj stopped at the junction of Bromley Common and Crown Lane and ran his hands through his thick black mop of hair. 'It's complicated, but they have a company where they undo wrongdoings for people at a price.'

'And that's legal, is it?'

Raj shrugged. 'I haven't delved into their affairs, and I'm not going to unless what they do interferes with what I do.'

'I wouldn't like to have a dispute with those brothers.'

'Big lumps aren't they, Petra, and yet they aren't thuggish. In fact, they come across as very intelligent and knowledgeable about the law and in general, so I guess whatever they do, they do it within certain boundaries of the law. However, someone has killed their little brother, so if they choose to stay above board, it's anyone's guess. But blood will be spilled if they find out who hurt Dixie. Let's pray whoever killed him isn't after Dixie-Lee. Not after everything the poor kid has been through.'

'Christ, no.'

'Thank goodness. Look, I can see a police car already here,' said Raj, as he pulled into the entrance to the college.

A security guard leaned into the window. 'You need a pass, mate, or you'll have to park elsewhere.'

Holland flashed her warrant card. 'Will this do?'

The guard waved his key fob and allowed the two detectives entry.

Raj parked directly next to the police car and got out, with Petra following suit. They headed towards the main entrance to the building. However, before going inside, Raj clocked Georgie rudely pointing in an officer's face.

He rushed through the doors to hear her saying, 'Don't fucking tell me I can't look for my daughter.'

'Please, Mrs Deacon, let us—'

The young PC didn't have a chance to finish. Raj jumped in. 'It's okay.' He held up his warrant card. 'I can deal with this.' He turned to Georgie. 'Is she here? What's going on?'

Georgie slapped her hands by her sides and said, 'They won't let me look around the college. Apparently, she is in a lecture, and so she isn't answering her phone, but I am frantic. And to make matters worse, this idiot jobsworth here doesn't want me searching for her myself.'

'Okay, okay. Right, where is her next lecture?'

'I don't know. They won't say. It's like I'm a fucking terrorist. I am her fucking mum, for Christ's sake.'

'I know, but listen, you wouldn't want the students in a college of this size not to be safeguarded, would you?'

Georgie nodded, but Raj noticed her hands were shaking. He turned to the woman at the desk. 'Right, you have a Tannoy, don't you?'

She nodded. 'But we don't like to use it because it interferes with the students—'

'Put a call out for Dixie-Lee Deacon, right away.'

'But, er . . .'

'Detective Raj, that's my name. Now, come on, chop chop. I haven't got all day.'

With her hair cut around her spiteful-looking face, the young woman curled her lip at Raj before making the announcement.

'There, now, that wasn't so bloody hard, was it?' he said, sarcastically, directing his look of exasperation at the young PC.

Georgie pulled her phone from the back pocket of her jeans and redialled her daughter's number.

This time, Dixie-Lee answered. 'What the hell is going on, Mum? I heard an announcement and realised that I had twenty missed calls. My phone is always on silent in a lecture.'

'Oh, thank God.'

'Mum, what's going on?'

'Just meet me at reception, will you.'

Georgie then realised that her fear of losing her daughter had totally consumed her, and now she would have to tell her that her father was dead. She hadn't mentally prepared herself for that conversation. She glanced at Raj.

Her eyes were so troubled, he knew she was about to crack.

'Let's take Dixie-Lee home, or at least away from here.'

Georgie nodded. 'I don't know how I'm going to tell her that her father is dead.'

Holland stepped forward. 'There isn't going to be an easy way to say it, but, I think, one step at a time. Let her absorb the words. I don't think she needs to know the full extent of the situation, though, the part about the revenge killing.' She shot a disapproving glance at Raj.

The double doors swung open, and Dixie-Lee stood there holding a bag and wearing a deep-green tracksuit, with her hair tied back away from her face.

Raj and Holland were both stunned to see how different she looked now that her face had healed. She was indeed a beautiful-looking girl.

'What has happened?' Her words were firm, but her eyes flicked from her mum to Raj and back again.

'Darling, can we get out of here? I need to tell you something.'

Dixie-Lee dropped her bag and threw her hands to her mouth, shaking her head. She didn't want to hear anything, yet she could sense something was gravely wrong.

Georgie quickly grabbed her daughter. She pulled her close and hugged her. 'Let's go home, and we can talk then.'

But Dixie-Lee pulled away. 'No, tell me now. Please, someone, tell me.'

Georgie pulled her daughter to her again. 'Please, we need to get out of here.'

Dixie-Lee glanced around, suddenly aware that all eyes were on her – a young PC, Raj, Holland, and the receptionist.

Silently, Georgie guided her daughter towards the car.

It was then that Raj noticed Dixie-Lee limping. It was true she hadn't fully recovered from her ordeal, and it was partly the police's fault. He wasn't surprised that Georgie had no respect for them, which was apparent in how she had just given the young PC hell.

Raj decided to follow Georgie home to make sure she and her daughter were safe. He was uneasy about their safety, especially since the latest news regarding the café. A family liaison officer would be assigned to Georgie, and, no doubt, before the day was over, they would be placed in a safe house.

As soon as Raj was inside the car, he called the police station on his mobile to get an update on the café fire. He had to know if anyone was killed because he knew Henry was there when he had left.

The chief superintendent took his call. He, too, had put two and two together and was convinced that the fire was connected to Dixie's murder. However, from what Fitzgerald was told, Henry was still alive and on his way to the hospital. A passer-by had heroically gone into the blazing café and lifted a large refrigerator off Henry, which was crushing him, and he was then able to pull Henry free. Henry, however, had sustained some injuries and was blue-lighted to the hospital.

Raj sighed. 'Well, Petra, at least I'm not going to have to tell Georgie that her boss, and I suspect her friend, is dead.' He sighed again. 'I dunno, I reckon we will have to pull in the Marxes, although, somehow, I can't see someone like Jasper or Riley taking revenge, and they're not known for running around with a shooter.'

'Do you think it's anything to do with this Ashby guy and Lieutenant Marston-Smith?'

After slowing down at the junction, Raj turned to face Holland. 'After we see Georgie, shall we go for a drink?'

Holland beamed because with every out-of-office date it was another step forward in their relationship. It had started with a little flirting and banter and then it had moved on to a few stolen nights here and there for a frolic between the bedsheets, but now, their conversation was becoming more meaningful. As partners, it wouldn't be ethical to date, but it worked for them, for whatever reason.

'Yeah, sure, I could do with a large prosecco or maybe a G & T.'

Raj nervously smiled because he wondered if he could trust her. She was sweet and eager, but she was a stickler for the rules, which on the one hand was a good thing, yet on the other, it could be a nightmare. Still, he was beginning to see the realities of life.

His mind switched to Petra again. He really liked her but could he trust her? If he divulged to his girlfriend any information about what he'd learned about Georgie, they could end up having a lovers' spat, and then she could easily go running to the governor and have his arse kicked out of the force. As it was, only he and Georgie knew the truth, and while that remained the case, no one could accuse him of hiding the facts.

By the time he reached Georgie's house, there were already two police cars, and, more surprisingly, his boss, Fitzgerald, who rarely ventured outside the office unless he needed to address the reporters.

He nodded at Raj and then flicked his head, as if to say, 'follow me'. Raj hurried over to him and past the officers who looked to be guarding Georgie's house.

'So what's going on, Gov?'

Fitzgerald, more affectionally known as Fitz, shook his head, a cloudy expression covering his face. 'I've been instructed from the big bosses to take on another team, but I have a strong feeling that personalities will clash.'

Raj nodded, unfazed, as he had too much on his mind.

'Gov, has there been any development concerning Dixie's murder? Any other evidence that may be linked to the Marx family? Because I assume they are the number-one suspects.'

'The cross carved in Dixie Deacon's head is the only link that I can see, but anyone with knowledge about the deaths of Todd and Eve Marx could have done that to pin it on that family. I had Matias Lamp check the press reports and he said that the details of the Marx murders including the crosses carved on Todd Marx's head were made public. If those details hadn't been put into the public domain, then we could take an educated guess that they were involved. But I am sorry. As it stands, the link is not substantial.'

Raj nodded. 'I understand, so, Gov, are we organising a safe house for Georgie and her daughter?'

Fitzgerald rolled his eyes. 'Well, I have assigned a new officer for the family. She's called Carol Lardon. She's from Tonbridge, part of the new team. Look, she's a cocky so-and-so, but I had little say in her recruitment. Anyway, the more help we have, I guess, the better.'

Raj glanced over at the dark-haired woman in her mid-thirties, who was a little on the chubby side and who probably wouldn't make an Olympic runner, but, as Fitzgerald had implied, the more help, the better.

'She can handle people. At least, I have been told she can. So I've assigned her as family liaison officer for Georgie.'

Raj wanted to laugh. He could imagine the response. 'And I guess that didn't work out well for you, Gov, did it?'

Fitzgerald straightened up, showing his authority. 'No, she's already told Carol to F off.'

'Yep, Gov, that's about right. How's Dixie-Lee, by the way?'

'In a bit of a state. The officer who was here before Georgie and her daughter arrived said the screams were bloodcurdling. It seems she was inconsolable, but what can you expect. That family, Raj. They've gone through so much in the space of six months. Tread very carefully, won't you.'

'Oh, yeah, absolutely. Gov, is there any news about the café owner?'

'Broken ribs, broken collarbone, and smoke inhalation damage, but it could have been far worse if that passer-by hadn't gone in and helped him when he did.'

'Right, Petra and I will go and sit with Georgie and Dixie-Lee and get them ready to go to the safe house.'

No sooner had Raj finished the conversion than a green Aston Martin drew up.

'Who's that, now?' asked Fitzgerald.

Raj sighed. 'That is Brodie Deacon.' *Now, this will be fun*, thought Raj.

'Oh yes, I remember him. And did we ever find out what the Deacons did for a living?'

'Yeah, they own a company where they undo wrongdoings, remember?' *Why is everyone so eager to know what they do for a living?* thought Raj.

'I recall that conversation, but I don't buy it.' Fitzgerald stared ahead, watching Brodie climb out of his car. 'Christ, look at the size of him. He seems to have grown in all directions.'

'No, Gov, he's always been a lump, although I have to admit he looks like he's been working out.'

'Okay, Raj, I need to get back to the station. Can you talk to Georgie? You know the drill, and, in the meantime, I will find out what's going on with Marston-Smith.'

'Do you think it's connected?'

'I have no idea yet, but Marston-Smith went on the missing list created by us, so you get inside and speak with Georgie. Find out what you can.'

'Okay, Gov, at least Georgie knows me. But even then, she still might snap my head off.'

Fitzgerald was already in the car before Raj even finished his conversation.

'All right, Raj, so what do we do now?' asked Holland, who had waited a few feet away while Raj and Fitzgerald spoke. She didn't want to put her foot in it and say the wrong thing because deep down she knew that the governor didn't like her too much. He often asked if she was up to the job, and he'd even whispered in her ear 'Don't keep telling tales. You will lose the respect of your fellow officers.' Not that she had ever ratted on Raj, but, inside, she was aware that it was part of her nature to go tittle-tattling. She assumed it would get her higher up the ladder of seniority. She aimed to be the police commissioner one day.

'We need to have a conversation with Georgie, take as much information as we can, and . . .' He paused and nodded in the direction of Carol Lardon. 'We will have to try to get her onboard with Georgie since she's been assigned as the liaison officer. Jesus, just look at her.'

Holland turned to see Brodie, a good foot taller than Lardon, with his hands on his hips. She was clearly blocking his entry.

Raj knew this wouldn't end well, so he marched over and flashed his warrant card. 'It's fine. This is Brodie Deacon, Georgie Deacon's brother-in-law!'

Brodie nodded an acknowledgement, but it was clear that the man was devastated. His eyes were red, probably from crying.

Lardon stepped aside. 'How was I supposed to know? He could have been anyone.'

'I'm Detective Sergeant Rajesh Raj. Call me Raj. And this is Detective Constable Petra Holland.'

Lardon looked Holland up and down and then focused on Raj. 'Yeah, I know, and I am the liaison officer, but for now, I am leaving Mrs Deacon to cool off. She's not too happy.'

With a sharp, sarcastic chuckle, Raj shook his head. 'Not too happy? Of course, she's not too bloody happy. Her husband has just been murdered. Tell me, Carol, do you know the backstory to Georgie?'

Unimpressed, Lardon frowned. 'Of course I do.'

'Good, then you will know she isn't too happy with the police.'

With an exaggerated roll of her head, Lardon replied, 'Oh come on. She can't treat us with contempt because she has issues with us, well, rather the system in general.'

'Oh no,' Holland said, 'you don't have children, do you?'

Lardon shook her head. 'No, I don't, actually, but what's that got to do with it?'

'Her daughter nearly died because we didn't do our job properly, so listen, I'm not having a go at you. I just want you to understand why Georgie is a little standoffish, shall we say.'

'Fair enough, but I don't appreciate being told to fuck off, especially in the presence of Chief Inspector Fitzgerald. I was made to look a right useless prat.'

Raj huffed. 'I am sure you weren't, and I am equally sure that Georgie doesn't want an officer in her face right now. So just a polite word of warning: tread carefully. Or the Deacons will shut us out completely.'

Lardon glanced behind her to see that the door was closed. 'Yeah, okay. I wouldn't want to get in that guy's way. Do you think they are capable of taking matters into their own hands?'

'Anyone is capable of that, Carol.'

CHAPTER THREE

Brodie put his arms around Georgie and held her tight.

There was silence for a few seconds before she felt his chest judder, and she knew then he was ready to let out a sob trapped in his throat.

He sat on the sofa, his hands over his eyes; his body was trembling with emotion.

Dixie-Lee came into the room and flew at Brodie, throwing her arms around him.

Georgie watched as they cried together.

When Brodie stopped and wiped his face, he said, 'I will kill whoever did this, you mark my words.'

Georgie glanced at her daughter. She was surprised to find her nodding as if it was the right thing to do; it was almost as if she expected no less from her uncle.

'I'll make a coffee, Brodie, yeah?'

Brodie nodded. 'With a dash of brandy.'

Georgie unintentionally listened to the conversation while making the coffee. Her daughter's sweet voice carried into the kitchen.

'Uncle Brodie, I didn't know my dad for very long, but I loved him. I *really* loved him, and some bastard has taken him away.'

Even though Dixie-Lee lowered her voice, Georgie could still hear her words, which were enunciated so emphatically.

'I'm worried about Mum. She's lost my dad twice, and she will grieve twice over.'

'Your mum is the strongest woman I know, and she will get through this, and you, my little Snow White, will too because you're young.'

'Does Nana Fin know?'

Georgie could hear Brodie's voice crack, and he coughed it away. 'Yeah, she knows. But your Uncle Rohan is with her.'

Deep inside, Georgie hoped that Rohan was on his way over from Ireland. She missed him, and she could only guess he missed her too, which was probably why he was deliberately staying away. She added a dash of brandy to the coffee and carried it in, placing it on the small but new coffee table.

Six months ago, the living room had resembled a war zone when Major Ashby had visited the property. Virtually everything had been replaced: the carpet, the rugs, and the sofa had been splattered with Finella's and Ashby's blood and so none of the furniture was fit to be left in the house. And even if everything had been professionally cleaned, the room would only have served as a stark reminder as to what had happened.

'Here you go, Brodie, and what about Mac? Does he know?'

Brodie took the cup. His hands were shaking, which shocked Georgie because her brother-in-law was usually so self-controlled. The news must have knocked him sideways.

'He is on his way over, but he is the most emotional one out of us all, so please don't be surprised if he wails like a baby,' said Brodie, before sipping his coffee.

Before Brodie could compose himself, the doorbell rang.

Georgie hurried to tell whoever it was to bugger off unless they were a welcome visitor.

As she opened the door, she saw Raj standing awkwardly with Holland, and with Carol Lardon looking equally uncomfortable. She knew why in her case. She'd already had words with her.

'Can't I have five minutes peace before you lot take over my home?'

Raj offered a genuinely sorrowful smile. 'I know, Georgie, but listen, the more you can recall right now, the more information we will have to go on.'

Georgie glared at Lardon. 'You don't need to be here. Or you, Petra. Just Raj.'

Lardon wasn't having a bar of it. 'Georgie, we all want your husband's killer found, so I need to be present. Two ears and all that.'

The cold glare put Georgie in a wild mood. 'First of all, don't call me *Georgie*. We're not mates, and I don't fucking *know* you. Secondly, I hate repeating myself, but I said Raj can enter my home but not you or Detective Constable Holland. And thirdly, I've already told you to fuck off. So do one, lady.'

Lardon responded before her brain had time to engage. 'And why is Raj allowed to enter your home and not me?' she asked, with an accusing tone to her voice.

'You *what*? Look, I said I want to speak to Raj. I'm *not* going to be interrogated by a fucking stranger. Now, get off my doorstep.' She glared at Raj. 'Are you coming in or are ya gonna stand there like a wet weekend?'

Raj could tell Georgie was not standing for any compromise, so he entered and let her shut the other two out.

'I'm sorry, Georgie. Really, I am.'

He followed her into the living room and politely acknowledged Brodie and Dixie-Lee again before he took a seat in the armchair. 'I'll get to the point, Georgie. The force want to know all the usual stuff. You know what I mean. Did your husband have any enemies? What were his movements during the last few days? Yada yada yada. And, of course, your whereabouts. The force will want your clothes for—'

'Gun residue. I get it, but I have three witnesses who will say I was working in the café. But, to save any argument, you can have my clothes.'

'You can't possibly think my mum killed my dad, can you?' spat Dixie-Lee, now jumping up from her seat.

Raj shook his head. 'No, not at all. Look, all I want to do is to eliminate her ASAP to keep you both safe because right now, we don't know who did this to your father.'

'Oh my God, it's my fault, isn't it? Someone wants revenge because I killed Ashby. They killed my dad in retaliation, didn't they?'

Raj leaned forward. 'Now, Dixie-Lee, stop torturing yourself. This situation, I am sure, has nothing to do with it.'

Before Dixie-Lee could respond, Raj's phone rang. It was the governor, Fitzgerald.

'Gov?' he answered.

'Where are you, Raj?'

'Inside Georgie's house with Georgie, Brodie, and Dixie-Lee. Why?'

'Take the call outside. *Now.*'

Raj felt the severe undertone, politely smiled at Georgie, and pointed to his phone. 'Sorry, I need to take this.'

He hurried from the living room and went outside. 'Go on, Gov, what's the news?'

'We have an eyewitness who saw two men in a BMW get out of their car. One of the men ran up to Dixie Deacon, shot him at close range, and as he fell to the ground, the other man pulled out a knife and cut Dixie's head.'

'Christ, did the witness get a good look at the perpetrators?'

'No. She said they each wore a balaclava. Dressed all in black.'

'Jesus, how do we start with that one? I mean, how many BMWs are there out there?'

'Only one with the particular personalised number plate. Get this, it's registered to a Mac Deacon.'

Raj stood there, stunned. '*What?*'

'Yes, you heard. Mac Deacon.'

Running his hands through his hair, Raj paced the short garden path. 'What was the description of these men?'

'The witness said they were both tall, but one was big built and the other fairly slim.'

'Slim? No, no, Mac is a big chap. I mean massive. He's got a forty-six-inch chest. No witness would describe him as slim.'

'Right, well, it was his car. So I suggest you get Georgie and her daughter out of the house and ready to take them to a safe house. Be mindful, though, because Brodie may well be in on it.'

'In on it? Nah, Gov, I don't buy that.'

'Raj, Dixie Deacon left that family as a teenager and never saw them again until six months ago. Do we know why?'

Rubbing his bristly chin, Raj was racking his brains. 'Okay, leave it with me.'

As he ended the call, he saw Carol Lardon and Petra Holland eagerly looking his way for an update. All he could do was wave, shake his head, and turn away. He really didn't want Petra inside with him. Not now, anyway.

Now uneasy, Raj slipped inside Georgie's house to find her with her hands on her hips, ready for war, and Brodie with his arm around Dixie-Lee. Brodie certainly didn't look like a man with a grudge against his own family.

'Georgie, can I talk with you alone?' Even before the words left his mouth, he knew the answer to that.

'No. Whatever you have to say, you can say it here with my family.'

Raj glanced at Brodie. 'Is Mac in the area?'

Brodie nodded. 'Yes. Why? Is he okay?'

Raj knew then that Brodie could hide his fear that someone had also harmed his brother Mac.

'I don't know. Tell me, has your brother sold his number plates or his car with the number plates?'

Brodie dropped his bottom lip and shook his head. 'No. Raj, spit it out! Why all the questions about me brother?'

'Yeah, bear with me. Mac is a big man, wouldn't you say?'

Brodie stood up. 'He was, but he's lost a lot of weight. He's been to the gym and he's eating rabbit food, he is. Now, why all the questions about Mac?'

'Because a witness saw your brother's car leaving the scene.'

'The scene?'

'Dixie's murder scene. I'm afraid I'm gonna have to take you to the station.' He held up his hands. 'Merely a formality, Brodie. I'm sure there's a major mix-up, but please just come without a fuss.'

'A major mix-up! You mean a great big feck-up of gigantic proportions. As if Mac would have anything to do with our little brother's fecking murder.'

Raj glanced at Georgie, who seemed a little distant. She suddenly grabbed her daughter's arm and pulled her close. Her eyes were wide and darting around, as if she was totally confused. It was so unlike Georgie.

'Mum, what's going on? Why is the detective taking Uncle Brodie?'

Georgie was silent as she watched Raj leave the house. He was followed by Brodie. However, before the door was even closed, Georgie heard a commotion outside. And when she hurried to find out what all the fuss was about, she was horrified to see two uniformed officers dragging Mac from his car. They were screaming at him to get down on the ground and to stay down.

Dixie-Lee was an inch behind her mother when she saw the officers kicking and punching Mac even though he was now on the ground and not fighting back.

Brodie lunged forward to pull one of the officers away.

But Raj intervened. He grabbed Brodie's arm. 'Don't get involved, Brodie. If you do, they'll nick you.'

Dixie-Lee, at only eighteen, wasn't going to stand by and allow the officers to act so brutally, when, in her eyes, her Uncle Mac wasn't trying to resist arrest.

'Oi! Why are you hitting him? He's already on the ground. Can't you see, or are you blind?' Her shrill voice had a pitch that compelled everyone to look her way.

One of the officers, whose knee was pushing down on Mac's back and forcing his wrists together, glared at Dixie-Lee. 'Come any closer and I'll arrest you for obstructing police in their inquiries.'

'Oh, you fucking will, will you? Well, I'm making a report. I'm putting in a complaint about how you two were so fucking brutal.' She paused to take a deep breath. 'You should be ashamed of yourselves, and you are not royalty, you know. You're civil fucking servants who work for us, and you think you are beyond any powers? Well, I will take your cockups and your brutality to the papers because believe you me, PC Bully, they will love to hear from me about how you guys left me for dead because you couldn't safeguard my hospital room from a killer. Also, I will tell them how the killer was able to come for me and almost murder me because you failed to believe my mother. And, now, how outside my home, you are viciously attacking my uncle. You are all fucking disgusting.' Dixie-Lee's tone changed. Her grief for her father had now turned to rage. All she could see was one of the men she adored, her sweet funny uncle, being attacked by the very constabulary that had failed her and her family.

Raj's head was all over the place. He was unable to decide who to go for first before this got entirely out of hand. Eventually, he decided to rush over to Georgie and Dixie-Lee. 'Go back inside, please, or this will end up in a shitstorm.'

'Are you off your fucking head, Raj? You want us inside, so we can't witness your bully boys punching and kicking a man who is clearly not resisting arrest. Fucking look at him, Raj!'

But when he looked over, he saw Brodie filming the incident.

'Georgie, call Hugh, will you? I'm not having this. It's all on film!' shouted Brodie, not taking his eyes off the incident.

As he stepped back to get clear footage, Lardon tried to remove his phone. 'You Brodie Deacon, are coming down the station. Now, give me the phone.'

It was at this point that Holland tried gently but firmly to hold Dixie-Lee by the shoulders to guide her back into the house.

'Get your hands off me, Detective, before I do you for assault.'

Holland instantly let go as if Dixie-Lee was a hot brick.

Brodie lifted the phone above Lardon's head. 'You can't do that, love. I would go peacefully, but it appears to me that you lot are gunning for a riot. And I am too smart to allow you to push me to the point I would later regret because I never want to regret anything.'

Lardon rolled her eyes. 'You're making matters worse, Brodie Deacon.'

His crisp Irish accent cut through the air. 'No, darling. I am helping to balance the scales of justice.'

Lardon's copper-coloured eyes snapped together in fury. 'You are interfering with an arrest.'

'Well, I'm not. I'm just filming a situation, and if you think their actions are within the rules, then why are you so worried?'

Lardon shook her head and gave him a bulldog face. 'I'm not worried.'

'No? Then why do you have beads of sweat on your moustache?'

Seeing Lardon release her handcuffs ready to arrest her Uncle Brodie, Dixie-Lee ran over to him. 'Give me the phone, Uncle Brodie, before she takes it and wipes the footage clean.'

'Go inside, Dixie,' hissed Lardon.

'Go fuck yaself, and my name is *Dixie-Lee*. My father was called Dixie, but he's just been shot dead, and you evil people are rag-dolling his brother around like a bloody criminal. You have no powers to tell me to go inside or to stop me from filming.' She took the phone from Brodie, turned it around, and grinned before she turned to face Lardon. 'Even if you take the phone, WPC Lardon, it's a live feed, so carry on, with what you were saying.'

Everyone was stunned that Dixie-Lee, who was quietly spoken and so sweet with it, had just lost her rag and morphed into a younger version of her mother.

'I can arrest you, Miss Deacon,' Lardon sneered.

'Yeah, go on then. And clearly explain why you are arresting me. I am studying law at college, so I know my rights, just so you know.'

Lardon stood with her hands on her hips, trying to intimidate Dixie-Lee, but her actions failed at every level.

'Looks to me like you don't have a reason, WPC Lardon.' Georgie stepped forward and inserted herself between her daughter and the aggressive-looking policewoman.

Brodie gently placed his hand on Georgie's shoulder. 'The footage is a live feed to Hugh.'

Georgie grinned. 'Perfect.'

'Who is Hugh?' asked Lardon, desperate to know what they were grinning at.

'You will find out soon enough.'

There was silence as the brutish officer in his thirties with blond hair who had kneed Mac in the back read him his rights.

'You are under arrest for the murder of Dixie Deacon. Anything you do say can and will . . .'

CHAPTER FOUR

Mac found himself handcuffed and held securely in the back of the police car. Brodie got into the second police car with Holland and another officer.

Shaking his head in disbelief, Raj walked with Georgie up her garden path and into her house.

'Georgie, this is a mess. Look, shall I make you a cup of tea or something else, perhaps?'

Georgie looked solemnly at him. 'I'll do it myself, Raj.'

She peered at her daughter, who seemed to have turned a sickly shade of grey. 'Hey, Dixie-Lee, are you okay, love?'

Dixie-Lee shook her head. 'No. I'm angry and devasted, and now I feel sick.' She held her hands out for her mother to see how much she was shaking. 'I have never spoken to anyone like that before. I swear I could have punched that officer. I was so mad.'

'I know, my darling, but you said what needed to be said, and I think maybe he will think about his behaviour in the future.'

'Yeah, if I'd had a knife, I would have stabbed him.'

Raj looked on, concerned. 'Dixie-Lee, listen, I will be the first to admit it was not handled in the best way, but please don't let it affect you. I'll have a word with that officer when I return to the station.'

'Why have they arrested my uncle?'

'Because a witness saw his car leaving the scene of the murder. Look, I am sure there is a reasonable explanation for all of this,' said Raj, 'but we have to do our job and eliminate him—'

'More like annihilate him,' snapped Dixie-Lee, before she stomped up the stairs to her bedroom.

'Georgie, I don't believe this has anything to do with Mac, but that's between you and me. Now, listen carefully. I believe it may be connected with the Marxes. I didn't want to tell you this, well, not today, anyway, but Henry is in hospital.'

Georgie gasped. 'What? Why?'

'There was a fire at the café, and the refrigeration unit landed on top of him. Luckily, some passer-by rushed in and pretty much saved him.'

With her eyes out on stalks, Georgie stared in disbelief. 'Where is he now? I must see him.'

'No, you and Dixie-Lee need to pack a suitcase so that we can take you to a safe house.'

'But didn't we just witness Mac being arrested? So why are we still in danger? Although, to be fair, I don't believe Mac killed my husband.'

'Really? Only I saw you pull Dixie-Lee away from Brodie.'

Georgie sighed heavily. 'I am a mixed bag of emotions at the moment. You can surely see that. My head is all over the place. And my first reaction is to protect my child, more so now than ever. But no way would Dixie's brothers have hurt him. I've seen how much they loved him.'

She walked away from the kitchen and into the living room. The small window at the far end looked out over the garden and the garages at the back. She stared out. 'I would never have thought Dixie was that homeless guy sleeping in my garage. I was angry with him when I found out he was my husband, and I tried not to be, but he'd changed so much, he wasn't the guy I married all those years ago.'

Raj slowly walked up behind her, and without much thought, he whispered, 'Did you have someone kill him?'

She spun around, a deeply furrowed frown almost distorting her face. '*What?*'

Unable to reply, he managed to look her in the eye. And at that precise moment, they shared something. It wasn't a romantic thought, but it was an understanding all the same. He knew something about her past, and now, it seemed, they shared a secret.

Calmly, she replied, 'No, Raj, he didn't do me any wrong. In fact, although I was angry, I knew he had been hovering in the background watching us. He tried to keep our daughter safe. He wasn't a bad guy. I was just disappointed and angry with the situation.' She pointed to the armchair facing the TV. 'He sat in that chair most nights just staring at the TV. His soul had died in the explosion all those years ago, so no, Raj, I would never have hurt that man, let alone have him murdered.'

Even though what Georgie had just said made complete sense, Raj was convinced she had killed before. Yet he wasn't going to arrest her for something he was pretty sure she had done in the past.

Besides, that particular case had been closed for over six months, and he was going to leave it that way.

'You'd better call Hugh Shields.'

Georgie nodded. 'Yeah, then I need to see Henry.'

'And this safe house. Will you be going there?'

Georgie shook her head. 'No, I won't, but I will send Dixie-Lee to her grandmother's in Ireland. She'll be safe there. No doubt, they will release Mac and Brodie.' She paused and chuckled. 'Christ, I'm looking at you like you're not a copper. Anyway, I'm staying. I want to know who killed my husband and who hurt my mate, Henry.'

He smiled. 'I see. So you're gonna go all detective on us now, are you?'

'You forget, Raj, I was in the Military Police. Anyway, I want to be here, and if Dixie-Lee can go to Ireland until the real culprits are caught, I will feel a whole lot better. And no disrespect to you, Raj, but a safe house? You couldn't keep Dixie-Lee safe in the hospital, could you?'

'I know. Okay, I think it's best if Officer Lardon stays with Dixie-Lee while you visit Henry.'

'Oh no. I'm liable to come home to find Lardon pinned to the wall and Dixie-Lee using her as a fucking dart board. No, I'll take Dixie-Lee with me.'

'And then you know what we have to do?'

Georgie felt her throat suddenly tighten. 'Identify his body?'

Raj nodded and gave her a sympathetic smile. 'Sorry.'

'I'm fine, Raj. Let's just visit Henry first, eh.'

***

Walking along the corridor towards Henry's ward, Georgie had flashbacks of when her daughter was there. It turned her stomach, but she wasn't going to spin around and leave. Henry had been so good to her over the years, so she wasn't going to let him down now.

While Raj waited with Dixie-Lee out in the corridor, Georgie went to see Henry.

Henry was propped upright with bandages around his head and large plasters on his face. His arm was in a sling, and he seemed dazed. He looked so different. Gone were his trademark T-shirt and apron. Seeing his NHS gown exposing his chest, she realised that he was actually quite a fit-looking man. His eyes suddenly lit up when he saw her.

There were four other beds in the room. Only one other bed was occupied, and that patient had the curtains around them.

Georgie hurried over, and for a moment, she didn't know how to hug him. He seemed to be pretty battered. She kissed him on the cheek before taking a seat.

'You found Dixie-Lee, all right?'

Georgie nodded, biting her bottom lip, and near to tears.

'What are you doing here, Georgie? No need, gal. You've got enough to deal with.'

'I can't bring Dixie back, Henry, but I can check on the living. What the fuck happened?'

'Someone poured petrol through the back door letterbox and then dropped a lighter inside. The place went up like a bloody bomb. The dessert fridge landed on top of me and broke my ribs and a few other bones, but I'm alive. This really decent guy, who must have been fucking strong, pulled the fridge off me and managed to get me out before the smoke choked me to death.'

'That was good of him, so you can send him one of your famous cakes when you get out,' replied Georgie, trying to keep the conversation light. But her attempt at doing so proved useless, she realised. She looked him in the eye and her smile evaporated. 'I'm sorry, Henry.'

Instantly, he moved his free hand and placed it on hers. 'You, my gal, have nuffin to be sorry about.'

'Yeah, Henry, I do. The people who killed Dixie did it for revenge, and I have a nasty feeling that they also did that to your café to get at me.'

'Stop it, Georgie. Look, the café is insured, so all's not lost.'

'Insurance is no good if you had died, Henry.'

'It will all go to you, anyway.'

That remark stunned Georgie. 'You what?'

'Yeah, I made a will, so everything goes to you. And if not you, then to Dixie-Lee.'

'Me, but why?'

''Cos, Georgie Deacon, you are the nearest I have to family.'

'But we've never been romantic like husband and wife, so I don't get it.'

'No, we're more like brother and sister. Georgie, you are my closest friend, and so there you have it. Anyway, I'm not dead yet. I'm merely wounded.'

His eyes looked beyond Georgie and he beamed. 'Oh, speak of the devil, here comes the hero of the day.'

Slowly, Georgie turned to see who Henry was referring to.

Dressed in blue jeans, a white jumper, and a black blazer-style jacket stood a man roughly six feet tall. For a moment, Georgie was starstruck. Not that the man was any kind of celebrity. But he was just extremely handsome. His thick blond hair was pulled back into a ponytail, and he had a beard, but what struck her was his piercing blue eyes and perfect white teeth. Suddenly, she became aware that she was ogling him. Never before had she felt lost in someone's appearance – except perhaps Rohan – but even then that was only once when she'd looked up from under her heavy eyelids and pushed through the curtains of despair.

Pull yourself together, Georgie. Her mind was all over the place. Everything was a mess, and now she was eyeing up Henry's rescuer. She had to leave and be away from people for their own safety and her sanity. However, the guy was at the foot of the bed, and she would have to walk around him. Maybe jumping up from her chair and scurrying away would look rude. So, slowly, she rose to her feet and smiled, acknowledging the handsome man.

When he returned the smile, Georgie felt her heart literally skip a beat. And worse, she could feel her cheeks burning. She quickly diverted her gaze to Henry. 'I will leave you with, er . . .' It occurred to her she didn't know the man's name, and now she felt stupid.

'It's Noel.' He reached out his hand. 'Noel Wade. Pleased to meet you.'

Georgie shook his hand and was instantly drawn into his eyes, especially when he winked.

'I'm Georgie Deacon. Er, I'm friends with, well, I work with, I mean, I work for Henry.'

Noel was still smiling as Georgie fumbled over her words.

'Well, it is nice to meet you, and thank you for saving Henry.' She managed by the skin of her teeth to regain her composure.

‘Oh, it was nothing. I just happened to be there at the right time.’

‘So I see you went home and got changed.’ Henry coughed. ‘I must pay you for the clothes that you ruined.’

Noel turned his attention to Henry and waved his hands. ‘No, don’t you worry about that, Henry. They were ready for the bin, anyway. It gave me an excuse to throw them out.’

‘Right, anyway, I must get going,’ said Georgie, as she leaned forward and kissed Henry on the cheek. ‘You rest and dream up more dessert recipes. I’ll be back to check on you.’ She turned to Noel with a genial smile, before she left the room.

Her face was still warm, and she could only guess her cheeks were scarlet. As soon as she opened the double doors at the end of the ward, she clocked her daughter being comforted by Raj. It was a cold poke of reality that made her realise that even though she could put her grief aside to address her anger, her daughter couldn’t. Losing her father must have been an enormous blow. And to see her two uncles taken to the police station was another one.

‘Is Henry okay?’ asked Raj.

‘Yeah, he will be. Thankfully.’

Raj got up from his seat.

‘Can you drive us home, Raj? I should have brought my own car.’

‘You need protection, regardless, Georgie, until we know for sure who killed Dixie.’

She smiled. ‘So you are adamant it wasn’t Mac, then?’

‘I can’t tell you why, but I have a gut feeling it wasn’t. Anyway, yes, I will take you back home. I’ll appoint temporarily an officer, and, of course, you have Lardon, the new officer. I believe she’s a detective from Tonbridge. I don’t know much about her, but, anyway, as she is your liaison officer, she will be inside the house with you.’

Since Georgie had other things on her mind, she decided not to argue with Raj. But if that Lardon woman spoke out of turn or looked at her the wrong way, she would throw her out on her ear. That wasn’t to say that her daughter wouldn’t do it first, though.

As they made their way along the corridor, Georgie glanced back, sensing someone was watching her. As she did, she saw Noel. She guessed he hadn’t expected her to look back, and she noticed his eyes widen before he waved and hurried to catch her up.

'Georgie, Henry said to tell you if you need anything to let him know.'

For a moment, Georgie frowned. *That was an odd thing to say*, she thought. Henry wasn't the type of man to send someone – a complete stranger – off to come to her with a message like that. She wondered if Noel was using it as an excuse to speak to her again, or maybe that was wishful thinking on her part.

'Okay, thank you, er, Noel.'

She then noticed that Raj and Dixie-Lee had stopped walking and were now facing her.

'Dixie-Lee, this is Noel Wade. He saved Henry from the fire.'

With her face flushed with grief, Dixie-Lee still managed to crack half a smile in polite acknowledgement.

Raj offered his hand. 'Pleased to meet you. And I am Rajesh Raj.'

Noel returned the gesture and politely replied, 'Let's hope you find the culprit soon.'

Raj nodded. 'Us coppers stick out like sore thumbs, do we?'

'Well, I assumed you would be a copper, considering what Henry told me.'

'Yeah, I am. Anyway, give Henry my best,' Raj replied, before walking away with his hand gently guiding Dixie-Lee.

Once Raj and Dixie-Lee were out of sight, Noel turned to Georgie. 'She's a pretty girl, but her red eyes tell me she is distraught. Give her some magnesium and lavender for the bath. It might help her sleep tonight.'

'Or a Valium.'

Noel smiled. 'Be careful.'

Georgie was drawn to him, and yet apart from his handsome face, she couldn't fathom why.

'Thanks again, Noel.'

'Maybe I'll see you on a visit.'

Georgie was thinking he meant prison. 'What do you mean, a visit?'

'A visit here at the hospital. I like Henry. I would like to stay in touch and try one of his famous desserts.'

Georgie blushed again, sucked in by his absolute charm, not forgetting his come-to-bed eyes. She was not normally attracted to men with beards, or even a man like Noel with his hair tied in a ponytail, but it suited him.

'I have to go. Nice meeting you, Noel.'

'Oh, Georgie Deacon, we *will* see each other again.'

'*What?*'

He laughed. 'When the café is repaired and up and running, I'm coming in for a cake.'

'Oh.' She laughed, now relieved. 'I see.'

With the night air biting at Georgie's face, she followed Raj to his car, keeping her head down to stop the wind from freezing her eyelids.

The thought of identifying Dixie's body was now playing on her mind, but she had to do it and get it out of the way. When they arrived at the coroner's office, Raj asked Dixie-Lee to wait in the car while he escorted Georgie inside the cold-looking building. Having phoned ahead, Kaleb, a member of the medical examiner's team, was there waiting.

Raj and Georgie paused outside the room while Kaleb made sure Dixie was ready to be identified. Once he returned from the room, he looked at Raj.

'Has the next of kin been informed of the . . . well, the condition of . . .?'

'I am the next of kin and I know what to expect,' Georgie interrupted.

Impatiently, she barged into the room, expecting to have this over with in a nanosecond. However, as soon as she laid eyes on her husband's face, she wobbled and had to grip the back of the only chair in the room. It was as if his scars had faded. And although his skin was pale, he genuinely looked asleep. The cross that had been cut into his head was horrific, and, in some ways, she was glad that whoever had done this despicable thing had done so after he was dead.

What struck her most, though, was that he looked so young, just like when they'd first met – when they were in love and ecstatically happy. But the tears that tumbled down her cheeks were for a memory. She approached his body, gently stroked his hand, and kissed his forehead.

‘I only hope you can find peace somewhere up there.’

CHAPTER FIVE

After leaving Georgie and Dixie-Lee in the hands of Petra Holland, Carol Lardon, and two uniformed officers, Raj hurried back to the station. Raging that the two officers, evidently part of the new team, who maltreated Mac did so in front of Georgie and Dixie-Lee, Raj believed that as young as she was, Dixie-Lee was right. The officer who had his knee digging into Mac's back was young and aggressive, and he had tried to make out that Mac was resisting arrest when evidently he wasn't.

Raj had two options: to stand by the officer or go to Fitzgerald with what he'd seen. Now, generally, he wasn't a snitch, but if he didn't do something, the situation had the potential to blow way out of all proportion.

Just as he entered the reception area, he clocked Hugh Shields, the Deacon family's solicitor, on his phone. He was dressed in jeans and a silk jumper. He looked nothing like a solicitor. And he seemed flustered as he paced the waiting area.

Raj decided it was best to escort Shields to the interview rooms before some stupid detective began questioning the Deacons without himself, or, more importantly, their solicitor present.

'Ah, Raj, good to see you. I believe you have Mac and Brodie upstairs,' said Shields, as he ended the phone call and stretched his hand out to greet the detective.

'Yeah, come with me, Hugh. It's a nightmare, and the sooner we can get the lads out, the better, although Mac has been arrested for murder. You did know that, didn't you?'

Shields raised his brow. 'Raj, Georgie called me and told me what she knew, including how the police in the line of so-called duty manhandled Mac. I saw the footage, Raj. It didn't look good. And while I remember, who the hell is this Detective Constable Lardon with the attitude? Shagging one of the officers, is she?'

Raj sighed. 'No. Carol Lardon has been transferred from Tonbridge. We have a few new members of staff who I have yet to meet. I only hope they are not as arrogant as her. I know nothing about her, except she shows little tact, especially for liaising.' He grinned. 'I thought Dixie-Lee was going to poke her one in the chest.'

'Dixie-Lee is such a sweetheart. I heard her threatening to go to the press, and believe this, Raj, she is a very clever girl. She's studying law, and I have spent many an evening with her helping her with her homework. She's going to make a top lawyer, and so when she threatened to go to the press, she may well do so. But she's not a girl to gob off, like many teenagers these days.'

'I know, and we both know she has a point and was kind enough not to go to the press six months ago. But if we, as in the force, keep pushing her buttons, she could open up a whole can of worms.'

By the time they reached the next floor, Fitzgerald was there to greet them. He was with another man who was dressed in a suit and wearing a sneer rather than a smile.

Raj suspected it might be the new detective, also from Tonbridge. They had the funds to replace ex-Detective Sergeant Kims. And Raj guessed he was looking at the new Kims. He only hoped this one wasn't so bent. He also prayed that this detective, who was supposed to be a rank above him, was someone he could get along with. He'd certainly never liked Kims.

Fitzgerald looked uneasy. 'Hello, Mr Shields,' he said, politely, acknowledging the solicitor.

In return, Shields gave him a generous smile. 'I think it's going to be a long night and a shedload of paperwork for you lot.'

With a furrowed frown, Fitzgerald inclined his head.

'The hullabaloo while your overzealous officer arrested Mac Deacon . . .' He paused. 'Ah, I can see by your face that you haven't been informed.'

'No, Mr Shields. What hullabaloo?'

Raj felt his stomach turn over when Fitzgerald shot him a concerned look.

'Oh, hang on. I think I have the footage on my phone.' Shields placed his briefcase on the floor and retrieved his phone from his pocket. 'Yes, that's it. It's a shocking state of affairs.' He held the phone in front of Fitzgerald to show him the footage.

Fitzgerald rolled his eyes but was stopped from saying anything when the man beside him leaned forward to take a closer look. 'Hi, I'm Detective Inspector Martin Drake. Can we discuss this later? We have two men in custody who we need to charge formally, and I am sure you will want to advise them of their rights, etcetera.'

Shields took one step back to make it clear that he was looking the detective up and down. He was tall and slim with an oblong-shaped head and dark hair cropped close to his head. He looked more like a villain than a detective, but, then again, Shields had met a lot of villains disguised as coppers in his time, and it was a shame because it gave the good coppers a bad name.

Ignoring Drake's comment, Shields continued. 'I think you will find that this footage demonstrates the brutality used before any arrest was made, so, Detective Inspector Drake, don't attempt to dismiss this because I won't let this go. Now, I want to see the custody records. And is this copper who arrested Mr Deacon still on duty?'

Fitzgerald nodded. 'Yes, he is in the incident room, no doubt writing up his notes. Why?'

'I want him breathalysed.'

'Breathalysed?' squawked Drake.

'Oh, come on, you don't think a person in their right mind and in their position would attack a man who wasn't resisting arrest unless they were drunk or drugged, do you?'

'What are you suggesting?' asked Fitzgerald.

'Nothing, except to say I want him breathalysed and tested for drugs, and I want the custody records and the bodycam footage because the track record at this station, need I remind you, when it comes to the Deacons, is hardly good, is it? So I want to ensure everything is done by the book, or you may not have a case to charge Mac Deacon.'

'Oh, I think we have enough,' growled Drake.

***

Mac had his head down when Shields walked into the interview room, and as soon as he lifted it, Shields flinched. 'Playing rugby, were you? How the hell did you get those injuries?'

Mac felt his swollen cheek and then his puffy eyebrow. 'These?'

'You're black and blue.' Shields slid his briefcase onto the table. 'Please don't tell me that copper on the video did that.'

'Yeah, he did. Two of them dragged me out of their car and smashed my face on the pavement. Luckily, I knew they were coppers, or I'd have turned them inside out so they could taste their own shit. Wankers!'

Shields sat next to Mac. 'So I take it they recorded all this at the custody desk? And took photos?'

Mac shrugged. 'No. They didn't record any of my bruises or take photos. The bastard who threw me to the ground was quite a tough man, but, Hugh, I tell yer, he went way over the fecking top.'

Shields flicked a speck of food off his jumper. 'Maybe it was his nerves, because as far as he would have been told, he was arresting a murderer.'

'It's all bollocks. As if I'd hurt me little brother. Jesus Christ, I can't get over the fact that when we found him alive, having searched for years, someone then came along and fecking murdered him.'

'Can you account for your movements today?'

Mac looked up again with his jaw shot forward. '*What?* Oh no, Hugh, yer don't think that I killed him, do yer, now?'

Shields showed the palms of his hands while vehemently shaking his head. 'Of course, I bloody don't. Listen, I need to get you out of here, and so, right now, you need to tell me where you were so that you have an alibi.'

'I was at Brodie's apartment in London when I got the devastating call that me little brother was killed. I drove over to Georgie's, and, before I knew it, I was being dragged from the car and assaulted by two fecking steroid abusing small-dick wankers.'

'Apparently, a witness took down the number plate of the car that was seen driving away from the murder scene.'

'And? So what. Feck me, can't you see? This is a fecking set-up.'

'I am beginning to think there is an agenda, but, unfortunately, we haven't been informed of the narrative. Raj is outside talking to another detective. Reading between the lines, it seems to be more about internal politics. Maybe the higher-ups decided Raj is too soft for the job because it doesn't look to me that he has been assigned to this case. Anyway, on a different note, Raj told me that Henry, the café owner, where Georgie works, was rushed to hospital . Someone tried to burn the place down with him in it.'

Mac sat up straight and glared. 'No way. Fecking hell, Hugh, where are Georgie and Dixie-Lee now? Are they safe?'

'Yes, Mac, they're fine. Now then, as far as I know, all they have on you is your car at the scene of Dixie's murder. I can get your clothes tested for gun residue, and we can check the cameras, and, hopefully, that will be enough to have you out of here by the morning.'

'Good because I want to be there for Georgie and Dixie-Lee. My ma is going to be beside herself. She would never cope having me inside as well.'

'Let's cooperate as much as possible and have you and Brodie out of here as soon as. This station makes me sick.'

'Brodie?'

'Apparently, there were two men in the car, so they have put two and two together and come up with five. But I'm not surprised, not with their track record.'

'Raj was there when they arrested me. Is he going to do the interview?'

Shields shook his head. 'No, there is a new detective. A prick with arrogance sewed into his soul.'

'Oh, for feck's sake. Okay, we'd best get this over with, then.'

***

When Drake bowled into the interview room with a new recruit, his sidekick Yan Evans, Mac sensed a deep foreboding as the atmosphere suddenly became very tense. He peered up and stared at Drake with an unblinking resolve, determined not to be in the least bit intimidated by the tall piece of piss with a badge and an attitude. Even the manner in which Drake walked into the room and dragged the chair away from the table said enough about the rude prick. And the short-arsed detective accompanying him was not much better.

Drake and Evans sat and loosened their ties before they both slapped files onto the table.

Mac grinned as he laughed inside. The film *Twins* with Arnold Schwarzenegger and Danny DeVito came to mind.

'I'm Detective Inspector Drake and my colleague is Detective Constable Evans. I want to start the tape for the formal interview.'

Just as Drake pressed the record button, Shields intervened. 'I asked for the custody report when my client was brought in. Only, he informs me that you didn't take any photos of his injuries, and you can clearly see he has them. The injuries are fresh, I might add, and witnessed by other people and recorded live.'

Drake flared his nostrils and chewed the inside of his cheek. 'Yes, I will get to that after this interview.'

'A little bit backward, wouldn't you agree?'

'What?' snapped Drake.

'The process. I mean, sorry, did you think I was calling you backward? No, Detective, I was saying the *process* is backward. Now, I would like to be assured that the custody records are as they should be and you are following PACE. Has my client been seen by a medical professional?'

Drake looked as though he was ready to blow his top. He shot Evans a look.

'I have called the doctor to look at his injuries,' said Evans, in a pert tone.

Shields looked at his watch. 'Great, so it's eight thirty now, and I take it that call was recorded before eight thirty.' He grinned. 'Because, Detective, you are sitting here now.'

Evans flushed red. 'Well, yes, I am sure it was made.'

'You just said you called the doctor – you – called – the – doctor. So, Detective Constable Evans, you would know if the call was made or not, or—'

'Mr Shields, what my colleague is saying is—'

Shields interrupted before Drake could finish. 'Please, Detective Inspector, try to be informed instead of opinionated, although I am sure you have been given that advice before.'

Drake got up from his seat, his eyes flicking from Hugh Shields to Mac Deacon, clearly in a raging temper. Pointing at Shields's face while the other hand rested on his hip, he barked, 'You need to be very careful with your insinuations, or I will have you done for . . .' He stopped when he saw Mac Deacon laughing.

'Oh, sit down, Detective. Your crazy is showing, and you might wanna suck that back in. Look, I'll give you that interview. Besides, I have nothing to hide. You need to remember Dixie is, I mean was, my little brother, not some nobody. So shall we start again? I need to get home to console my family.'

Suddenly, the tense atmosphere in the room subsided.

Drake then began the interview by asking Mac to go over his movements at the time that his brother was shot.

‘I was at me brother’s apartment in London going through some business when I—’

‘What business?’ interrupted Evans.

‘Me brothers and I have a company. We settle disputes.’

‘Sounds dodgy to me.’

‘Does it? And your point is, Detective?’

‘What do you mean by settle disputes?’

‘Have you sharpened your crayon and is your helmet tight enough?’

Evans grinned, bearing his cigarette-stained teeth. ‘Ah, so you’re being funny, are ya?’

Mac leaned back on his chair. ‘Why am I explaining what settling disputes means? Because as far as I can recall, we learned about that in nursery school.’

‘*His* business, Detective Constable Evans, is not *your* business. He is not here for any other reason than a murder charge, so let’s focus on that, shall we,’ intervened Shields.

Drake had been listening and staring at Mac. ‘No, actually, his business may well be connected to the murder.’

‘Oh yes? How?’

‘Well, did your business, this company, employ your brother Dixie? Was he involved in any shape or form?’

Mac shook his head.

‘So your company is owned by three brothers, but that didn’t include your youngest?’

‘That’s right.’

‘So why not Dixie?’

Mac shook his head. ‘You haven’t done your homework, have you now? Because if you had, then you would know that Dixie wasn’t in our lives until six months ago, and our company has been up and running for well over twenty years.’

Evans smiled like he had farted and got away with it. ‘And that’s my next question.’

Shields knew immediately where this was heading. ‘Detective, we are going off on a tangent. If you haven’t got enough evidence to hold my client, then . . .’ He paused and checked his watch. ‘We have a family to console. And to make arrangements for. Because with your track record, a safe house won’t cut it.’ He had to get the dig in because he couldn't stand the smug look on Drake's and Evans's faces right now.

However, he was surprised when Drake leaned forward, and, in a menacing tone, slowly replied, 'Oh, Mr Shields, we do have more evidence, and probably enough to go to the CPS and have your client in court first thing tomorrow.'

Mac glanced at Shields with utter amazement written all over his face. 'What evidence?'

'We will get to that, Mr Deacon, so I will ask you again. Why did your brother walk away from all of you and stay away for . . . Er, how long? Er . . .?' He opened his file and whizzed through the notes. 'Twenty-four years.'

'What information, exactly, are you looking at, Detective?' Shields asked. Although he was annoyed by this seemingly irrelevant questioning, he remained calm, determined not to show his annoyance.

'The notes from when we had Georgie Deacon on a murder charge six months ago.' He pointed dramatically to his file. 'They're in here.'

Shields could feel his heart beating so fast inside his chest that he was silent momentarily.

'It's simple really, Detective. My stepfather hurt me brother, and so Dixie ran away, joined the fecking British Army, got fecking blown up, suffered amnesia, and by the time he got his memory back, he was a fecking broken man, so he lived as a vagrant, sleeping in Georgie's garage. So that's it in a nutshell.'

'And that's not a story you just plucked out of thin air, is it? I mean, who sleeps in a person's garage for years without getting noticed? It doesn't add up to me.'

Mac glared. 'No, you seem like the kinda fella that can't do their additions, let alone subtractions, and I bet you're completely fecked doing percentages, but hey, senility for you, I am sure, would be a smooth transition.'

'Oh, I see. Trying to be witty is your way of deflecting the question, is it, Mr Deacon?'

'No, not at all, but I feel Evans here likes playing fecking ping pong with idiotic comments. So I thought I'd keep him fecking amused.'

He was certainly entertaining Shields, who wasn't at all surprised by Mac's quick wit. It was a trait that all the brothers shared. However, Brodie, being the sharpest of the brothers, tended to be more cutting with his repartee.

Drake opened his file. 'Right, Mr Deacon, can you tell me what this photo shows?'

Mac took the photo and stared. 'A black jumper – a cheap black jumper at that – a pair of black trousers, and a balaclava.'

'Good! Are they yours?'

Mac sneered. 'I've never worn a balaclava in my fecking life or a jumper from Primark, so, no, they're not mine.'

'Are you sure? Take another look.'

Shields took the photo and slapped it down on the table. 'My client said they are not his, so move on.'

'Well, we found them in the boot of your car, along with this.' He removed another photo from the file and slowly and deliberately slid it under Mac's nose. 'I'll let you take a good hard look before you say this is not yours.'

Mac's eyes momentarily widened, but Evans had seen enough.

'You've seen that gun before, haven't you, Mr Deacon? Because your surprised expression spoke volumes.'

'Was that the gun used to kill me brother?'

'Er, Mr Deacon, we ask the questions, not you.'

Shields was still seething. 'Right, my client will not answer any more questions until he has seen that doctor you called for, and I will accompany you to the custody suite to see for myself the time you supposedly called the doctor. And I want to witness his injuries getting formally logged if they haven't already been.'

'We are in the middle of the interview. I am sure it can wait,' spat Drake.

'Unless your name is Dr Martin Drake, then you are not qualified to even judge if my client is fit for interview now. I am advising my client not to answer any more questions until the formalities have been dealt with according to PACE. I am not letting your police brutality slip through the net. We have enough of that going on. Wouldn't you agree?'

'I wouldn't agree, but I will accompany you to the custody desk.'

'Good, and you, Detective Constable Evans, might be wise to offer my client a warm refreshment. His injuries look so bad that Mr Deacon could suffer shock at any moment.'

***

The custody sergeant was red-faced when Shields arrived, and right away, Shields knew the police were up to no good.

'This is Sergeant Kerns. He was here when Mac and Brodie Deacon were brought in.'

Shields smiled. 'Great. Can I see the custody records, please?'

'Is there an issue?' asked the large sergeant with a bald head and a moustache.

'Well, for your sake, let's hope not. I want to see where Mr Mac Deacon's injuries are listed, the photographs of his injuries, and the actual time the doctor was called. It should all be logged.'

Kerns flicked through the custody record book and stared, clearly trying to find an excuse for not having recorded them.

'I am in the process of writing everything up.'

'Not the right way to go about it, so, tell me, what injures are you recording?'

'Er, a bruised eye.'

Shields stared. 'Left or right?'

'Right.'

'Nope, it was his left eye. And . . .'

'Oh. Well, I will have to speak with Mr Deacon again, and we will arrange to take more photos.'

'And what time did you call the doctor?'

'Oh yeah, I rang him about an hour ago.'

'Oh, did you? That's odd. Only Detective Constable Evans said *he* made the call, so, anyway, let me see the record of it, including the time.'

'We don't record that. We just call the doctor.'

'Hmm, well, it's been an hour, and my client has head injuries.' He looked back at Drake. 'He clearly isn't a nurse, and you clearly are not a doctor, so why is my client sitting in the interview room with his face black and bloody blue, and with no one knowing if he is even fit for interview?'

'If you have a problem, then you should take it up with the IOPC.'

‘Oh, I will, and my job as his solicitor is to ensure that he is legally and fairly treated, and as I see it, he isn’t, so I would be challenging this situation with the CPS and IOPC and naming you, Sergeant Kerns. So I would suggest you quit the slapdash attitude and get a move on, or I will have more to add to my complaint. Now, where’s the governor, Fitzgerald? I would like a word with him.’

As Shields walked away, Drake was on his heels. ‘He did it, you know, and I will prove it. I saw the look on his face when I showed him the gun. That’s his gun, and when the prints come back, they will show it. You can have your doctor and your photos and put your bloody complaint in, but it won’t change the fact that Mac Deacon shot his brother. And Brodie Deacon was with him.’

‘Detective, I want to remind you that this station messed up big time when they arrested Georgie Deacon and were grossly incompetent when they failed to protect her daughter, so tread very carefully. Don’t treat this case as a notch on your bedpost for a murder conviction because, again, the press will cover this story. It involves Dixie-Lee, the murdered victim’s daughter. The public will follow her as they did before, all the time she was in a coma. This is just another saga, so make sure you do everything by the book, or you will go out as your predecessor did.’

CHAPTER SIX

Raj followed Fitzgerald into his office. He didn't wait to be asked to take a seat. He was too angry, and now looking at the governor himself, who always looked calm and in control and who never broke into a sweat, he seemed out of sorts. His otherwise very healthy tone had paled. His hair needed a cut, and Raj noticed a tiny bloodstain on his shirt, probably from shaving, and, by the looks of things, with a blunt razor.

'Raj, I need you to be on board with me. I get it. Drake, Lardon, and Evans have joined us, and I'll be the first to admit it: they are not ideal, and I understand that their attitude is somewhat different from ours, but . . .' He leaned forward with his hands balled under his chin and his elbows resting on the desk. 'But I had to take them on. The fact is I didn't have a choice.'

Raj tilted his head to the side, waiting for any further explanation, but Fitzgerald wouldn't give him any eye contact; instead, he momentarily glanced at his computer screen.

'Gov, why? I mean, if I am going to work with these guys, then you could be honest with me and tell me why you had to have them on the team. And all from Tonbridge.'

Fitzgerald rubbed the back of his neck. 'Lord Drake.'

'Is that what you call him?'

Fitzgerald shook his head. 'No, Lord Drake is Martin Drake's uncle. I know you would never believe it, by the way the man carries himself. He has serious connections, but Martin pissed a few people off at Tonbridge, so he and a few others were transferred here. I tried to get to the bottom of it but my conclusion is we may have acquired the dregs who they can't sack because of Martin Drake's connections. Who knows? Let's hope I'm wrong. Anyway, the upper echelon want them out of Tonbridge, so we're stuck with them.'

Raj rolled his eyes. 'So this Drake bloke is now *my* boss. Is that right?'

Fitzgerald swallowed hard. 'Sorry, Raj, but yeah, he is. And, by the way, you have to call him Gov.'

'Bollocks.'

'No, Raj, Gov.'

'Oh, that's funny.'

'Leave Drake and Evans – Jesus, that man needs to go on a hygiene course – to concentrate on the Deacon case. I want you to look into the Marston-Smith inquiry.'

'Gov, isn't that Margate's problem?'

Fitzgerald shook his head. 'No, they want us to have a hand in the case. When I say a hand, I mean more like a little finger.' He could see from Raj's reaction that he wasn't buying this hard sell. But he himself had little choice. He was close to his retirement and he wasn't prepared to mess that up over a decision from above. 'Look, it's only because his death was so inextricably linked to Georgie Deacon. Find out what you can about her movements a week ago. We have to show we have dotted the i's and crossed the t's.'

Raj steepled his hands together. 'You don't think she had anything to do with it, do you? I mean, we established that Ashby killed two of the Marx siblings, and it was Ashby who was after Georgie. Marston-Smith was involved in the arms deals along with Ashby, but other than that, why would Georgie kill him?' He was determined to test Fitzgerald to see what his thoughts were.

'He raped her. It must have been at least twenty years ago, but, nevertheless, he raped her.'

'Yeah, so do you think she would kill him after all these years?'

'Why not? She would have a motive.'

'Gov, this is so weird. A more likely scenario is that it is someone who was in on the arms deals with Marston-Smith and who may have wanted to silence him so he didn't turn out to be a military informant.'

Fitzgerald stared unblinkingly. 'Hmm, your point about a possible associate is an interesting one, but, let's face it, Raj, it was an international operation involving various companies. So, the Army have ruled that scenario out. Look, we have to consider that Marston-Smith has a family, so we have to be seen to be doing *something*.'

Raj nodded in acknowledgement. He knew Fitz wouldn't budge on the matter. 'So I'm off the Deacon case. But not completely, Gov, because the Marston-Smith case could be linked . . . er, possibly, and what about the arson attack on Henry's café?'

Fitzgerald nodded. 'Yeah, sure, I guess you can call it attempted murder.'

'*Guess?* Of course, it was attempted murder.'

Fitzgerald loosened his collar. 'I'm going to take a few days' leave, Raj. Do us a favour. If there is anything I should know, then call me. I need to—'

'Go on, Gov. You do what you need to do. I'll call if it is urgent.'

Fitzgerald had taken a real liking to Raj. His beaming smile and realistic attitude meant a lot to him. Not prying into his own private affairs was a respectable trait, not always found in the average copper, and certainly not by the likes of the three Tonbridge coppers he had just taken on.

'Thanks, Raj. You're one of the good ones.'

It was a strange comment, and it compelled Raj to question if the 'Tonbridge Lot' were bent.

'Before you go, Gov, I know I'm not on the Deacon case, but the arson attack on the café was connected. I'm sure of it.'

Knowing that he couldn't stop Raj from having some input regarding the Deacon family, Fitzgerald merely smiled and nodded.

Raj knew then that his boss had the world on his shoulders.

After leaving Fitzgerald's office, Raj walked along the corridor and into the incident room to find Drake going through his filing cabinet. 'Unbelievable,' he muttered, under his breath.

'Can I help?'

Drake spun around with a heavy load of files in his hands. Clumsily, he dropped a few, and the contents flew across the room.

'Yeah, get me the Georgie Deacon case file, will you? I want everything there is on that family.'

His tone was harsh, but the complete disregard for the mess he had made was more shocking. And without even an apology, he stepped over the scattered files and left the room.

Opposite Raj's desk was Matias Lamp, a man in his forties but with the face of a teenager. He was a genius when it came to IT. He stared with his mouth open.

'Gov, I told Drake to wait until you returned, but he just ignored me. What a wanker! I take it that guy is our new boss – Martin Melonhead Drake. And he thinks I will cooperate with his every request when he snaps his arthritic fingers? He can fucking suck my dick. Ya know, he hasn't even called a meeting to introduce himself, and there was me thinking that you would be heading up the team. Gutted I am! Fucking gutted!'

'Do you know anything about Drake?' asked Raj, as he bent down and scooped up the files from the floor.

'Well, what I have been told about him is that he is a bully. Apparently, he has more informants than I've had caramel lattes, and . . .' He lowered his voice. 'Again, I've been told he is on the take. He got close to being investigated, so I believe that's why he has been moved here.'

'So why has he got away with it if it's true?'

Matias moved his floppy fringe out of his eyes and leaned back on his chair. 'He is a Drake. That's the problem.'

Raj shrugged. 'Means nothing to me.'

Matias gave Raj an exaggerated roll of his eyes. 'Drake and Drake, the company law firm? His grandfather is the CEO of Drake Pharmaceuticals, and his uncle sits in the House of Lords. Not sure if he is Lord Drake or a lord on his mother's side. But your new boss holds all the aces, I'm afraid.'

Raj slapped the files on the desk. 'So he is the dropout, the family member who became the school bully – the wannabe gangster – the black sheep. Fuck!'

'Yeah. The less you know about that guy, Raj, the better, if you know what I mean.'

'How do you know so much, Matias?'

With his cheeks flushed, Matias glanced around, ensuring no one else was in the room. 'He's married, right.' He looked around before continuing. 'But I've seen him in the Crash Club. It's a members-only gay bar. The dirty ol' codger likes a young man. I mean the pretty-boy type. West says he is a right creep.'

'That's your boyfriend, isn't it?'

Matias waved his hand. 'Yeah, he is *now*. Well, actually, he is my fiancé. Anyway, Drake had a thing for West. A little bit of pillow talk and all that. My West loves to talk. And, apparently, Drake was so pissed that he let a few things slip. You know what I mean, right?'

Raj grinned, thinking that West surely wouldn't get a word in when Matias was off on one. 'Does Melonhead still frequent this gay bar, then?'

Matias nodded. 'Usually most Thursdays, but you won't get in, if that's what you're thinking. As I said, it's for private members only.'

'Me?' Raj poked himself in the chest. 'No, I was thinking, perhaps, West could suck some more details out of him because' – he pointed to the files – 'I think ol' Melonhead is going to make our lives hell.'

'Yeah, sure. Luckily, he doesn't recognise me. Mind you, Raj, I do look very different when I'm out and about. It's amazing what a little bit of lippy, a set of false eyelashes, and a red wig can do.'

'Very pretty, I'm sure. Now, Dolly Parton, let's see what else West can discover as long as he doesn't put himself in danger. Oh, and a selfie inside that club would be good. Are you okay with that?'

Matias winked. 'I like where you may be going with this.'

'Matias, we need every bit of dirt we can dig up, and I am straight as they come, my friend, but you can't fight fire with a fucking paper wand.'

'I'm on it, Raj, and I know West will be in his element if he thinks he is playing detective. I mean, he loves role play and—'

'Yeah, Matty, I get the picture and I don't need the details. Not those kind, anyway. Oh, Matty, would you be a darling and fetch me a caramel latte and one for yourself.' He placed a ten-pound note on the desk.

Matias jumped up, grabbed his flight jacket – the most masculine one he owned – and shot off to the local Costa. He paused, his hand hovering over the note. 'Er, Raj, the club that my West works at . . .'

'Go on,' said Raj.

'Well, the thing is, my West is handing in his notice at the end of the month. He said the club has become an unsavoury place to work. It's run by a coterie formed of the elite. You know what I mean. Persons in power. They have slowly taken over, and now they pay his wages. He implied to me that they were running a racket.'

'What sort of a racket? Drugs?'

Matias looked down and then up and through his long lashes. 'No, young men, homeless or troubled kids, a rent-boy racket.'

'Christ, why didn't you say? I can have the place raided.'

Matias shook his head. 'No, Raj, this type of crime has been around forever, and the kids, unless they look eighteen, are not in the club.'

'And is Drake part of this elite group?'

Matias shrugged. 'I wouldn't like to say, but I can ask West to do some digging, although in a couple of days we will be off for three weeks. Australia, here we come.'

***

Raj waited until Matias was out of the room before he opened the middle drawer and found Georgie's file where he had hidden it under the main floating files. He knew if he filed it in the archive now, it would be listed as a recent addition, and Drake would become curious and open a Pandora's box. The old file, including Georgie's redacted Army records, was in the archives, and no one, apart from himself, was aware of the most recent Army file, which had surfaced six months after the murder of two of the Marx siblings. He decided to hide the latest file in his briefcase, and, for the first time in years, he used the combination lock.

Just as he was about to stand up to put his coat on, Drake stormed into the room again. 'Well?' he snapped.

'Sorry, what do you mean by "well"?'

'Georgie Deacon's files. Where are they?'

'I don't have them. They are stored in the archives. But you must have known that her case was closed. She was found not guilty of the Marx sibling murders, so all the files are stored away. I can give you codes, etcetera.'

'I understand there was an MOD file. I want to go through it.'

Raj rose from his chair. 'Do you think Georgie was responsible for her husband's murder?'

'I won't rule out anyone, especially the Deacons.'

Raj frowned. 'The Deacons? Why them?'

'Oh, come on, Raj. Don't play dumb.'

'No, seriously, you've lost me.'

'I looked into this business of theirs. On the surface, it all looks above board. It is a legitimate business. It is registered with Companies House. According to them, it is established as a consultancy firm.'

Raj shrugged. 'So?'

'It rakes in fucking millions, mate. They are worth a fortune. You can't tell me they earn that through consultancy work. No, Raj. They are dodgy fuckers, the lot of them, and as for Georgie Deacon, working in a café, when her family are stinking rich, I don't believe it.'

'Well, she does work in a café and has done for years, so what's your point?'

'She's hiding something. I reckon this plain Jane effect is simply that: a fucking con, because behind the scenes, I bet she is up to stuff. And I for one, will find out what's going on. And I can wager it has something to do with Dixie Deacon's death.'

Raj laughed. 'Next, you'll be telling me she's an ancient alien.'

'Don't fucking mock me, Raj, or you'll be staring at a computer screen watching CCTV footage for a month.'

Raj nodded. 'Yeah, that doesn't surprise me.'

'What d'ya mean by that?'

Raj stared with a poker face. 'Nothing, nothing at all. I have a case to investigate and a victim to question, so if you'll excuse me, Gov, I must be somewhere else.'

Drake stormed out of the room, almost banging into Matias, who was holding two coffees.

'Fucking look where you are going, or you'll have a dry-cleaning bill on your hands.'

Matias was gripping a cellophane-covered chocolate muffin by his teeth and holding a cup in each hand.

Having witnessed Drake's harsh behaviour, Raj hurried over and held the door open, while relieving his colleague of one of the cups. 'Please tell me, Matias, that that prick's bark is worse than his bite.'

Matias removed the muffin from his teeth. 'I think as a kid, he had some kind of inferiority complex.'

Raj laughed. 'Yeah? Well, in my opinion, it was fully justified. He is the prime example that shit can grow legs and walk.'

Matias took a seat and peeled the cellophane off the muffin. 'Fancy a bite, Raj?'

Raj smiled. 'Not from you, mate, and I don't like muffins either. I'm off home. I'm going to see Henry from the café first thing tomorrow, so I won't be in. Er . . . Matias, I don't normally ask this, but would you, er . . .' He paused and picked up his briefcase. 'Never mind.'

'I will keep an eye out and take notes. That fucking goes without saying. If he leads a trail of breadcrumbs, I'm following them, and anything else, Raj, you just say the word.'

Raj winked and left.

CHAPTER SEVEN

Georgie listened to her daughter's sobs, but she could do nothing to help. No amount of hugs would bring her father back. She poured a nip of brandy into her coffee and stared out of the window; it was pitch-black.

For some time, her eyes had been drawn to the garage at the bottom of the garden. And they were now. She knew she would never see that candle light up again. In that moment, it was as though he had never moved in. As if her memory of her husband was locked up in that garage. She had loved him once upon a time, but that was so long ago.

Alone in the living room staring out, she tried to recall how many times she had seen her husband, as he was then – the homeless guy. Certainly, he wasn't there every night, but he had been there on and off over time. Had her romantic idea that he had genuinely been hovering in the background to keep an eye on her and their daughter been exaggerated? Because as far as she was aware, he had only been there on the odd occasion. A reality check compelled her to think about the facts. Yes, she had made soup and bought an ex-Army sleeping bag for him when the winter had turned bitterly cold. And yet, when she had ventured into the garage there was only that makeshift bed – no real home comforts or belongings. She shook the thoughts from her mind and tried to address the fact that he was dead – murdered.

Her mind returned to the garage. Dixie had taken on the job of securing the garage when he finally moved in. He'd insisted they keep it locked so that it wouldn't get vandalised. At some point in the future, he'd told her he would use the garage for his hobbies. Whatever that meant. She hadn't been interested enough to ask. A chill went down her spine. *Was that the problem between them? Had she neglected him, his needs, his interests?*

When Dixie-Lee's sobs finally subsided, she crept up the stairs to her daughter's bedroom and peered in. The lavender in the bathwater and shot of brandy must have done the trick. Dixie-Lee was fast asleep. *Well done, Noel*, she thought.

Her daughter must have cried her heart out, judging by the size of the wet patch on her pillow. And in the orange glow cast from the landing light, she could make out Dixie-Lee's swollen cheeks and red eyelids. Anger suddenly whipped through her like a fast train. Not for herself or even for her husband, but for her daughter's pain. She would kill whoever took her daughter's father away from them. Tiptoeing around Dixie-Lee's bed, she peered out of the window. She could make out the police car and the unmarked car with Carol Lardon and Petra Holland inside. The interior light from the car lit up their faces; they were chatting and not paying much attention to their surroundings.

Georgie's mind returned to the set of keys and the garage. Maybe she could find something there that would be a keepsake for her daughter. Or perhaps Dixie had something of interest – like a diary. Because if she was honest with herself, there was more to her husband than an introductory short story of what happened to him after the explosion that had left him with PTSD and amnesia. She'd been evading the questions because she didn't want to know the answers. But also, at the time, she simply hadn't cared. But now? Now, Dixie was dead – and not even cold in his grave. So she wished she could go back in time. Because she needed answers. Answers that might lead to Dixie's killer. Was it someone from the Marx family or somebody else? It was all so baffling. And she didn't hold out much hope that the Bromley police would find the killer.

After creeping back to the living room, she took her phone from the coffee table, unlocked the back door, and removed the bunch of keys. Sliding her feet into her slippers, she gently closed the door behind her and made her way to the garage at the bottom of the garden. All the garages were merely concrete shells, and the drive between the houses and garages was an overgrown jungle of weeds. That was probably why the police weren't guarding the back. They may have not realised there was an alleyway. And she wasn't going to tell them because her back door led straight into her living room, and she didn't fancy a copper gawking in.

Using the torchlight on her phone, she lit the way. A rat stopped dead and peered up at her, momentarily startled; he was a big one, and his eyes looked red with the light shining directly at them. She wasn't scared of rats although she didn't like spiders much. In fact, the only thing she feared was anyone hurting her daughter. 'Shoo.'

The rat scurried away and left her to get on with her mission. But as she reached the garage door, she suddenly stood dead still, listening. She closed her eyes, knowing that her hearing would become heightened, and then she heard a very gentle sound of breathing. With the bunch of keys held tightly in her hand, she felt for the penknife, and with a fluid movement, she flicked it open but remained calm. A faint and subtle smell permeated her nostrils. It was a man's aftershave – JOOP! – a sweet perfume that happened to be her favourite. Rohan used it. Her heartbeat increased, not through fear but possibly excitement. Had he arrived here to see her? The excitement instantly vanished when she remembered he was at home with Finella and there was no way he could have arrived so quickly anyway. Not from Ireland. So who was lurking in the shadows? And who, if they wanted to hurt her, would even be brave and daring enough to come to her home with the police outside?

Slowly, she turned around to ensure no one was near her back door. When a dry twig snapped, her instant reaction was to point the beam in that direction, but all she saw was an urban fox with a dead rat in its mouth. The sweet smell had gone, though, and so had the sound of breathing.

Was she tired? Perhaps she was imagining things? Keeping the knife open, she relaxed her shoulders, mentally explaining away the smell of JOOP! She decided any one of the neighbours could have had a bathroom window open and the scent could have simply travelled out into the cold night air.

Using the phone torchlight to get a closer look at what she now saw was a new garage door, she was surprised and peeved to find that Dixie had used heavy-duty steel to reinforce the frame. Even the padlock on the garage was huge. No one would be able to use a hacksaw through that. Then, as she peered up, examining the new frame, she spotted a tiny black button-shaped object that she couldn't reach. As she stared at the object, she realised what it was – it was a camera.

What the hell was inside? Stepping back, she contemplated returning to the comfort and safety of her home and leaving whatever secrets that garage held in the past.

But curiosity won the battle. She tried all the keys on the key ring to open the padlock. Some she couldn't even remember what they were for or even if they had always been on the key ring. *So where would you hide a key?* Once again, Dixie had left her with another unsolved mystery to add to her list.

Another twig snapped, and a fox screamed, making her jump out of her skin. She hurried back to the house and locked the door, before running up the stairs to check on her daughter. Dixie-Lee was in the same position and fast asleep. When she looked out of her daughter's window, she noticed that the detectives' car had gone. But the police car, with two uniformed officers inside, was still there.

It was so late that she had to get some sleep, or she wouldn't function properly. She was about to close the curtains when something caught her eye, a movement outside. Her bedroom window faced the garages. Sure enough, someone was out there. She turned her light off and peered out. She could make out a figure wearing a dark hoodie and a thick jacket. He was of medium height, slimly built, and he appeared to be trying to mess with the lock to the garage door.

Georgie felt sick. She wanted to run outside and tell the police, but then she would have to notify them that she had a back alley and access to the back of her house. She sighed and thought this guy was probably an opportunist. Perhaps he had merely come across the overgrown alleyway by chance. Besides, all the garages were unused shells because they had been regularly broken into, so no one used them or even used the rear alleyway that divided the garden from the garages.

Holding her breath, she watched and saw him turn on his phone. The light shone into his face, but it wasn't a face she recognised. It seemed to be disfigured, although she couldn't be sure, being so far away, and the light from his phone cast shadows. He shone the light on the ground, and to her surprise, he began hopping about before he took off. 'Ah, so, Mr Nosey Parker, you're scared of a rat.' He didn't sprint like a fit man. Instead, he hobbled.

After peeling her clothes off, she climbed into her pyjamas and sat on the end of her bed, her mind flying in all directions, but there was so much to think about. She was fully aware that she needed to sleep first before she blew everything out of all proportion.

***

Blinded by the morning sun, Georgie placed her hand over her eyes. She had forgotten to close the curtains. Jumping up so fast, she had to take a deep breath to compose herself. Her first reaction was to look towards the garages. There was no one there, and her garage was intact. Also, she could see the large padlock from the window, which was still firmly in place.

It was the voices downstairs that must have woken her up. She glanced at the alarm clock; it was nearly eight o'clock.

Throwing on the clothes she wore yesterday, Georgie flew down the stairs. Her heart was beating so fast, she thought for a moment she would be sick. But with every horrible thought running through her mind, she was almost pleased to find Lardon there. Not that she liked the woman, but at least it wasn't the man she saw last night.

'What the hell are you doing in my house at this time in the morning?'

Lardon put her hands up, indicating she came in peace. 'I'm sorry, Georgie. I saw the kitchen light on, so I thought—'

'You thought you'd jump at the chance to get inside my home.'

'Please, Georgie, can we start again.' Her fake smile and fake voice made Georgie shake her head with frustration.

'Why, Detective? Did you wake up with a different personality this morning?'

'Mum!'

'Dixie-Lee, you may be a sweet, forgiving young lady, but I am not.' She turned to face Lardon. 'So say what you need to say, and then don't let that door of mine slap your arse on the way out.'

'Fair play. I understand that what happened to Mac outside the house yesterday looks dreadful from your perspective.'

'From my perspective? Are you insane? Your arresting coppers were punching Mac when he was clearly restrained, so don't you fucking dare come at me with your pathetic defence.'

Lardon was looking at the floor and feeling attacked. She waited for Georgie Deacon to stop ranting, and then she peered up. 'I'm sorry. Look, you took it the wrong way.'

'You fucking amaze me, Ms Detective, how flexible you truly are. I mean, you have your foot in your mouth and your head up your arse all at the same time.' She paused. 'Now, I told you once.

You don't get to call me Georgie. It's Mrs Deacon to you. So say what you need to say and leave.'

'We have a safe house ready for you and Dixie-Lee.'

Georgie crossed her arms and tapped her foot. 'You don't listen, do you? I told you I'm not *going* to a safe house. Your lot fucked up the safety of my daughter once before, and I'll never entrust you to protect my child ever again.'

'I understand, but you have to think of the safety of Dixie-Lee.' Lardon turned to her. 'What would you like to do, Dixie-Lee?'

'That's enough, Detective. How dare you go over my head. She is *my* child, not fucking yours, and *I* will be organising a safe place for her.'

Lardon went red in the face. 'And we will need to know where that is.'

'Well, I won't tell you because I don't know you.'

'Come on, Mrs Deacon, we are officers of the law and—'

'Yeah, and so was Detective Sergeant Kims! You do you know about Kims, don't you?'

Lardon was struck silent.

'My point, exactly. Now, please leave.'

With Lardon's patience wearing thin, she couldn't hold back. 'Well, Detective Inspector Drake wants to interview you himself, so I am charged with escorting you to the police station. My colleague will watch over Dixie-Lee.'

'Am I under arrest?'

Lardon's face flushed pink once more. 'No, but—'

'Well, there is no way I am leaving my girl here with your lot.'

'Mum, please, it's fine. I will be okay.'

Georgie looked at her daughter's puffy face and red eyes. 'I'll go when I've got you sorted, safe, and away from here.'

Dixie-Lee nodded. She wasn't going to argue with her mother. She never had, and she certainly wasn't going to start now.

As Georgie opened the front door, gesturing that Lardon must leave, she was confronted by Raj, who was ready to tap on the door.

'Hi, Georgie, may I come in?'

Lardon remained rigid to the spot, not stepping over the threshold. 'What are you doing here, Detective? I understood you weren't on this case.'

Raj smiled. 'And good morning to you, Carol. And you are quite right. I'm not, and I wonder why,' he replied, sarcastically.

'So why are you here?'

'I am here on another matter.'

'Oh yeah? What's that, then?'

'I not at liberty to say.'

'Well, if it is linked to our case, then—'

'It's not, so don't stress yourself.' He looked at Georgie. 'May I?'

'Yes, Raj, come in. Detective Constable Lardon was just leaving.'

As soon as the door was closed, Georgie sighed. 'I can't take much more of that woman. Just her face riles me up. She looks like a dog looking into a spoon.'

Raj chuckled. 'Yeah, she does a bit. Anyway, er, Georgie, listen. I have no idea what's going on, but please don't say too much to those guys. I shouldn't be telling you this, but I reckon Lardon and the two new detectives on your husband's murder case are bent.'

He walked into the living room, and, like mates, he felt comfortable enough to sit on the sofa uninvited. Yet having dealt with her case six months ago and having read her files, he felt he knew her so well. In fact, he did. He knew her only too well.

The sound of Dixie-Lee marching up the stairs had Georgie rolling her eyes. 'That kid is devastated.'

'And you, Georgie. How are you doing?'

'Holding it together, I suppose. Excuse me for being so frank, but you look shattered, Raj.'

'I am drained. I was up all night trying to figure out what exactly ex-detective Kims and Marston-Smith had going on between them. I know Kims was working for Marston-Smith, but I would like to know how deep their business went. Who else was involved and so on.'

He loosened his tie and unbuttoned his coat.

'I didn't kill Marston-Smith, if that's what you are concerned about. Although I am glad he's dead.'

Raj stood up and removed his coat. He was sweating. 'I want to tell you something, Georgie. Now, believe me when I say this is strictly between me and you. No one else.'

Georgie sat beside him on the sofa. 'You have my word.'

'Firstly, I know what you did back in the summer.'

Georgie could tell merely by the look in his dark-brown eyes that he knew, but she still felt she had to keep up a pretence. How could she admit to murder. 'I don't know what you mean,' she replied, with a deadpan face.

'Okay, let me explain. You see, you knew that the first thing Kims would do was request your records while you were in the Army because, Georgie, you were in the Military Police, so you and I both know that would be his first reaction. And, of course, he did. He emailed the MOD and requested your personal file. And, sure enough, when it arrived at the station by courier, no one questioned the validity of it, even me. I assumed it was real because it was authentic, except it wasn't the complete file, was it, Georgie?' He lowered his voice. 'You knew your file from the MOD would take six months to arrive, but . . .' He paused for effect. 'But I guess you knew that by the time the original file arrived – with everything documented inside – your case would be closed and that MOD file would be placed in the archives and someone like me would have assumed it was a duplicate and nothing more. But I read all of it, Georgie. I read how you were accused of murder and how your case was dismissed. But more important than that, I read the details of your original charge. It was a mirror image of the Marx murders.' He stopped talking and looked for her reaction.

'Do you want a cup of tea or coffee, Raj? You look like you need one.'

Aghast at Georgie's calm demeanour, Raj stared silently for a moment before he replied, 'Yes, please, Georgie. One sugar and a dash of milk, and surprise me. I like both tea and coffee.'

Eager to see if there were a few squad cars outside, Georgie hurried to the kitchen window and peered out. Her blood was pumping around her body at a rate of knots because there was no way she could deny what she had done. And Raj was spot on about all of it. She had assumed that the original file – the unredacted version – would have been automatically archived. She had also assumed that no one would ever read it.

There were no extra police, no additional cars. So maybe Raj wasn't having her arrested. She made the tea, contemplating what he wanted. *Was it money?* she wondered. However, she wasn't loaded, and she thought she knew Raj. He didn't seem the sly type. Clever – like her – maybe. She had to admit he'd stunned her.

For the very first time, her hands shook with nerves. It was so unlike her. But then this moment seemed so surreal. Her sodding liberty was on the line. So many thoughts were going through her mind, but she tried to maintain her cool demeanour, as she handed Raj a mug of tea and retook her seat.

After a sip of his tea, he was about to place the mug carefully on a coaster when he spotted a printed notice on it. He almost laughed out loud at the notice: *Don't fuck up the table.*

'I can see what I have just told you has finally sunk in. You look worried. Please don't be.' He opened his briefcase, removed a file, and placed it on the table.

Georgie stared at the leather outer cover, the same one as her own file, which she'd had couriered to the police station, except this one was twice as thick. The complete file was inside. Lifting the file onto her lap, she flicked through it. Sure enough, it was the original.

'What are your intentions, Raj?'

'I don't know yet.'

Even though it was cool in the house, Georgie wiped the beads of sweat from her brow. 'I can't live with worrying what you intend to do, Raj. And all hell has broken loose, as I am sure you're fully aware. I've just lost my husband, I've got my daughter in pieces, and I won't have a job to go back to because some bastard has tried to kill Henry and burned the bloody café down in the process.'

'Listen, let me make one thing clear: there are no other copies of that file. You have the only one in your hands, and I would suggest you burn it.'

Georgie pulled the file to her chest. '*Really?*' She frowned. 'And what do you want from me? I hope this isn't a flaming shakedown, Raj. In case you haven't noticed, I'm not loaded.'

Raj nodded. 'I know, but listen. I signed for that bloody file, and if it is found, and I haven't reported it, which I haven't, then I'll be in the shit. The best thing to do is to burn the bloody thing. The case is closed anyway, and I would have to bring it up again, and something inside me tells me not to, so there you have it.'

‘But you said you haven’t decided what your intentions are.’

‘Sorry, I was referring to whether or not to leave the force, and that brings me to this detective from Tonbridge. The guy called Drake. Something isn’t kosher about him. So please, Georgie, be very careful what you tell him and what you say when you are around him and Carol Lardon. Oh yeah, there’s another detective, Yan Evans. Just watch them all, okay?’

‘What’s going on, Raj?’

Raj chewed his bottom lip. ‘I don’t know yet, so please don’t mention this to anyone, but after this case, I will probably leave the force. It’s too corrupt for me.’ He grinned and light-heartedly said, ‘Maybe there’s a job for me working in this company your brothers-in-law own.’

CHAPTER EIGHT

By the time Raj had left Georgie's home, he felt more at ease with himself. So much so, that if he only had the nerve to hand in his notice right there and then, he would do it. However, there was something he felt he needed to do first. That was to get to the bottom of Dixie Deacon's murder even though he wasn't part of the investigation.

As he walked towards his car, he spotted a man he thought he'd seen before heading towards him. 'Hi!' said the tall well-built man, with striking bright-blue eyes and a Hollywood smile. 'I am looking for Georgie Deacon. I'm a friend. Well, I'm the man who rescued the café owner from the fire.'

The penny dropped. 'Ah, yeah, I remember you now. We were in the hospital. Noel, isn't it. Sorry, I was miles away.'

Raj looked the man up and down. He had to admire the clean cut of his cashmere coat, and tucked around the collar was a very expensive-looking scarf.

Noel smiled again. 'No worries,' he replied, holding out a gloved hand to shake.

Raj smiled. 'Nice to meet you. And well done for saving Henry. The estate would be devastated if anything happened to him.'

'Well liked, is he?'

'His desserts are a culinary work of art.' He rubbed his belly. 'I put this extra baggage down to his delights.'

'I see. Well, it is nice to meet you. Is Georgie alone? I don't want to intrude.'

'Only Georgie and her daughter are at home, but good luck getting past the gatekeeper.'

He nodded to Carol Lardon, standing with her feet evenly apart and her hands clasped together in front of her as though she was guarding the Crown Jewels.

'Oh, I only wanted to pass on a message from Henry.'

'I can do that if you'd like, Noel.'

Noel looked around and leaned forward. 'I really wanted to see her again. I know it's not the right time, but I want to make sure she's okay. You know, sometimes an outsider can help.' He shrugged. 'And if she's not interested in that, then nothing is lost.'

Raj could relate to what Noel was saying. He reminded him of an old neighbour he barely knew who had comforted him when his grandmother had died. He had found it easier to talk to practically a stranger than to his own parents.

'I understand. Tell that detective over there that Raj said it was okay. She might listen, but then again, she might not.'

Noel gave a salute and bowled over to Georgie's front door.

***

Looking at the property, Noel concluded it needed a lot of work. The front gate and the window frames hadn't seen a lick of paint for years, he noted. But the front garden was tidy.

'Good morning. I came to speak with Georgie.' He glanced over his shoulder to see Raj nod. 'Raj said it was okay.'

Lardon was staring into the man's eyes. She imagined him throwing her around the bedroom and fucking the life out of her.

'So if you don't mind,' said Noel, indicating that Lardon needed to step away so that he could knock.

'Who are you?'

'Noel, a friend of Henry's. Georgie knows me.'

Lardon was still captivated by the celebrity-looking man. She had already pissed off Georgie, so she stepped aside and allowed the handsome man to knock.

By the time Georgie answered the door, she was calmer. She'd just received a text from Rohan. He had bought a ticket for Dixie-Lee to join them in Ireland. All she needed to do was to get her daughter to the airport. Rohan would be there to meet her when she arrived in Ireland. And from there, they would stay in a holiday home they owned that no one knew about, so she would be safe.

To her surprise, there, with a welcoming smile, stood Noel.

'Oh, er . . . hello. How did you know I, er . . .? Sorry, what are you doing here . . .?'

Noel grinned. 'I can go. I don't want to intrude. But I wanted to check you and Dixie-Lee were okay.'

Georgie flashed a look at Lardon who had turned around and was clearly earwigging. Georgie glared at her and flicked her head for Noel to come in.

He politely wiped his feet on the doormat. 'I'm not interrupting anything, am I?'

Georgie shook her head and closed the door in Lardon's face. Suddenly, she felt very self-conscious. She looked down at the clothes he had seen her in yesterday. But it wasn't just what she was wearing that was the problem. She'd not taken care of herself. Her hair hadn't even been brushed; it was now a messy bun on the top of her head. She then realised she hadn't washed her face or cleaned her teeth. 'Please go through. I will just be a minute.'

Noel smiled and casually walked straight through into the small living room.

Georgie bolted up the stairs and hurried into the bathroom. The mirror never lied, and today, she didn't look her finest. After washing her sweaty face and cleaning her teeth, she sprayed deodorant under her arms and peeped into Dixie-Lee's room.

Her daughter was lying on her bed facing the window with her earbuds in. So, she gently removed one of the buds and whispered, 'You need to pack a bag. Get your passport because Uncle Rohan has organised a flight for you to go to Ireland, to their holiday home.'

Dixie-Lee spun her legs around to face her mother. 'Was that Uncle Rohan who knocked? Is he downstairs?' Her eyes lit up in anticipation.

'No, darling, it's Noel. You know. That man who rescued Henry.'

'Oh yeah, that nice guy.'

'Right, you'd better hurry, darling. You won't need to pack much. Your grandmother will undoubtedly have a completely new wardrobe of clothes for you. Plus, it will help her having you there. And I am sure it will help you too.'

'What about you, Mum?'

'I'll be okay, love.'

'No, Mum, I mean, how are you? And I understand how you must be feeling but don't pretend for my sake. I'm not a kid, Mum, and I know you didn't love Dad like you probably did when you weren't much older than me.'

For a second, Georgie was startled. 'You are too mature for your own good. But I did love him.'

'I know, but not like you would if you'd been together for twenty years. All I'm saying is don't pretend to feel something you shouldn't.'

A sad smile tugged at the corners of her mouth. 'I was thrilled when Dad came back. It was like a whirlwind for me, but I also felt so sad for you and Uncle Rohan. I believe that Dad coming home actually put an iron curtain between you two. I'm sorry, Mum. I'm treading on ground that's probably sacred and not my business. I just wanted you to know I understand.'

Georgie felt the lump lodged in her throat. She couldn't wish for a kinder and more understanding daughter than Dixie-Lee. She kissed her daughter's forehead and smiled. 'Get packed, babe. We need to leave in half an hour.'

Noel was staring at the photo of Dixie in his uniform. He looked up. 'So your husband was in the Forces?'

Georgie nodded. 'I'm having a coffee. Would you like to join me and tell me how Henry is faring?'

Once the butterflies in her stomach had calmed down, Georgie felt more confident and found her tongue. There was something about this man that made her legs turn to jelly. Being in the kitchen away from his come-to-bed eyes, she managed to compose herself.

'Sugar?' she called out.

'Not for me, thank you.'

For a second, she thought she heard a slight twang of an Irish accent; however, moments before, she had been imagining Rohan, and she always thought of him with his sexy Irish brogue.

As she stirred the coffee, her heart felt heavy thinking about Rohan's text. It was so matter of fact, with no kisses. She understood he was using a burner phone, but he could have rung. In the last six months, he had kept his distance between them, and even when she had visited Finella in Ireland, he had made his excuses not to be there. Maybe he felt guilty for liking her, but, in her eyes, there was nothing wrong with that. And besides, they hadn't actually done anything inappropriate – not sexually, anyway. They'd all thought Dixie was dead. And now her husband *was* dead, and Rohan being the real gentleman he was, she assumed he wouldn't want to even think about anything romantic, not now. She guessed he would feel as if he was betraying his brother.

By the time Georgie entered the living room, Noel had removed his coat and placed it over the back of the chair. On top was his scarf but not his gloves. He had them on.

'Hope you don't mind, Georgie. I get very hot. I am an outdoors kind of man.'

So why are you still wearing your gloves? she wondered. 'No, it's fine. Here, this is yours, no sugar.' She handed him a mug of coffee and indicated to him to sit on the chair. After she had sat down on the settee, she asked. 'So, how is Henry?'

'He is getting better, but I imagine he needs therapy. It was a shock, I can tell you. The explosion was frightening for anyone, but the fire and being trapped under a huge fridge, is not your everyday experience, so, all being well, his body will heal and then his mind will too.'

'You talk like you have experience in the medical field.'

'I work in rehabilitation. Anyway, enough about me, Georgie. How is your daughter?' There it was again, that slight Irish accent.

'She keeps herself to herself most of the time. She likes listening to her music, but I sense inside she is very angry and bitter. She's a good kid. She studies hard and has the biggest heart.' Georgie paused and bit her bottom lip to stop the tears. 'I am dying inside for her. If I could take her pain away, I would.'

'Yes, I bet as her mother you *would* die for her. Right?'

Georgie raised her brow at that remark. 'Yeah. But wouldn't most mothers?'

'I guess so. Did you try the lavender?'

'I think it worked. Sadly, she sobbed herself to sleep.'

'Look, Georgie, I know we don't know each other, but Henry has talked for hours, mainly about you, and now I feel I do know you. Is there anything I can do for you?'

'Why would you want to help me? Because you're right, we don't know each other. Sorry, I didn't mean to be rude.'

He chuckled. 'Henry said you could be quite direct. I am going back to Ireland, and since meeting him, albeit under horrific circumstances, I know that when I return in a few weeks, I can call on him, and, well, he is like a mate now. We shared an experience, if you get what I mean.' He winked and sipped his coffee.

That wink had Georgie's stomach doing backflips. 'I should imagine you have plenty of friends in England.'

'Not really. They are all clients, and they tend to be overly friendly at times because after telling me their inner demons, and shedding the overbearing bricks from their shoulders, they suddenly feel elated and link that feeling to me.'

Georgie was listening, but, in her mind, she suspected that many of his clients befriended him because he was so good-looking. His chiselled jaw and long eyelashes sucked her in. She saw herself as a together woman, so if any female found herself potentially broken, he would be their fantasy, and he sure would be hers.

'I have a vision of you as the Pied Piper.'

He laughed again. 'I can't play the flute.'

The clock chimed; it was ten o'clock. 'Oh, it's time to scoot. I need to get my daughter packed.'

'Packed?'

'Yeah, I am taking her away from here. The police want her in a safe house, but they are as useless as windscreen wipers on a donkey.'

'Safe house? Are you in danger?'

'Well, as you know, my husband was shot dead. They believe it was a revenge killing.'

'Oh, from the business a few months back?'

Georgie tilted her head, wondering how he knew about that.

'Henry told me all that you've been through. I am surprised you aren't seeing a therapist. You know, you can always come to see me when I return from Ireland. It will be my pleasure.'

Georgie waved her hand. 'I don't do therapy. Never have.' She looked at his eyes as they slowly blinked and then realised she shouldn't look a gift horse in the mouth. 'But maybe it's time I started, and I would love to take you up on your offer. Perhaps it *is* time I spoke to someone.'

'You were in the Army, weren't you. Didn't you have therapy then?'

Georgie suddenly felt cold. Her mind momentarily flicked back to Marston-Smith, when he had injected her, before he and another soldier raped her.

'Hey, are you okay, Georgie? You looked far away just now. Did I say something wrong?'

'No, it's fine. Sorry, er, look, I need to get my daughter to the airport before this bloody detective carts me off to the station for an interview. Anyway, was there any other reason you came to see me?'

'Oh, yes, sorry, Henry has lost his phone, and all his numbers were stored there. I've bought him a new one and left him setting it up. He asked me to check up on you and to get your number for his phone.'

The sudden expression on Noel's face had changed. He looked softer, almost angelic.

'That was so kind of you. I'll get a pen and paper.'

'Oh, okay. You don't want me to have it on my phone?'

'Sorry, Noel, I wasn't thinking. I didn't sleep very well.' She stood up and looked out of the window towards the garages.

'Lavender didn't help you either, I guess. Maybe you should have had a chamomile tea.'

'No, it's not that. There was a man down the end of the garden who was snooping around last night.'

Noel leaped up from his chair. 'Are you joking? What did the police say? Did they catch him?'

'No, I didn't tell them.'

'Why?'

'Because the truth is, I also discovered something new to me. The security on the garage has been updated and there is now a padlock on the door that was never there before. And if the police open that garage, they may learn more about my husband than perhaps I even know. It's hard to explain, but I feel like I am entitled to know the truth before anyone else.'

'The truth?'

'Well, maybe not so much the truth but perhaps a little history before the police start poking around. It's weird, I know.'

'It's not odd. It's a natural reaction. Henry told me you thought your husband had died. What was it? Eighteen or so years ago?'

Georgie nodded, feeling relaxed in his company.

'And how he lived in the garage for all those years.'

'Well, did he? That's the question I never asked him. You see, it wasn't plain sailing. I was so caught up in my emotions and how I would ease Dixie into our lives for Dixie-Lee's sake, that I probably didn't use the right tactics to understand his past. Still, one thing I do know is he wasn't the same man I married. He was quiet. It was as though he always had something on his mind. Even working with the scaffolders, who often came to the café, he couldn't commit to working full-time, only part-time. He said he needed to go to therapy, so he often disappeared for a whole day and even two days without coming home. I assumed he found it hard being enclosed in this small house when he'd had the freedom of the outdoors for so long.' She stopped when she realised she was talking to a complete stranger about her feelings.

Unexpectedly, she felt his hand on the small of her back, his breath on her neck. 'You must never beat yourself up over anything. You were brave enough to try to make a marriage work after all those years of not knowing Dixie. I can help you. I'll open the garage and if the shutter remains open, then no one will, as you put it, poke around. And you will get the answers you need.'

There was something about the feeling of him being so close that she suddenly felt she craved. It was madness. How could she enjoy this man's company so much when her husband wasn't even buried? 'It's kind of you, but I have to get Dixie-Lee ready. I'm sorry, Noel. I do have a million and one things to do, but please take down my number.'

'Georgie, I can help. Where do you need to take Dixie-Lee?'

'The airport. She has a flight to Ireland.'

'I can do that for you.'

'No, God, no. I don't know you.'

For a moment, Georgie felt she had been too easy with her words; she shouldn't have told Noel, but something about him made her feel so at ease.

'No, of course. Christ, what was I thinking. Listen, you have my number. I'll give Henry yours, and if you need me, I'll help if I can. It was lovely to meet you again, and maybe you would be wise to tell the police about the garage. You must stay safe, Georgie. At the very least, lock your doors.'

He grabbed his coat and slipped it on before grabbing the scarf. Georgie chewed her thumbnail, grappling with whether to trust the man.

She watched him pick up his mug from the coffee table and take it to the kitchen.

'You didn't take my number.'

'Oh, no, I haven't, have I. Are you not going to write it on a piece of paper?'

'No. Put my number on your phone and give it to Henry. Maybe I could book some rehab with you.' She gave her best cheeky smile before reeling off her number. However, before he had a chance to say goodbye, there was a hard rap at the door.

Georgie rolled her eyes. 'That's a copper's knock.'

Noel raised his brow. 'Maybe they have some news. I'd best be out of your hair. Let's hope they have found the culprit, so you don't have to live like this.'

Georgie pulled open the door to find a tall man in a suit and a shorter guy with mangled teeth. He looked like the rat she saw last night. Even the startled expression was the same. 'Can I help you?'

'I'm Detective Inspector Martin Drake, and this is my colleague, Detective Constable Yan Evans.'

Georgie stared silently.

'May we come in?'

'I have company. What do you want?'

'We need to talk. I understand that you don't want to come to the station, so I came here. I need a formal interview from you, and we need you to move to a safe house.'

'I will be the judge of the places I go to, and a safe house isn't one of them.'

'Georgie—'

'It's Mrs Deacon. I don't remember us being pals, let alone being formally introduced.'

'Mrs Deacon, may we come inside? It's cold, I'm tired, and I am working very hard to find your husband's killer. I want to eliminate you from our list of suspects, and I need you to go to our safe house before the press swarm your house and cause mayhem.'

Georgie folded her arms. 'Maybe trial by the press wouldn't be such a bad idea since your lot messed up last time. I served time, my daughter was nearly tortured and killed, so there you have it.'

'Mrs Deacon, not cooperating will only hinder our investigation, so I will ask you nicely. May we come in?'

Georgie was fed up with arguing, so after stepping aside to allow the officers into her home, she indicated they should go through into the living room. She went into the kitchen.

Noel had just finished washing up his mug. 'I'll let you get on with it, Georgie, and again, if you need my help, please call.'

She glanced at the clock. 'Damn!'

'What's wrong?'

'I need to get my daughter away from here to the bloody airport, and judging by their attitude' – she pointed to where the two policemen were in the living room – 'I won't be going anywhere anytime soon.'

'The offer still stands. I can take her there now, and I will watch her like she is my own daughter.'

Georgie searched his eyes to ensure he was being genuine. But she finally nodded. 'I really appreciate this. Where is your car parked?'

'I parked it around the corner. I couldn't get parked outside, what with the police and all. It's a white Mercedes. I'll wait for her. If she has the flight details, I can check to make sure there are no delays. I always do this when I'm back and forth visiting my mother in Ireland.'

Before she could even say thank you or goodbye, he had kissed her on the cheek and hurried out of the front door.

Georgie closed the door behind him and walked into her living room to find the two detectives already seated. 'Ah, take a seat. Oh, I see you already have,' she said, her voice laced with sarcasm.

'Mrs Deacon, who was that who just left?'

'A friend. Now, if you will excuse me for a minute, I need to talk with my daughter.'

She snatched her phone from the table and skipped up the stairs.

Dixie-Lee was almost ready. Sitting on the bed, with her thick teddy coat on and her gym bag beside her, she was lacing up her trainers.

Georgie noticed that the tiny scar on her forehead was now barely visible, but it was still a reminder to her. She hugged her daughter tightly. 'Now, listen. You talk to no one. Be vigilant and do whatever Uncle Rohan says. He will be at the other end to meet you. Okay?' She opened the text message that contained all the flight details, and her daughter used her phone to take a picture of it.

Dixie-Lee's eyes filled with fresh tears. 'Will you be okay, Mum? Call me every few hours so I know you are safe. And don't go fighting the Marx family. Let the police find out who killed Dad.'

'I will do, darling. Noel, Henry's friend, will take you to the airport. He has parked his car around the corner. It's a white Mercedes.'

After a final hug, Dixie-Lee raced out the door and Georgie breathed a huge sigh of relief. Her daughter would be in Ireland. She would be away from this lot, the police outside the house, the dodgy man who'd been poking around the garage, and, in general, the sheer doom and gloom of it all.

'Right, now what is it you want me to do?' asked Georgie, as she entered the living room.

'I need to go over your movements for the last few weeks, and I want you to take us through what you know of your husband's activities, his associates, everything that we may use to find his killer.'

'Well, have you spoken with Billy from the scaffolding firm where my husband worked because he would know a lot about his whereabouts? And if Dixie wasn't working, he was sitting in the armchair with the remote glued to his right hand, catching up on *Coronation Street*, I wouldn't wonder. Anyway, before I go through everything, have you released Mac and Brodie because there is no way they had anything to do with my husband's murder?'

'We can't give out any information.'

'So if you think you have your killer, as in Mac or Brodie, then why are you here?'

'Oh, come on, Mrs Deacon,' said Drake. 'You know how it works. You were a copper yourself, well, a military copper.'

'You say that like it is inferior to your role. But never mind that. All I know is that my husband went to work and when he wasn't at work, he was taking long walks, going to therapy, or at home watching the TV.'

Evans had his notebook out ready to write a long list of details. He looked up to see Mrs Deacon shrug her shoulders.

She smiled. 'That's it. That's all I know.'

Despite being grilled further by Drake and Evans for what seemed like hours, although it was actually only minutes, the questioning led nowhere.

Georgie wouldn't give anything away, not the Deacons' business, that was for sure.

CHAPTER NINE

With the interview inconclusive but over, Drake and Evans felt utterly washed out. Once they left the house, they looked at each other and shook their heads.

'She is bright and clued up. Maybe it was part of her training as an officer in the Military Police that gives the woman her astuteness, but one thing for damn sure is she knows more than she is letting on,' said Drake, still in awe of Georgie Deacon, yet at the same time annoyed.

Evans opened the passenger door to the unmarked car and climbed in.

As soon as Drake drove away, Evans said, 'I noticed she was adamant that she didn't know anything about the Deacon family's business. That's a lie. It has to be. She is the sister-in-law. Of course, she knows. And I don't buy the fact that her husband spent most of his time in a fucking armchair watching the soaps. I reckon she knows damn well who killed her old man, and I bet the brothers do too, and it's only a matter of time until a family like that seeks the killer out, and as their company motto states, they will undo a wrongdoing, if we don't find a way to stop them.'

Drake shook his head. 'We have them in custody, and they ain't going anywhere. As soon as we have the DNA match on the balaclavas and have the ballistics specialist check out the gun and the bullet that went clean through Dixie Deacon's head, the sooner we will know what the hell is going on here.'

'Gov, tell me, why are you so desperate to find out what the Deacons do? Is there something I should know?'

Drake stared ahead and didn't bother stopping at an amber light.

'Gov?'

'Okay, Yan, listen. Someone from the very top wants those brothers looked into. And it's a matter of fucking urgency, okay. That's all you need to know.'

'Who? Fitzgerald?'

'No, he is small fry. No, someone at the very top.'

'The Prime Minister?'

'Shut up trying to guess, all right. Look, I'll tell you. It's someone in MI5.'

'Fucking hell. MI5? Are they looking into Dixie Deacon's murder? Was he a spy or something? What's going on?'

'You're like a kid with the questions. No, this has nothing to do with Dixie Deacon's murder. They want to know about the Deacon brothers and what their company is actually all about. The fact we have them in custody and have good reason to question the likes of Georgie Deacon puts us in their favour if we can get some answers. But if the brothers are as reluctant as that bitch Georgie to tell us what we need to know, then MI5 will want to take over. I certainly don't want that to happen, if you get what I mean.'

Evans tapped the side of his nose and winked. 'And I take it you, and if I'm in on it, we, Martin, will be compensated for, let's just say, a job well done, will we?'

Drake suddenly swerved and pulled over, clipping the kerb.

Evans leaned away, knowing that there would be a backlash.

'You want to shut that trap of yours. There is *no* fucking money changing hands, *no* lining of back pockets. This is merely us doing the right thing. So stop hankering after finances.' He pointed his finger in Evans's face. 'You need to be aware that when I say the man at the top, I mean just that. He will just as easily have you fucking pulled down from your post.'

'All right, Gov. All right. This ain't personal, is it? I understand you're related to someone at the top? Is that right?'

Drake suddenly grabbed Evans's face and squeezed it. 'Don't you dare imply that I'm involved.' He instantly let go of Evans who flushed bright red.

'Fucking hell, I was only asking. And what do you mean involved? Involved in what?'

'Nothing!' he snapped.

'Martin, we've worked together for years, mate, and I've never known you to be so tetchy, so what is it?'

‘Shut up and mind your own business.’

‘Martin, I heard you talking about someone going missing.’

‘Are you fucking spying on me?’

‘No, Gov, of course not, but I’m not deaf, and you know me. I will help if I can.’

‘No, Yan, you only help me when I’m lining your pockets.’

‘That ain’t fair, Martin. You ain’t even bought me a pint for keeping me mouth shut when your missus calls me wanting to know where you are. There’s been plenty of times when I’ve been your alibi. I only hope this bit on the side is worth it.’

‘Yan, do yourself a favour, mate. Keep your fucking nose out of my business.’ He glared with a sour look. ‘And while I think about it, buy some dental floss *and* some deodorant.’

‘That wasn’t called for.’

‘I wasn’t having a fucking dig. I was stating a fact. I am fed up with people offering you mints.’

***

Georgie bent down, removed the MOD file from under the sofa, took it upstairs, and hid it under her wardrobe. She would burn it later.

Once again, she was drawn to the view of the garages from her bedroom window. That padlock was bugging her, let alone the reinforced frame and the new door. Why go to those lengths? What was inside that was worth making the place so theftproof? Why hadn’t she noticed it before? Then again, she hadn’t been down to the garage because there hadn’t been a need. She hadn’t ever used the garage for storage. But one thing vexed her. What was the deal in having a new garage door, the huge padlock, and the reinforcement frame? And all that camera stuff? *What was that all about?* she wondered. Once again, she cursed Dixie for not telling her more about his past. But now he was dead, she was left to work out everything for herself. *Life was such a bitch.*

She returned to the living room to get the bunch of keys, but they were missing. She spun around. Her eyes scanned the mantelpiece, the coffee table, and the nest of tables. She felt inside her pockets but the keys weren’t there.

Searching the kitchen with no success, she then went back upstairs, thinking that after last night she may have taken them with her. And that would be a first, as the keys were always left in the back door. She tried to remember where she had put them, but her head was so full of problematic stuff, she couldn't. However, what bothered her the most was the back door wasn't locked, and she would never have gone to bed without checking the back door, especially when she'd seen some creepy bloke lurking about outside the night before. She pondered over the idea of it being one of the Marx tribe. They were a large family with many cousins and uncles and most had an unsavoury reputation.

The outside air was bitter. She wondered if it was a warning that snow was on its way. Pulling her cardigan tighter around her, she ventured outside and traced her steps to the garage, hoping to find the bunch of keys.

But she was out of luck. She stood in front of the garage and looked up at the small camera. Although it was out of reach, she could see it more clearly in the daylight. It was a camera that could be linked to a phone or a laptop. Why would Dixie have had it and what was inside that garage? Or did he know someone was coming for him? A sudden rush of anger filled her veins. *What the hell had he been up to?* She glanced down at the padlock and noticed that someone had tried to use a hacksaw to cut through it. *It wasn't like that last night,* she thought to herself. The police were useless. Surely, if the police had done their homework properly, they would have known there was a back alley, yet all they did, it seemed to her, was to sit inside their police cars playing games on their iPad.

She bent down and gripped the padlock in her hands and tugged. The padlock was secured. But it was the camera that she was more intrigued by. If Dixie had a laptop or phone inside her home, she would find it.

Once she was back indoors, she leaned a small table against the door because she couldn't lock it now and she didn't want the cold getting in. She peered around the living room and knew there was nowhere he could hide a phone or a digital device. Her living room was small and basic without bookshelves or cabinets. *Where did you keep your phone, Dixie?*

Making her way upstairs to their bedroom, Georgie felt a little uneasy by the idea of snooping through his stuff, which he'd accumulated very quickly in the last six months. She had never questioned where his belongings had been stored prior to him moving in.

Opening his wardrobe door, she suddenly felt self-conscious that she was doing something rather sneaky. It made her look behind her as if he would suddenly appear and catch her out. Slowly, she turned back to the wardrobe, which contained a number of boxes, but ignoring those, her eyes focused on the long well-worn coat that she had seen him in when she knew him only as the vagrant. Something was poking out of the pocket. Sliding her hand inside, she retrieved a blue baseball cap; it was a child's. Turning it around in her hands, her thoughts turned dark. *Why would you have a child's cap, Dixie?* A cold feeling ran through her, and she had the urge to close the wardrobe door and run. But she didn't. Instead, her mind went back to the garage and that camera fixed outside. *Where was the phone or iPad he'd used to check the garage was secure?*

Thinking the device must be in the wardrobe, she gingerly removed the first battered shoebox from the top shelf above the shirt rail and was surprised it was so light. After emptying the contents on the bed, she found an old pair of small-sized trainers, which were clearly not his. And tucked away in one of them was a small plastic bag. She held it up and her blood turned cold. Inside was a minute action hero figure. She slid her hand inside the other trainer and pulled out a lock of hair and a bag of baby teeth. *What the fuck were you really all about, Dixie?*

Unable to find an iPad or a phone, she decided to look downstairs again. She was just about to check the armchair where Dixie would sit for hours and look out of the window – *was he watching the garage?* – when her phone rang, making her jump. Removing it from her back pocket, she saw Rohan's name on the screen. At first, it didn't dawn on her that he wasn't using a burner phone. With her heart racing, just seeing his name, she answered right away. 'Hi.'

'I'm so sorry, Georgie, I wanted to call yesterday, but Mum was in a terrible state. How are you?'

'I'm okay. It's Dixie-Lee I am worried about. She cried herself to sleep, and I know she'd fallen in love with her dad, so losing him now goes into the realms of cruelty. Anyway, I am sure she will feel a little better when she sees you and Finella.'

'That's such a good idea. Why don't you send her over to Ireland?'

'*What?*' Georgie's body suddenly turned to ice. 'What do you mean, Rohan? I've seen your text this morning.'

'Georgie, what's going on? I didn't text you.'

With her hands shaking uncontrollably, she staggered back to the sofa. Her mouth was bone dry and she could barely answer. 'Sh – she – she's gone to the airport on a flight. You sent me the flight details. Please say you did. Please, Rohan.'

'Christ, Georgie, I didn't. What the hell's going on? Where is she now? Get off the phone and call her right away. Tell her to go home.'

Georgie cut him off and dialled her daughter's number, but Dixie-Lee didn't answer. Her heart was in her mouth. She felt as though she was being strangled as she gasped and gasped for breath. After calling the number again, she listened and waited while the phone rang. But when Dixie-Lee still didn't answer, all her worst fears came to the fore. Trying to fight the rising panic, she couldn't help that evil feeling of dread gnawing away at her insides.

Suddenly, she remembered she had a tracker app to trace her daughter's phone. She scrolled through her apps. As she was still getting used to her smartphone, she still needed to learn what each one did. Almost by accident, she came across the one she required – the tracking app. She clicked on it and watched as the map opened. As it homed in, the map enlarged, and she realised that Dixie-Lee's phone wasn't on the M25 heading to Gatwick Airport but instead it was stationary around the corner. *Thank God*, she thought. *Her daughter was here.*

Opening the front door, Georgie barged past Detective Constable Lardon, hurtled along the street, turned left first, and instantly stopped dead. The road was empty, with no white Mercedes. The only car was a green MINI that had never shifted from that parked position in all the years she had lived there.

Georgie glanced at the app, and as she walked along the street, she could see she was closer to the phone, and there it was: it was on the road by the kerb. She picked it up and held it to her chest before she fell to her knees as fear throbbed inside her.

Lardon was behind her. She helped her to her feet. 'What's happened?'

Georgie's eyes were blurred, but she managed to pull away from the detective and run back to her house.

But she couldn't slam the door shut because Lardon jammed her foot in the door. 'Let me in, Mrs Deacon. For fuck's sake, what's just happened?'

'My daughter's gone. They've taken her.' She wiped her nose with the sleeve of her cardigan. 'They've fucking got her.'

'Who?' yelled Lardon. 'Give me a name! Anything!'

'I don't fucking *know*. The guy who rescued . . .' She paused, her mind now going back over the visit. This Noel guy hadn't removed his gloves all the time he was in her house. And he'd washed up his mug. She tried to recall his features, and straightaway, she focused on his hair. It then dawned on her that it was in a bun and heavily jelled into place. The bastard had tried to prevent any traces of his DNA. 'That man who was here. He was supposed to take my daughter to the airport, but I found her phone by the kerb.'

Lardon rolled her eyes. 'Kids are always losing their phones. It doesn't mean this man has kidnapped your daughter. He is probably on his way to the airport. Let's calm down and check the flight details. I can call the station, and they will check to see if your daughter is on that flight. Do you have the flight numbers?'

Georgie was still trying to process the facts. 'No, listen, there is no flight.'

'What do you mean?'

'I had a text this morning from who I thought was my brother-in-law to say he had booked a flight for Dixie-Lee to go to Ireland to the Deacon family's holiday home, but when I spoke to Rohan Deacon just now, he told me he hadn't sent that text. Jesus Christ, I swear to God if anyone has hurt my daughter, I will fucking eradicate them.'

But it wasn't anger that was directing her mood. She felt guilty. Why had she trusted a complete stranger, for God's sake? And even worse, why had she been sucked into this Noel bloke's handsome face and believed his bullshit about his caring job and his charm. Charm was one thing she'd never fallen for in the past, and now she had allowed it to cloud her judgement. At this precise moment, she was convinced her actions would lead to the gravest consequences.

'You should have let us take her to a safe house.'

No sooner had Lardon said those words than Georgie's eyes widened with rage. Grabbing Lardon around the throat, she lifted her off the floor and rammed her against the wall. 'Shut your fucking mouth, you piece of shit.' Dropping the detective like a hot brick, she stared with horror at what she had done to the officer.

Lardon fell to the floor, gripping her throat while she coughed and spluttered. 'Mrs Deacon, I – I – am arresting you—'

'My husband has been murdered, my daughter is missing, and you want to fucking arrest me? Well, do it then, you ugly shit stain! Fucking do it, and I will make sure that you and your cocksucking colleagues will be known all over the press because the best way to find my daughter is by going to them. Believe you me, darling, I will fucking use everything I have to find her. And the fact that you lot failed to protect her before is the reason I haven't trusted you this time, and that's the fucking reason she is missing, so arrest me, you bitch. Just fucking do it!'

Lardon stepped back and rubbed her hands around her neck. She stared while they locked eyes like two predatory lionesses, daring each other and mentally planning their next move.

Lardon had never been scared like that before. Even when she had arrested the biggest brutish men, she'd never felt she was so close to death. Georgie Deacon would have killed her, and she knew it. She was so strong, like a man, and her movements were so deliberate and precise.

'You know you could have killed me, don't you, Mrs Deacon?'

Georgie nodded.

'Army training?'

Georgie shook her head. 'Escaping my mother's perverted boyfriends, and, I guess, military moves. But I didn't kill you. I barely touched you.'

Lardon rubbed her neck again. 'You fucking lifted me off the ground, though.'

'But I didn't kill you and I didn't leave you disabled. In fact, you don't even have a red mark around your neck now.'

Georgie looked at the back door debating whether or not to make a run for it. She had to find her daughter.

‘Okay, I won’t arrest you. But if you scarper and I find you, I will.’

‘Just do your job, Detective. I will tell you and that weasel Drake everything I can about this bloke, but you must already have his details. He rescued Henry from the fire.’

Lardon frowned. ‘That case is Detective Sergeant Rajesh Raj’s. He is looking into that, but the two incidents could be connected.’

Georgie shook her head in despair. ‘*Obviously*, they are fucking connected. Now, I need people around me who I can trust and who can make enquiries themselves, so I hope to God, knowing this, you will look at releasing Brodie and Mac.’

Lardon raised one eyebrow. ‘Is this a set-up to get the Deacons released?’

Georgie’s eyes were wide again, glaring at the officer with undisguised utter contempt. ‘You what? How fucking dare you.’

Lardon raised her hand. ‘Okay, I need to call this in. Do you have the man’s number plate?’

‘His name is Noel, and no, I don’t.’

‘You let Dixie-Lee go off with a stranger and—’

‘If you continue stating the obvious, like you’re my mother, you will be arresting me for grievous fucking bodily harm. Now, please, either help me or fuck off.’

‘You are treading on thin ice, Mrs Deacon. You need to calm down and let me do my job. I’ll call Detective Inspector Drake.’

Georgie could hear Lardon on the phone, but she couldn’t hear Drake’s response. Every so often, though, she noticed Lardon glancing at her, and finally, she moved away from her out of earshot. However, she did hear her mention Raj and then she sighed heavily. The body language was a dead giveaway. There was evidently contention between Raj and the new team.

Before Georgie could ask what Drake had said, her phone rang. It was Rohan.

‘Any news, Georgie? Have you found her?’

His voice moved Georgie so much that her tears felt like hot rivers rolling down her cheeks. ‘*No!* She’s *gone*. Her phone was on the kerb around the corner from my house.’

‘I’m on my way. Ma will stay behind for now, in case, for whatever reason, Dixie-Lee manages to find her way here.’

‘When will you get here?’

‘As soon as I can book a chartered flight.’

Now feeling relieved she had Rohan’s support, Georgie slumped onto her sofa, placed her hands over her face, and cried.

Realising that Mrs Deacon needed some personal space, Lardon made her way to the kitchen and put the kettle on. After making a sweet tea, she returned with two steaming mugs to find Mrs Deacon rocking back and forth and sobbing quietly.

‘Here, I’ve made you a sweet tea. Can I get you anything else? Er, paracetamol, er . . . ’ Lardon faltered clearly not knowing what to say. Georgie Deacon had gone from almost murdering her to now crying like a baby.

Georgie took a few deep breaths to compose herself before she took the mug of tea and swigged the piping hot drink. ‘Thank you. Now, I heard you mention Detective Raj.’

‘Hmmm, well, apparently, he is on his way to interview this Noel guy again. No one thought to take a formal statement because this Noel was viewed as the hero of the day. They only took an address for him, which was confirmed. Apart from that, we really don’t know anything else. Detective Inspector Drake is sending Raj a message now. He has also sent two officers to meet Detective Sergeant Raj there.’

Georgie drummed her fingers against the mug. ‘I can’t sit here and do nothing.’

‘There is nothing you can do except sit and wait. We also don’t want to worry about where you are.’

Georgie placed the mug on the table and rose to her feet. ‘Excuse me.’ She barged past Lardon and straight out through the front door.

Lardon was behind her. ‘Wait, listen, you can’t just go off.’

‘I’m not. I’m going to knock on a few doors to ask them if they saw my daughter.’

Lardon grabbed Georgie’s arm. ‘Don’t! Let the *trained* officers do the house-to-house search.’

Georgie threw a warning glare before looking up and down the road. ‘Well, where are they, Carol? They are not even bloody here and don’t insult me by saying the word *trained*. You forget what I did in the Army!’ she yelled.

‘No, we haven’t. We know exactly what you did there.’ Lardon spat the words out with such profound emphasis that it compelled Georgie to stop in her tracks and stare at her questioningly.

Lardon blushed. Once again, she had put her foot in it.

‘What do you mean?’

‘Nothing.’

‘No, Carol, tell me what you mean, or I will get straight on the phone to the fucking press now, and I will be mentioning your name.’

‘Word went around about how you accused the top brass of rape, and a soldier took his own life because of your claim.’

‘That’s bullshit, absolute bullshit. That never happened, so you can go back and tell your gossiping mates that they are all misinformed and not to say such rubbish without the facts. You’re like a bunch of kids in a playground.’

Lardon looked away, feeling pretty stupid – not for repeating what she knew but for not choosing her words carefully enough.

CHAPTER TEN

With Petra in the front passenger seat, Raj flew through the streets towards the address Noel had initially given the police. He'd instructed Matias to search for any information he could find on Noel Wade. All Raj could give Matias was the description: long hair, which may be tied up in a bun, a beard, and blue eyes. The guy could have walked straight out of a men's magazine dressed in a designer suit.

When they reached the address – an apartment at the posh end of Bromley – Raj waited for the backup. Holland had only spoken to him to ask what they were doing. He knew she was annoyed because he'd been sharp with his words and not given her much attention, but he didn't want to be distracted; his mind was on finding Dixie-Lee alive. Besides, he recognised that perhaps Petra Holland wasn't the woman for him. He found her a little easily led, especially by the new team. Her few comments made him think she was kowtowing to the enemy as he saw them. It was just another reason why he felt he should quit the force.

He surveyed the outside of the apartment. It was the top half of a grand-looking Victorian house. The front had been painted white, and the upstairs had Juliet balconies. As soon as the uniformed officers arrived, Raj got out of his car and hurried to the steps, remaining vigilant. Several supporting officers ran around to the back and two remained at the front.

Before Raj had even reached the middle step, the front door opened, and a middle-aged woman appeared. She had grey hair cut perfectly around her face. Almost too perfect, in fact. She didn't wear any make-up, and her bland outfit consisted of a black jumper, a long black skirt, and a long cardigan with pockets. Before she managed to spin around and go back inside, he called out, 'Who lives there?' Desperate to find Dixie-Lee, he ditched any polite introductions.

The grey-haired woman stepped back when she realised the house was entirely surrounded by police. 'Er, Noel, er . . .' she tentatively replied.

'Wade?'

She hesitated before nodding. 'Yes, but he is not here now.'

'And you are?'

'Oh me, I'm just a cleaner.'

'Key?' said Raj, holding out his hand.

'Oh, er, yes, okay,' the woman replied, digging deep into one of her cardigan pockets. 'But do you have a warrant?' she asked in a gentle, mild manner.

'Do you have something to hide?' snapped Raj, having ditched his usual caring personality.

'Sorry, no, I don't. Please go ahead.'

Raj flew up the stairs and opened the door to find the apartment stinking of bleach, the level of which made his eyes water. The place looked immaculate. The bed was made as if by a soldier, it was so perfect. There was not a crease, not a wrinkle, and the wooden floorboards were polished enough to see your face in them. As he turned around, the woman was behind him. 'I don't know if he even slept in that bed. He kept the place so clean and tidy. I don't know why he needs a cleaner. There's very little for me to do. He is such a nice man. What are you looking for? Maybe I can help?'

'A teenage girl.'

'There's no teenage girl here.'

'And do you know what time he left?'

She shrugged. 'Oh, I don't know. Now, let me think. Perhaps nine, maybe ten. Oh dear, dear me. I *am* forgetful these days.'

Raj stepped aside as the support officers hurtled past him and into the apartment. However, there wasn't much to check. The property had four rooms consisting of a lounge, a kitchen, a bathroom, and a bedroom.

'My colleague will take a statement from you.' He looked at Holland, who seemed away with the fairies, as she gazed up and down the street.

'Petra!' He waved her over to him.

'Raj, there are no cameras on this road.'

'No, love. There is only one when you join the main road towards Catford,' replied the woman.

Raj was impressed and intrigued. Why would a middle-aged woman, who was reasonably well spoken, know about APRs?

'Sorry, what's your name.'

'Er . . . me . . . it's Mrs Silvia Serval.'

'Petra, take a statement from Mrs Serval. I want every little detail. I want to know everything there is to know about Mr Wade.' He turned to face Mrs Serval. 'Did you know him well?'

'Not at all. Only that he was charming. He was such a lovely man for—'

'A kidnapper,' said Raj, as he finished her sentence for her.

'Oh gosh, no. He seemed like a kind, sweet man to me.'

Raj glared at what appeared to be a smirk on the woman's face. Or maybe it was just the way she looked at him.

Raj nodded to Petra. 'Please escort Mrs Serval to the station. I want a statement.' He saw the fear creeping along her face, and her eyes widened.

'Oh no, please, if anyone should see me in a police car, I would be mortified. I run the women's refuge group and work in the church. I will be thrown out. Oh my God.' She placed her hands to her throat. 'This will ruin me. You don't understand. I have a reputation. I have a responsibility. I am a trustee at the animal rescue centre. I am in charge of the local Cats Protection League . . .' Her voice petered out as she held out her hands, expecting cuffs.

'Sounds to me like you are a very busy woman. Look, no one is going to restrain you. I just want a statement, that's all.'

'He has done something bad, hasn't he?'

'We believe he may have. So please, help us as much as you can. Any detail, no matter how small, may be huge to us and may lead us to where he has taken an innocent teenage girl.'

Mrs Serval nodded, her eyes glassy. 'I'm sorry.'

Raj watched as Holland led the woman away towards a police car, but something bugged him. Mrs Serval walked as though she was elderly but she looked more middle-aged, so he wondered if she was acting like a much older woman for a reason. He glanced about him and noticed that parked outside was a brand-new white Mercedes. He had been informed that Noel may have driven Dixie-Lee away in a white Mercedes.

'Wait. Mrs Serval, who does that car belong to?'

She turned around, looked at the car, and then back at Raj. 'Oh yes, it's mine.'

It was quite a sporty-looking car. It was not the type he would expect a very plain woman – like Mrs Serval – to drive. However, he couldn't say such a thing.

'Did you lend your car to Mr Wade at any time?'

'No, I wouldn't ever do that.'

'What car does he drive?'

She looked at the sky. 'Er, I think it is a blue Audi, maybe a BMW. I can't be sure.'

Before he could ask another question, the lead officer called over. 'Nothing here, Gov.'

Raj waved them on. Apart from Silvia Serval's account, there were no clues or evidence that Noel Wade was even here. However, something about her bothered him, although he couldn't put his finger on what it was.

***

Raj arranged with one of the officers to take Holland back to the station once she had finished. He needed to speak with Drake before he went back to see Georgie. The case was now joint, and they would have to join forces and work as one team. He dreaded the thought because he disliked Drake and Evans immensely. To him, they were like two unprofessional and disrespectful detectives who should be on some dark comedy, not leading a murder investigation. And the fact he suspected they were bent didn't help matters.

The station was busier than he'd seen in the last few months, now they had a murder and a kidnapping, and the kidnapper had walked away right under their noses.

However, before he reached Drake's office, his phone rang. It was Matias. 'Raj, did you infer earlier that Noel Wade looked like he'd stepped out of a men's magazine?'

'Yes, why?'

'Well, I am looking at him on my screen right now. I don't know what men's mags you wank over, but believe me, Noel Wade, who owns that apartment, is three foot and a fag paper tall, with a bald head, Coke-bottle glasses, and a nineteen seventies porn star moustache. And he is currently on a sabbatical in Thailand. Jesus, he's an idiot. Why are people so stupid as to put their whereabouts on social media?'

'Shit, we need to talk to that cleaner again.'

'Well, that was my next comment. Petra called in Mrs Serval's address after she shot off in her Mercedes. The property, my friend, is owned by a Lady Guthrie, not a cleaner by the name of Silvia Serval.'

'Did she get the number plate?'

'Sorry, Raj, she didn't, but listen, don't be too hard on her. I think she's got a lot of stuff on her mind.'

***

Yan Evans was hurrying along the corridor. He was so engrossed in reading notes contained inside a grey file that he was unaware of those around him.

Raj noticed that Evans held the file with one hand and a hot drink in the other. He pulled out his phone and pretended to be talking to someone while deliberately bumping into Evans. Files and papers went everywhere and coffee was splashed over Raj's coat, but the incident was more of a shock to Evans, and he instantly hissed, 'You fucking knob.'

'Shit, sorry, mate,' said Raj, as he bent down to pick up the file.

'Leave them!' yelled Evans, but he was too late.

Raj swooped down and retrieved two pieces of paper, and before Evans could rip them away, Raj managed to clock the heading of one piece. It was from the ballistics testing department, and the other was a note, and at the bottom, he noticed the name Lord Cecil Fairly.

'That was quick. Shit, I normally have to wait a few days, sometimes weeks, for a ballistics report.'

Evans, like a child, snatched the papers and hid them behind his back. 'You need to keep your nose out.'

Raj smiled from ear to ear, completely unnerving Evans. 'Really? And why is that? After all, we are all coppers at the end of the day, and sharing information helps us to catch the bad guys, so do you want to tell me what you mean by keeping my nose out?'

'It's not your case to be sticking your beak into.'

Raj took a deep breath and looked up and down the corridor. 'Hmm, so the thing is, you have clearly been left in the dark, mate. This *is* my case. You see, I was handed the arson attack on the café and all that went with it. And it is now linked to the Deacon murder, but you knew that, didn't you? So I have the authority to see what you see.'

Evans frowned. 'By whose authority?'

'By Fitzgerald, *and* your boss. Funny, I was just about to call him as well. Anyway, I have a kidnapped kid out there who happens to be Dixie Deacon's daughter. And the man who helped Henry from the fire is my number-one suspect. See where I'm going, mate? So that ballistics report is as much for me as it is for Martin Drake. So while you are here, I'll have a look,' said Raj, who had left his softer side at home in bed along with his sweaty bed linen.

Evans tried to imitate the beaming smile, but he only highlighted his need to see a dentist. 'I'll show Drake first, and then I should think he will call a team meeting.'

Raj looked up and down the corridor again. 'Is the solicitor representing the Deacon men still here? His name is Hugh Shields.'

'Why?'

'Well, he will want to know how to advise his client since the ballistics report is back. Of course, he will want to know because that's all you are holding his client on. And if his prints are on that gun and he had gun residue on his clothes, and if it was that kind of weapon used to murder their brother, then you may have a good case for the CPS. You seem to be smiling, so I take it you do have that information. Is that right?'

'Wait for the team meeting, Raj.'

'Oh, I see. You can't fart unless Drake says so. Is that the case?'

'Fuck off, Raj.'

Raj smiled as he watched Evans storm off with the hump and mumble under his breath.

As soon as Raj entered the custody suite, he spotted Shields, who was on the phone. His face was white, and his eyes were circled with black rings.

He looked at Raj but remained on the phone.

Out of view of the custody sergeant, Raj gestured to Shields if he wanted a cuppa.

Shields knew what Raj was doing. He clearly wanted to have a conversation away from the station. He waited a few minutes, then he left the custody suite and made his way to the coffee shop in Bromley High Street. They had enjoyed a coffee there before. As soon as he reached the shop, he saw Raj at the counter ordering the drinks.

Shields removed his coat and slid it along the cold plastic seats. Seeing Raj approach, he offered him a smile.

'I need a coffee. They are so bloody hostile in the station, and I am sure they think I'm a villain.'

'They are a bunch of wankers, Hugh. Sorry, that was so unprofessional, but, to be honest, I'm done with being the nice guy.'

'I take it you don't like them? This new lot, I mean.'

'No, I don't. There is something fishy going on. Anyway, they have the ballistics report back, but Evans didn't want me to see it.' Raj slid the cup of coffee in front of Shields and offered him a slice of carrot cake. 'You haven't slept, have you?'

'No, I haven't.'

'What's going on, Hugh?'

'I am worried sick about Dixie-Lee. I've grown quite fond of her, and when her mother says she is a beautiful girl inside and out, she isn't wrong. And I've got the two brothers raging inside your nick, when they need to be with their family. Firstly, they need to grieve for Dixie and secondly they need to . . . Well, they are men of the world, and they will have their own contacts who may be able to track Dixie-Lee down. As you can imagine, they have no faith in your team, not that we include you, Raj.'

Out of the blue, Raj said, 'I'm leaving the force, Hugh. I'm done with it. You know, that Evans prick wouldn't show me the ballistics results. It's like working with Kims all over again. So, anyway, after we find out who killed Dixie and we get Dixie-Lee back, I'm quitting.'

'Fair enough but please don't quit yet, Raj. We need you in there to ensure Mac and Brodie aren't being set up because, trust me, Mac wasn't the one who killed Dixie. He wouldn't have. I've known the family for years and represented them for years, and a man like Mac wouldn't kill his own brother. Which means he is being set up.' He sipped his coffee, placed the cup down, and rubbed his face with both hands. 'What a fucking mess. We need to go back in. I want to see what they have to say about the ballistics because I know the truth.'

Raj frowned. 'What do you mean?'

'Jesus.' Shields leaned back on his chair. 'I hope to God, you are being straight with me, Raj.'

'You have my word, Hugh, because, between you and me, I know something shady is going on.'

'Okay, when Drake showed Mac the photo of the gun found in his car, Mac did recognise it. It was his own gun.'

Raj's mouth dropped open. 'You are joking.'

'I say *was* as in the past tense. That gun was taken from him many years ago by a family back in Ireland. The Olivers. They're a nasty firm. Long story short, the Olivers ambushed Mac one night. They beat him about the head, threw him into the boot of a stolen car, and were going to teach him a lesson. Still, one of the Olivers, a lad called Eamonn, well, he'd had a drink – one too many – and showing off to his brothers, he drove the car. The others were following. They drove around a sharp bend with a steep drop on the other side leading down into a lake. Eamonn took the bend too fast and shot over the side and into the lake. Lucky for Mac, the impact forced the boot open, and he managed to swim to the surface before the car reached the deep depths of the lake. It was dark, and so no one knew he'd escaped. All the Olivers knew was their youngest brother was fish food, and they blamed Mac. They bandied it about that Mac had managed to get into the back seat from the boot and forced Eamonn off the road.'

'Bloody hell's bells, that's a story for grandchildren.'

'Yeah, that didn't sit well with the Deacons. So, Brodie being Brodie, he took the eldest brother, Chubs, to a disused farm and they had a fair fight, but, of course, Brodie won. The Deacons and the Olivers called a truce, but you see, the thing is, the Olivers had removed Mac's gun when they'd ambushed him. So he assumed it went down to the bottom of the lake with the car.'

'And he was sure it was the same gun the detectives found in his car?'

Shields sighed and nodded. 'There were markings that caught Mac's eye. However, he said the gun was clean when he had it. It couldn't possibly have his prints on it. He hadn't touched that gun in years.'

'Shit, so if Drake pretends otherwise, then we know for sure he *is* bent, and not only that, but someone is after having Mac behind bars for their own purposes.'

'Yeah, so now can you see why I have to get the Deacons out of custody so they can do their own investigations, and believe me, Raj, they are shit-hot at doing that.'

'Maybe they will give me a job in their company.'

'I think you would be an asset.'

CHAPTER ELEVEN

Georgie had almost worn the carpet out as she paced the floor. She'd used a box of tissues to wipe her face dry and felt that she had fallen into the depths of helplessness. Yet that wasn't who she was. Right now, with the police seemingly waiting for the kidnapper to make a demand or for a dead body to turn up, she had to do something herself.

She believed the only people to hold a grudge against her were the Marx family. Her husband's murder and the cross carved into his head could be seen as a revenge killing, as Raj had put it, but the only link was them. She was aware that they were an extensive tribe, with more second cousins than the British royal family. And what was Riley doing at the college? There were questions that only the Marxes could answer. However, while she had to admit that Noel Wade looked nothing like them, maybe he was a throwback from when someone in their family was good-looking because the rest of them looked like sly-eyed pigs.

As soon as the sun went down, Georgie checked the front of the house. She noticed that Lardon had gone and only two officers remained; they were sitting in a police car. She couldn't blame them; it was freezing cold. She turned the light off in the kitchen and hurried upstairs, where she got changed, wearing only black, with a black beanie that completely covered her hair.

Finally, she turned off all the lights in the house and peered out of the front window again. The officers were eating a Chinese takeaway, and she could see they were both watching something on an iPad because the light reflected their faces. 'Useless fuckers,' she mumbled, under her breath.

After selecting a recently sharpened knife from the kitchen drawer, she opened her back door and surveyed her surroundings. It was pitch-black. None of the neighbours had their living room lights on which could throw light onto the gardens, and she knew none had sensor lights. She hurried along the alleyway past the ghostly-looking tree where Eve and Todd Marx had been murdered. She then sprinted across the field, so she didn't have to pass the police car. Once she'd pulled her beanie down over her ears, she hurried back onto the estate and weaved through the streets before coming to the Marx family's house. She had to ensure no one could see her before she scooted along the side of their house and into the gateless back garden. She pushed herself against the wall next to the back door that she knew led into the kitchen because she was aware of the layout. All the houses were the same except for her terraced house, which was a two-bedroomed property with two rooms downstairs. The house where the Marx family lived was a three-bedroomed semi. The back door led into the kitchen, and from the kitchen, there was a short hallway and the living room to the right.

She didn't have a watertight plan because she didn't know who was in the house or even their whereabouts, but she wasn't going to sit behind a parked car and wait. The air was still, the temperature was probably below freezing, and the thought of her daughter being held captive somewhere outside in this bitter cold forced any ounce of fear, for what she was about to do, to the back of her mind.

After pushing herself away from the wall, she snuck past the back door and peered in through the kitchen window. There was no one there. The smell from fried burgers and chips seeped through the partially opened window and Georgie could see the piled up dirty plates and teabags slung on the side. There was a light illuminating the hallway. And then she heard a girl's voice laughing; she guessed that would be Yasmin's.

Then she heard a man shout, 'Turn the telly up. I can't hear what that tart is saying.'

'Oi, Jasper, you've got the remote, ya fucking div.'

Georgie also knew that voice. It was Sheila's, the mother of the Marx family and the breeder of evil.

The sound of the TV suddenly drowned out any other noise. Georgie was about to slide past the window when the kitchen light came on, and she spotted Yasmin saunter in. She was in a set of bright-pink Barbie printed pyjamas and had her hair pulled up in a messy bun. Without her ton of make-up, she looked very different. Minus those thick black false lashes, her eyes seemed to disappear into tiny slits. And her skin was peppered with red pimples. She watched as Yasmin held the kettle in one hand, turned on the tap with the other, and then removed the lid.

Georgie flew past the window, opened the back door, and, in a flash, she was inside the kitchen, clamping her hand around Yasmin's mouth while poking a knife at her neck.

'Fucking move, and I will slice your throat wide open,' she hissed, through gritted teeth while keeping her voice just below the sound of the TV.

Yasmin's eyes were the widest they could be, but still, they were filled with horror. She froze on the spot. In her mind, she believed that Georgie Deacon was capable of such a thing even though they themselves had done nothing much for six months except gather the family together and discuss how they would exact revenge on the woman. They believed that no one other than Georgie had killed their brother and sister, and to make matters worse, they had been tormented by the fact that the press had accused their brother of being the serial killer.

Hate for the Deacons had coursed through their veins. Her name was the one that had constantly crossed their lips. Her mother had vowed to kill Georgie as soon as she could get her hands on a gun. However, the family knew that Sheila couldn't have a gun for several reasons. Firstly, she needed to go to the optician but refused because it would spoil her looks. Secondly, because of the frame of mind she'd been in, she could shoot anyone who pissed her off. And thirdly, she could quite easily turn the gun on herself. So her threats had gone now to calling upon all the members of the Marx tribe to make sure that Georgie's life and the lives of all the Deacons would be a nightmare, including that daughter of hers – Dixie-Lee Deacon – because it had all started there.

'Who is Noel?' Georgie asked, as she slowly removed her hand from Yasmin's mouth.

Yasmin was so terrified that she couldn't speak.

A tinkling sound compelled Georgie to look down, and that was when she realised that Yasmin was so scared, she'd wet herself. Maybe the horrific way in which Yasmin's brother and sister had died had put the fear of God into her.

'Don't shout or scream, Yasmin. I'll ask you again. Who is Noel?'

Eventually, Yasmin swallowed and found her voice. In an act of survival, she turned her efforts to pleading. 'Look, please, I never meant to hurt Dixie-Lee. I swear I never meant for her to get hurt that bad. I didn't do it. It was Kimmy, I swear.'

She dropped the kettle into the sink and held up her hands. 'Please, Mrs Deacon. Don't hurt me.'

'Forget Kimmy. All that's history. Who the fuck is Noel Wade?'

'I swear on a stack of bibles, I don't know anyone by that name.'

Yasmin blinked, and that was when Georgie saw the tears streaming down the girl's face, but she herself had no respect or compassion for any of the Marx family. None whatsoever.

'Who's in the house?'

Yasmin glanced to the side of her. 'Just me and Mum.'

Knowing Yasmin was lying, she grabbed the girl around the throat and held the knife a millimetre away from her eyes. 'I'll blind you in one fucking move. Now, who is in the house.'

Yasmin swallowed hard. 'Mum, Riley, and Jasper.'

'Where are they?'

'Mum is in her armchair, Riley is opposite, and Jasper's on the sofa.'

'For fuck's sake, Yas, what are you doing out there?' Sheila croaked. 'You're gonna miss the fucking end! Bring me another packet of fags, will ya.'

Georgie grabbed Yasmin's hair and moved the knife to her throat. 'Now, we are gonna walk into the living room nice and slow. Don't try anything silly because one false move and you will be redecorating your mother's house in claret.'

Yasmin didn't attempt to fight back as the two of them walked slowly into the living room.

The second they were in the doorway, Sheila looked up and instantly gasped, throwing her hands to her mouth. She knew it was Georgie Deacon even with a hat covering her hair. She had dreamed of slicing that face of hers to ribbons.

Jasper jumped up from the sofa, but Riley was reading a book, so he didn't notice his sister, who was still being held by Georgie Deacon.

'What the fuck are you doing here?' asked Jasper, the mouthiest of the brothers.

Sheila, the dregs of the earth with a mouth like a sewer, rose to her feet. The initial shock had clearly worn off, and she was now standing in a daring stance, her hands on her hips and her head tilted to the side. 'You think you can come into *my* house with *my* family here and walk out of here alive, do you?'

Georgie was silent as she surveyed her surroundings. Then she turned to Sheila and smiled. 'It looks to me like the first person who could easily get killed here is your daughter, 'cos, Sheila, I'm the only one with the knife, and right now, it's at your daughter's throat. Oh, and understand this, love. I ain't afraid to use it. You know that I'm military trained. I've been in a warzone, and I've seen more blood, guts, and killings than you've had fags. So shut the fuck up with your empty, in fact, stupid threats.'

'Put the knife down, bitch, and we'll see how fucking hard you are. Let's have a one-on-one, shall we?' shouted Jasper, putting his fists up.

Georgie ignored him. 'Sheila, who the fuck is Noel Wade?'

Sheila inclined her head. 'Who?'

'Noel Wade!'

Jasper was hopping around like an epileptic Michael Flatley baring his fists. 'I said drop the knife and fight me.'

Georgie turned to Jasper with a cruel smirk. 'There's no need to repeat yourself, you total arsehole. I fucking ignored you the first time. Take note, dipshit, there are 'as-beens and there are a never was. You are a never was, so sit your arse back on the sofa and shut it while I talk to your mother.'

'I swear to God, I will kick the fucking fanny right out of you, Georgie Deacon!'

Georgie yanked on Yasmin's hair, pulling her head back and showing the knife pressed against her carotid artery. 'Jasper, we all know there isn't a single brain cell in that head of yours, but if you make one more bad decision, you will be responsible for your sister's death. Look at my knife. Have you ever seen what a mess it makes when you cut through this artery?'

'No, please, please, no, don't!' screamed Sheila, as she dropped to her knees, with her hands in a praying position. 'Don't, she's my baby. You killed my two kids. Please don't kill her. I will cooperate. Just don't do anything stupid.'

'You've been bandying about to anyone who will listen that I murdered Eve and Todd, but the police say otherwise, don't they? Yet, still, you wanna believe it was me who killed them.'

Sheila glared with a blackness that could turn the saint into a devil. 'I fucking *know* it was you. I know what you did, but still, you weren't nicked for it, and to make matters worse, my Todd, who did fuck all to you, ended up not only dead but his name in ruins. A serial killer, ha! As if. And now my whole family's name is shit because of you.' She glared at the knife at her daughter's throat. 'If I knew who this Noel Wade person was, don't you think as a muvver, I would tell you when you are holding my gal's life in your hands. Believe me, I don't know any Noel.'

'My girl has been kidnapped, and your family is the only one I know who hates me. 'Cos, Sheila, you have told everyone who would listen what the fuck you would do to me, and now I wanna know who has her.'

Jasper suddenly put his fists down by his sides and glanced at his mother. 'What's she talking about?'

Sheila got to her feet and shrugged. 'Listen, I have had nuffin to do wiv any kidnapping. Jesus wept. I know you murdered my two kids, and as much as I might swear and shout about what I would do to you, I wouldn't have your girl kidnapped because I know you're a nutcase and you would come after my surviving kids. I ain't that fucking stupid.'

Georgie stared into Sheila's eyes and wondered for a second if she was actually being honest. If so, that was a first. 'Give Yasmin your phone with your passcode.'

Sheila snatched her mobile from the side of her chair, opened it with a simple four-repetitive-number code, and handed it to Yasmin. As soon as she passed the phone, she could feel her daughter's fingers were like ice.

Slowly, Georgie allowed Yasmin to straighten up.

'Go to messages, Yasmin, and scroll down.'

Yasmin didn't answer. She simply did as she was told.

The only relevant messages that Georgie could see were from Jasper, Yasmin, or Riley. There were a couple from random relatives, all about buying hooky gear or asking for one of them to bring home a loaf of bread or a packet of fags. But there was nothing that would suggest Sheila had been speaking to anyone of importance.

But then she found a text from Riley.

'Stop scrolling,' Georgie hissed into Yasmin's ear. 'Go back to your mother's conversation with Riley.' As she made her demands, she looked at Riley, who had placed his book on his lap and was nervously watching Georgie.

'Actually, you, Riley, tell me what's in that text about my daughter.'

Sheila shot at look at Riley.

Riley went as red as a beetroot. 'I just told Mum that Dixie-Lee was at college.'

As Yasmin began to scroll down, Georgie stopped her and peered up. 'So, Riley, you'd better explain these texts because I swear now that if you lie, I will slit your sister's throat.'

Georgie could see Riley was sweating. Beads of moisture were popping up on his forehead.

'What have you done, Riley? Have you hurt my daughter? Tell me!' Georgie bellowed, making everyone jump.

'No! God, *no*.'

Georgie looked back at the texts. 'I'm looking at this message to your mum. It says, "seen Dixie-Lee again at college", and then your mother replies, "don't go near her, not today".'

Sheila shook her head. 'He likes your girl, for fuck's sake. My dopey boy is infatuated with her. He wants to ask her out, and I keep telling him not to.'

'You actually said, "don't go near her, not today". To me, that suggests you are lying.'

'Yeah, okay. Go through all the messages. You will see I say it nearly every fucking day. That twat's in love with her. Jasper, show the woman Riley's art book.'

Riley tried to snatch back the sketch pad before his brother had a chance to show the pictures inside, but it was too late.

It was Georgie's turn to gasp. As Jasper turned the pages, every picture was of her daughter. She had to admit they were good. In fact, they were excellent. Riley had managed to enhance every pretty feature of her daughter. He'd even left out the small cross carved into her forehead. She glanced back at Riley, who had his head down, seemingly embarrassed.

‘I swear to you, Georgie,’ said Sheila, ‘I don’t know who took your gal. I only know it weren’t none of us.’

Riley got up from his seat, seized the sketch pad off Jasper, and unexpectedly held it out. ‘Here, Mrs Deacon. You can have it.’

Georgie was stunned because she knew that Riley genuinely meant it. And what was even more surprising – he showed absolutely no fear of her. But as she was about to take it, she was hit by the best kept secret of the year.

‘Me muvver’s right. I do like Dixie-Lee. I like her a lot. She’s a good kind girl, and pretty. I talk to her sometimes.’

Georgie’s eyes widened. ‘You *what*? And does she reply to you?’

‘Yeah, I’ve walked to college with her, and I sometimes have to wave the bus down to stop ’cos of her bad leg. She can’t run just yet. This Noel, how do you know he kidnapped her?’

‘Because he was the last person to see her, and he was supposed to take her to the airport, but it was all a lie. There was no flight, and now she’s gone, and the only person or person who hates me enough to take my kid are you lot.’

‘I won’t let anyone hurt her. She’s a sweet person. How do you know he was called Noel?’ asked Riley.

‘He said his name was Noel. He saved Henry from burning to death in the café fire. Yeah, I bet that was your fucking doing.’ Georgie shot a glare at Jasper.

‘Me?’ He poked himself in the chest. ‘Set fire to the café? Nah, the only thing we ever did, well, not me but me cousins, was to smash the window, but that was months ago. No way did we set fire to the café. I saw it cordoned off. I just thought his ovens had caught alight. Look, arson ain’t our style. That carries a longer bird, so you will never catch me with a fucking box of matches.’ He paused then laughed. ‘Looks like you’ve been well and truly fucked over. And now, Mrs Deacon, you are more fucked than ever ’cos you have no idea, do you, who has your girl.’

Georgie knew he was right. She didn’t have a clue. Yet as much as this family were evil, she sensed they weren’t responsible for her daughter’s disappearance.

‘Shut up, Jasper. Shut the fuck up. Dixie-Lee is missing, and I’m gonna find her!’ yelled Riley.

'Don't you tell me to shut up. Who the fuck do you think you are? I—'

Riley punched his brother clean in the mouth, knocking him back onto the sofa. 'I said, shut the fuck up. Dixie-Lee ain't part of any of this. She's innocent. She was terrified of that geezer who was going to kill her, and now I bet she's frightened all over again, so shut up. I don't care what you' – he pointed to Jasper and then to his mother – 'or you think. I'm gonna help Mrs Deacon find her.'

'You mug!' mumbled Jasper, as he felt his fat lip.

Sheila's shoulders dropped. 'Well, I suppose the girl has been through a right ordeal. She don't deserve to get kidnapped.'

Georgie removed the knife from Yasmin's throat and pushed her away. 'Try anything, and I won't hold back. I'll kill one of you.'

Sheila shook her head. 'You've got bigger fish to fry than us for now. So where is your husband? Why are you here and not him?'

Georgie suddenly realised that they had no idea he was dead. Lardon had told her they didn't want the public to know, so the press had been kept well and truly out of it. However, she wasn't going to do what the police wanted.

For the Marx family to ask that question, it confirmed the fact that they couldn't have been a part of this. But the cross on her husband's head suggested otherwise: if so, it was yet another attempt by someone to lay the blame at this family's feet.

'He is dead. He was shot at point-blank range.'

Sheila staggered backwards. '*What?*'

'Someone shot him and then carved a cross in his head.'

'So just like my kids, then. They had a cross carved in their heads too.'

Sheila reached for her cigarettes and found they were empty. She clicked her fingers at Riley who threw her one of his. Her hands shook as she lit up and took a deep drag. 'You don't think we did that, do you?' Her face was pale, and her lips took on a blue tinge. ''Cos we never did, ya know. I don't even own a gun.'

'Nah, I don't think you did. I don't think you have the guts.' She looked at Jasper, who was dressed in a fake Nike tracksuit and scuffed fake Nike trainers. 'And assassins don't come cheap.'

Jasper could feel Georgie eyeing him over, and he slid his cuff over his fake Rolex.

Selling knockoffs never paid well, thought Georgie. Her eyes cast down to the well-worn carpet. And the coffee table had serious coffee-stained rings on it. The sofa was uneven. Georgie suspected the springs had gone. Looking around the entire room, Georgie deduced that the rest of the place was generally tired and cheap. This family didn't have money; all they had were their foul mouths. Their main man Todd was dead, and their reputation had died with him.

Georgie saw no point in standing there or wasting her breath. She had to get back and make other plans. Snatching the sketch pad off Riley, she turned to leave, but as she reached the kitchen, she could hear the footsteps of an angry man. It was Jasper. Before he could lay his hands on her, she spun around, grabbed one of the dirty dinner plates, and using it like a discus, she whacked him in the throat. He was stunned momentarily before he hit the floor clutching his neck.

Sheila was behind him, screaming, but as her son went down, she panicked, 'Oh no. Please no.'

'He ain't dead, he's just wounded, but he's a fucking lucky man. I could've killed him. Now, hold him back and leave me alone. If he or any of your lot call the police or knock at my door, I will come for one of them.'

Sheila was on the floor helping her son when she looked up and nodded in defeat and acknowledgement.

By the time Georgie had reached the end of the road, tears were streaming down her face. Then she heard footsteps, and as she spun around, she saw that it was Riley.

He held his hands up. 'I'm not your enemy, ya know. I really ain't.'

She stopped. Her shoulders slumped and she nodded for him to approach.

'Please, Mrs Deacon, if there is anything I can do to help, please let me. I get it. Our families are, well, they're enemies, I guess. But I'm not like them. I promise you I'm not. I've started college to get a good job. I was never the cleverest, but I want to become someone, and it was your Dixie-Lee who said I could be anyone I wanted to be, and I could break the mould. She encourages me. I will do anything to find her. Please take my number. If I can help, I will.'

Georgie stepped back and looked Riley up and down. She realised he looked different from when she'd first met him. At one time, she'd laughed at his name tattooed on his head, but now his hair covered it. And looking closely at him, she could see that he was trying to dress more smartly. And even when he spoke, he was doing so without swearing and mumbling.

Georgie nodded. 'Okay, I'll take your number, and I hope to God, if I need your help, I can trust you or—'

'Yes, I get it, Mrs Deacon.'

He gave her his mobile number. The fact was he could see she'd been crying and he felt embarrassed, as he couldn't comfort her, although he wanted to.

Georgie walked home. She wondered if she'd imagined the last hour.

CHAPTER TWELVE

The sky was clear, but the night air was still bitterly cold. Georgie would have marvelled at the beauty of the stars, but not this evening. If wishes came true, she would have wished on every star up in the sky, but she was a realist, and the only way to find her daughter was to wait until Brodie and Mac were released and then to make a plan with them. There was nothing more she could do except wait, for now.

She thought Rohan may have a better idea when he arrived. *Please, God, let her be alive.* Her eyes were stinging from the cold, and her nose began to run, so she wiped it with the back of her sleeve.

She was so deep in thought, she didn't notice the man hiding behind the ghostly-looking tree at the end of her road. It was in an area of waste ground, and to most people, they would never have guessed that opposite the tree and along the side of the end house was an alleyway that separated the garages from the houses. She glanced down the road to see if the police cars were still parked outside her home. She clocked the two officers; they were still inside their vehicle with the white light from an iPad. She shook her head. She'd snuck out of her house, walked to the Marx family's house, had a confrontation with them, and was now walking back, and yet they hadn't even noticed her missing. *What a fat lot of good were they?*

She passed the tree and shuddered. Her mum always said that was when someone steps on your grave, but she knew that it was something deeper. She tended to shudder when she thought of the men her mother had invited into their home. The men her mother was too out of it to entertain. Their eyes always roamed in one direction – hers. The only thing she had learned from that was how to fight and how to run. Now with her thoughts on her daughter, she felt proud that she had taught Dixie-Lee all she knew. She just hoped to God that Dixie-Lee wouldn't need to use any form of defence strategy.

Hurrying along the back of the terraced houses, she reached her own. But when she glanced at the garage, she had that niggling feeling that the heavy lock and that camera were not just to protect the garage. So what the hell were they for unless Dixie had been keeping something of extreme value or a dark secret from her? Because Dixie hadn't even fixed up a camera for the house. She suddenly paused, thinking she could hear footsteps. But as she listened, she couldn't actually hear anything, and there was nothing to give someone's presence away, such as a light hint of body spray, aftershave, or body odour.

She continued up the garden path, past the broken swing, and through her back door. Quietly closing it behind her, she headed straight to the kitchen, where she peered out of the window to the street to check on the police. 'Ha! Why the fuck am I checking on them?' she said, aloud.

After removing her coat and rechecking her phone, she poured a whisky, gulped it back, and headed upstairs. Without getting undressed, she lay on her daughter's bed and gripped the pillow until her knuckles were white. Soon the tears came and with them a gut-wrenching, throat-closing sob. The crying eventually subsided, and her eyelids felt heavy until she dozed into a light sleep.

It was less than ten minutes later when a noise suddenly awakened her senses. Startled, her eyes shot open. There, standing in the bedroom, was a man. Because it was dark, she couldn't make out who he was, but he was bent over, clutching his stomach, and breathing heavily.

As she jumped up and on to her feet, the man fell to his knees. 'Please, Mrs Deacon, it's me, R . . . Riley.'

Georgie could see right away that he was not there to hurt her. She flicked on the light to get a better look and was mortified. 'Jesus Christ!' she shrieked, as she tried to help Riley up. 'What the fucking hell happened to you?' She was still half-asleep and assumed that his brother had given him a clump for siding with her.

Riley allowed her to help him on to the bed. He was shaking all over. Someone had given him a proper beating. Blood poured from the deep gash in the side of his face. His nose was smashed to pieces, and he'd lost a front tooth. However, it was the way he was holding his side that concerned her more. She unzipped his jacket, kneeled beside him, and tugged at his shirt. 'Let me see what they've done to you.'

Riley helped her lift the shirt and then fell on his side, his bloody face resting on the white broderie anglaise pillow.

‘Can you breathe okay, Riley? Because it looks like you’ve got a few busted ribs. I’m telling the police. We need an ambulance. This is bad, Riley.’

She was about to leave the room to call the police, but he stopped her. ‘Don’t go. Don’t tell the police because if you do, Dixie-Lee will get killed.’

‘You what?’ A sudden cold shiver touched the top of her spine. ‘So you lot are behind this, you fucking—’

‘No, not me, not us, but a man. I don’t know him.’

‘A man? What the fuck are you talking about? You mean your family didn’t do this to you?’

‘No. I was attacked by some bloke. He was . . . He . . .’ Riley tried to catch his breath, but his broken ribs were making it hard to breathe, let alone talk.

‘Listen, Riley, I know you’re hurt, but you must help me. Can you sit up and tell me exactly what fucking happened? For starters, how did you get into my house?’

‘I had to run. He was going to kill me. I didn’t have to bang on your door. Your back door was unlocked.’

Georgie glared at him. Standing straight, she folded her arms, trying to recall if she had locked the back door. But then she remembered. Of course, she hadn’t. She hadn’t had the key.

‘The state of you, I can’t see you running the fucking Olympic 200-metre sprint. This guy would easily have caught you, so he wasn’t going to kill you, then? I assume he wanted you to give me a message. So what was it, Riley? And I reckon he knew you were coming to my house. He went over the top on your face for a reason.’

‘I don’t know. All he said was, if . . . if I call the police, he will kill her. I came to p-post this.’ He struggled to pull a rolled-up piece of paper from the back of his jeans. It was torn, battered, and covered in dirt. His hands trembled as he handed it to her. ‘I worked hard on this. I wanted to give it to her, but . . .’ He stopped as he tried to catch his breath again.

Georgie took the rolled-up piece of paper and opened it out. She was shocked to discover that the lad had sketched a portrait of Dixie-Lee. It was so perfect it could have been a black-and-white photo. The sketch spoke a thousand words. From the drawing, it looked as though Riley truly loved Dixie-Lee because he had so carefully and in such a gentle way captured her inner beauty.

'It's beautiful.' As she glanced back at Riley, she noticed the blood still running down his face.

'We'd better get you to the hospital.'

She was about to lift him off the bed when he grabbed her wrist. 'No, listen, the doctors will call the police, and this guy said if they got involved, he would kill Dixie-Lee. I believe him. I do. Look what he did to me.'

'But you are fucking bleeding badly. That cut needs stitching.'

'No, you must believe me. He will kill Dixie-Lee. He nearly killed me. I saw him follow you down the alleyway. He was hiding behind the big tree where Todd and—'

'Yeah, I know. Go on.'

'I saw him creeping towards you but he didn't see me. I ran after him and grabbed his shoulder to spin him around. I said, "What the fuck are you doing sneaking after Mrs Deacon?"'

He coughed and whimpered as he clutched his ribs.

'He had something in his hand, and he belted me hard across my face, and then I tried . . .' He paused as tears filled his eyes. 'I swear to you I tried to fight him, but he was like an animal. He wouldn't leave off. He grabbed my hair and kept punching me. Then he lifted me into the air. He was like the Incredible Hulk. He kicked me until I was lying in agony on the ground and then he said that if I call the police, he will kill your daughter, but he knew who I was, an' all. He said, "You're a fucking Marx. I'm surprised you're sticking up for her." He pulled that drawing out of my jacket, opened it, and laughed a really nasty laugh. He threw the picture on the ground, and as I went to grab it, he trod on my hand and said, "If you tell the police, I will come back and cut your fecking hand off, and you will never draw again." When he removed his foot, he kicked me, and I slid down that small bank down to the path. But the grass was wet, so he slipped too. I managed to run, and that's all I know, Mrs Deacon. I swear to you.' He stopped to try to take a gentle breath. 'Oh and I think he must be Irish, unless he has a fake accent.'

Georgie could feel the fear rolling around in her stomach. She gripped Riley's face and moved it from left to right. 'Okay, Riley,

I'm so sorry you've been caught up in this. Look, I can glue together this wound. It may not hold, but it sure as hell will sting.'

Riley gently ran his fingers over his cheek. 'It stings anyway. Look, I can't go to the hospital, so please, if you've got some PVA or whatever, just patch me up.'

She grinned. 'I think you mean superglue, Riley. I can't see PVA doing the trick, somehow.'

'Whatever. Please just do it. I can handle pain, but I can't handle fear.'

Leaving Riley to rest on the bed, Georgie hurried down the stairs to fetch the medical box, a bowl of warm water, and the glue. She was on her knees rooting through the cabinet under the sink, looking for the Dettol she used for cleaning, when she heard someone behind her.

Knowing it wouldn't be Riley, she also knew it wasn't a friend because they would announce themselves. She didn't move but looked for a tool. The only one was a set of plumbing grips she had used when the sink had leaked. She kept them there for when they might be needed. With her hand firmly gripping the handle, she slowly backed out of the cabinet, and, in one fast movement, she swung the tool and hit the legs of the person behind her. As the intruder instantly went down, she managed to get to her feet. With the metal grips in her hand, she was about to club the man over the head, but she was perplexed when he grinned, showing his perfect white teeth. She could see it was Noel, yet his eyes weren't blue, they were hazel, and he'd shaved his beard off, which had previously hidden a deep scar along his jawline. He hadn't cut his long hair although it did appear darker.

She clenched her jaw and flared her nostrils as rage ripped through her like a hurricane, ready to destroy everything in its wake.

'I wouldn't if I were you, Georgie, because if I don't come out of here alive, my men will kill your daughter and you will be burying her along with your husband.'

Georgie tried to control her temper. She could hear the drumming sound of her blood pumping in her ear. She wanted to kill him. Mentally, she pictured smashing him repeatedly in the face. 'If any of you so much as hurt a hair on her head, I will come for you one by one, and I will torture the fuck right out of you. Where is she?' she hissed, through gritted teeth.

His eyes had an unflinching resolve when he stared, as if he feared nothing. She'd met men like him, and they were called psychopaths. Like Ashby. She swallowed hard because she realised that this man had no conscience. He would kill her child and think nothing of it. That cold stare and fixed grin made her go cold. Perhaps he had worn the contact lenses and grown the beard to soften his features. Whatever the reason, she felt she was now seeing who he really was. And there was no way she could penetrate his coldness. She hated herself for thinking that he had genuinely liked her – how utterly foolish she had been.

'What the fuck do you want from me? I have nothing. Absolutely fucking nothing. I live in a council house, and I work in a café.' She watched him get to his feet and brush himself down.

'Good move. I can see you were military trained, and you taught your daughter a few moves as well.'

'Have you fucking touched her?' She held up the weapon, ready to hit him.

He shook his head and laughed. 'Me? No. My men, they tried, but she's good. I'll give her that. She's like her mother.'

Georgie's breathing increased, her anger intensifying. A myriad of emotions played across her expressive eyes.

The anger he expected but the sudden chuckle threw him.

'I assume you laugh through fear,' he said, still stunned by her reaction. 'It must be so frustrating for you to think that I'm here unarmed, and you have a weapon, and you would love to kill me, but you can't, because if you do, your daughter dies.'

Georgie held the plumbing grips by her side, and she smiled back. For effect, she slowly replied, 'I don't want to kill you. I want to hurt you really, really badly.' She placed the tool on the side and held up the palms of her hands. 'But you are so fucking right. I won't because your life means nothing to me, but my daughter does, so get to the fucking point because I am sure you didn't kidnap her for the fun of it.'

'No, we didn't. Now, you will be told what to do, and if you think you can outsmart me for a minute, then you go ahead and take that risk. But know this, Georgie Deacon. I can quite easily chop her head off. I'm a bit like you, Georgie. I don't give a shit.'

'You're *nothing* like me, Noel. You are a fucking psychopath.'

'And your point is?'

'What do you want?'

'I wanted first to establish that we have an understanding. I have your kid, and in order for you to get her back all in one piece, you need to do something for me.'

'How do I know my daughter is even alive?'

Noel wagged his finger. 'Oh, I see. You want proof?'

Georgie nodded.

'And if I don't have proof, you'll still go along with the plan because I know how much you love that girl, so I can bank on the fact that you wouldn't take a chance.'

With hate running like lava through her veins, Georgie had to count to ten mentally, or she would have killed him with her bare hands.

'Where is she? Is she outside? Is she warm?'

With a sarcastic chuckle, Noel replied, 'There it is, the motherly instinct to protect her child. Is she warm?' he said, in a childish voice. 'Yes, she's warm. I'm not a fecking farmer keeping her in a barn. She is in a flat, and it is warm. She has food and her teeth intact to eat it. There is also a TV. The door is locked, but she isn't hurt. My men, however, are injured because the little bitch can bite and kick and . . . well, it doesn't matter. She is okay for now, that is. And know this, Georgie. Business is business. I don't need to tie her up or treat her with disrespect. However, if you so much as put a step out of place, I will do more than tie her up. I'll put her somewhere outside in this freezing weather with a few nasty wounds to lick.'

'Okay, what do you want?'

'Ha! Yes, what do I want? Well, the first stage, as I mentioned, is to get clarity that you are on board. That you know it's me who has your daughter, and it's me who will be making the fecking demands, and you, Georgie . . .' He used his gloved hand to lift her chin. 'You are going to do as I say.' He let her go and clapped his hands. 'I will make contact again with instructions.'

'Why, me?' she asked, as he was about to turn around to leave.

'Because you are Georgie Deacon.'

'Is this to do with Ashby or Marston-Smith?'

He grinned. 'No.'

'Did you kill my husband?'

'If I said "yes", would that make you take me more seriously?'

Still stunned by his response, she didn't answer. Instead, she merely watched him walk through her living room and out of the back door as if he had been a guest.

Hopelessness settled in her chest like a cement block. She glanced around the kitchen before realising why she was there in the first place. 'Shit . . . Riley.'

Gathering the things she needed before Noel had arrived, she took the stairs two at a time to find Riley lying on his side on the bed. Blood was still seeping from his wound, and his skin was pale despite the claret all over his face.

'Let's get you cleaned up and that gash closed up before you paint the bedroom red.'

Riley was still dazed but he managed to sit upright. 'Were you talking to someone downstairs?'

At first, Georgie was going to say 'no', but Riley was involved. He had risked his life for her, so she wasn't going to shut him out – not for now, anyway. 'Yeah, it was that Noel guy. He slyly snuck in and told me the same as you. I'm not to go to the police but to wait for instructions.'

'He won't hurt her, will he?'

'I don't think so. I'll do whatever he asks of me, so hopefully, she will be home soon.'

She dabbed the wound with warm water to clean it enough to see the extent of the damage. He didn't flinch. He allowed her to do whatever was needed to be done, and, at that moment, they made a silent pact.

'I was never like them, you know, Mrs Deacon. I've never ever wanted to be like them, but you have to understand this: when you grow up in a big family with everyone all thinking the same and acting the same, if you don't go along with it, then you are the enemy, the black sheep. They've always treated me like I am the thicko, the dopey one. I'm not, ya know. I am just quiet. I even pretend a lot of the time to be stupid, just so they don't ask too much from me.'

Georgie pinched the wound together and then began layering the glue.

He smarted for a few seconds and then relaxed.

'Riley, I have to ask. Why did you tattoo your own name on your head?'

'That wasn't me. That was Eve and Jasper. They got me drunk and then they drugged me, so for a laugh, they used Toddy's tattoo gun. They said they were tattooing a wolf's face, but when I was sobering up, they showed me what they had done in the mirror. Then I saw my name. They thought it was funny. I hated it, but I couldn't hide it because when I tried to, they pinned me down and used the clippers to shave my head.'

'You really aren't like them, are you?'

He shook his head. 'No, that's why I go to college. I want to better myself. I'm not surprised Dixie-Lee hasn't mentioned me. She wouldn't want to worry you. I guess you went through a lot, and Dixie-Lee wouldn't have known what happened to you because she was in the hospital.'

'Dixie-Lee would have known that I would be worried, but, in truth, mate, I reckon you are a good egg. Right, I'm going to make you a sweet tea and get you some painkillers. You can sleep in this room, and, hopefully, you will feel better by the morning.' She glanced at the clock. 'It's two thirty. Will your mum or Jasper be bashing my door down worrying about where you are?'

He smiled. 'No, not at all. My mum is nuffin like you, and she would only worry if I went out to buy her fags and didn't return.'

By three o'clock, Riley was in a pair of Dixie's pyjamas, his face was cleaned, and the glue had stopped the bleeding. The strong painkillers had taken the edge off the pain, and he was comfortable and warm in Dixie-Lee's bed.

Georgie took one last look at Riley, whose eyes were heavy and ready to close. She wondered how on earth she could ever describe what had just happened. The last few days had been beyond bizarre.

CHAPTER THIRTEEN

Raj sat bolt upright in his bed. He'd taken a sleeping tablet at eleven o'clock, and it had knocked him out, but now, it was three o'clock in the morning, and he couldn't close his eyes. Too much was rolling around inside his head; in fact, there was so much that he couldn't settle, so, after a strong coffee, he headed back to the station. It was pointless tossing and turning in his bed.

The streets were empty but inside the station it was busy. Raj ignored the fiasco in the custody suite. A drunken brawl in a local pub had ended up with everyone fighting, so the police on duty were busy processing the men and women who had been involved. From the state of their faces, some certainly needed the hospital. However, Raj didn't even want to ask about it. He hurried towards his office where he hoped to catch up with the team if they were working through the night. And he also wanted to see if Mac was okay and to get more information on the Oliver family. However, as he walked along the corridor, he realised he had forgotten his phone. After patting himself down, he knew he'd left it in the car. He swiftly made a U-turn and marched back towards the car park.

It was still freezing and still dark outside, and he expected the police car park to be relatively quiet. However, he noticed three cars slowly drive in and park by the side door. The windows were blacked out, and as he looked closer, he clocked five men in suits exit the cars and walk in through the side entrance of the building. They were too far away for him to recognise any of them, but he could almost smell the stench of MI5. But what on earth they were doing in Bromley Police Station would be a question he was sure no one would answer. Not to him, anyway. It briefly crossed his mind that perhaps one of the street brawlers was actually a security officer working undercover or something of that sort.

After retrieving his phone, he hurried back inside the building and passed the custody suite – where the crowd were still hooting and hollering – to get away from all the noise and to calm his mind and try to think straight. It was so early that no one would likely question his business. And yet he felt that he was such an outsider now; it almost seemed as though he had no place in the station. He shook the paranoid thoughts from his mind and decided he would go and pay the Deacons a visit before Drake started to demand answers and stick his great beak in.

As he approached his office, he expected it to be empty and in darkness. No one would be in at this early hour in the morning. Matias often worked late, but he was never in before seven. When Raj spotted the light on, he held back and carefully peered in through the window of his office door. The light was coming from his desk lamp, and there, trying to break into his private drawer, which only he and Matias had a key to, was Drake.

The sly detective was so engrossed in trying to use his tool to get inside that he wasn't aware that Raj had quietly opened the door and was standing there staring at him.

Drake cursed and banged the top of the desk before he looked up and then jolted as if he'd seen a ghost.

'What the fuck! What are you doing, creeping up on a man like that? You made me jump.'

'Clearly, Drake.' Raj waited because he knew he had the upper hand catching Drake trying to break into his drawer.

'I was looking for a file.'

Raj turned the main light on. It pinged and buzzed before it illuminated the room.

'And what file would that be?'

'A file on Georgie Deacon, that's all.'

'Hmm, and you thought you would find it in my personal drawer, did you?'

Drake grinned. 'But it's not personal, is it? My colleague saw Matias, or whatever his name is, put a file in your drawer, so it's hardly private, now, is it?'

'Martin—'

'Gov, to you.'

'Tell me, *Gov,* do you have a key to that drawer?'

Drake shook his head. 'You fucking know I don't.'

'But your colleague, when spying on Matias, saw him put something in my drawer?'

'He wasn't spying, but yeah, he did. Why?'

''Cos that, Detective, would suggest that Matias has a key and if Matias has a key, then he has access. In other words, he has permission to use the drawer, but you, *Gov*, you don't. You don't have a key. Now, tell me why you would think I have a file on Georgie locked away in my personal drawer?'

'I believe some of the files are missing. The evidence on Georgie Deacon regarding the Marxes and her interview.' He flipped the tail of his suit jacket and placed his hands on his hips.

'Nothing is missing. Like I said, they are all in the archives. The case was closed. And, anyway, I can't see what it has to do with the Dixie Deacon case.'

'Well, her husband is dead, and her daughter is missing, and for all we know, she may have something to do with it, so I want to see her old files.' He pointed a finger at Raj. 'I know you had a meeting with their lawyer in the coffee shop. I want to know what that was about.'

Raj didn't move; he stood staring at Drake. 'I went for a coffee, and Mr Shields joined me. He was anxious to know if the ballistics results had come back because he will be arranging his own ballistics guy. Listen, Hugh Shields isn't our enemy or even a suspect. He is a bloody solicitor, so if I want to have a coffee with him, I will do. He and I both want the killer of Dixie caught, and, of course, we want Dixie-Lee found, and I can assure you that Georgie would never hurt her daughter.'

'People do the strangest of things, and, Raj, *as a detective*, you should know that.'

Deciding not to continue this ridiculous argument, Raj sighed in defeat. 'If you are genuinely looking for Georgie Deacon's paperwork for a crime she was not found guilty of, then, like I said, you need to check the archives because the case was closed, and everything was stored down there.'

Drake tilted his melon-shaped head to the side. 'Genuinely?'

Now agitated, sensing that Drake wasn't giving up, Raj raised his voice. 'Yes, *Gov*, because you should know the files are archived. Why on earth would they be in my office? You've already fucking ransacked it, and now you're trying to prise my drawer open. Something stinks, and I'm not afraid to admit it. I don't fucking trust you, Drake, or Evans, so you can take that to whoever the fuck you like!'

'You want to be very careful. I am your boss, so remember that. And since I am, I want you to open that drawer. Matias placed a file inside, and I want to know what it was. And I also want to know why it is in your personal drawer.'

Raj slapped his hands by his thighs. 'My key is at home, but you must get permission first from Fitzgerald, and then I will gladly open it.'

Drake glared before storming out of the office and slamming the door behind him.

Raj waited until he could hear the stomping of footsteps way off in the distance before he pulled his chair out from his desk and sat heavily. He was tired, but his brain wouldn't switch off. That conversation felt as though it had taken years off his life. *Thank God he'd taken precautions earlier.* Taking the key out of his pocket, he opened the drawer and saw a file in there which was new to him. Glancing up at the door, he checked no one was watching before he opened it.

His eyes almost popped out of his head. *Is this supposed to be a joke?* Inside the file was a photo of a young man in a pink bikini who was strapped to a chair with a bondage mouth gag and a blindfold.

Raj leaned back grinning, because, for a moment, he assumed Matias was messing around, maybe to put a smile on his face. But, when he turned to the next page, he had to pull the photo closer. His heart almost fell into his stomach. This certainly was no joke. It was sordid and shocking. The man in the bikini wasn't a man but a teenager. Probably no more than fourteen years old. His blindfold had been removed, and the expression of terror in his eyes was sickening to look at. Holding his breath, he turned the page to the next one. Another young man, a small lad, again possibly fourteen or fifteen years old, was naked and tied up. The last photo was of a few men in suits at the bar of a club. They were middle-aged and he thought he recognised one of them. Not that he knew him well, but he had brushed shoulders with him once upon a time when Fitzgerald had invited him to his gentlemen's club, where he drank with a few of the members of the House of Lords. However, this guy wasn't from the House of Lords. He was a bigwig in MI5. He turned the photo over; there was nothing on the back. When he looked at the corner of the paper, he realised that Matias had used the photocopier in the office to copy the photos. He quickly placed the file inside his briefcase. Then, he read the note that had come with it.

Raj, once you've seen it, get rid of it. I need to talk privately with you, away from the office. Don't trust Drake. I may be wrong, but he could be linked to this paedophile racket. West has more photos. But I am afraid if they get into the wrong hands, there could be serious consequences.

After hiding the note in his briefcase and using the combination lock for added security, Raj paced the room, feeling uneasy. What did Matias mean by consequences? And *consequences for whom?* Something was going on. Matias wasn't joking around. He was on to something, and it had clearly bothered him.

Raj could tell by the tone of the note that for Matias not to end the note with an X was a clear sign that this matter was extremely serious. As much as he didn't like Drake – he assumed he was a bully and probably bent – he now wondered if there was far more to this than he'd thought. Were Drake and Evans part of some unthinkable paedophile ring or was Matias being overly dramatic? Considering that Drake wasn't particularly kind to him, was Matias looking for a reason to bring the man down?

Turning off the lights in the office, Raj quietly closed the door behind him and hurried past the incident room, hoping no one would notice him. He shouldn't have worried. Officers were busy doing whatever it was Drake had instructed them to do. He quickly looked through the large window, but although he didn't see Drake or Evans, he assumed they were somewhere in the building. Their cars were in the car park, and as he hadn't passed either detective on the way out or back in, he reasoned then that they must be here. As he walked towards the flight of stairs that led down to the police cells, he had to pass Fitzgerald's office. The door was ajar, which was odd because as far as he was aware, the boss was off for a few days, so that should have meant his office was off limits to members of the force.

Without even giving it much thought, he opened the door and there inside were Drake and two of the suited men. Having seen the photos of the men in the club, and with these on his mind, he took note of the two men in the office and recognised they weren't the men in the photograph.

Drake shot Raj the dirtiest of looks and hurriedly slammed the door in his face.

Raj just managed to remove his hand from the doorframe before losing his fingers. Then spotting one of the suited men, with an earpiece, he now knew that they were from the Security Service, otherwise known as Military Intelligence, section 5, or MI5 for short. Although he wondered why they were engaging with Drake, he knew that on rare occasions, MI5 would work with the police to bring suspects, who were planning a serious crime against the security of the country, to trial. However, he would have been told if such a person was being detained at the station. Something was not quite kosher, so he decided not to wait around and continued down to the cells.

The officer on duty looked up from his phone. 'Hello, Detective, what can I do for you?'

Raj smiled. 'Mr Deacon's solicitor asked me to check on him.'

'He is fine.'

Raj nodded and chewed his bottom lip. 'Yeah, he may well be, but his solicitor is making waves about his injuries, so I take it you've been checking on him every thirty minutes, have you? I assume you know he sustained an injury earlier. Right?'

The young officer's eyes widened, and he glanced at his watch. 'Well, I did check thirty minutes ago.'

'Great, so is it all logged?'

The officer gave Raj a slightly worried nod.

'Great, now I don't want this solicitor to cause us problems, so I will do as I was asked and check on him because my name is on the line. You understand, I hope?'

'Oh, er, I was told to, uh . . . let him rest.'

'Oh, is that right? So how do you do the rouse check?'

'I look through the window. He is fine, Raj.'

Usually, Raj would accept anyone calling him just by his name, but now in this police station, he was done with being nice. 'It's Detective Sergeant Raj, to you. Now, open the door. I want to check for myself, and I want to see the custody records. I want to see what has been said and check the timings.'

'Well, the custody sergeant is busy and . . .'

'You know what? I don't give a flying fuck, mate. If I want to see that this prisoner is being treated as he should be because his fucking lawyer asked me to, then that is exactly what will happen. Now, I have asked you once, and I won't ask again.'

The officer was now on edge; he had never known Raj ever to swear or be so cold, so he was aware that the detective was angry about something. He opened the door and stepped back, allowing Raj to go in.

But when the door closed, and Mac tried to sit up straight, Raj gasped. 'Bloody hell! What the fuck's going on?'

Mac's right eye was closed up, his right cheek was swollen and purple, he was holding his ribs, and when Raj looked down at Mac's bare feet, they were black and blue.

'Get us a drink, Raj, mate. I'm fecking dying in here.'

'Who did this?' asked Raj, as he stared at the blood coating Mac's teeth.

'I don't know, Raj. They took me to the hospital. The nurse cleaned up my wounds and agreed I was fit for the police to interview me. And then, two plain-clothes officers cuffed me and pushed me into a fecking black van. I was a little dazed at the time, so I didn't overthink it until the bastards put a bag over me fecking head and . . .' He paused, holding his chest. 'One of them said, "this is for starters". And they then told me that if I didn't answer their questions, they would beat me brother Brodie but ten times worse.'

'Who were they, Mac?'

'I didn't recognise the man's voice, but I, well, the thing is, I fecking fainted. I was out cold. Then, the next thing was I woke up in here. Beaten to a pulp, I was.'

Raj looked up at the camera inside the cell. It was weirdly angled straight down. 'Fuck me, and you have no idea who did this or what they want?'

Raj heard footsteps coming along the corridor and knew by the marching sound it was Drake. Raj quickly whipped out his phone and began taking pictures. 'Lift your top.'

Mac didn't object; he stood up as straight as possible and turned around.

Raj winced at the state of the man's back. Mac then pulled his tracksuit bottoms down, and again, Raj was dumfounded at the black marks all over him. He clicked away, capturing as many shots as he could, before the door finally opened.

'What the hell's going on?' yelled Drake.

Raj couldn't believe the man's audacity. 'Er, shouldn't I be asking you that question, *Gov?'*

'He fell down the stairs because the doctor gave him some medication that made him dizzy. It's all in the custody records, but I will ask again: what the hell's going on?'

Raj smiled sarcastically. 'I needed to ask Mac Deacon a few questions.'

'You're not on the Dixie Deacon case, so hop it, Raj.'

'I'm not on the Dixie Deacon case, but I am on the Dixie-Lee Deacon case.'

Mac pulled his tracksuit bottoms up. '*What?*'

Raj glared at Mac. 'Has Hugh Shields not told you?'

Drake quickly recovered his composure. 'No, and I would appreciate it if you left us to our inquiries. You have no reason to be in here.'

'What do you mean, you're on the Dixie-Lee case? You'd better tell me that she's okay,' growled Mac.

'See, Raj, now you have the man worried. You need to leave well alone.'

'And that, Gov, is why I'm here. Mr Deacon, here, may be able to help me with *my* inquiries.'

'Will someone tell me what the feck is going on? What's happened to Dixie-Lee?' Mac yelled again.

'You have no idea, Mac?' asked Raj, with a profoundly concerned frown.

Mac shook his head and placed his hands on his hips.

Raj looked at Drake. 'Now, hang on a minute. His solicitor was in the custody suite. We had coffee in the coffee shop, as you know, and he was coming back to talk to Mr Deacon, so what the fuck's happened, Drake? Why didn't his solicitor see him? Why was he denied access? Because I am guessing he was.'

'Mr Deacon was at the hospital when his solicitor wanted to see him. He can come back later this morning because, by then, I am sure Mr Deacon and his brother will be before the magistrate to hold them on remand for the murder of their brother.'

'Raj, what has happened to my niece?' Mac's voice had a grave undertone that made Drake take a step back.

Staring at Drake, Raj raised a brow, as if to say, 'Are you going to tell him, or shall I?'

But Drake ignored the gesture. 'I need to question Mr Deacon, so, Raj, I'm sorry, but your case can wait.'

Shaking his head, Raj replied, 'My case is about the living, hopefully, so I am not acting like a kid in the playground, but I was here first.'

Mac grasped what was going on and right away jumped in. 'Look,' he said, turning to Detective Inspector Drake. 'If you want to question me, then I want my solicitor to be present, and, believe me, Detective, I have a lot to tell him, so I reckon he will have a lot to say about these fecking injuries.' Without waiting for a reply, he turned to Raj and dropped his harsh tone. 'But if you want to question me, Raj, then I am happy to cooperate. Because I want to fecking know about my niece.'

Drake suddenly acted like a spoiled child. 'And why do you want to answer his questions and not mine?'

'Off the record?' asked Mac.

Drake nodded.

'Well, 'cos you're a goon. He ain't. Is that simple enough for your tiny mind?'

'Cut the insults, Mr Deacon. Why will you answer his questions but not mine?'

Mac shook his head and laughed. 'Really, Detective? I am battered to feck, and you wonder why I won't be questioned by you without Hugh Shields present. Seriously, mate, were your fecking parents related?'

Drake didn't bother to stand there and argue. He stormed out. However, Raj placed his finger to his lips for Mac to remain silent while he listened.

Unless Drake had removed his noisy boots, he was outside the room. Raj knew only too well that the sound outside the cells carried. It was how the corridor was built, and he could hear everything.

Drake was telling the officer to go to Fitzgerald's room and ask for one of the men to come downstairs so they could take Mac to the courts.

'Right, listen, I'm calling Hugh now. I need you in the interview room, and I need to visually tape and record the interview. I don't want them taking you to the courts or anywhere until Hugh arrives.' He leaned into Mac. 'Something fucking dodgy is going on.'

'Is Dixie-Lee okay?'

Raj shook his head. 'She's been kidnapped.'

'*What!*' Mac almost screamed.

'Please listen to me. I'll talk when we get to the interview room. Just go with the flow. I'm cuffing you to me.'

He opened the door and saw Drake standing there.

'Where are you going?'

'Interview room four.' It was the room with the audible and visual recording.

'Four?'

'Yeah, four. Excuse me.' Raj stormed past Drake, showing that he had Mac handcuffed to himself. He clocked the angry yet agitated look on Drake's face, and, for a second, he felt a smile lift his cheeks.

As soon as they were on the stairs, Raj spotted two MI5 men. He casually smiled and hurried along the corridor.

'That's fucked them. They can't say anything to me, Mac, but they were going to take you off somewhere. They want something out of you. I don't know what, though. Maybe you can help me with that.'

As soon as they were in the room, Raj turned on the audible and visual tape. 'For the record, I have Mr Mac Deacon in the room. It's five a.m. on . . .'

He then pulled out his phone and dialled Hugh Shields. The phone rang twice. 'Hugh, it's Raj. I am with Mac, so ASAP, get to interview room four.'

'I'm on my way. I'll be there in thirteen minutes.'

'Hugh, grab a coffee for Mac.'

'Done.'

CHAPTER FOURTEEN

No sooner had Raj turned the audio and visual on than he realised he was now into something far above the actions of a few bent coppers. This was on a whole other level, and suddenly he felt sweaty and uneasy. 'Can you show me your bruises, Mac?'

Mac turned to face the camera and lifted as much of his top as possible because Raj was cuffed to his left hand. He then leaned down and pulled up part of his tracksuit bottoms, demonstrating the lumps, bumps, and heavy bruising on the lower part of one of his legs. But he hadn't finished; he turned around and asked Raj to lift his top, and that was when Raj winced again. There were long stripe marks across his back. He didn't doubt that Mac had been beaten with a tool. He was surprised that the man could still stand. He knew if it had happened to him, he would have died.

'Okay, let's sit down. Hugh will be here in a moment. While we are waiting for him, I need to talk to you about Dixie-Lee.'

Mac nodded. Knowing that Raj was one of the good guys, he went along with whatever the detective asked.

'First of all, we believe that your niece has been kidnapped by the man who rescued Henry, the café owner, from a fire.'

Mac stared, his eyes unblinking.

'He befriended Georgie and offered to take Dixie-Lee to the airport because Georgie had received a text that she assumed was from Rohan, and it stated that he had a ticket for Dixie-Lee to get a flight to Ireland. But it was only a while later, once Dixie-Lee had left the house and Georgie assumed she was on her way to Ireland, that she received a call from Rohan. It was evident he had no idea what Georgie was talking about. Georgie then used a tracking device to hunt for Dixie-Lee's phone, only to find it a few yards around the corner from her house.'

Mac's eyes welled up. He ran his free hand through his hair. 'Who?' was all he managed to say.

'We have no idea, but I was hoping you do. Hugh mentioned this family, the Olivers.'

'The Olivers? But that was years ago.'

Before Raj could delve deeper, the door flew open and in rushed Drake. His face was burning as he almost fell over a chair to get to the recorder. He slammed the off button and yelled, 'Take the cuffs off, Raj! Now!'

Raj was stunned by the fury slapped on Drake's face and the over-the-top aggression from his actions.

Before Raj could do anything, the door opened again, and this time, two of the suited men came in. He assumed they were MI5. Their muscles almost popped out of their fitted suits, and their black ties seemed to disappear into their necks.

Raj spotted the clear resin earpieces and imagined they were acting like robots taking orders from above. And one of the meatheads, a fair-haired younger guy, had an odd button on his jacket, so Raj knew then he was wired and filming everything.

But it was Mac who jumped up. 'You're the hard men who had to fecking put a sack over my head and beat the feck out of me when my hands were cuffed behind me fecking back, you cowards! I bet you wouldn't fecking fight me with me hands free, 'cos for sure, I would leave you crying for your mammy if you had a jaw left to fecking talk.'

The two men smirked as if what Mac had said was small beer to them.

'You don't know what happened, Mr Deacon, because you were given a sedative. As I told you before, you fell over.'

Mac glared at Drake. 'Fecking hell, not you again with your bullshit. Christ, I could eat a tin of alphabet soup and shit a better line than that.'

Drake nodded. He wasn't going to get into a pointless slanging match. 'Detective Rajesh Raj will be removing the cuffs. Mr Deacon, I want you to answer a few questions for these guys.'

'I'd rather shit in me fecking hands and clap than help you. Now feck off. Go and find some cheese and crackers to go with that fecking whine of yours.'

The two suited men sniggered, which infuriated Drake. 'Raj, take the cuffs off.'

But Raj didn't move. 'Gov,' he said, his voice laced with sarcasm, 'I'm waiting for his lawyer, and before you cart him off to the magistrates, which is unheard of at this time of the morning, you need to have enough evidence to send to the CPS. So unless the ballistics report shows that Mr Deacon here used the gun, I'm not sure what proof you have. And if I ask that question, you can be cocksure Mr Shields will be asking the same one.'

Drake smiled. 'Raj, I don't have to justify anything to you. Mac and Brodie Deacon are now going to be subjected to questioning by MI5.'

Raj would have looked shocked, but he wasn't. He had an inkling that there was something else going on. 'Oh, I see. They wanted to fuck him up first and then ask questions later. Is that it?'

Drake was stunned that the mention of MI5 hadn't had Raj standing to attention.

The darker haired younger suit stepped closer and leaned across the table to whisper something in Mac's ear.

However, Mac was still reeling from the beating he had taken. He had no intention of letting that go unpunished. With his free hand, he gripped the hair at the back of the guy's head, before viciously smashing his forehead across the bridge of the man's nose.

The noise was so loud it made Drake cringe.

But before the other suit could get involved, Mac repeatedly butted the man, like a woodpecker on a mission. As soon as the dark-haired man's head flopped, Mac let go and watched as the man slumped to the floor. The second suit tried to get to Mac, but Mac used his knee to lift the table, causing it to tip over. The fair-haired suit pushed the table aside and went for Mac, but, to his horror, Mac took a fast swing and clumped him hard around the jaw, and he, like his colleague, went down like a sack of shit.

Raj, in the meantime, had had his arm almost wrenched from its socket.

'Sorry, Raj, but' – Mac turned to face Drake, who was now stunned by Mac's actions – 'I don't know who those men are. They didn't introduce themselves, and they fecked me over, and you saw it! That fair-haired prick was going for me again.'

Drake stepped back towards the door. 'You attacked those men, Mr Deacon, and—'

'No, he didn't! They attacked him! I am the closest witness because I have the handcuffs still on. In case you've suddenly gone fucking blind, Gov.'

Drake looked at the wrath on Mac Deacon's face, and like the weasel he indeed was, he bolted from the room to call for backup. The moment he pressed the emergency button, he spotted Hugh Shields running towards the interview room.

Within seconds, three burly officers appeared from the side rooms and tore towards Shields, savagely pushing him against the wall as they hurtled past him.

By the time Shields reached Drake, he was out of breath. 'What's going on?'

'Not a good time, Mr Shields.'

'I'll be the judge of that. Is my client inside that room?'

He didn't need an answer from Drake. He saw the three officers grappling with Mac on the floor and Raj trying to remove his handcuffs. As soon as his handcuffs had been released, the three officers pinned Mac to the ground, cuffed his wrists behind his back, pulled him to his feet, and marched him out of the room and back towards the cells.

Shields's mouth almost hit the floor when he saw the state of the two men in suits. He guessed right away who they were. But they were out of the interview room before he could question them. One was trying to straighten his jaw while the other was pinching his nose. The blood poured like two fast-flowing streams.

Raj cast his mind back to when he had clocked the five members of MI5 who had exited their cars, including one man who looked like a senior member of the security service. Raj suddenly glared at Drake. 'Where are the other MI5 officers or shall I call them agents?'

With much satisfaction, Drake smirked.

'Where is my client, Brodie Deacon?' demanded Shields, once the penny had dropped.

But, again, Drake grinned as though he had the winning lottery ticket in his hand.

'Detective, where is Brodie, my client?'

Drake's smile widened even further. 'I believe personnel from MI5 are interviewing him.'

'Torturing him, you mean,' growled Raj, who was now fuming.

Shields put his hand up to stop Raj from ranting. 'Detective, that doesn't mean my clients' rights to a lawyer have been relinquished because it happened to be some bod from MI5, so enlighten me, Detective Inspector Drake. Has the law changed overnight?'

'Mr Shields, you know that MI5 have greater powers than I have. They take command from Parliament, so you can take your grievances up with them.' He smirked again.

'I cannot see what my clients have done to influence or breach national security. They're not the IRA or Al-Qaeda, so what's really going on here, Detective?'

'I am not at liberty to say, but as you've just pointed out, the words "national security" come to mind, so it's best that they interview the Deacons because evidently they believe they are subjects of importance.'

'And by interviewing them, you mean bashing seven bells out of them. Is that right?'

'Mac Deacon fell down the stairs, like I said.'

Shields flicked his head for Raj to follow, but he glared back at Drake and gave a slow nod as if to say, 'I have your number.'

As Shields and Raj walked out of the room and along the corridor, Shields said, 'Can I visit Mac in the cells? I am so concerned. I mean, what the hell is going on? MI5? Listen, Raj, I'll be straight. I know practically everything the Deacons do regarding their work, and there's no way they have got involved in anything that deep.'

'Well, let's go and see Mac. You have the right since he is your client, and I also have a right because we still have his niece somewhere missing and presumed kidnapped.'

They both hurried down the stairs to the holding cells to find Evans there, who had suddenly made an appearance. He was with another officer, and by the way they looked at Shields and Raj, they showed they were expecting them.

Evans was more than happy to announce the news. 'The Deacons have been taken to the courts.'

Shields was now fuming. He stepped forward, invading Evans's personal space. 'And where is the ballistics report that shows Mac fired the gun, and while you're at it, what is Brodie Deacon charged with?'

'Ballistics report?' Evans gave an exaggerated frown.

‘Yan, I saw you had the report,’ Raj interjected. ‘You said a meeting was scheduled, so am I blind? Because, mate, I’m not stupid.’

‘You must have been mistaken.’

‘What’s really happening here? Have MI5 taken the Deacons away?’

Evans looked from left to right and then back at Raj and Shields. ‘Yeah.’

‘Where?’ snapped Raj.

‘Take the angry look off your face. They want to question them.’

‘About what?’ asked Shields.

Evans chuckled. ‘Well, that’s the thing. We aren’t in the loop. You know how MI5 work. It’s all on a need-to-know basis.’

CHAPTER FIFTEEN

Hearing from one of the uniformed officers that he would be going to court early, Brodie knew something was odd when two men in suits escorted him to a black van. Initially, he assumed there was some kind of strike by police officers. If that was the case, he surmised that the Army, as they often were on these occasions, had been called in. But when he thought more of it, he hadn't known Army officers to wear suits. He was taken from the station towards a black van by two men, one on either side of him. Then, still cuffed, unexpectedly, a sack was put over his head before he was aggressively bundled into the back of the van. The vehicle was off within seconds of him being pushed down on a side bench and the back doors slammed shut. Brodie remained calm and sensible because he had absolutely no idea what the deal was. He had a good guess that the two men in suits were either CIA or MI5. He had nothing to say to either of them. When the van slowed down, he could hear breathing; he suspected the two men in suits were accompanying him.

After an hour or so, the van stopped, and the back doors opened. One of the suits, who had a deep scar from his eye down to his chin, removed the ties that held the sack in place so Brodie could see. They had brought him to an empty building on an industrial site. There were two chairs and a small office room on the back wall. The smell of gassy diesel and grease and the oil stains on the floor made Brodie think it was probably a disused garage. He tried to take in everything before he was dragged across to a chair and forced to sit down. He knew that even though his hands were cuffed behind his back, he could possibly still take down the two men. He looked them over as he tried to devise a plan.

Having listened to their conversations, he knew that the taller and slimmer man was called Adie. He had black cropped hair, was toned, and he stood confidently.

The other man, with the deep scar, who he now knew was called Mendel, was a big musclebound man. He was so big that he struggled to place his arms by his sides because his biceps were in the way.

But Brodie knew this guy wouldn't be fast enough if it came to a one-on-one fight.

However, Adie was sleek and could be into martial arts, so Brodie thought he could be harder to bring down. He glanced at another chair only a few feet away.

So they were expecting company. He took a wild guess and assumed it would be his brother, and if that was the case, between them, they could take on four or even five men. They had done it before.

He watched the two suits standing opposite him merely staring, in a weak attempt, he thought, at intimidation. He smiled back but didn't speak. Mentally, he was planning an escape because when he looked down, he saw the bloodstained concrete. These men were serious and if they were from one of the security agencies – MI5 or CIA – they could shoot him dead and cover his disappearance up.

Groaning in the background was the sound of a van. As the vehicle got closer, he clocked the men nodding to each other. One waited while the other walked towards the van that had reversed into the building and was now stationary.

Brodie heard doors opening and closing before he saw two different men walking towards him and dragging another man. From Brodie's position, he could see that his head was slumped. At first, he didn't realise it was Mac. But, seconds later, when his brother came into view, the anger compelled him to leap up from his chair ready to fight, even with his arms cuffed behind him.

Mac was battered, and his hands were black and blue. Brodie could see blood dripping from his head, and when they stopped dragging him and stood him up, he saw the damage to his brother's face. It was almost unrecognisable.

Mendel grabbed Brodie by the shoulders to force him back onto the chair, but without any hesitation whatsoever, Brodie headbutted him across the bridge of his nose. As the man threw his hands to his face, Brodie fly-kicked him in the chest. Before he could do any more damage to the man, Adie ran over, and using a Taser, he brought Brodie to his knees.

The suits then dragged Brodie onto a chair and did the same with Mac.

'I see, Brodie Deacon, you have recovered instantly from that voltage. You are a very hard man,' said Adie.

Brodie didn't answer; he was so angry that he didn't want to talk. He always liked to be in control, but the state of his brother's beaten face was stirring his inner killer instinct.

Controlling his breathing, he turned to his brother, who although conscious could hardly open his eyes because they were bulging like two huge purple plums. 'Did these men do that to you, Mac?'

Mac's head was slumped forward, bloody dribble running from his lips. 'They've taken our Dixie-Lee.'

Brodie paused, taking in his brother's injuries and the idea that these men had kidnapped his niece. He looked up and directly at the man with the Taser. He smiled, shook his head, and flew off the chair, diving on top of him. They both fell to the ground.

Brodie straddled the guy, ready to nut him hard.

However, Adie stuck the Taser into Brodie's ribs.

When Brodie bit down hard on Adie's neck, the voltage caused Brodie to shake and go rigid without him being able to unclench his jaw.

Adie screamed like a child so loudly that all the men hurried to try to pull Brodie off, but the Taser was still going off because Adie hadn't been able to release the trigger. Finally, Mendel grabbed the Taser and pulled it away.

Brodie then fell onto his side with a mouthful of muscle and skin between his teeth.

Adie jumped to his feet, but instantly, he began staggering while gripping his neck. The blood seeped between his fingers, and he was back on the floor before he could do anything. The blood was now pouring out. His face was white and clammy, and he couldn't even speak, let alone scream.

Brodie sensed the men were now in panic mode when they carried Adie to the entrance where a car must have been parked because as soon as he could get his senses back, he heard wheels spinning. He spat out the lump of flesh and gasped a few times before his light was fully on.

A different suit, a red-haired freckly man, who Brodie had heard Mendel call Barry, pulled him to his feet and hissed, 'Try another stunt like that again, and your brother will get another few rounds with my bat. It's your call, Mr Tough Guy.'

Brodie didn't answer but allowed himself to be taken back to the chair.

The door to the office at the back of the building opened and out strutted a tall black-haired woman, who was dressed in a dark-grey fitted coat, a checked scarf, and black leather gloves.

Brodie guessed by the sudden positions of the men that this woman was in charge. The sound of her heeled boots echoed as she approached.

'I can assume you want to know who we are, Mr Deacon?' She stopped and rolled back and forth on her feet while she rubbed her hands together. There was a pause as she waited for Brodie to answer, but the silent response intrigued her. 'Oh, I see, so you don't want to speak to me?'

Brodie had clocked the confidence ooze out of every pore in her body. Clearly, she was used to commanding attention. He could assume she was clever to hold this position, and without a doubt, she was strikingly beautiful. However, he noticed her skin was a little glossy and too perfect, concluding that she was wearing a ton of make-up to try and pull off the natural look. Being a genius at evaluating a person's character, he found analysing her a piece of cake. A cocky woman used to men falling at her feet. She loved herself, she was beautiful, but she knew it, which, in his eyes, made her ugly. And there was something else about her. She hadn't come from nothing. No, she held herself too much like a lady. Her voice was private school, university, privileged – Daddy was rich.

'Where is my niece?'

The woman rubbed her hands together again and sniffed the cold air. As she did, a plume of winter breath left her mouth as if she was smoking a cigarette.

'Hmm, now that's a question I'm not sure I can answer.'

Brodie leaned back and turned his head to the side. 'Well, sweet cheeks, if you can't tell me, then I'm conversing with the wrong bitch. Get the person who can, and then I might feel obliged to have a conversation.'

'Oh, sorry, Mr Deacon, I can see that you thought we would be up for negotiation, or, as you put it, conversation.' She smiled and two dimples appeared. 'This isn't that type of meeting.'

Brodie didn't answer. He glared, knowing he would be better off saying less and listening more.

'I want to keep this simple, and I was hoping without violence. I hate a mess, you see, Mr Deacon.'

She smoothed back a loose lock that had slowly fallen from her tight bun onto her face. 'But, sometimes, it is a case of needs must.' She pointed to the men standing like combat soldiers.

With a deadpan expression, Brodie continued to stare, hardly blinking.

'What is your association with a Mr Rodney Potter?' she asked, before she began to pace the floor. The sound of her heels echoed like a constant tapping to his brain.

Brodie looked up to the ceiling as if he was thinking. 'I've no idea who you are talking about.'

'Hmm, I was afraid of this.' She turned to the scar-faced musclebound man, who was still dabbing the blood from his nose, where Brodie had butted him. 'Mendel, drop the rope.'

Mendel nodded, marched to the back of the van, opened the doors, and retrieved a substantial heavy-duty cord. After attaching one end to the tow bar at the back of the black van, he then pulled the remainder towards the centre of the room. With one good swing, he launched it over the steel beam that ran the entire length of the building.

When Brodie realised the end was tied in a hangman's noose, his stomach churned, but his anger outweighed the fear, so he held everything together.

Mac, however, was regaining his composure and coming around after the kicking he had received in the cells and in the back of the van on the way to this place.

'Hanging me won't give you answers.'

'No, Mr Deacon, but hanging your brother may loosen your tongue,' she replied, in a sharp tone.

'I really don't know a Rodney Potter.'

Brodie watched the woman flick her head to Mendel and Barry. As if they had done this before, the two suits grabbed Mac and dragged him to the rope. What they hadn't expected was the backlash. They stupidly assumed that the beatings Mac had been given would have given anyone a severe concussion. They hadn't factored in that Mac had a head like a bullet.

And as they dragged him towards a steel pillar where the end of the hangman's rope rested, Mac suddenly straightened his back and used his feet to throw himself backwards almost in a summersault. The surprise threw the two men off balance, and they came crashing down. Mac took the opportunity to wade in using his size twelve feet, even though they had already been smashed with a bat.

Brodie saw two other security agents, who'd been hovering in the background, rush to help, and that was his chance to go for the woman, but as he ran to bowl her over, she pulled out a gun. 'You've had your fun, Brodie Deacon. Now, sit back down and call your brother off.'

CHAPTER SIXTEEN

Brodie stared at the gun and decided he wasn't going to argue with it; he knew that trying to fight these men was probably the fastest road to getting himself killed.

'Mac! Stop!' he yelled.

Mac instantly ceased kicking the second he saw the gun being pointed at Brodie. He knew he might well be the one pulling the trigger if he didn't stop lashing out.

'Good. Now, Mr Deacon, we may get somewhere.' She smiled in a supercilious, almost arrogant, manner for effect. 'And I want you to know I am not averse to hanging people. But I prefer to shoot. It's quick, it's easy, but it's also bloody messy. Suicide is a good way of closing a case. Or, of course' – she paused and smarmily grinned – 'slapping you two behind bars for a very long time would be another option. You see, Mr Deacon, we can make shit stick. I am sure you know what I mean.'

'Look, Miss, er, what's your name?'

'Call me James.'

Brodie yawned. 'I bet that's not your real name, is it?'

'Yes, it is, actually,' she replied, with a slight edge of irritation to her tone.

'Ha! So, you see yerself as a James Bond type of girl, rather than Miss Moneypenny, do you?'

Insulted, she glared, her turquoise eyes glowing with hate. 'It's a name that will do for you.'

So much was going through Brodie's mind, but, oddly, he was fixated on the woman's appearance. What he could see through the unbuttoned coat was an expensive pristine suit. Her heeled boots were made from soft leather, but as he stared, he noticed that she had one foot larger than the other by a good two sizes. She did, however, have other distractions, like her oversized watch, which probably cost in the range of fifteen to twenty thousand pounds. However, what really surprised him was James's mouth, which showed an overload of unnecessary teeth, which even a decent set of veneers would have sorted out. He knew then that James's

Achilles heel was pain. It was obvious to him that she had never been to the dentist.

'Right, James, I get the picture, and I can assume that you are MI5. What I don't understand is how the likes of my brother or me can be a threat to our country. Fecking hell, I'm not linked to any factions, illegal rackets, the IRA, or anything, and I have never heard of Rodney, whatever his last name is.'

'You're not giving me the right answers, Mr Deacon.'

James looked over at Mendel. He and two others were dragging Mac back to his chair. 'No, Mendel, hang him up and let's see if Brodie will answer my questions then.' She tutted. 'And don't let him loose again.'

For a moment, Brodie was panic-stricken. He couldn't think quickly enough.

This time, because Mac wasn't struggling, the men managed to haul him to the rope and place it over his head.

Brodie glared, terrified that they would go through with the threat.

But Mac didn't fight. He was also afraid that James would shoot Brodie.

With his brother's face like a purple bowling bowl and his feet now swollen like a drowned cadaver, Brodie wanted to cry. He'd never seen his Mac so brutalised and he could tell he was in a lot of pain.

When Mendel tightened the noose, Brodie suddenly jumped up.

He turned to James. 'You do know I'm not all about violence. I'm not a villain, a gangster. I'm a businessman and I'm used to having a normal conversation, especially regarding a subject, which, right now, I can tell you're very passionate about.' He glanced at his brother and then back at James. 'If I wanted to know if someone knew a person, I would consider the fact that they may not know them by a particular name. Has that crossed your mind, Miss Fecking Moneypenny?'

James nodded but she kept her eyes closely on Brodie. 'Lift him up. I haven't got time to fuck around.'

Brodie watched as Mendel and another man pulled the rope, lifting Mac until he was on tiptoes.

'Wait! If you do that, I will panic over me brother's fate and I won't think straight. I'm like that, you see. But you don't know me, and I don't know you.'

'I know you love your brother,' she said, tapping her foot, as she folded her arms.

'I do, but that isn't enough to pull information on a Rodney Potter out of my arse. However, if you lower that rope, I might think straight. If you don't, you'll probably end up with two dead men and no answers.'

James waved her hand, and Mendel lowered the rope.

Brodie could hear his brother gasping for breath, and he wanted to run at James and kill her, but, instead, he remained calm and kept himself together.

'You visited Rodney in prison.'

Brodie frowned. 'Tell me, when was I supposed to have visited him in prison?'

'A week ago.'

Brodie shook his head. 'No way. I haven't visited anyone in prison in the last year, so either your information is wrong, or you have the wrong Brodie Deacon.'

'You booked a visit two weeks ago for last week. You arrived at Rochester Prison and visited Rodney.'

Brodie smiled. 'Okay, so now you are telling me that I went to a prison which I fecking know I didn't. Doesn't the visiting room have a camera? You would then see it wasn't fecking me.'

At that point, he saw a shift in her demeanour. He knew then that they didn't have CCTV footage on him specifically because if they did, she would have jumped all over it.

'Doesn't the prison visit room have CCTV footage? I would have thought so, wouldn't you?' he mocked.

'It appears one of the cameras wasn't working that day, but that means fuck all.'

'Listen, James, now I will help you because if there is an issue of national security, then I'm not out to hinder your investigation or whatever the feck it is. Still, there is no need to hurt my brother or myself. It may be your way of doing things, but it's not ours.'

'Really? I think your company does! Ha! *Undoing wrongdoings*, it says on the Companies House profile. You must use unsavoury methods because you're not a lawyer. You have a tidy sum of money in your accounts, nice fine properties to your names, and you, Brodie Deacon, own an Aston Martin, no less.'

When her serene expression suddenly took on a wildcat look, she yelled, 'Who the hell do you believe you are? An equalizer?'

'James, darling, I watched that series when I was a kid, and what we do, I guess, is a bit similar, but we're not fecking actors. Our clients pay us to help them get their own back on someone who has done them wrong.' He held up his hands. 'Not in a violent way, but a way in which both parties benefit.'

'Ha, both parties benefit? What a load of bollocks. Anyway, we know that you or one of your brothers visited Rodney, and I can assume he employed your services.'

'Oh, I see, now. It's gone from me to possibly one of me brothers.' He smiled. 'Well, James, it seems to me that you don't know who visited this Rodney chap. I am not a Mac or a Rohan—'

'Stop stalling. I don't care which one of you visited him. What I want to know is what kind of service he asked for!' She rubbed the gun with her other hand and then held it with both hands as if she was about to fire it. 'And just so we're straight, I know you Deacons all work together in your *company*. You all know what's going on unless you hold secrets from each other.' She laughed, glanced at Mac, and said, 'Which I doubt very much. So now the truth, Brodie Deacon. You're the top guy in the company, the eldest, and I have been told, the smartest.'

'I see, Miss Moneypenny. So you think you have done your homework, but, evidently, not that fecking well, because you would know that none of us visited Rodney. And why the interest in a man who's in prison?'

'Oh, come on, Mr Deacon, you know why.'

Brodie sensed there was anger behind the calm seductive tone in her voice.

'Don't you fecking think I would tell you if I did. Understand this: my company does earn good money, and, yes, it's based on secrecy and loyalty.' He narrowed his eyes. 'But believe fecking me, money means nothing to us compared to family. You may not have empathy or a conscience, but there is no way I would keep me mouth shut and risk the safety of me niece or me brother.'

James tilted her head to the side. 'Really?'

'You haven't got a daughter or a niece, I take it. And, James, if you had done your homework, and, come on' – he grinned – 'MI fecking 5 are the best at that, aren't they, you would know everything about me, wouldn't you.'

As he shot a look at Mac, he realised that the poor guy was about to collapse. Even through the bruising and swelling, his face wore a grey pallor.

'James, look, I'm going to come clean with you. Maybe Mac did visit Rodney. You see, there are a few days when he said he had some business to attend to.'

Before he could continue, everyone was distracted by what happened next.

Mac was dangling loosely on the rope. But the noose was still around his neck. And it had tightened. His eyes were now bloodshot and he wasn't breathing.

'Boss!' shouted Mendel, who was now trying to hold Mac up, but his dead weight was too much.

James spun around and saw what was happening. She couldn't have Mac Deacon unconscious because she was on a mission, and if it *was* Mac who visited Rodney, then she needed him alive and fit for questioning. 'Hold him up and cut the fucking rope, you idiots!'

It took two men to hold up Mac while the third cut the rope.

For a moment, James was caught off guard, and as she turned around, Brodie was there in her face.

'He'd better not be dead, James,' he hissed, before he hurried over to Mac. Seeing his brother breathing, Brodie let out a dramatic sigh of relief.

James knew Brodie could have headbutted her or kicked her off balance, but he hadn't.

'He needs a hospital, now, James.'

But James was feeling for a phone in her pocket. 'Shut up!'

Brodie stared at Mac's pale and lifeless body. 'He's dying, you evil cow. Call an ambulance. Get him to a hospital.' His frustration was hitting the roof. He could tell that James appeared to be in a dilemma.

'James! For feck's sake, we will help you, but Mac can't, if he is dead, can he? Now, please, call an ambulance.'

'I said, shut up!'

'For feck's sake, woman, grow a pair of balls to go with that name of yours and make the decision now!'

But she ignored Brodie and continued to dial a number. She walked away out of earshot, only to return a few seconds later, looking more frustrated than ever.

'Mendel, get him in the van!'

'He needs a fecking ambulance!' yelled Brodie, before one of the men grabbed his shoulder and pulled him back.

James shot a look of fury. 'That is not an option. Mendel will drive him to a hospital. Either that or he dies.'

'Take me as well.'

'No, you will remain here with me.'

'I fecking knew you weren't the boss. You, strutting around on your high fecking horse holding a gun. But I know women like you. All the gear and no fecking idea, eh! You're all mouth, and under that coat, you're wearing a pair of trousers that you hope won't make your arse look big. And as hard as you think you portray yerself, you hate pain, don't you, Miss Moneypenny. You're terrified of pain.'

She listened to every word, knowing that he was bang-on, but she wasn't going to back down. 'Pain doesn't bother me, Brodie Deacon,' she replied, in her calmest voice.

'No? Then get yer teeth fixed because they let the rest of your face down.'

***

Dixie-Lee hadn't slept a wink. Even though the room was clean and warm, and the bed was comfortable, she was still too afraid to close her eyes. The fight earlier had left her on edge, and her blood was alight with adrenaline. She'd trusted Noel until he'd bundled her into the back of his car with the ugly greasy-haired man, who had then belligerently pushed her head down so that no one could see her in the back of the vehicle. She'd bitten his hand, but, in response, he'd clumped her hard on the side of the head and stunned her. Her level of fear at that point had risen to such a pitch, it had sent her head spinning. 'What do you want with me?' she'd yelled, her voice cracking in terror.

However, the ugly man had hissed in her ear, 'Shut the feck up, and stay quiet.'

Her face had throbbed and stung from the punch, and so she'd thought it wise at that point to do as she was told.

Dixie-Lee guessed Noel had driven for half an hour before he descended into an underground car park. When they pulled her from the car, she noticed that there were only a couple of vehicles there and those were concealed by car covers. Other than that, the place looked empty.

The door that led from the car park to the main building opened and there dressed in jeans and a baggy T-shirt was another man, who was equally as ugly. His skin hung loosely around his jowls, and a belt held up his baggy jeans. She assumed he'd lost a severe amount of weight and not bought a new set of clothes. He seemed to be in charge, and as he held the door open, he flicked his head. 'Take her to her room. It's all ready.' Unlike the accent of her uncles, which was gentle, his was harsh.

Dixie-Lee glared, showing disdain by curling her lip and snarling, 'What do you want from me?'

The man she wrongly assumed was in charge glared at her. 'Any more noise from you and I'll fill your mouth with me dick. Now, you, missy, do as you are told.'

'There's no need to be so crude.'

Noel chuckled. 'She's studying to be a lawyer, Chubs.'

Chubs gave Noel a narrowed eyes glare. 'You've just used my name, you thick twat. Just take her upstairs, will you now? We've plans to make.'

'Don't get mouthy with me,' snapped Noel.

But before Noel stepped forwards, Chubs gripped Dixie-Lee's face with one hand, and with the other, he grabbed her between her legs. 'You will do as you're fecking told. Lawyer or not, Miss Fecking Fancy Pants!'

Dixie-Lee's legs weren't very strong, but her hands were. She shot a two-fingered prong into Chubs's neck beside his collarbone. It was so fast and precise that it instantly forced him to let go of her. She grabbed his wrist and bit down hard before kneeing him between the legs. 'Don't ever touch me again!'

She'd caught him where it hurt the most. His balls were now throbbing like hell, and she'd managed to bruise his ego. In a fiery reaction, he backhanded her, knocking her to the ground.

'Oi, Chubs, fecking leave it out. What the fecking hell's the matter with you. She's a kid,' growled Noel, as he reached down to pull Dixie-Lee to her feet. 'The girl wasn't supposed to get hurt.'

'She bit me.' He shoved his wrist under Noel's nose. 'Look. Would ya fecking look. And she's no kid. She's fecking eighteen. She's not a child, and I'm no fecking paedophile, so shut it, Noel. And I will treat the woman as I choose, and you' – he poked Noel in the chest – 'will do nothing about it.'

'Don't you ever talk to me like that again, Chubs.'

Noel had to admit she had done some damage, but as far as he saw it, it was Chubs's fault, and he deserved it. He shook his head and nodded for Dixie-Lee to walk on.

Chubs sulkily pushed past Noel and the other guy and stormed towards the lifts.

It gave Dixie-Lee time to survey her surroundings. The building appeared tatty, the carpets in the corridor had seen better days, and the wallpaper was 1970s flock and peeling at the edges. The lift was old-fashioned with external black buttons, and the smell was musty. So she guessed that at one time this place was possibly a hotel but it was now being used for homeless tenants. She'd heard about a similar scheme from a college project they had been given. It was to cover tenancy laws, part of her curriculum.

From Noel's reactions, she felt he would protect her; then she ground her back teeth. She was never going to fall for her captor. She knew about the Stockholm syndrome, and although momentarily, Noel had defended her, she still hated him. And she knew how much her mother would be absolutely in bits. As well as the fresh grief she'd already suffered from losing her dad, she hated everyone right now – everyone outside her family that was.

When they reached a flat, they locked her in the room with the ensuite bathroom. She tried the windows, one in the bedroom and the other in the bathroom, but they had both been nailed shut, and she didn't have a tool to open them. She checked to see if the bed had legs, but it was a divan, and so, as she slid the mattress off the bed, she saw that underneath there was a metal grid. So there were not even wooden slats that she could snap and use as a weapon.

Hearing the sound of whispering coming from the room next to hers, she pricked up her ears. Chubs was obviously talking and the vile words coming out of his mouth made her feel sick. Right now, she didn't care if she died. She was not going to let Chubs anywhere near her. If he did to her what he was saying on the other side of that wall, then he would be having sex with a corpse. He would have to kill her before she gave in to an ugly middle-aged creep like him. It was bothering her that she couldn't hear Noel's voice, though. Maybe he was asleep. If so, she would scream her head off if Chubs entered the room.

She was kidding herself; Noel wasn't asleep. He probably wasn't even in the flat. A sudden cold sweat coated her skin, and she dry-heaved before rushing to the bathroom and emptying the contents of her stomach. She gasped a few times before running the tap and sloshing ice-cold water around her mouth. Once she had caught her breath, she clocked the tap dripping at the point it was attached to the sink. She stared at the sink and the pedestal underneath and noticed they were two separate units. Crouching down, she tugged with all her strength at the pedestal until it came away from underneath the basin. The basin then dropped forward, pulling the plaster off the wall. However, she managed to support the basin before it hit the floor and caused an almighty racket.

She listened, but she couldn't hear Chubs. Quietly, she closed and locked the bathroom door. This was her chance, and she would have only one.

Her mother had taught her how to fight and use a weapon if she ever needed to, and once again, she was in a position where she did. She eyed the towels and was surprised to find they were brand new. She shuddered again. They had planned this. Even buying fresh towels. So it crossed her mind that they planned to keep her here for some time.

Her rising anger, mixed with fear, gave her the strength to lift the pedestal. Raising it above her head, she aimed for the window. After taking a deep breath, she hurled the pedestal straight at it. The sound was like a bomb going off. The glass didn't shatter, but it splintered. The windows hadn't been updated with toughened or laminated glass, fortunately for her. Immediately, she grabbed a couple of towels and wrapped both hands before she removed two of the most prominent shards of glass from the broken window.

She heard Chubs trying to smash open the door. 'Open up, you little fecking bitch!' He banged hard again, and then she listened to the voice of the guy whose hand she had bitten in the car.

'Chubs, what if she has jumped out of the window?'

'Shut up, Jerry. She'd be fecking splattered.'

Dixie-Lee stood with her legs evenly apart and with the shards of glass, one in each hand, ready to fight.

'Move aside, Jerry. I'm gonna smash the fecking door in, and then I will give her what for. The fecking poxy family. They think they're so hard and even the girl seems to reckon she has what it takes.'

'Hold up, Chubs. You heard what Noel said.'

'Feck him. And why are we still calling him fecking Noel?'

Dixie-Lee jumped when Chubs kicked the door. She gripped the glass tightly.

'Chubs, what are you gonna do?'

'I'll make a woman of her if she ain't one already. Know what I mean?'

'Oh yeah? So you're gonna feck her, then, are you?'

'I'll do more than feck her. Now, stand back. I'm smashing this door in.'

Dixie-Lee took a deep breath and stood her ground.

As the door flew open, the handle shot off, just missing her. But what struck her immediately was the smell of whisky, and she clocked that Chubs was swaying slightly. He was drunk. Her mother's words rang in her ears. The bigger they are, the harder they fall. Use their weight and speed to your advantage, she'd told her. She'd shown her the moves when she was five years old. It was a game. Her mother chalked out a sumo wrestling ring and taught her how to do it. Maybe it wasn't a game, but she was learning from a young age. And right on cue, Chubs launched himself at her. She swiftly stepped to the side and used her elbow to whack him in the back, increasing his momentum so much so that he barely stopped short of the broken window. She spun around, hoping to be able to push him out. However, the bottom of the window was just above his waist, so he didn't fall by being top-heavy.

Nonetheless, his instinct was to put his hands out in front of himself, which didn't end well for him. His two wrists slid over the spiked glass that stood like an alpine mountain range on the bottom window frame.

Dixie-Lee heard the cry but she was now facing Jerry, who seemed to think she was a joke. He laughed, shaking his head. 'Put those down, you silly little girl, or I will split you in half, but not with a piece of glass.'

As he stepped forward with no fear of her whatsoever, she could also smell the whisky on his breath and see the glazed look in his eyes.

'Get a towel, Jerry. I'm fecking bleeding to death.'

Dixie-Lee glanced to the side of her to find Chubs trying to stop the blood from squirting up the walls like a fountain.

'Shit, Chubs!' gasped Jerry, as he attempted to scoot past Dixie-Lee.

But she was experiencing a fight-or-flight moment, and rage was kicking in. His disgusting words rattled around her brain, taking her back to the day six months ago when Major Ashby stabbed a knife into her grandmother's leg and threatened to torture her. The fear and rage back then were just how she felt now. She hadn't thought twice about killing Ashby. She didn't regret it, and she would have done it all over again.

'Grab her, Jerry, the fecking little bitch.'

Dixie-Lee was moving from foot to foot as though she was ready to serve out a game of tennis, but it wouldn't be a tennis ball if he came any closer. Stupidly, the whisky had given him Dutch courage because he lunged forward at her. With his outstretched arm, he attempted to grab her around the throat.

Dixie-Lee may not have been the fastest on her feet, but she was faster with her hands than the joker Jerry. She swiped his wrists as if she was swiping a credit card, and yet for some reason, he hadn't felt it. He continued towards her and managed to clutch her neck and squeeze it. The fear that she would get dragged to the ground compelled her to push him away. However, both her hands were gripping the glass, and so naturally, she plunged the broken pieces into his chest.

For a moment, he just stared at her. With a gentle flicker of a frown, his pupils narrowed, and his head tilted gently to the side until he stepped back, the shards of glass disengaging from his chest.

All Jerry could hear were Chubs's cries echoing inside his head to fetch a towel. Now stunned and terrified and feeling the warm blood running down his chest onto his beer belly, he staggered back, away from Dixie-Lee's pretty but cruel expression. He knew then that in minutes he would die, and to be killed by her was adding insult to injury. He wondered if he saw her lips curl into a smile or was he now hallucinating?

CHAPTER SEVENTEEN

Dixie-Lee felt drowsy from sleep deprivation. Her head was spinning, and she was suffering from a low constant buzzing sound in her ears. She looked back to see Chubs still trying to stop the blood squirting from his wrists. Jerry was lying on the floor. His chest and stomach were completely covered in claret. Everything seemed to be moving in slow motion, but the sight of the blood and gaping wounds forced her to get a grip, clear the fuzziness from her head, and run away before she suffered any more horrors.

With her mouth as dry as a bone and her heart racing, she bolted from the bathroom into the bedroom and then into the living room. She hadn't paid much attention to her surroundings when she first arrived because they'd quickly dragged her into the bedroom. But the glimpse she caught now told a story of the kind of people they were. There was porn showing on the TV, tissues at hand on the armchairs, and on the floor there were empty pizza boxes, crushed beer cans, two empty whisky bottles, and an overflowing ashtray on a long glass coffee table. Next to the ashtray, there were old Nokia burner phones, a knife, a belt, and some cable ties. The sight alone made her shudder, and as she yanked on the door handle to get out of this hellhole, she panicked. In her absolute terror, she lost concentration and thought the door was locked. 'Oh God, please open.'

Taking a deep breath, she turned the knob the other way, and the door flew open, knocking her backwards. When she was back on her feet, she ran frantically down the corridor, but she froze to the spot when she heard the lift door suddenly open. Looking down at her hands, she realised that she had thrown away one shard of glass to open the door but not the other. The blood-soaked towel was wrapped around her hand, and she was still gripping the glass. It was the murder weapon.

Her heart stopped racing, and she almost had to laugh when she saw a middle-aged woman, who was dressed in a long black skirt and a long thick cable-knit cardigan with deep pockets, step out and walk towards her. Her face was sweet, and Dixie-Lee estimated her to be about sixty. Dixie-Lee immediately put the shard of glass behind her back and smiled before trying to hurry past.

With a beaming smile, the woman said, 'Well, hello, there. Are you all right, my darling?' before she unexpectedly clutched Dixie-Lee's arm.

The woman's hand was strong and determined. But Dixie-Lee thought nothing of it. She turned to her. 'Yes, yes, I'm fine, thank you.'

'You don't look like it, though. Can *I* help you?'

'No, honestly, I'm fine, thank you,' Dixie-Lee replied, trying to shake her arm loose.

'I don't think you're fine at all. Come with me. I'll make you a nice cup of tea. Now, sweetie, where have you come from?'

'Well, I, uh, I don't live here. I was just, um . . . visiting, and now I have to go. Please, um, I'm sorry. I have to go.'

'I don't think so. I know exactly who you are, sweetie, and you can come with me, *Dixie-Lee*.'

Hearing the sound of her own name turned Dixie-Lee inside out. With wide eyes, she glared. The vision and the notion didn't match up. Surely this gentle-faced 'granny' couldn't possibly be involved with these evil kidnappers, could she?

However, once the woman poked a gun into her side, Dixie-Lee realised that this was indeed the case. 'You will come with me, and, like I said, I want you to have one of my teas. Now, I wouldn't argue with me if I were you. Firstly, this gun is loaded, and secondly, I can fecking fire it. That's for sure.'

The sudden change from an English to an Irish accent, and a harsh one at that, had Dixie-Lee tensing up. But she had one thing going for her. She was still managing to hold the shard of glass in her hand behind her back.

'Now we will walk side by side, back to the flat, and after I give me two sons a talking to, *the useless fecking pissheads*, for letting you escape, you will go back to your bedroom. A good dose of my tea will help you to relax because you look like fecking shite. Like a horror film character.' She chuckled. 'I bet I know why you haven't slept.'

Dixie-Lee was shocked by Jerry and Chubs's mother's peculiar behaviour. She went from a demonic Irish gremlin to a soft-spoken Londoner. But, more importantly, she had no idea that her sons may well be dead by now. But Dixie-Lee couldn't mentally make a plan, and she certainly couldn't with a gun digging into her side. All she could do was go along with it until the right time arose to either wrestle the gun from her or run if the mother didn't kill her first.

'You're much prettier than I imagined, though you look much whiter than I thought. I guess that comes from shitting yer fecking knickers.'

Dixie-Lee didn't understand why she kept switching from Irish to this soft, mild voice, like a modern version of Mary Poppins. By the time they reached the flat, where the door had been left open from her hasty exit, she almost buckled. The sight of the cable ties and the knife played out like something out of a slasher flick.

'Chubs!' his mother yelled.

A groan came from the bathroom. 'Mam, I'm in here. Help me.'

'You get inside.' She waved the gun for Dixie-Lee to move into the flat.

With the shard of glass still behind her back, Dixie-Lee walked into the living area, but she was conscious of keeping the weapon out of this crazy mother's eyesight.

'You move, and I'll fecking shoot you!'

Chubs's withering voice rang out. 'Mam, help me.'

Dixie-Lee was surprised that the woman had just left her standing there. The knife was still on the table, so, in a flash, she dropped the piece of glass and grabbed the blade. Just as she was about to sneak out of the room, she heard the demented mother scream, 'Oh Mary, Mother of God. No! Jesus, not my baby.' Her voice changed from a high-pitched scream to a low masculine demonic tone with a dog's growl thrown into the mix. 'Give me strength!' she screamed. 'I'll fecking kill her!'

'Mam, don't leave me. Please . . . help me stop the bleeding.'

'All right, Son, I'll use me belt. Shush, Son, save your strength, love.'

Dixie-Lee ran from the flat knowing she didn't have time to reach the end of the corridor before the woman appeared and fired off a shot at her. Hiding in an alcove, she caught her breath, believing that Jerry and Chubs's mother would soon appear like a rabid dog determined to kill her. At that moment, she heard her in the hall shouting, 'If I catch you, Dixie-Lee, I'll slit your throat, you evil bitch!'

Just as Dixie-Lee was about to relax, thinking this nasty piece of work would return to her son, she heard the lift door open.

As Noel stepped out of the lift, his mother yelled down the corridor, 'Oh, Son, hurry up. One of your brothers has been murdered. You have to help me get Chubs to the hospital, or he'll die an' all. The little bitch is a nightmare. She just broke out.'

'You what? When?'

'Just now. She must still be in the building!'

Dixie-Lee felt her guts moving. The man she knew as Noel was fit and had the strength to fight her, and he probably had a gun. She tried to control her breathing so he couldn't hear her, but all she could do was keep swallowing. Her vision was slightly blurred, and her head felt on fire. Hearing him running along the corridor, she pressed her back against the left-hand wall and prayed he didn't see her. She felt the rush of a breeze as he shot past her. He didn't stop running.

Hearing that his brother had been killed had completely thrown Noel off guard, and his sharp gaze was now truly dulled.

Dixie-Lee needed to decide whether to run or stay put. She could hear their voices in the distance and then there was silence. She assumed they were inside that flat. This was her chance to escape, but the door opposite opened. There stood an elderly man in his late seventies, slightly stooped, and holding two empty wine bottles. His clothes were clean, but otherwise, he looked unkempt. She hoped and prayed that he had nothing to do with the deranged family that had kidnapped her. With a quick movement, she was at his side. 'Please let me in, sir.'

The man looked up, clearly startled. He hadn't seen any pretty girls in the building, and this one – standing almost in his face – was stunning. No one had called him 'sir' in many a year. He knew instantly by the trepidation in her eyes that she was scared. He stepped aside and let her enter, looking up and down the corridor before closing the door quietly.

The moment she was inside the flat, she collapsed in a heap, sobbing uncontrollably.

‘There, there,’ said the old man, ‘nothing in this world is that bad. Come into the living room, and I’ll make you a drink – coffee, tea, or would you like something with a kick to it?’

Dixie-Lee turned her head to look at this kind man. She felt such incredible relief, and his gentle words moved her to cry fresh tears.

The old man kneeled down beside her, putting his arm around her shoulders. ‘Come away from the door. The walls are paper-thin in these flats. Come into the living room. You’ll be safe there, dear.’

Dixie-Lee took a few deep breaths before she got to her feet.

As she did so, the old man spotted the knife, and his grey hooded eyes widened.

The last thing Dixie-Lee wanted to do was to scare the poor guy. ‘Sorry, I’m not going to hurt you. I was only holding it to protect myself.’

He led her into the living room and gestured for her to sit down.

This flat was bigger than the one she had just escaped from, and the living room was so cosy. A colossal bookcase, crammed with books, whose visible spines ranged from the traditional red, green, and orange leather bindings to the modern reissues of the classics, dominated the room. On the opposite wall there was a fake wood-burning stove with a gently flickering flame that looked real. The green Chesterfield suite was worn and polished. On either side were two high-backed plaid chairs, and beside one there was a small side coffee table on which he had a glass of wine, a pipe, and a newspaper. She could tell so much about the man in his sitting room, and what gave him away were the photographs, of which there were so many, all very similar, many in black and white. He was standing next to a class of students who were wearing immaculate uniforms, unlike the school she had attended. He was a former teacher – perhaps a headmaster – but what made him special was his broad smile and gentle eyes. Every photo showed him with his chin up and proud to be standing there with his pupils. She knew she could trust him.

‘I am so sorry to barge in on you. I . . . I was kidnapped . . .’

The old man gasped. ‘Oh gosh, let me call the police right away. Who kidnapped you?’

Dixie-Lee wiped her face and took another deep breath. 'I actually don't know. But it was a family. Well, a man called Noel – I don't know his real name – kidnapped me and brought me here. Then there are two of his brothers called Chubs and Jerry.'

As Dixie-Lee peered up, she saw a sudden change in the old man's face. His soft features hardened, and he pushed his glasses further up his nose and glared. 'What did you say your name was?'

Dixie-Lee felt every hair on her head stand on end. There was an evident shift in his demeanour. 'I, er, I didn't. Why?'

His smile returned. 'Oh, sorry, no reason. Now would you like a cup of tea? Let's get you settled before we call the police.'

Dixie-Lee clocked a landline phone on the occasional table. 'I would love a coffee, Mr . . .'

'Oh, it's Mr O'Shea . . . I mean Mr Shanklin. Sorry, I didn't put my teeth in properly.'

She watched him disappear into a room she assumed was the kitchen. Then she glanced back at the photographs. Something struck her – it was the name of the school. Kerry High School for Boys, Ireland.

There was another photograph on the mantelpiece above the fake fire. It was of a young woman. More than likely, it was his daughter, judging by the way he had his arm around her, kissing the top of her head. Suddenly, her heart was in her mouth, her stomach contents rose, and a hot feeling shot up her spine, which made her head momentarily spin. She recognised the woman and knew she had to escape. This place was a trap.

Slowly and quietly, she crept towards the front door, and as she passed the kitchen, she could hear the old man making her a drink. She knew then she had an opportunity to make a dash for it. She figured that as soon as he realised she was gone, he would be on the phone to the woman – the insane mother of Jerry, Chubs, and Noel. This old man could well be their grandfather. Gripping the knife, she opened the door and peered up and down the corridor. It was quiet. She guessed she didn't have long to get out of the building before one of them caught her, and so she wasn't going to hang around. Knowing she had murdered one – possibly two sons – she knew they would kill her if she stayed any longer.

Was this building filled with tenants who were all related to this Irish family? The well-worn carpet, the peeling wallpaper, the madness of it all, was pretty creepy. Everything she had seen added to her fear. She felt compelled to run like the wind.

After her attack six months ago, she had been held back because her leg just wouldn't work properly. Her physiotherapist had told her that it wasn't a physical issue but a mental blockage. However, fear must have cleared the blockage, and she sprinted like a 200-metre Olympic runner. The more she ran, the faster she got until she finally reached the last door on the right, which had a fire escape sign above it. She opened the door and hurtled down the stairs until she was one storey up from the car park. At that point, she could hear Noel's voice. She guessed he'd gone down in the lift while she was in the old man's flat.

Holding her breath, she listened. It was apparent that Noel was on a mobile phone talking to a person called Jared.

'She must be in the building, Jared. She couldn't have got away already. The kid can hardly walk, let alone run. Pops said she'd scarpered just seconds ago, but you know Pops. He's a little bit daft. He's probably drunk some of his own tea. Get here ASAP. I need every room in this hellhole searched. And tell Jonas to guard the fecking entrance. If she gets away, we're all fecked. Kill her, if you have to.'

Hearing Noel return from the car park to the bottom of the stairs, she leaned back so that he couldn't see her.

'Fecking lift. Hurry up,' he mumbled, as he punched the button on the wall.

As soon as the lift opened and closed, Dixie-Lee hurried down the stairs to the car park, hoping that Jared and Jonas weren't already in the building, or, more importantly, in the car park. Cautiously, she opened the door and peered around her. To her amazement, Noel had left his car right under her nose and with the driver's door open. As she ran around to look inside, she saw the keys and then saw that it was an automatic. She hadn't passed her test yet, but she knew she could drive this car.

Without hesitation, she hopped into the driver's seat, closed the doors, locked them, started the car, and looked in the rear-view mirror. To her horror, there was a huge man, built like the side of a house, who was running towards the car and waving his arms. For a split second, it crossed her mind that he may have been there to help her. But when he pulled a gun from his back pocket and aimed it at the car, she knew he was the enemy. And it very much looked like he wanted to kill her.

Ramming the car into reverse, she slammed her foot on the accelerator, and the car, being a sports model, flew backwards at such force it slammed into the monster of a man, knocking him over. She then thrust the gear selector into drive and shot forwards. Her adrenaline, now surging through her veins, gave her the gumption to reverse over the man again, with the intention of finishing him off. She had lost all empathy but had maintained her logic. This family wanted her dead, but she would fight for her life, and it wouldn't be for the first time. Fury came from her feet and raised up through her body to her head. She slammed the gear selector into reverse and shot back but she was surprised when she felt no lumps or bumps.

A glance in her door mirror told her that he had rolled out of the way, got to his feet, and was standing right beside the passenger door window aiming his gun at her.

But she had her wits about her. She ducked and pushed her foot down on the accelerator again. The car reversed so fast that even when the man fired the gun, he missed. She was now looking in the rear-view mirror again, steering the car in reverse up the ramp to the barrier. It was now down.

The man shot at the car a couple of times, but Dixie-Lee managed to stay in control and reverse the car at such a speed it took the barrier off, which then bounced over the car and rolled down the ramp. She clumsily managed to swing the car around, the second she was on the road.

Luckily for her, no car was coming along the road. She straightened up and then tore off. It didn't matter if the police stopped her; she was away, free, and heading home.

CHAPTER EIGHTEEN

Dixie-Lee had barely settled her racing heartbeat when she realised she had absolutely no idea where she was. Nothing around her looked familiar. However, she had to get away because without a doubt the Irish lot would be following her. She slowed down when she became dangerously close to hitting a car. She'd been having driving lessons in a tiny Fiat 500, and this car, compared to that one, was a beast. As she reached the lights, she saw a sign for the M25 and knew then that she could find her way home once she was on that. As she tore along the A roads, she heard the car beeping and a flashing light appeared on the dashboard.

'Damn! Damn!' she yelled, before running her hands over her sweaty forehead. She was nearly out of fuel and didn't have her purse on her. As she slowed down in the inside lane of a dual carriageway, she glanced at the side pocket in the door and the centre console before opening the glove compartment. She nearly jumped out of her skin when a wallet and a gun fell out. She hoped the wallet had some money inside, enough at least to get her home. Thankfully, there was a filling station up ahead, so, slowly, she pulled in, and not knowing which side the petrol cap was, she took a lucky guess. Leaning over to the front passenger seat, she picked up the wallet and opened it to find there were credit cards and a couple of fifties. 'Fanbloodytastic.'

She was feeling lucky. Lucky to have escaped, lucky to have stolen a car, and lucky to find a few quid to fill up. And also, as she opened the door, she was fortunate that the cap was on her side, and she wouldn't have to pull the nozzle right over the roof of the car.

Once she'd filled up, she grabbed a bar of chocolate and a bottle of juice to boost her energy levels. She knew she was running on fumes herself. When she glanced over to the till, she spotted a problem. A queue was suddenly forming. It seemed the till wasn't working. *Had her luck just run out?*

The guy behind her was huffing and tutting. 'The bloody bridge is closed. The traffic using the Dartford Crossing is gonna be a nightmare,' he muttered, to anyone listening.

Dixie-Lee sighed heavily; perhaps she'd jinxed her good luck. She grabbed another bar of chocolate and two more bottles of juice before she joined the queue.

After she finally managed to pay, she was back on the road again within minutes. The man who'd been in the queue behind her was right. The traffic was terrible because there were some issues on the bridge, so everyone was diverted through the tunnel. Her tiredness had made her unable to think quickly. She realised once she was in the traffic jam that she should have asked to borrow someone's phone to call her mother to let her know she was okay. She opened the juice and drank it so fast, she was almost sick. The traffic wasn't moving, and she was now worried that her mother would think she was still kidnapped, or worse – dead. The loud engine roar of two motorbikes shooting past made her jump. The noise was followed by an overwhelming feeling of dread. She was stuck in traffic, but what if Noel and these other guys were on their way to her house and now on motorbikes? They would get there before her. What if they knew a quicker way? There were so many what-ifs, her mind was awash with all kinds of nasty scenarios. Still, each one returned to the idea that going home wasn't the best way forward. Noel, his gang, and even his nutty mother might be there waiting for her. So, she decided to go to the last place anyone would expect her to go. Once she had made up her mind, she chowed down on a large bar of Cadbury Dairy Milk Wholenut and drank another juice.

By the time the traffic had cleared, and she was through the tunnel, she was focused, had also become more familiar with the car, and felt she could drive like she owned it and not like she'd nicked it.

With her wits about her, she cruised into the estate and parked a few metres away from her destination.

As soon as she stepped out of the car, the bitter wind stung her burning cheeks. Having been in the car for hours with the heater blasting, she had become accustomed to being as warm as a furnace, and so the sudden drop in temperature made her shiver relentlessly. She glanced nervously about her before she gingerly knocked at the door. The wind caught the tall green dustbin and tipped it over. Instantly, she hurried to grab it before it escaped and caused mayhem in the street.

However, just as she stood the bin upright, the door opened, startling her. 'Oh, er, I'm so sorry to bother you—' She knew this was Sheila, although she hadn't seen her so close up. Sheila's reputation on the estate, though, was legendary. Her gnarly features and clawlike hands would put the fear of God into any human. Time clearly hadn't been good to her, judging by the profound lines that radiated from the corners of her eyes and the deep furrows around her mouth that deepened when she glared with a strangled expression. One eye widened while the other twitched. *She could win an Oscar for playing a character in one of Roald Dahl's books, merely on looks alone*, Dixie-Lee thought.

'What the fucking hell are you doing here? And leave me fucking bin alone.'

Dixie-Lee was suddenly near to tears. She had made a mistake even thinking that for one minute the likes of the Marxes would entertain her.

'I am sorry.' A tear escaped and trickled down her frozen cheek. 'I'll go.' She turned to hurry away.

'Hold up. You're that Dixie-Lee, ain't ya. You can't fucking knock at my door and then piss off. Come here.'

Her harsh words and sour tone made Dixie-Lee stop and spin around. 'I really don't want to cause any trouble.'

Sheila's face softened. She glanced up and down the road before she beckoned Dixie-Lee inside.

The warm air inside the hallway was welcoming; however, the smell of cigarettes and burned fat was overpowering. Still, Dixie-Lee was grateful to be inside.

Sheila closed the door. 'Now, what the hell is going on? Your muvver was here with a knife at me baby's throat demanding to know where the fuck you were. And here you are, as bold as brass, on my doorstep with bruises down ya face and a look as if some gangster seagull has fucked off with your hot dog.' She placed her hands on her hips. 'Does your muvver know you're here?'

Dixie-Lee wiped the tears away, trying to keep up with the speed at which Mrs Marx rattled off her words. 'No, no, not yet. This man, this mental family, kidnapped me. I came here because they might go to my house and—' She guessed she sounded absurd, like a five-year-old expressing their imagination.

'Well!' interrupted Sheila, now looking less than empathetic. 'I can't have fucking shit happening at my doorstep. You'll have to leave. As you know, I've had enough grief to last me a lifetime. Go on, get going.' She shooed Dixie-Lee towards the door, like a stray cat, mumbling, 'As if I'm a flaming rescue centre.'

'Wait, Muvver! Leave her alone,' said Yasmin, as she skipped down the stairs.

Dixie-Lee was shocked beyond belief. From what she had been told, Yasmin was partly responsible for her ending up in the hospital. Yasmin had spread it around that one day she would come for her to hurt her good and proper. Not that she herself was afraid. But now, it seemed, Yasmin was sticking up for her.

'Muvver, Dixie-Lee's had a shit time, right? She never killed me bruvver nor me sister, and she came here for help. You saw how frantic her muvver was, and I know because she held a knife at me throat.'

Dixie-Lee looked at Yasmin and saw someone completely different. Yasmin wasn't the spiteful cocky girl she once knew. She appeared to have drastically changed. She wasn't wearing a ton of make-up for a start, and her hair was a natural blonde, not the bleached blonde she used to be.

'Thank you, Yasmin. Look, I don't want to be a bother, I swear, and no one will come here for me.' She looked at the floor ashamed.

Turning to face Sheila, she said quietly and respectfully, 'No one would dream that I would knock at your door, but I am desperate. Please, these men were cruel. They, er . . .'

'Enough, you don't need to tell me, okay? Come into the living room. Yasmin will make you a drink. Yas, put the kettle on, will ya.'

Unexpectedly, Dixie-Lee gently clasped Sheila's hand and held it. 'I am so very sorry about Todd and Eve. Truly, I am. Having me in your home must be hard, and for that, Mrs Marx, I am so grateful.' She sniffed back a tear.

'Yeah, well, it's fucking freezing out there. I can't have me door open letting in the cold air, and I s'pose you're right. This is the last place anyone would look to find you.' She grinned. 'So if I killed you, no one would know, eh?'

Dixie-Lee's eyes widened.

'Muvver, shut up. Can't you see a joke like that ain't funny? Go into the living room, Dixie-Lee. I'll fetch you some tea, yeah? Sugar?'

Dixie-Lee nodded. 'Yes, please, Yasmin.'

Cautiously, Dixie-Lee sat on the sofa while Sheila sat on the chair to the side. She sparked up a cigarette, offering Dixie-Lee one.

'No, I'm good, thank you.' She guessed that saying 'I don't smoke' might sound a bit snobbish.

'Right, so who kidnapped you, then?'

'I don't know who they were. This man, Noel, said he was taking me to the airport so I could fly to Ireland to stay with my grandmother, but as soon as I got in the car, there was another bloke who made me get down so no one could see me. Then these guys took me to a flat in this old hotel.' She stopped talking and began to shake all over. Her head was hot. She could visualise the knife and cable ties. The image was so vivid, and so frightening. She could hear Sheila's voice in the background. Her words sounded fuzzy and strange. At that point, she knew she was about to faint and could do nothing to stop it.

When she came around, Sheila was fanning her face with a newspaper, and Yasmin was shouting up the stairs for her brother Riley to come down and help.

'Are you with us again? Fucking hell, girl. You gave me a fright. I thought you were dead. You just switched off and looked like you'd keeled over.'

Yasmin returned to the living room. 'The lazy bugger's probably asleep.' She looked at Dixie-Lee. 'You fainted. It must be the shock or something. You ain't diabetic, are ya?'

Dixie-Lee shook her head. 'You're right. It's probably shock. I'm sorry. I am causing such a fuss, aren't I?'

Sheila smiled. 'No, gal, no more than usual in this house. Now, sit yaself up, drink that sweet tea, and let's see what you wanna do.'

The sudden relief had Dixie-Lee more relaxed enough to drink the sweet tea without spilling a drop.

'Yas, get the gal a biscuit. She's as white as a ghost.'

'Thank you. I'm fine. Honestly, I just feel shaken up, that's all.'

'How did you escape?'

Dixie-Lee stared at nothing, trying to recap, but she knew she couldn't tell Sheila or Yasmin that she had killed a man, possibly two. 'I used a pedestal to smash the window, and then I climbed out and ran.' She deliberately left out the part where she stole a car to get here.

'Do you want to call your muvver? She is worried sick. I can tell you that much.'

Dixie-Lee looked at Yasmin. 'I will do. Er, she didn't hurt you, did she? I mean, she wouldn't. She was in the Army, ya see, and so she can get a bit GI Jane, if you know what I mean.'

Yasmin suddenly burst out laughing 'You're a bit of a laugh, Dixie-Lee. I never saw you as a giggle. I always thought you were stuck up your own arse.'

Dixie-Lee assumed that somewhere in that remark there was a compliment.

'Our Riley likes you, ya know,' said Sheila.

'I like Riley too. We walk to college together. He is so good at art. He's got a painting in the foyer. You must be so proud, Mrs Marx', said Dixie Lee, turning her attention to Sheila.

A glow suddenly coated Sheila's face, and her cheeks flushed a pink colour. 'I never knew he had stuff in the foy, whatever it's called. He never said nuffin about that. Blimey, so our boy's an artist, is he? I mean, I know he draws pretty good. Mind you, I didn't like the fucking one he did of me. My face looked like a decomposing arse.'

'But, Muvver, can't ya see? That's exactly how our Riley *sees* you. It's a modern artist thing, ya know.'

Suddenly both Sheila and Yasmin burst out laughing, and Dixie-Lee was stunned. She hadn't taken Sheila for the type of woman who would laugh at herself.

Sheila giggled. 'Oh, shut up. I'll have you know, Yasmin Marx, that there were many a man following me around in my day.'

Yasmin laughed and slapped her thigh. 'Yeah, it's called morbid curiosity.'

Dixie-Lee smiled at the extreme turn of events.

'You can laugh, Yas, but the sketch of you looks like something that came out of a slow cooker.'

Joining in, Dixie-Lee said, 'I wonder what he would make of me, then?'

Sheila stopped laughing, and her face became serious. 'Have you never seen the pictures he draws of you?'

With a nervous smile, Dixie-Lee replied, 'No.'

'Well, gal, I won't lie. He draws you like you have the face of an angel.'

Waiting for the joke, but with a half grin, Dixie-Lee said, '*Seriously?*'

Yasmin nodded. 'Yep, he has lots of pictures of you. Don't get me wrong. He ain't a weirdo. Well, he might be a little bit weird, but he ain't a letch. Well, he might be a bit but nuffin too deviant. I think he finds you easy to draw, and I will admit, he does have a bit of a crush on you.'

Dixie-Lee nodded. She had always thought as much.

Sheila lit another cigarette. 'Dixie-Lee, do you want to call your muvver?'

'Yes, please. Do you mind?'

Sheila pointed to the phone on the wall. 'Be quick about it. My phone bill is sky fucking high with this lot.'

Yasmin hopped up from the arm of the sofa and reached across for the phone before handing it to Dixie-Lee. 'Take your time. Ignore Muvver. She's only joking.'

Dixie-Lee glanced back at Sheila, who winked, and at that moment, she realised that a lot of Sheila's mouth and aggression was probably a front.

She dialled her home phone and waited, but it just rang and rang. The answerphone didn't kick in for some reason. But she wouldn't have left a message even if it had. A feeling of despair came over her. What if Noel and those other men had got to her mother?

'No answer?' asked Sheila, as her forehead furrowed into a deep frown.

Dixie-Lee shook her head. 'Can I call her mobile?'

'Sure. Maybe she's at the police station.'

Dixie-Lee shook her head and said, 'No, she doesn't like the police.'

Still feeling uneasy, Dixie-Lee dialled her mother's mobile and waited, and again, it rang and rang. When it went to voicemail, she didn't risk leaving a message. A cold sense of dread crept up her spine and dried her mouth.

'What's up, Dixie-Lee?'

'She's not answering her mobile. I know something is wrong. She knows I've been kidnapped, and yet she ain't answering the phone. They've got to her. I know they are waiting for me to go home, and I don't know why, but they want me for some reason.' Feeling her chest heave, she knew she was about to break into a sob, so she bit on her bottom lip. 'They wouldn't tell me why they'd kidnapped me, but I guess it's because they either want my mum or my uncles—'

'But why you?' Yasmin interrupted.

However, it was Sheila who answered.

'These men wanted Dixie-Lee because she's probably the most precious thing to her mother and those uncles of hers. They wanted to use her as a bargaining tool. Now, the chances are they've got to her muvver. They want her to do something for them, I betcha.'

Dixie-Lee nodded. 'I think you're right, Mrs Marx.'

'Oh, stop with the Mrs Marx. Call me Sheila. I was never a schoolteacher, so don't make me feel like one. Now, mind you, I reckon I would have been a good school—'

'Leave off, Muvver. Let's sort out Dixie-Lee's situation.' She rolled her eyes. 'Schoolteacher? You never even went to school.'

'I'll have you know I left school with a good education, my gal.'

'You left school with a bun in the oven and a first-class honours degree in a shitty attitude.'

Sheila grinned. 'Better than nuffin.'

'Call her again, Dixie-Lee.'

After another attempt and with still no answer, Dixie-Lee stood up. 'I'll have to go home. I know they've got her. I just know it. And they are ruthless men, trust me.'

'How could they get to her, though? I mean, I walked near your road, and there were two cop cars outside.'

'Yeah, well, the police haven't considered that we have that back alley, and my mum won't tell them. She doesn't trust them. They've arrested my two uncles for the murder of my father, and there is no way they would do that, not in a million years.'

Sheila coughed and blew a choking ball of smoke into the air. 'The filth probably got them in the nick to drill them over other matters, no doubt. They did that with my lot many a time, the fucking bastards.'

'I'll have to go and find out what's going on. I can't just sit here.'

Sheila stubbed out her cigarette and stood up. 'No, love, you wait here. I'll go and see what's afoot.'

'Muvver, you can't do that. What if—'

'Stop fussing, Yas. Get Riley up. He can come with me. Jasper's at work.'

While Yasmin ran up the stairs, Sheila turned to face Dixie-Lee. 'When my ol' man died, it crucified my kids. They were inconsolable, and what you've been through, well, I suppose I feel sorry for ya.'

'Thank you, Sheila, for being so generous, but I'm tougher than I look.'

'I blamed your muvver for my kids' murders, but I had to have someone to blame and hate, and trying to accept that this Ashby geezer went to such lengths to make out that your mum was their killer when really he was responsible, well, it didn't seem possible, so I truly believed your muvver killed 'em.'

Dixie-Lee was unnerved by the seriousness of this conversation, knowing that if Sheila didn't believe it, she would hate the family so much she could be capable of anything.

'I lay in me bed night after night planning how I'd kill her, ya know. But now I have come out the other end of that hateful fucking fog I was in. I can see that now, after what that Major Ashby did to you, your muvver, and your grandmuvver. And, well, of course, he killed my two eldest kids. I suppose I just got used to hating your muvver. Anyway, it's time for amends, I reckon.' She smiled. 'I just hope she don't think I'm a foe. Well, we're hardly mates.'

'Muvver, Riley's not in his bed, and he ain't slept in it either!' Yasmin yelled, before she entered the room.

Sheila frowned. 'The last time I saw him, he was running after your muvver with a drawing he did of you. Oh Christ, you don't think he was caught up in all this, do you, the daft little fucking sod?'

Sheila looked at her daughter and then back at Dixie-Lee. 'I would call the police, but I'm a bit like your muvver. I can't stand 'em. I wish I had a fucking gun.'

Yasmin rolled her eyes. 'A gun? You'll end up shooting yaself or the wrong person.'

'Whatever. Right, I'll go by meself and cause a stink. I'm good at that. And if these geezers who kidnapped you are there, well, then we will know, and I can tell the police because you will be here safe and your muvver won't have to worry about you.'

'But what if—'

'Shush, I need to think. Yas, get me coat and me fags. I'll be back in twenty minutes, and if those men have hurt my boy, I won't need a fucking gun to kill 'em. I will rip their heads off with me bare fucking hands.'

Yasmin passed her mother a long thick black coat, clearly two sizes too big for her, and then her cigarettes and a reggae lighter.

Dixie-Lee watched as Sheila slid her feet into a pair of black fur boots, pushed her shoulders back, picked up her brolly, and marched out the front door.

'God help 'em, is all I can say,' said Yasmin, watching her mother storm off along the road. 'It will take the entire fucking British Army to stop her, once she's on her mission. And if they have hurt my bruvver, she will stop at nuffin to bash the fuck out of 'em.'

'And I believe you,' replied Dixie-Lee, as she stared at the woman thundering ahead.

CHAPTER NINETEEN

Brodie stared at James. 'You do know, darling, that if my brother dies and I'm still alive, I will come for you and kill you, and I warn you, it won't be quick. I will turn your stomach inside fecking out.'

Brodie noticed that even though it was bitterly cold, James had broken into a sweat.

'Well, that was graphic. It sounds to me, Deacon, you have killed before.'

The words came out calmly, but Brodie sensed an unease.

'I never said that, but believe me, James, I can play out every fecking last gruesome detail in my mind. Even how you will scream for your mamma.'

'Threats won't get you anywhere.'

Brodie grinned. 'But you, James, you fecking rely on them, bullying and blackmailing and threatening. I bet you did a stint in Guantánamo Bay detention camp. As a fecking torturer.'

'No, I didn't, but you and I are very similar, Deacon.'

'Ha! You're delusional, and there is nothing similar about us, James. You see, you're a bully, and me, I hate bullies. That's how I started my company, from people who'd been bullied and needing my help.'

James nodded. 'Yes, and I can guess you even the scores when you and your brothers wade in teaching the bully a lesson, yeah?' She sneered. 'Am I right?'

Brodie smiled. 'Wade in? Oh, darling, you couldn't be more wrong.' He smiled again. 'Let's get back to this Rodney chap you seem so worried about. Who is he?'

'I ask the questions, Deacon.'

'Oh yeah, and how's that working out for yer?'

'You will see how I get answers, once your brother is fit for an interview.' She turned the gun around in her hand. 'I'll get the answers I need because, Deacon, that's my job.'

'For what it's worth, James, I do believe you have the wrong Deacon family. I haven't visited a man called Rodney. In fact, I don't know any men called Rodney. And me brothers don't either. And if I did and my relationship with this man was in any way a serious threat to the country, I'd tell you.'

James smirked. 'Really?'

Brodie nodded. 'I think the issue for you is what my brothers and I do for a living. I don't think you understand what we're about. You completely misunderstand our business. So, assuming that's the case, perhaps that gives you a tiny reason to believe that we could be far more dangerous than we are. But I have no interest in endangering innocent lives. That's not who I am or what I fecking stand for.'

'MI5 are not set up for the sole purpose of national security. No, we deal with far more than that.'

'Like what?' probed Brodie, hoping James would get to the point of why he was being held in the disused manufacturing garage.

'Ah, I see what you're doing, Deacon. You want me to run my mouth.'

Brodie shuffled about on the hard seat until he was comfortable. He stared at James for a moment before he frowned. 'James . . .' He paused for effect. 'James, if you believe that I visited Rodney, and evidently you do believe that . . .' He paused and waited for a response.

James nodded, wondering what was coming next.

'Then that being the case, you wouldn't have a problem telling me why I was there and what my relationship with Rodney is, would you?'

James didn't answer; she merely glowered.

'See where I'm going with this? And that tells me one thing, James. You don't really believe it was me or me brothers, not now, not since you were about to hang Mac in front of me when I still couldn't give you answers. So basically, you know full well that you're pissing in the wind.'

Brodie didn't expect James to respond with any further information. However, he was stunned when she uttered the words, 'Okay, I will level with you.'

Brodie sat up straight, prepared to be all ears. 'We're levelling now, are we?'

'Rodney Potter was locked away for murdering his daughter and grandson. He got a life sentence without parole.'

Brodie shrugged. 'And?'

‘He claimed he found the bodies in his spare room. He said he didn’t know they were there until there was a smell. You know what stench I mean.’

Brodie shook his head. ‘Nah, darling, I don’t know. But I get the picture, all the same. But what’s that got to do with MI5?’

James looked to her left. There were two officers standing there and then she looked to her right at the van. One officer was standing with his arms clasped in front of him.

James stepped towards Brodie, but she left a six-foot gap between them. Once again, she held her gun in both hands. Lowering her voice, she said, ‘He killed them both. There is no question about it.’

Brodie was nodding, hurrying her to get to the point.

‘He was arrested and taken to Tonbridge Police Station, where he made some wild accusations. He claimed he knew who killed his family and he would make sure they paid.’

Brodie could only guess where this was leading. ‘And you believe he hired my company to take revenge?’ He shook his head. ‘That’s not what we do. However, James, if someone like Rodney truly believed he was wrongly accused and he asked us to do a bit of private investigation work, we would undertake that for a fee and then hand over our findings to his solicitor. We’ve done that before, but I honestly don’t know a Rodney Potter, and I’m not familiar with the case . . .’ He stopped abruptly and silently studied her face. Tilting his head to the side in suspicion, he made a statement. ‘I’m not familiar with the case because it wasn’t in the press, was it? I mean, come on, the press would have been all over a story like that. Father kills daughter and grandson.’

James began chewing her bottom lip, and Brodie understood then that she realised she had underestimated him. He guessed, she had taken a good look at him and assumed he was an uneducated thug.

‘Now, I assume it was hushed up, kept out of the paper because . . .’ He paused for effect before a smile beamed across his face. ‘The man who Rodney accused of killing his family is, er . . .’ He paused again. ‘One of you guys!’ He sucked air in through his teeth making a whistling sound. ‘But the thing that puzzles me, James, is how can this circumstance be one of national security?’

Brodie could tell he was hitting a nerve with her; the pulse in her cheek was prominent and she was grinding her back teeth. But James wouldn't be the first person to underestimate his intelligence.

'Unless, James, whoever went to visit Rodney actually carried out Rodney's threat, in which case, the person he accused of killing his family is either dead and you have no body, or he or she is missing, because, again, you have no body. Now, I can see in your eyes that it's dawned on you that I'm not the daft bastard you thought I was. So, darling, am I on the money?'

'There are a million scenarios, Deacon, but it makes me think that you're our man because you seem to know more than you should.'

Brodie huffed and shook his head. 'Well, James, it's clear to me, you are used to, let's just say, less intelligent people, but now . . . now, you've met someone with a little more than fecking common sense. So you give me a different scenario if you believe there are more than a million. And please, James, give me a feasible one.'

'Okay, let's stop with the games, Deacon.'

'Good, I agree. Now then, love, am I right that Rodney accused one of your men of being the killer, and I suspect a high-ranking man. In which case, Rodney will be a very angry man. I know I would be, wouldn't you? Some geezer kills his family and then has him locked away for their murders.'

James rolled her eyes. 'Carry on.'

'So I bet angry Rodney wanted this man hung, drawn, and quartered, wouldn't you say?' Brodie waited for an answer.

'Yes.'

'So this issue with national security runs much deeper than a double murder and an angry father. Let's just call the person who Rodney believes killed his family Mr X. If Mr X killed my family and I killed him or had him killed, then that could be hushed up, yeah? You can make it all go away, can't you?'

When James's eyes twitched, and she licked her lips, Brodie guessed then that he was getting to the truth. Inside, he was laughing, knowing that she wasn't the formidable powerhouse she made out she was.

'Me, James, I believe there is so much more to it. Rodney has something over your guy, Mr X, and it's more than just murder. Maybe Rodney's visitor holds the truth, and that's why you have me with my hands behind my back, your men surrounding the building, and a rope over the steel beam, ready to hang me or Mac to extract information as to what we know.'

'Yes, Deacon, you're spot on.'

'Well, there we fecking have it. Only, James, you have been on a wild fecking goose chase, because, as I said, I don't know a fecking Rodney, and I didn't visit him in prison. But from the look on your face, while I was putting more meat on the bones of my scenario, your facial expression gave a lot away. You should go on a course for that. Anyway, I digress. Sorry, can I ask, have you found a body? Wait, wait, let me answer that for you.'

Feeling like a fool, James replied, 'Go on, then.'

'You haven't found a body, have you? No, you haven't found your chap because old Rodders has had him kidnapped. Mr X, your top person, is probably being held hostage, and much like this situation, the kidnapper is trying to extract information from him. And no doubt information that could implicate any one of you guys, maybe even you, love. And that, James, darling, is the reason that this is now a breach of national security. I mean, Mr X could be divulging all sorts to God knows who. But, Miss Moneypenny, be sure of this. Mr X has not divulged anything to me or my brothers, because we're not the kidnappers.'

'How can I be sure?'

'See, ol' Rodders, he has absolutely nothing to lose. I mean, Christ alive, a fecking little grandson was murdered.'

'He wasn't little, he was fifteen.'

Brodie saw the sudden regret slapped across her face. He stared and raised his brows. 'You think that a little fecking fifteen-year-old is a man? He was a kid, just fifteen. He would have been at school. It's obvious you're not a mother, thank God for small mercies. But even as a woman, you still said he wasn't a kid. Hmmm, interesting.'

'No, I was just saying he wasn't little. He was fifteen. It was not like he was just five.' She shut up, knowing how stupid she sounded.

'And that makes a fecking difference? I'll tell you this for nothing. My niece is eighteen years old, and to me, she's my little niece. And, see, just the thought of anyone hurting her sends me insane. So listen, James. There is no way that this Rodney guy is guilty, because if he is, he'd be in a secure mental prison, not fecking Rochester Prison in Kent, for Christ's sake.'

'Not all kid killers are insane.'

'No, you're right there, so why was this hushed up, eh? We all know how the press are. They run their own kangaroo court, so why, James? Tell me why was it hushed up, eh? Why, love?' Brodie shook his head. 'No, don't tell me. I'll tell you. It was because the fecking man was innocent, I bet. Anyway, like I said, he had nothing to lose. But I, James, have a fecking lot to lose, and so does Mac. I've got a nice life and people alive that I love dearly, so that's the truth. Now, it's my turn to ask a question, and I want honesty, James.'

He lowered his head as pain morphed across his face. 'Why did you kill my little brother? He was just a fecking part-time scaffolder, and he was innocent. The poor man who served in the fecking Army got blown up and suffered from PTSD. Why kill him? Why?' he cried. 'Surely to God, you didn't think it was him who went to see this Rodney bloke, did you?'

She sighed and lowered her gun. Her arms were aching. 'We didn't kill him. It wasn't us.'

'Bollocks, you bitch, you're lying.'

'I'm not lying. His death has nothing whatsoever to do with MI5, and I can assure you of that.'

Brodie frowned. 'And my niece?'

'We know nothing about your niece.'

CHAPTER TWENTY

An hour earlier

Georgie felt drained. She peered into her daughter's room to check on Riley. It seemed that the tablets had completely knocked him out. Looking closely at the wound, a small smile graced her face. She was pleased with the job she'd done and only hoped that Riley would be too, once he had rested and had a chance to recover. She only hoped he wasn't suffering from a serious internal head injury. But after listening to his breathing, she sensed he was gently purring, which put her mind at rest.

Catching a glimpse of herself in the small mirror glued on the wardrobe door, she noticed that there was some blood in her hair and on her face. After a quailing shudder whipped through her bones, she decided to go for a shower.

Since the bathroom was so tiny, the shower itself was merely a handheld 1980s contraption that she'd hung on the wall over the bath. And so as not to soak the floor, she had hung a shower curtain along a metal rail she'd fitted years ago. She stared at the rust on the pole and automatically peered out of the window to the garage below. Even on a wintry day, the smidgeon of sun caught the brilliance of that vast new padlock. Tutting, she looked away, turned on the taps, pulled the knob up that sent the water to the makeshift shower, and stripped off. The door had never locked, but she wasn't worried that Riley might walk in. He was zonked out.

Initially, the fierce, sharp spray felt ice-cold until the water eventually warmed up. With the help of some zingy shower gel, she felt more awake. The smell penetrated her nostrils and even made her feel hungry.

Her mind turned to her daughter. She hoped that she was fed and looked after as much as a captive could be. If only she knew what this Noel wanted from her. She would do anything to get her daughter back – anything.

Just as she rinsed the shampoo out of her hair, she saw the door open very slowly through the pastel pink curtain. She snatched the towel that hung over the curtain rail and grabbed the only weapon to hand, a wooden back scrubber. Her heart raced as she partially covered her body with the towel using her left hand. With the other, she gripped the back scrubber. But, to her horror, the curtain was ripped back.

It was Noel and he was holding a gun with a silencer attached.

Noel grabbed her by her hair before she could lash out. In one aggressive and fast move, he pulled her out of the bath and pressed the gun against her cheek. 'Fecking scream, and I'll shoot you.' He threw her hard to the floor, where she smashed her head on the toilet.

Dropping the back scrubber, she felt the back of her head, and then, when she looked at her hand, she saw it was covered with blood. But, worse than that, she experienced a ringing in her ears that always accompanied dizziness.

This man was strong and merciless. There was no point in trying to fight him.

Pulling the towel tighter around herself to cover her body, she saw Noel scoop up her clothes and throw them at her. 'Get dressed. I'm not interested in fecking you. You're not my type.'

Georgie snatched her jumper and jeans and waited for him to turn away.

'Don't look at me like that. I'm keeping my eye firmly on you, bitch. Now you can either get dressed or don't bother. Either way, you're coming down the stairs with me.'

Georgie got dressed in record time while clocking the smell and the sounds from downstairs. The whiff of cigarettes masked with a sweet tang of JOOP! aftershave, permeated the air, but it wasn't coming from Noel. Looking over his shoulder, she was relieved that her daughter's bedroom door was shut, so they wouldn't know Riley was still here. She didn't want the boy involved because she figured he was likely to have a go at Noel. That wouldn't end well for Riley, though.

Noel lunged forward; he viciously gripped Georgie's arm and pushed her out of the bathroom and down the stairs.

Georgie almost tripped when he kneed her in the back. *What the hell had rattled his cage?* she wondered.

As soon as they were in the living room, she faced two other men. One was a big fat man with medium-length wavy hair. His shirt was gaping open so much at the seams, she reckoned one false move and one of his shirt buttons would have her eye out. The smell of cigarettes was from him. She could tell by the yellow fingers and the rotten teeth. There was something goofy about his expression; clearly, he was a few cards short of a full deck.

The second man was a weasel-looking character with eyes that darted about like a racoon on speed. He was around five feet two and wafer-thin. Even though he wore a hoodie, it didn't completely hide the scar on his face. He swayed from side to side. *He looked to be another character who was not the full ticket*, she thought. And then she recognised him as the creepy guy who had tried to get into the garage. *So this was the JOOP! man.*

Appraising them more carefully, she thought she could take on the big oaf. After all, the bigger they are, the harder they fall. As for Mr Weasel, he would be a doddle to sort out. She reckoned she could snap him in half.

But Noel wouldn't be such a pushover. He would probably beat her in a fight. He was solid and fast and had a predacious persona that simply didn't match his handsome features. Not that she was attracted to him anymore, but it would be disingenuous to describe him as less than handsome. However, she would have to add the term psychopath to finish the description.

'Sit!' Noel demanded, as though he was talking to a dog.

Georgie didn't rush to comply with his demand; instead, she casually sat down on the chair he pointed to, opposite himself.

'Oh, I get it. You want to show me who's in charge. Well' – he said, as his lip twitched – 'I'm in charge, Georgie. I've got the gun.'

Georgie smiled and nodded, totally calm and serene. 'So how is my daughter?' she asked.

'You tell me, Georgie.'

'You're the one who took my child, so where is she?' Georgie growled, her eyes burning with anger.

'Shut the feck up and listen to me, Georgie Fecking Deacon.'

The landline phone rang, and before Georgie could answer it, the fat man rushed to grab it.

However, Noel stopped him. 'Don't touch the phone, you stupid prick. Look, Jared.' Noel pointed to the phone. 'It has an answering machine. Use your half-pea brain and listen.'

He glared at Georgie. 'If it's your daughter, phone her back, ask her where she is, and tell her to come home. Any funny shit and I'll have no qualms in pulling the trigger, and then when I do find your precious girl, I will sell her to the lowest scummiest bidder and pack her off to Eastern Europe. I have friends, yer see, in very low places. What they wouldn't give to roast a pretty little thing like her, is anyone's guess.'

The way Noel had berated Jared the oaf gave Georgie the sense that the men were related. She eyed them both over but there didn't seem to be any family resemblance. Still, then again, among a sizeable ugly family, you may get a good-looking one, possibly a throwback. Either Noel must have been a throwback, or this oaf was. Regardless, she didn't care. They were both evil in her eyes.

Georgie flared her nostrils. Her insides were burning. If that gun wasn't loaded – and she assumed it was – she would have clawed Noel's eyes out and bit his carotid artery right out of his neck. She remained still, watching, taking in every little detail of Noel, the oaf, and the weasel.

Once the phone stopped ringing, Noel stared at it, waiting for the caller to leave a message, but there was no further activity. The caller had ended the call. But then, Georgie's mobile phone began ringing a few seconds later.

'Jared, fetch the phone. I can hear the thing ringing in the kitchen.'

Waddling like a fat duck into the kitchen, Jared returned with the phone still ringing. He showed Noel that it wasn't a name but a private number. The caller had presumably pressed 141 both times.

'I bet that's her, the clever little bitch,' he snarled.

With her heart beating so fast, Georgie couldn't help but feel proud of her daughter. Dixie-Lee wasn't stupid. If she had escaped these nutters, she must have used every ounce of savvy she possessed. She only hoped her daughter would stay away and not come to the house with any heroic ideas.

The last time she had looked out of the front window, there was only one police car and a drippy-looking copper who couldn't have been much older than twelve. She sighed, realising that considering her husband had been murdered and her daughter, as far as the police were concerned, was still kidnapped, her family wasn't really a priority for them. She speculated this present predicament she was in was down to Lardon. Clearly, there was something amiss with that woman. Still, what did it matter now? At least she could feel relieved that her daughter was away from Noel and these creepy men.

'So where *is* my child?'

'You shut yer mouth, and you listen to me. I do the fecking talking, and you answer my questions. Other than that, you say, yes fecking sir.'

Georgie was raging inside, but her anger was mixed with joy, knowing that Dixie-Lee was out of their clutches. 'Yes fecking sir? Who do you think you are, Noel? I mean, you fucking hurt Henry, you evil bastard. I bet my life you set his café alight, and then you took my daughter and—'

'Shut yer mouth!'

'No, Noel, I won't shut my mouth because you can't use me. Not now. Because you don't have any leverage.'

'I will do, though. She'll turn up here. That's a given. And when she does, Georgie Deacon. I will fecking hurt her so badly, she will want to die, if you don't do as I say.'

'But you can't hurt her, can you. And you can't kill her because, Mr Flash Prick, you don't *have* her.'

Georgie could see the sudden implication play out in Noel's eyes. 'Penny dropped, has it, Noel?'

'Shut the feck up, or I will shoot you. You don't bother me, Georgie Deacon. You're just another member of that family, so I won't lose any sleep over your death. Still, I would if it was quick. I want you to know how your daughter dies before I kill you.'

'Well, Noel, it will be a very long wait because, like I said, my Dixie-Lee ain't coming back, but I am interested in how she got away.' She looked at the oaf and the weasel. 'None of you speak, then?'

Jared looked questioningly at Noel, but the weasel looked down and stared only at the floor.

When she looked back at Jared, she noticed that tears in his eyes were welling up. He stamped his size twelve foot and pointed a fat finger at her. 'Your kid killed me brother Jerry. She's a little bitch, and if Noel doesn't kill her, I fecking will.'

A horrible thought crossed Georgie's mind. Her daughter would only kill someone to protect herself. If this Jerry had touched her, she would piss on his grave. 'Why did she kill him? What the fuck did he do to her?'

‘Fecked her up the arse, I hope.’

She glared at Noel, who was twitching again. ‘What the hell did he do to her for her to kill him? My girl’s no killer.’

But Noel didn’t answer. His eyes were ping-ponging between Jared and the weasel as if he was miffed about something.

‘I assume there was more than one person guarding my daughter. Is that right?’

‘Yeah, there was. But so what? Shut up. I need to think.’

‘If she killed one, where is the other?’ She looked at Jared. ‘Is it you?’

Jared screwed up his face so much, it looked like an overfed French bulldog. ‘No,’ he replied, sounding like a miserable teenager.

‘You, then?’ She nodded at the weasel.

He shook his head without making eye contact.

‘I said, shut up!’

‘If it wasn’t these two, then who else was with my daughter? Are you sure one hasn’t killed the other, and my girl escaped in the pandemonium? Because, let’s face facts, she’s only eight stone, she’s got a leg that doesn’t work properly, and she’s . . . well, she’s not like me, that’s for sure, ’cos you would have two of your crew dead.’

‘I said, shut it. Now, fecking shut it.’

Georgie got up from the chair, sensing that as much as Noel was a hard bastard, he wasn’t going to shoot her, and there must be a reason for that. Perhaps he had some kind of grudge against the Deacons, or she would be dead by now.

‘Your kid killed me brother, that much I do know. Look around you, Georgie. Why aren’t the police all over this place with guns aimed at our heads?’

Georgie frowned. ‘What?’

‘Your girl hasn’t called the police because she knows what she did. She will be locked up for murder, so she hasn’t called the police.’

Georgie smiled, shaking her head, before she placed her hands on her hips. ‘I think your fucking reality check bounced, mate.’

Noel raised his hand, pointing the gun straight at her, but the fearless look in her eyes compelled him to think twice about putting a bullet in her. ‘Well, why didn’t she come home then?’

'Because she knew you'd be here, and she didn't call the police because firstly, I hate them myself, and secondly, she wouldn't want to put my life in danger, knowing your first port of call would be here. She probably guessed you'd be armed. She's bright, my kid. See, Noel, we're not all like your brothers or whoever they are. Look at him.' She pointed to the weasel. 'He looks like a fucking letter with no address on it, just standing there with his head down, inwardly wondering where his village is, because clearly, Noel, he is the bloody missing idiot.'

The moment she said those words, the weasel yelled, lifting his hands up in a clawlike pose, like a child losing its temper, and launched himself at her.

Georgie leaped back while Noel grabbed his brother, holding him at bay. 'No, Jonas, leave it.'

'Aw, it seems I've upset the plankton member of your deranged fucking family.'

'Don't push it, Georgie, because you will feel his fecking wrath if I let him loose on you.' But even Noel knew he sounded like a joke after seeing Jonas acting like the guy in the *Karate Kid* movie in a praying mantis pose.

She laughed. 'His *wrath*? Oh fuck me, Noel. Ya know what? I was beginning to take you seriously, what with you armed with the gun and that fancy silencer, but you blew your reputation with that comment.' She laughed again. 'The plankton's wrath. I would be warier of ol' bulldog features over there.'

Noel let go of Jonas and pushed him towards the back door. 'Stay out there and tell me if anyone comes.' He shot a death stare at Jared. 'And you, Jared, keep Jonas company. I need a word with this bitch.'

Jared lifted one side of his mouth, and a cruel grin slithered across his face.

For the first time, Georgie felt unnerved. 'What is it you wanted from me in the first place?' She huffed. 'Before you went to great lengths to kidnap my child.'

'Oh, trust me, Georgie, with or without your daughter, you will still do as I say.'

'Will I now?'

He nodded and smiled. 'Yeah, you will.'

Georgie didn't like his confident expression; it made her feel uneasy, as if he knew something that she didn't.

'What exactly do you want from me?'

'Good, now we're getting somewhere. Rohan, I can only imagine, is on his way here now. All the way from miserable fecking Ireland, and I want you to bring him to me.'

'Why?'

'Because he and I need to have a talk.'

'Nah, mate, I'm not buying your shit. You could phone him. You could ask him to meet for dinner or for coffee . . . Unless, of course, he doesn't want to talk to you. But, presumably, you already know that.'

He smiled and stepped back, looking Georgie up and down. 'I would also like to talk with Finella.'

Georgie shook her head. 'Rohan is coming alone. Finella is too grief-stricken to come over, so that chat must be done over the phone.'

'And I thought you were smart. Thanks for the info. It looks like I won't need you after all. Me brother back in Ireland can pay her a visit. The lonely old crow. When she is screaming like a fecking banshee, then Rohan will be all too willing to meet with me. He loves his ma. He won't have his brothers to protect him. 'Cos they will be fecking rotting in jail for murdering Dixie.'

Georgie saw the sudden deranged look in Noel's eyes, and his outburst of a high-pitched chuckle made her jump.

'I don't need you or your child, wherever she is, but I promise you this, Georgie Deacon, I will find her and take her life, just like she took my brother's!'

CHAPTER TWENTY-ONE

'I'm going to get into that garage,' Jonas mumbled to himself, but Jared overheard him.

'Leave it, Jonas, for fuck's sake. We're not here to nick their stuff.' He blew a long plume of smoke into the air. 'Come back here, gravel.'

'Call me that again, and I will cut you up, Jared.'

'Sorry, mate, I forget you're touchy about it now,' Jared replied, in a genuine tone, before he took another deep drag on his cigarette.

Two minutes later, while watching Jonas trying to get into the garage, he glanced up the alleyway towards the old eery-looking tree and spotted a woman who seemed to be stomping her way towards them, as if she had a bone to pick with someone.

'Jonas,' he called. 'Get back here. One of the fecking neighbours is coming.'

Jonas straightened up from trying to unpick the padlock and looked towards who he assumed was the neighbour. He hurried through the back garden to Jared, who was standing only a few feet away from the back door, and practically hid behind his lump of a brother. 'Why isn't she using the front door then, Jared, if she's a neighbour? This alleyway looks like it's not been used in years. It's all overgrown.' He gripped his brother's arm. 'Oh shit, Jared, she's coming our way.'

'Go inside. Tell Jesse.'

Jonas hopped up the steps, opened the back door, and only poked his head in. 'Jesse . . . I mean Noel, there's an old woman outside. I think she's coming here. She was looking straight at us.'

Jesse's eyes widened, and he turned to Georgie. 'Who is it?'

Georgie genuinely had no idea. She shrugged. 'I don't know.'

***

Sheila knew the back alley from when she was young. Her aunt had lived in a house just a few doors along from Georgie's, so she knew exactly which place Georgie lived in. As she passed her old aunt's place, she quickly looked to see if it was the same. Surprisingly, the old rose bushes were still there. They were far more straggly than when her aunt had the place, but they were there, nonetheless.

Sheila cast her mind back to the conversation she'd had with Georgie's daughter. If Dixie-Lee's story was to be believed, the only reason for interfering in this issue with Georgie and a potential kidnapper was the notion that her youngest son was involved. All the way to Georgie's, her anxiety had risen to a level that would take twenty bouncers to stop her from getting inside Georgie's house to find her son. With every determined stride she took, she thought over how she'd lost her eldest children. She would not lose one of her youngest, not her Riley. He was the son she'd always told to shut up, to make the tea, and to fetch the shopping. Tears in her eyes welled up when she thought about how she had made him the butt of most of their jokes, probably to the point where she'd been cruel to him. She could see that now.

***

As she headed towards Georgie's house, her thoughts turned to the past. She saw herself as the hard mother who was responsible for raising a fierce take-no-shit type of family, especially after her husband had died. They were running the estate, earning money through exerting maximum fear, and she had loved it. She'd also loved how the men in the pub had always bought her a drink because they dared not upset her.

After all, in her younger days, her husband was a force to be reckoned with. Between them, they had raised a fearless brood, and they never went without. When she'd asked for a pint of milk to be put on the tab, she'd got it, knowing that she would never have to settle any debt. No one would dare to ask her for money. And after her husband's death and when Todd was alive, he had taken her husband's position, and so she was given the same favours. But now, he and her beautiful girl were dead.

So much had changed. Her children, with the exception of Jasper, were distancing themselves from a life of crime. Yasmin was starting college next year to be a hairdresser, and Riley was already there. Her kids even dressed differently. In fact, they were turning into what judges would deem to be productive members of society, and – she had to admit it – she was proud of both of them. If only she hadn't pushed Yasmin and Riley to live on the wrong side of the law. It hadn't been right. With all the technology, cameras, and computers, the filth had the edge over old-fashioned villains like her family. So she and her brood were risking time in the nick. It was all about risk versus reward. And there was fuck-all reward for them.

Her heart felt heavy because although she'd never say it out loud, deep down she was ashamed of how she'd approached motherhood. Not having that motherly mindset and being raised by a father and uncles, she had more of a man's mentality. Still, at that time, the villainous men and her husband were of that breed too, a match made in heaven, she used to say, but now, now she was older, she realised that it wasn't that at all. In fact, it was probably a match made in hell.

She thought about Georgie Deacon and her pretty, polite girl Dixie-Lee. She was kind and soft, a sweet thing, and she couldn't help but think about how Dixie-Lee had gently clasped her hand. She, herself, wasn't used to affection; she'd never hugged her kids.

And then her mind turned to how Georgie had had the brass balls to storm into her house and hold her Yasmin at knifepoint looking for her daughter. She had to admire the woman. She was doing what most mothers believed they wanted to do, but would any of them really do it? She wondered if even she would have. Still, today, she would take a leaf out of Georgie's book and do whatever it took to get her son back.

Looking at Georgie Deacon's back door, she clocked two men hovering outside. *So, Dixie-Lee was right, then,* she thought. *She hadn't been exaggerating.* Not only that, but Georgie's daughter must have a telepathic mind. She had certainly played her cards well. If she had gone back to her house, she would have walked straight into the lion's den.

This genuinely was a serious situation. Gripping her old faithful umbrella – which used to be her husband's – to any copper, it looked like a lady's folded brolly, with its walnut handle, and the fabric of the cover showing an old-fashioned floral print. What harm could an old umbrella do? Unless, of course, it wasn't an umbrella but a cleverly disguised lump of metal. Her husband had used that tool many a time and returned with the cover drenched in someone's blood and bone fragments. She had ended up with a hundred brollies, all without the covers in order to replace the bloodied ones. At one time, the kids made camps in the garden with all the brollies, just like a Japanese scene, with every colour and pattern littering the garden.

Before he had used the short stubby metal cosh brolly, her husband had used a different one. She shuddered, thinking about it. The blade that was attached was cleverly hidden. It was a nasty weapon, and it was how Henry from the café had got his scar. She had felt gutted for the man at the time, and still did, even now. Yet, if she'd questioned her husband or eldest son, Todd, she would have undoubtedly suffered the same fate. So she put a smile on her face, patted her husband on the back, clapped louder and laughed harder, and showed that she was on his side because God help her if he thought for a second that she wasn't.

She had been just twenty years old when she stupidly made that mistake. It was the first and last time she'd ever questioned her husband's motives. She recalled it only too well, as though it was yesterday. It was strange because that day had been a cold, blustery day, just like today. He'd returned from a night at the Queen's Head covered in someone's blood and was laughing as he told the story. The young lad, Simon, the milkman's apprentice, had told a milkman's joke, which grabbed her husband's attention. The other lads were laughing, but her husband didn't find it funny. Of course, it would have been hilarious if he had told the joke, but he was in a mood because Jasper, who was only a toddler then, had emptied three packets of his tobacco down the toilet. The poor milkman was dragged outside and had his face rearranged. By the time her husband returned home, he was pissed. After relaying the story, Sheila remembered saying without thinking, 'Aw, did you have to? He's a kid. He's my mate's son.'

She recalled regretting those words for weeks. In a flash, he snatched her night dress, and then, in one clean sweep, he ripped it off her back and yelled, 'You dare question me? See this fucking house and everything in it? It's 'cos of what I bring in.'

She'd assumed that all the time his mouth was engaged, he would eventually burn himself out, go to bed, and sleep off the endless pints of strong lager. Only he didn't. He grabbed her arms, pushed her up against the wall, and nutted her across the bridge of her nose. She'd heard the crunch and felt the blood trickling down the back of her throat. The fury in his eyes terrified her. He lifted his head back and was about to nut her again when Eve yelled, 'What ya doing, Dad?'

He stopped hitting her, then, but he hadn't finished punishing her. Pushing past Eve, he dragged her downstairs and opened the back door. 'You will understand that going against me, Sheila, will cost you everything. Now, you wait outside until I can say it's okay to come back into my fucking house, and then you might feel a little more grateful.'

She begged him to let her back in or at least give her a coat. How could she knock at a neighbour's door naked? The idea that it would be her last night on earth crossed her mind as she shivered relentlessly, her feet numb and her skin stinging as though it was being rubbed with ice cubes. And the pain never ceased. Her broken nose throbbed, and her heart ached. How could he do this to her? She was the woman he was supposed to love with all his being.

That cruel night, she'd come to the realisation she was just something he owned. She was his property. End of. And it didn't help her case at all that she was a looker in her day. She knew that but so did he. And so did the entire community. And that proved to be a problem because she knew that if she even looked at another man, all hell would break loose. It was all about what he owned, so anger raged through his veins because he was a jealous man. He wanted everything, from the flash cars to the big house, but the fact was, he wasn't clever enough to get a job and pay for it. And he wasn't the most competent villain, either. The plain truth was he was a thug and a bully. If he wanted something, he got it. And that included herself. But all those years ago, she knew no different. She fell for his charms.

Now reaching Georgie's back garden, she felt the tears on her cheeks. She never cried. She didn't even when her husband died. But that wasn't because of the way in which he had treated her. It was because his cruelty and feelings for others had rubbed off on her. Tears were for those who showed weakness. But now? Now she was shedding a tear. Several. They were significant. She could now admit to herself that her husband was a heartless man. And she wasn't the same person anymore.

Suddenly a million thoughts were invading her mind. Had she truly loved her daughter or was it a fake emotion, like the one she'd had for her husband? She knew she had been jealous of Eve. He had been her favourite. She knew that as well.

Wiping away the tears, she felt the bitter cold on her face. Just like that night. She had shivered and was near to hypothermia before he'd slept off his drink and allowed her back in. But what had hurt her more than the pain of the cold was seeing Todd and Eve looking out of the kitchen window. They were smiling and pointing at her, just as if it was all a big joke. Not once did it occur to them to unlock the back door for her. True, they were young, but that look in their eyes told her so much about what they would become. They were their father's children. And that night, she knew they would be just like him.

She remembered barely being able to climb the stairs to the bathroom. Her bones felt as though they had been glued together at the joints. When she saw herself in the mirror, she wanted to cry. There wasn't one part of her skinny body that wasn't blue. The hot bath had almost sent her into shock. Nonetheless, when she had finally warmed up, she cleaned the cut on her nose, applied make-up, and put on her warmest clothes before going to the kitchen and preparing their regular Sunday roast dinner. From that day forward, she had hated the cold and had never liked winter. It was then that her drinking and heavy smoking began.

***

As Sheila approached Georgie's back door, she clutched the brolly handle with purpose. Those dark memories of a wasted forty years or so disappeared in a flash as she prepared herself for what lay ahead. She still hadn't devised a plan. That was another of her problems. She was never really good at organising or planning anything. Eyeing up the two men, she marched towards them and instantly recognised their unease.

'Excuse me, lads, but I need a fucking word with Miss High and Mighty.'

Storming forwards, her heart was racing at such a pitch, she thought at any minute she would keel over. *Get a grip, Sheila. You're a Marx*, she said to herself.

The bigger of the two men could have easily pushed her over, but, instead, he glared at the woman. 'Er, no, Missus, you can't go in.'

‘What? Get the hell out of my way. I don’t know who the fuck you are, but you don’t tell *me* what to do.’

Jared grabbed her arm, stopping her from opening the back door, but she froze and glared at his hand on her arm. Then she looked up at his face. ‘You had better take your hand off me right now, boy, or I will cause such a fucking stink and give you such a hiding, you won’t know which part of yourself to mop up first.’

Jared was stunned. But he was even more shocked that this middle-aged woman was talking like this. He wanted to laugh but instead he nervously smiled in disbelief.

‘You think that’s funny, yeah? Move out of the way, fat man,’ said Sheila, as she spotted the skinnier man step aside as well. She clocked he looked a little strange.

But before she could barge past, the back door opened.

Sheila’s eyes widened as she observed Georgie standing there with a tall man behind her. The resigned look on Georgie’s face told her that the woman, who always had so much gumption, was not in a good place. In fact, she seemed almost defeated. So she guessed that the tall guy was sticking a gun or a knife into Georgie’s back.

Although Sheila wasn’t usually a quick thinker, she suddenly got with the game.

‘You, Georgie Fucking Deacon, have crossed the fucking line when you came to my house and held a knife to my *son’s* throat. Do ya think I’m gonna let that go?’

Instantly, Georgie realised that Sheila was giving her some kind of message because she hadn’t held the knife to her son’s throat at all. She had threatened Yasmin. ‘I’m busy, Sheila. Anyway, your *son* asked for it. Why don’t you fuck off.’

Sheila knew then that Georgie was also in the game. She glared at the tall man. ‘And what are you gawping at? You think you’re gonna stop me from smashing her face in? Who are ya? Another one of her gobby in-laws, are ya? Well, you don’t scare me, you long, lanky streak of piss. I’ve put bigger lads than you across my knee and given them a good larruping.’

Sheila knew it was all or nothing, although she was wary of Georgie. Lunging forwards, she grabbed Georgie’s hair. ‘Outside, you! You’re coming with me, and we’ll fight this out fair and square, you bitch. Think you can hurt my kid!’

Georgie was absolutely flabbergasted. All of her military experience just went out of the window. What the hell was she supposed to do? She didn't want to hit the woman even though she had sussed out that this was a ploy. Deciding to play along, she allowed Sheila to grab hold of her and shake her about like a rag doll, while she yelled, 'Get the fuck off me, you old hag. I'll smash your face in. Ahh! Get the fuck off me.'

Georgie hoped that Sheila wouldn't stop. She needed to get out of that house. In a dramatic attempt, she deliberately tripped over the back doorstep and tumbled down onto the path, with Sheila falling on top of her.

Noel, who Georgie now knew was called Jesse, panicked. He shoved the gun into the back of his jeans, jumped over the two fighting women, and legged it through the garden and up the alley. Jared and Jonas, who were only used to taking orders from Jesse, suddenly realised that he was waiting for no man, so they ran after him. Jonas tripped over his feet and had to straighten up before limping away.

Sheila was on top of Georgie, gently tugging at her hair but calling her all the names under the sun until she saw the three men bolting up the alleyway. 'Thank fuck for that,' she said, gasping for breath, as she climbed off Georgie.

With her mouth gaping, Georgie stared at Sheila, totally bewildered. The woman was actually laughing. That was a first.

'Your girl's safe. She's at mine, Georgie. She realised that would be the last place anyone would look for her.'

So out of character, Georgie flung her arms around Sheila. 'Thank you, Mrs Marx. Thank you so much.'

Sheila was completely taken aback. The warmth of Georgie's arms and the feeling of genuine relief made her return the hug.

'I need a cup o' tea after that. Put the kettle on, Georgie, and please tell me my boy's all right. He followed you home last night.'

'He's okay. That long streak of piss, as you called him, beat the granny out of the poor boy. I've patched him up and given him some knock-out pills. He's snoring in Dixie-Lee's bed. I'll take you up to see him.'

For a moment, Sheila smiled, and then she laughed until she cried.

Georgie had to join in because the situation was so bizarre, no one could have made it up.

Georgie bent down and picked up the brolly that had been dropped in the pretend fight. 'Blimey, this weighs a ton.'

Sheila winked. 'Yep, it's useless when it rains but handy when you want to take someone's whole set of teeth out.'

Raising her eyebrows, Georgie said, 'Whose? Mine?'

'No. I didn't know how many men I needed to bash. The thing is, I've got a touch of arthritis in me hands. And that tool comes in handy.'

'Come in, Sheila. Let's have that cup of tea. Is Dixie-Lee okay? They didn't hurt her, did they?'

'I don't really know. She's bruised, but if she's anything like her muvver, she probably gave them a good hiding.'

'Let's have that cup of tea.'

CHAPTER TWENTY-TWO

By late afternoon, Raj was spitting feathers. Neither he nor Hugh Shields had any idea where the Deacon brothers were. And to make matters worse, when he checked the court listing, they weren't even on the hearing list. He had a pretty good idea that the ballistics report was in Mac's favour, and he assumed that if that was the case, there would be no prints or DNA of his on the gun or on the balaclava. Mac's clothing would have had some gun residue on it at the very least if he had fired it.

It was time to call Fitzgerald. He dialled the man's personal number and it continued to ring. He then dialled his home number. It was something he would never do unless it was an emergency. In fact, he couldn't remember ever needing to phone him at home before. As with his mobile, the landline phone simply rang and rang. It was not even going over to answerphone.

He looked at Shields and shrugged. 'That's not like Fitz. Come with me, Hugh. Let's go for a drive.'

As they were about to exit the building, Drake ran up behind them. 'Er, wait up, Raj. Where are you going?'

Raj paused before he spun around. 'Why the question?'

'I want to know as your acting supervisor. I have the right to ask that question, so, again, where are you going?' Placing his hands on his hips, he glared at Shields. 'And why is the Deacon family's solicitor accompanying you?'

'Why aren't the Deacons in court as you insisted they would be?' Raj replied, completely ignoring Drake's question.

'I asked you a question, Raj.'

'I know you did, and I asked you a more pivotal one, so mine trumps yours. Now, something very fishy is going on here, and I intend to get to the bottom of it, starting with why the Deacons aren't in court today. They have been held long enough.' He pointed rudely at Drake. 'So you know you have to charge them, or you have to let them go. Right?'

Drake ran his tongue over his top teeth. 'What are you, Raj, a copper or Mr Shields's lackey?'

Shields had had enough of Drake. 'Oi, now, that's very unprofessional, Detective Inspector Drake. I suggest you answer the questions because they are *my* clients we're talking about.'

Drake sighed. 'You know that MI5 are questioning them, so what they do supersedes what I do, and that's all I have to say to you.'

'All you have to say or all you want to say?' said Raj.

'Don't play with words. I'm a straight-up kind of guy.'

Shields raised his brow. 'And I beg to differ. Now, Inspector, I understand the ballistics results are in.' He grinned. 'And I want to see them. I want to know exactly for what crime you are holding my clients. As I understand it, you have one witness, for whom we have no details. The evidence seems a little bit thin to me. I can't see the CPS approving this. And, just so we're clear, Inspector, I am a straight-up kind of guy too.'

Drake chewed his bottom lip as his eyes ping-ponged between Raj and Shields. 'We . . . er, haven't got all the results in, so—'

'So that's fine. I will see what you have got,' said Shields, before he sighed. 'Look, understand this: I am not only their lawyer, but I am a good friend to the whole family, and, believe me, if Mac and Brodie killed Dixie, I wouldn't represent them. I grew up with them. We attended the same school, we lived in the same street, and shared everything. So now can you see where I'm coming from?'

Raj could see Drake mulling over the conversation. And he knew he had to intervene before Drake spun on his heel and stormed off. 'Gov, let me go and question this woman who claims she saw Mac and Brodie in the car. Just in case it's a set-up.'

Drake grinned. 'Be my guest, but why on earth would a middle to elderly woman, who works for the church and the Cats Protection League – and you know the type – floral dresses and a grey rinse – want to make up something like that?'

Stunned, Raj's mouth dropped open, and his eyes widened. 'Are you kidding me?' he asked, in a high-pitched voice.

Drake frowned. 'No, why, what's going on?'

'Why would she say she worked for the Cats Protection League? Not only did the name change to Cats Protection a little while ago, but why, Drake, would she go into that kind of detail if not to make you and/or your colleague think she was a sweet church-going lady who rescues cats? And while I think about this, did she say anything about doing charity work?'

Drake shrugged. 'She may have.'

'And she reckons she worked for the church, as in the church right next to where Dixie was shot, yeah?'

Drake nodded, feeling annoyed now that Raj had something over him because it was clear that whatever he'd said had turned on not a light bulb but a whole bloody chandelier.

'And you've checked her name against an address, have you?'

'One of my officers took the statement.' He ground his back teeth. 'And obviously, he took her details. The name matched the address.'

Raj scratched his forehead with his thumbnail. 'Can you get the details for me?'

'Raj, are you going to tell me what's going on? Because I am leading this case, not you.'

Raj smiled like the cat that got the cream. 'This information is relevant to Dixie-Lee going missing because I believe it's the same woman who was pretending to be the cleaner at Noel Wade's apartment.'

Drake shot his jaw forward. 'No way. That's just ridiculous.'

'Is it, Drake? Is it really? So tell me this. How many women do you know who work for the Cats Protection *League* and arrange the flowers in the church, oh, and in two different bloody areas?'

Drake looked down, puzzled. 'I'll get the details.'

'Good, email them to me while I visit the vicar.'

'*What?*'

But it was Shields who responded. 'We are going to see the vicar, and while I'm there, I believe it would be prudent for you to have the ballistic records checked and double-checked, ready for me on my return. And if this woman is connected to Dixie-Lee's kidnapper, I think we can see, when it comes to my two clients, you, Martin Drake, have been cocking your leg up the wrong fecking tree.'

Raj was surprised to hear an Irish twang in Shields's voice.

Drake didn't hang around to take any more humiliation; he knew he couldn't stall Shields any longer. He had to get the details, or someone above Fitzgerald would want answers. He was also sure there was no way Raj could contact the boss because

Fitzgerald had wangled extra leave, so he would not be accessible, even by phone.

Not waiting for Drake to change his mind or to hold them back any longer, Raj and Shields hurried to Raj's car. Within fifteen minutes, they were pulling up outside the church. To Raj's dismay, they had taken down the crime tape. The place looked as though it had never been a serious crime scene. The scaffolding was still on the church roof, but there were no signs of any bloodstains, so he assumed this spot where Dixie Deacon died had been professionally cleaned.

Shields stared at the scaffold poles on the ground and a pair of soaking wet workman's gloves. 'I wonder if this marks the spot where Dixie died?'

Raj consciously slowed down his usual impatient and quick movements, giving Shields time to look and think. After all, Dixie was also friends with Shields.

'This is killing Finella, you know. She has to say goodbye to her son twice now. It's shocking, and we still don't know why.'

'Come with me, Hugh. We will get some answers, starting with the vicar.'

As soon as Raj stepped inside the small freezing church, he stopped dead. With all the rushing around and his mind working at a speed of knots, he was now in an alien place. The thick stone walls made the air eerily cold and much colder than outside. It was more of a chapel than a church. He looked around. The place consisted of two rows of pews, an altar, and a few stained-glass windows. Even so, the fact that it had been standing for a few hundred years gave it a sense of presence. The smell of damp, along with stillness, added to the atmosphere, and as he stepped onto the stone floor, it echoed.

Shields was behind him. 'I don't think it's like a church where the vicar spends most of his time here. It's probably run by someone who may well be responsible for a number of parishes.'

A sweet-sounding voice came from behind them. 'That's right. Our vicar is only here every other Sunday and on a Tuesday evening.'

Shields and Raj turned to find an elderly lady with a silk scarf covering her thinning white hair and wearing a thick brown overcoat and brown loafers. Over her arm was a 1950s-style black bag with the gold clasp and no authentic fancy design to it, and in her gloved hand, she had a roll of black refuse sacks.

'Hello, I'm Detective Raj, and this is my colleague Mr Shields.' He couldn't think fast enough about what to call Hugh, but he guessed it wasn't important now.

'I suppose you are here about that awful killing here. The poor lad. He was such a lovely chap.'

'You knew him?' asked Raj, surprised.

'Yes, he had been putting the scaffolding up on the roof. He said he was not a professional scaffolder. He told me he used to be in the Army. My father was in the Army, so we spoke a bit. I made him tea. He liked three sugars. I made tea for the two other workmen too. Very nice chaps they were. They helped me move my furniture around without any trouble at all. Not even a quibble.' She smiled sweetly, and as she did so, her faded grey eyes sparkled.

'May I ask, Mrs, er, sorry, what's your name?'

'It's Mrs Wright. I look after the church. You know, I arrange the flowers, sweep the leaves that blow in, that kind of thing.'

Feeling his excitement rise, he asked the burning question on his mind. 'Are you the only one who arranges the flowers here?'

'Gosh, yes. I've been doing it for years.'

'Did you see who shot the young man?'

Mrs Wright put her hands to her chest, and a tear sprung from her eye. 'No, no, I wasn't here. Oh, gosh, that poor young man. It was the vicar who told me, but, fortunately, I was at the hospital at the time. I don't think I could have coped with witnessing such a terrible thing.'

'May I ask, did you ever speak to a police officer?'

'No, never. In fact, Detective, I believe you are the first policeman I have ever spoken to about what happened to the workman.'

'And one last question. May I ask where you live?'

'Of course, Detective. I live there.'

She pointed to the small cottage opposite the church.

'And you are sure no other lady comes here to fix the flowers?'

Mrs Wright frowned. 'Oh, officer, this is only a tiny church. I'd know if another lady was meddling with my flower arrangements.'

That was enough for Raj to be convinced that the woman who gave a brief statement was a plant.

'Excuse me a moment,' he said, as he opened his phone to check the emails. There, as clear as a bell, was a photo of the officer's notes. The address was the cottage across the road, and the name was Mrs Wright. So their suspect, an accessory to murder, was a middle-aged woman who could have passed herself off as a sweet churchgoer.

Shields was quietly taking in what Raj was asking the lady as he tried to piece things together for himself.

'Mrs Wright, did anyone ever ask you about your job?'

Deep in thought, she looked up to the ceiling while drumming her fingers on her handbag. 'You know what? There *was* a lady who came to the church the day before the terrible incident. She asked the vicar if she could do some flower arranging, but he explained that there was no need as I live across the road, and I attend the church in his absence.'

'So you think it was likely that he gave your name and address?'

'I shouldn't think he'd have to give my address. He would have pointed to my property, just like I did to you.' She chuckled. 'Everyone knows me. My family used to run the sweet shop on the corner. It has done for fifty years, and my mother tended the church before I took over due to her ill health.' She stretched her arm towards the cottage. 'And if you look at that tiny plaque, it says Wright's Cottage. It has been in the family for years. Probably more than three hundred years.'

'Wow, now that's history. How lovely for you, Mrs Wright. Well, you have been so helpful. Hopefully, now, with your help this morning, we may actually get to the bottom of that poor young man's murder.'

'Really?'

'Yes, Mrs Wright.'

As soon as the men left the church, Raj headed for his car. 'Hugh, whoever killed Dixie has a middle to elderly woman in tow. How crafty and premeditated are these killers? I have no doubt these are the people who kidnapped Dixie-Lee. Can you think of anyone, now, who'd want to hurt the Deacons?'

Shields shook his head. 'There could be several people. Let's face it, it was a family of four boys, although Dixie, as you know, left the family years ago. But his brothers could fight, and they did at one time or another. And don't forget the company itself. The work they do would piss a few people off.'

Raj unlocked the car and climbed in.

Shields took one last glance at the small alleyway where Dixie was shot down.

'And what do you suppose all of this has to do with MI5?'

Raj pushed his hair out of his eyes. 'I feel as though we are dealing with two cases, and, as you say, the Deacons' company could easily make enemies, maybe to the point where they even encroach on MI5's toes.'

Shields huffed. 'Not likely. They're not into big-time stuff, not on an international basis, but I think you might be right about one thing. MI5 and a little old lady rowing in the same boat? No, it doesn't seem credible to me.'

'So we both agree that Dixie's murder and the MI5 shenanigans are probably unconnected, then?'

Shields nodded. 'Shit, this is a nightmare. Raj, what are you doing? You've got me in the car treating me like I'm your sidekick when it should be Petra who is with you. Are you seriously going to quit the force?'

Raj drove away. 'Petra isn't the woman I thought she was. She's now irritated the frigging life out of me. I wish I'd never had that first drink. Still, it's not that I can't trust her. It's just that she's a jobsworth. Not only that but I get the feeling she's after my job. There's something not quite a hundred per cent right about her.'

'And me, Raj? You have me in the car, while making your inquiries. Why?'

'Yeah, well, you are more than the Deacon family's solicitor. So there is no reason why you can't help me with my inquiries.'

'I suppose not, when you put it like that.' He smiled. 'Would you be so kind as to take me to Georgie's? I want to sit with her for a bit. Rohan's plane has been delayed, and I am sure the poor woman will be biting her nails down to the quick. She lives for that kid, you know. Dixie-Lee is Georgie's be-all and end-all. It's funny because I can trust you, Raj. I have never trusted many coppers before.'

'Cheers, Hugh. I am a trustworthy kind of guy, unlike some of the coppers currently down the nick.'

'Yeah, I get that.'

CHAPTER TWENTY-THREE

Having built a trusting relationship with Raj, Shields felt comfortably quiet in his presence. And as bizarre as it was, Shields tried to determine what role Raj played at Bromley Police Station since he certainly wasn't on Drake's side.

As Raj slowed up outside Georgie's house, he tutted. 'It's unbelievable. One police car and one officer, and yet we have a murderer and a kidnapper on the loose. For Christ's sake, Georgie needs protection, and all they send is a kid who barely has the cradle marks off his arse to protect her. Look at the little prick. He's not even standing outside Georgie's house. Why is he sitting in the car?'

'My question, Raj, is why are they stepping down the protection?'

'That's a very good question, and I don't have the answer. It seems I don't have a lot of answers for this family. This suffering family.'

Raj and Shields both exited the car at the same time and were instantly stopped by the young officer, who had quickly dived out of his car and was marching towards them while abruptly holding up his hand. 'Who are you and—'

Before the officer could finish the question, Raj flashed his warrant card at him. 'Detective Sergeant Raj. Is Mrs Deacon inside?'

The officer suddenly looked uncomfortable. 'I think so. She hasn't left since I've been here.'

Raj shook his head in annoyance. 'And you haven't called to check she's fine?'

'No, I wasn't told to check. I was told to wait outside and stop anyone going in.'

'And that's it, then, for you, is it?'

The officer frowned. 'What do you mean?'

'What I mean, sunshine, is you won't get promoted if all you can do is what you are told without understanding your greater role, which . . .' He paused before leaning closer and raising his voice. 'Which is to protect Georgie Deacon, not spend time googling unimportant bollocks.' He was enraged by the smirk that had suddenly made the young officer look like a little annoying smart arse.

'Give me your phone and passcode. And your name!'

'It's Matthew Level,' he said, with a smile, as he tried to shove his phone into his pocket.

But Raj had his hand out, curling his fingers, to request the phone.

'Phone, Matthew Level, and by that arrogant grin, I assume your father is Matthew Level senior.'

Level nodded.

'Well, Matthew junior, your father has retired, and I'm afraid he no longer carries clout in my station. Now, hand me your phone.'

Level's face suddenly looked like a tomato. It glowed red as he tentatively handed over his phone. 'The code is all nines.'

Raj snatched the phone and eyed the embarrassed young officer, who looked as though he was turning inside out. After taking a deep breath, he realised he was taking his frustration out on the wrong person. 'Here, take your phone, and if I pull up again and find you on it when you're supposed to be vigilant, then I will do more than look at your browsing history.'

Level took the phone. 'I'm sorry, Gov. It won't happen again.'

'Why weren't you outside?'

'It's freezing, Gov, and if anyone came, I could see them from the car.'

'But could you hear them?'

Level blushed again. 'I think so.'

'No, Matthew, you couldn't hear them. So if Mrs Deacon was yelling for help, you wouldn't hear her.'

'I'm sorry, Gov.'

Raj stormed past with Shields directly behind him. He knocked at the door and called through the letterbox. 'Georgie, it's Raj and Hugh Shields.'

The door opened, and there, with a smile on her face, which was a massive surprise to Shields and Raj, stood Georgie.

She stepped aside as they entered. Shields felt a little twinge of excitement because the expression on Georgie's face was one of relief, possibly even happiness.

'What's going on?'

Georgie offered both men a seat on the sofa. Once they had sat down, she glanced from one to the other. 'Raj, please tell me that I can trust you.'

But Shields answered. 'We can, Georgie, I promise you that. Raj is one of the good guys.'

'Dixie-Lee is safe.'

Shields leaped up from the sofa and clapped his hands. 'Yes!' he yelled, as if his football team had just scored a winning goal. 'Sorry, I'm just so pleased. Is she okay?'

Georgie looked at Raj. 'She is okay. I haven't seen her yet, and I won't go near her until these men who kidnapped her are captured. I reckon they will follow me to her.'

'Where is she, Georgie?'

'The last place you would expect her to be.'

Raj suddenly got up and looked around him. 'Then I can guess where she is. She is at the Marx family's house, which means they will guess that too, so she needs to get out of there. Believe me, Georgie, this family is so well organised, they will suss that out. For six months, we saw how the Marxes and you were at loggerheads. It all played out over the news, so they will fathom it out, just as I did.'

Georgie's face lost its colour until she grinned. 'No, they won't guess. I mean, Sheila came here when they were here. She pretended she wanted to fight me. It's a long story, but we ended up having a ruck, and because she was shouting and swearing and drawing so much attention, the three men legged it.'

Raj was dumbfounded. 'These men are bloody reckless, which makes them dangerous. Look, we need to get Dixie-Lee to a safe place, for starters, until I get to the bottom of it all.' He glanced around the room. 'So these men were here?'

'Yes, look, this guy who has been calling himself Noel smashed up Riley Marx last night. Surprisingly, he was on his way here.'

'Why was Riley on his way here?' Raj asked, with a suspicious undertone.

'He had a sketch of Dixie-Lee, which he'd drawn. He thought I might like it. Anyway, the poor little sod got caught up in the crossfire.'

'And what exactly did this Noel guy want?'

'He said he would return with instructions for me. Of course, at that time, he had my Dixie-Lee, so I said I would do whatever he wanted for the return of my daughter. Well, anyway, he came back but that was because Dixie-Lee had escaped. So my daughter managed to get to where Sheila Marx lives, and because I didn't answer either of my phones, Sheila decided to help me. I have to give it to her: she is a bloody good actress. So these evil bastards scarpered. Sheila then took her Riley home.'

Raj was still gobsmacked. He was trying to process it all before making his next move. 'And how the hell did Sheila get past that copper outside?'

Georgie shook her head. 'For some reason, Raj, they don't know I have a back entrance, or rather they haven't realised there is access to my house from the back alley. I mean, I know it's all overgrown, but they still haven't posted a copper there.'

Raj shook his head. 'This poxy Tonbridge lot are fucking useless. Er, excuse my language.'

'Or, Raj,' said Shields, 'they don't care enough. They have bigger fish to fry, as in Brodie and Mac, but why, God only knows.'

'Listen, it doesn't matter. I must get Dixie-Lee to a proper safe place, and no disrespect, Raj, but the police are as much use as tits on a fucking fish. I need to know she is a hundred per cent safe because they made some pretty alarming threats, and I suspect this flash prat Noel, whose real name is Jesse, is the man behind all of this. Sorry, I could have mentioned his name sooner. Too much is happening at once.'

Suddenly Shields gasped. '*Jesse?*'

Georgie nodded. 'Do you know him?'

'Does he have a scar down his jawline?'

'Yeah, he does. He had a beard when I first met him and blue contact lenses, but when he came back, he'd shaved his beard and tossed the lenses. His eyes were brown, and believe me, when I say I really do think he is a psychopath or possibly a sociopath.'

'Fuck me,' said Shields, shaking his head. 'Now, excuse my language, but that is one family you don't mess with.'

Georgie felt like someone had stabbed her with a pitchfork. She straightened her back. 'Maybe, but no one, I mean no one, messes with my family.'

Shields sensed Georgie had taken his comment as undermining her, but that was far from the truth. He knew how tough she was, and Jesse Oliver had probably met his match. He carried on, now he had her attention. 'I had a suspicion when that photo of the gun Drake showed Mac was the same one that Mac had years ago. He has never used it, mind you, and the Olivers took it off him before they drove him to what was supposed to be his death. However, the youngest member of the Oliver family, Eamonn, was adamant he would show his brothers that he could handle someone like Mac. So when Mac was shoved into the boot of a stolen car, Eamonn took off, driving like an idiot, until he hit a sharp bend and ended up in one of the deepest lakes in Ireland. What no one could have anticipated was that the boot popped open, and Mac was able to escape. But I thought the Deacons and the Olivers had drawn a truce. Something must have happened since to bring the Olivers out of the woodwork.'

'I think I need to sit back down for this,' said Raj.

'First things first, we need my girl taken to a safe place.'

Before Georgie even had her hands on the landline phone, it rang. Everyone turned to it, knowing it could be one of the Olivers.

'Hello,' she said, calmly, before she put the phone on loudspeaker.

'Georgie, it's me, Sheila. Dixie-Lee has gone.'

'You what? No!'

'Calm down, Miss Fiery Knickers. She said she felt she wasn't safe because this Jesse guy would guess her whereabouts soon enough. So she's gone with my Riley in a car she said she'd used to drive to my house. She said to call you 'cos you'll be worried, and she will call you later, using Riley's phone.'

'Did she say where she was going?'

'No, she didn't. I guess trust only stretches so far. I gotta be honest, she was probably better off not telling me in case they come and torture me.'

'They won't,' said Georgie, but as soon as she said that, she knew she didn't believe it. 'Listen, go and stay in a hotel. I'll cover the cost.'

'Really? Well, in that case, I'll check out the rooms at The Dorchester. I fancy myself as a bit of a lady.' She chuckled.

'They don't allow pets or livestock, so you're better off booking into a cheap bed and breakfast.'

'Cheeky mare. I'll be okay, Georgie. I've got a few weapons to hand, and I've plenty of families to go to. I'll call again if I hear any more. Let me know if the police catch these bastards.'

'How is Riley, now?'

'He perked right up when he saw your girl. He's okay, just a bit bruised. He'll keep her safe, if he can.'

'I know he will, Sheila. Cheers, speak soon.'

'She's bright, your daughter. I'll give her that,' said Raj.

'But she's not invincible. Now, tell me about this fucking Oliver family. Why would they come after us? I take it, this feud with the Deacons was some time ago?'

Shields nodded. 'It was about sixteen years ago. The Olivers held a gun to Rohan's head and demanded . . .' He paused and looked at Georgie, hoping this wouldn't change her opinion of Rohan before he decided to go into detail. 'Let me go back a bit. You see, Rohan had briefly dated their sister, Elspeth.' He coughed, clearing his throat. 'A small Irish town, everyone knew her, and they knew her well. How can I put this without it sounding derogatory? She wasn't the sweetest, most innocent little Irish girl. All that going to church was a front. She was . . . well, you know what I'm saying.'

Georgie sat on the chair opposite Shields, eager to hear the whole story.

'Having seen Elspeth hanging around, Brodie had warned Rohan not to get involved. But Rohan was young. He didn't listen to Brodie, well, not that time, anyway. So Rohan took Elspeth to the pictures. They had a couple of drinks afterwards, and with the Irish police being strict on the drink and driving, Rohan decided to catch the bus. However, they missed the last bus. Rohan couldn't get a cab and certainly wouldn't call his brothers, so they had to walk home. Elspeth got home very late. Anyway, a month or so later, she announced to her brothers that she was expecting a baby, so they assumed Rohan had got their little sister in that condition, and she didn't deny it. You see, the Deacon brothers were quite a catch for a poor Irish girl with no prospects.' He shook his head. 'And as far as her brothers were concerned, she was a sweet and innocent little thing, and he had taken her virginity. And being Irish

Catholics, the only way to handle the situation would be for Rohan to marry Elspeth.'

Feeling very jealous at hearing this story, Georgie had to lick her bottom lip to stop her mouth from drying up. Her heart was heavy as she listened to the story.

'I remember being in the kitchen when Finella sat Rohan down and asked the question: "Is the baby yours." Rohan answered: "No way. I never even touched her. She really isn't my type." Now, I know Rohan well, and he wouldn't have lied about that, even if they had held a gun to his head. Livid, Finella paid the family a visit but she was physically pushed out of their house and then pushed over onto the gravel. She cut her chin and lip, so you can imagine what happened next.'

'The feud began.'

'Yeah, and in a big way. It went on for months. Jonas, a prolific car thief of the family, burned down Brodie's garage with his best car inside, but he was caught red-handed, and Brodie, in a temper, used his lasso, which he liked to use for fun, and caught Jonas by the ankles. Brodie then dragged Jonas, who was screaming his head off, away from the garage a good few hundred feet along their dusty gravel drive, taking the skin off Jonas's face. I mean, the whole feud got way out of hand, and that's when they somehow cornered Mac, beat the shit out of him, and threw him into the boot of a car they had stolen to take him to a disused airstrip where they planned on murdering him. They were really after Rohan, but Rohan was in London on business. So Mac was their next target. And the rest is history.'

'What happened to Elspeth and her child?' Georgie asked.

'Ah, see, that's the thing. After Brodie met with Jesse, I assumed it was all settled. Elspeth seemed to have disappeared off the face of the earth. I reasoned at the time she'd found her way to London and had an abortion. You can't do that in Ireland, you see. And I thought maybe she'd made a life for herself elsewhere.'

'I sense a but,' said Georgie, now enthralled by the story.

Shields took a deep breath. 'The last I heard was that she did have a child – a son –
and . . .' He paused, staring Georgie squarely in the eye. 'She called him Rohan.'

'Really? And Rohan denies this child is his?'

Shields nodded. 'Rohan wouldn't claim he is the boy's father if he is not, even if the boy had the same name.'

'Had?'

'Yes, I read in the local paper back in Ireland that he died from a drug overdose. But, again, that was a year ago, so I can't see how any of this has to do with the Deacons and the kidnapping of Dixie-Lee. It just doesn't make any sense.'

'And Rohan never spoke about it?'

Shields shook his head. 'No, it was a taboo subject in the Deacon family's household.'

CHAPTER TWENTY-FOUR

Brodie was sweating. With his hands still tied behind his back, he could only rub his forehead on his shoulder. The unknown was killing him. He watched James pace the floor like a predatory black panther sizing its kill.

'Can't you call one of your men and get an update on my brother?'

'They will call when there's news, all right?' She threw him an evil scowl.

'James, by the look on your face and the determination in your voice, I think this is more than a day at the office. This is personal.'

She stopped pacing and pointed the gun at his head. 'Shut up. This is my job, which I do with passion and I am damn well good at it. It's *not* personal.'

Brodie's eyes carried a charming sparkle even though he knew he was insulting her. 'And you feel you need to tell me this? Most people don't need to brag about how good they are, especially when it's common knowledge. So you might want to leave the compliments for your colleagues to throw around.' He glanced over at the two suits. 'Although they don't look like they could walk and talk at the same time. Anyway, I still think this is more than work. As I said, this is personal. It is, isn't it?'

She sensed him mocking her. 'I don't answer your questions, so button it.'

'Hmmm, I tell ya what, James. Think for a minute about this scenario. My brother and I are completely innocent. We've never met a Rodney or gone to visit anyone in Rochester Prison, and' – he sighed heavily – 'your men bashed my brother to within an inch of his life and held me prisoner. Just imagine that, James. Two very innocent men being tortured and terrorised over a notion that you got gravely wrong.'

When she lifted her chin, straightening her posture, Brodie knew he had got to her, but he could tell she wanted to fight back. He surmised she wasn't used to being called out. And he guessed she was spoiled rotten. So much so, that he wondered if she'd got her job because her dad had connections. He decided to probe. 'Is Daddy proud of you?'

Those words had an unexpected catastrophic effect. Instantly, her eyes widened, and she flew at him, grabbing him by the hair. She poked her gun viciously into his temple. 'You bastard, it *was* you. You did visit Rodney in prison. So where is he?' she screamed.

'Wow, hang on, lady. What the feck just happened? I only asked if your dad was proud of you. Feck me, I was only winding you up.' He paused and bravely turned his head to look at her. Her face wasn't so glossy now; it was red and contorted with rage.

As his green eyes burned with intensity, she returned her gun to her shoulder holster in surprise. She hadn't intended to behave so emotionally. Her boss, Lord Cecil Fairly, had warned her not to take on the case; his advice was to leave the interrogation to someone not so closely connected. But he wouldn't argue too much considering who her father was, if, of course, he wasn't dead. She'd got on her knees and prayed to God that her father was alive; he had to be. If he had been killed, then her life would turn upside down. They would rip the job right from under her. The house, the villa in Cyprus, and the fat bank accounts were already in her brother's name. She despised her mother for that little stunt. And when her mother passed away, her father had told her he would make an appointment with the solicitor to change the will to include her. However, she knew he hadn't had the chance to change anything yet before his disappearance.

Brodie could hear her breathing intensify and sensed her anguish. 'Listen to me, James, I'm good at reading people, and I shouldn't have to tell you that, but just now, you held that gun to my head. So I need to explain something to you before you jump to conclusions and blow me fecking head off. I genuinely was winding you up. I was going to say what father would be proud of a daughter who tortures innocent people? Still, you flew off the handle, and so clearly, sweet cheeks, your father must be mixed up in all of this. And I know what I'm about to say is built on supposition, but your reaction screamed a few facts to me. I take it your father has gone missing, and you believe it's to do with Rodney Potter. Who, we know, is inside for murdering his grandson and his daughter.'

If Brodie's attempt at placating her had been aimed at reducing the tension in the room, it hadn't succeeded. Her serenity hadn't returned. She felt her face. She knew it would be bright red. It wasn't a great look for someone who was supposed to have top credentials in the security force.

'You wouldn't know anything, Deacon, if you weren't involved.'

He raised his brow. 'You implied that Rodney had professed his innocence and accused another man.' He smiled. 'So I assume the other man is your father. Am I right?'

In a flash, the gun was out of her shoulder holster. Gripping the weapon with both hands, this time, James aimed at his face.

'You can't shoot the wrong man just because you are angry that your father is missing, and you, the one person who could find him, have drawn a blank. Shooting me or torturing me brother won't suddenly bring him back.'

She didn't move her body, but her hands holding the gun were shaking.

'Why would this Rodney accuse your father? Maybe, we can collect a few clues.'

'We? *We?*' she squawked.

'Yeah, why not. Look, I need to prove I'm not involved, and you need to find your father. I can help you, so let me.'

With a sigh, she lowered the gun, and, once again, she placed it back in her shoulder holster. The immediate problem was lack of sleep. Too many sleepless nights worrying about her dad had gnawed away at her senses. She was constantly on edge, so Brodie Deacon's attempts at needling her had succeeded.

Brodie Deacon, she now recognised, could be right. And torturing the Deacon brothers would not bring her father back. Even though her mind was full of anxiety and she wasn't mentally sharp enough for this operation, she'd had time to process everything he'd said. And he was almost certainly the genuine article. Cursing herself for approaching this operation in the way she had, she now believed she had the wrong Deacons. *What a complete fuck-up*, she said to herself. *I have no fucking plan B.*

Although Cecil Fairly, her direct boss, had warned her not to get involved, in hindsight, the warning had been pretty feeble. It was more of a polite gesture. The more she thought about it, the more she realised now that Cecil, being in a position one rank lower than her father, would have more to gain if her father wasn't found. He would naturally be promoted into her father's position. And, on top of that, she had always sensed he'd never liked her father. He mocked him but in very subtle ways. Ways in which he could easily distance himself, if necessary.

Her mind was now running away with her. She wished she hadn't met Lord Fairly for lunch and listened to his half-hearted pleas for her not to head the search; he had also plied her with three large glasses of his expensive brandy.

Now with her hands shaking once more, she was, she knew, a complete wreck. She needed to leave and recharge her batteries before she made another wrong move. However, before she could go anywhere, she had to be sure that Mac Deacon was alive because if he died, she would have to kill Brodie. There was no way she could leave any traces of the men. And taking Mac to the hospital was never going to be an option. She knew it and her men knew it. So, he was either a corpse or regaining consciousness in the back of the van somewhere outside.

As if Brodie had read her mind, he said, 'James, please find out if my brother is okay, and I will help you if I can. Rodney is nothing to me, so I have no loyalties to him.'

James could feel her lips cracking and her mouth bone dry. She had to think straight, but it was becoming increasingly difficult. She licked her lips.

'James, love, get a drink before you become dehydrated and end up with a migraine.'

She narrowed her eyes. 'What? Shut up for a minute.'

She didn't shout this time. She was in a different place, a state of confusion. Her head was already pounding, and she felt sick, but she refused to give in. Everything Brodie was saying was right, but there was something about him that she really wanted to prove wrong; maybe it was the fact that he was so much like her brother. However, not in looks because Brodie was, without a doubt, extremely handsome. He was the type of man she would hook up with in a bar if he looked her way. She liked her men broad, toned, and with eyes that would coax her into bed, and Brodie certainly had those features, although she really preferred older men. But Brodie's level of intelligence and his skill in reading people went far beyond hers, if she was truthful to herself. That was the trait she wished she had been born with, but, no, sadly, that was her brother's characteristic; hers was more in the good looks department, which she had got from her mother.

Swallowing hard, she forced a tiny amount of saliva down her throat. *Was this nerves?* she asked herself. *Or was it the thought of her failing on this assignment?* Her mother always said she would amount to nothing. Her mind turned to her mother, which was unusual because she had learned to block her out. But for some reason, she could hear her mother's harsh voice. *You're a disgrace to the family name. You thought your good looks would compensate for your failings, but they won't last forever, and then you will be simply a dull middle-aged woman with no career, no talent, and a bored husband looking elsewhere for his fun.*

Her face burned as she tried to get those thoughts out of her head, but, moments later, they were back again, tormenting her. Those sharp aristocratic tones were like needles stabbing her eardrum. *If you don't return to university and learn to be someone of stature, I will ensure your father cuts you off from the will. I will never acknowledge a daughter who has so much disregard for our family and herself, for that matter.* That shrill tone in her mother's voice was forever embedded in her brain. She shook her head, trying to blank her mother out of it. When they buried her, she assumed the memories would go six feet under, but today, they were back. *You should be more like your brother. Christ, you don't see him sleeping with my friends, do you? So, Miss Spoilt Brat, stay away from your father's. It's so bloody embarrassing.*

'James, please call the hospital. I need to know that Mac is okay,' said Brodie, interrupting her thoughts.

'*What?*' she viciously sniped. She was suddenly not in a good place; everything seemed a little fuzzy around the edges. Sliding the phone out of her pocket, she realised her vision was blurred. She couldn't see the numbers, and her head felt as if it was pulsating.

'Call Mendel and find out Mac Deacon's status!' she shouted to the two men standing by the van.

Brodie mumbled, 'Cold-hearted to add to the mix.'

'*What?*' she screeched again.

'I said you're cold-hearted. Why you couldn't find out how Mac is, not his status, as though he is a commodity, I really don't know. He's not, you know. He is an innocent, a really nice guy, and you have had him tortured.'

James tried to swallow but she coughed. Her mouth was still dry and her tongue felt brittle.

'James, listen to me. You are looking a bit pale. I can see you need some water. Get a drink before you fall over and that fecking gun goes off and kills me.'

Having heard the conversation, one of the suits left his post, hurried to the small office area at the back of the building, and returned with a glass of water. Without saying a word, he handed the drink to her.

She snatched it, spilling some of the contents. She tried to sip the water gracefully, but her thirst suddenly peaked, and she drank it like a man in a beer-drinking contest.

Brodie decided not to comment on it. 'Tell me, James, why do you think this Rodney chap has accused your father of killing his family?'

James didn't answer. Her eyes were glazed when she stared back.

Sensing James was wrestling for control, he slowed down his voice and lowered his tone. 'Okay, you know, but don't want to say, and that's fine. Tell me this: where did Rodney Potter live, and what did he do for a living?'

She ran her tongue across her teeth and took a few deep breaths before answering. 'I believe he worked in a garage near his home in Chatham Kent fixing old cars. Why?'

'Hang on. Another question for you. Is your father a rich man, like a titled man? You know what I'm saying.'

James shuffled from foot to foot. 'He is a lord and he holds a high position in MI5. But I am sure you've guessed that already.'

'So let me get this straight. Rodney Potter, a low-paid worker with a daughter and a grandson, accuses a well-respected member of MI5, a lord – no fecking less – of murdering his family. This is the thing. How does a man like Rodney Potter even *know* a man like your father?'

Brodie, James knew, was getting to the crux of the matter, and she suddenly felt exceptionally uncomfortable. In any scenario, she could hide her emotions, even though she was trained to. However, something very odd was stirring inside her. Maybe she had suppressed her true feelings for too long and was reluctant to voice her suspicions and certainly not to her father. Her father was everything. Rodney Potter was a liar. *He just had to be, didn't he?*

'When you say old, did this Rodney fella fix prestige or vintage cars? Maybe he fixed your father's car? I mean a lord, I should imagine, would own a decent car, a Bentley perhaps. Is that how they met?'

Even though Brodie asked the question in a matter-of-fact way, he had an ulterior motive for asking it. He had always been keen on vintage cars and the workings behind them. He owned a few, aside from his Aston Martin. And the one thing he did know was the location of each and every garage that specialised in restoring or repairing vintage cars. There was no such garage in Chatham. If she agreed to his questioning statement, then she was lying through her arse.

James blinked a few times to clear her vision. The water was having an immediate effect. She could feel the pulse in her head settling down to a gentle rhythm rather than it playing the drums.

'Yes, that's exactly it.'

Her gentle smile told Brodie that she was feeling a little better and even relieved that she could get away with not being honest about her father.

'Well, it sounds to me as if this Rodney was chancing his luck, and when the police caught up with him, he used your father's name, the first name that came to hand,' Brodie said, going along with this made-up notion. 'I hardly doubt that this Rochester inmate from Chatham could afford an assassin. They are not the cheapest service.'

'And how would you know that?'

Brodie laughed. 'That's not hard to work out, is it? Killing for a living has to be lucrative. Think about the risk involved. Anyway, I think this Rodney chap wouldn't have employed an assassin . . .' He paused and leaned forwards. 'He's no lord, is he? No, darling, if your father was taken, it would have been by his own kind, a rich man, an influential man, with a grudge to bear. I can tell you this: it wasn't a mechanic from Chatham.'

James was going back to her dark thoughts. Lord Cecil Fairly was top of the list. He was a lord, he was rich, and he would want her father's job. Maybe her father had something on Cecil, and this

Rodney's visitor was not related to Brodie Deacon's family at all but was simply another person with the surname Deacon. Maybe a pal from Chatham, or an associate of Cecil's. And the fact that Rodney refused to say who had come to visit him was most likely a scheme to piss her off and nothing much more than that. And it was Cecil who had planted that seed about her father being a little deviant and then laughed as if it was a joke.

She snapped out of her thoughts when she heard her phone ringing. It was Mendel. 'Yes,' she said, in a cold voice.

'Mac Deacon is alive and conscious. What would you like us to do with him?'

Brodie felt his heart in his mouth. James was close enough for him to hear the gist of the conversation. Holding his breath, he was willing her on to order Mac's release.

'Take him back to the police station.' She looked at Brodie. 'He fell over and rolled down the stairs.'

Brodie nodded. 'He sure did, James,' he replied, with relief but with a bitter taste in his mouth.

'Hmmm, okay. They will take you back to the station, Brodie,' she said, looking defeated.

'And my niece?'

James frowned. 'Oh yes. Sorry, we genuinely don't have your niece. Her disappearance is nothing to do with us.'

She flicked her head for the men to hurry to help Brodie to the van.

'Can I ask, James, why you haven't mentioned me brother Dixie, who was killed a couple of days ago?'

She shrugged. 'Our investigation showed us that he was estranged from you for at least twenty years. He was homeless and worked part-time for a scaffolding company. There is no link between your late brother and Rodney Potter whatsoever. The details about your company pricked our ears, but I guess we got it wrong.'

'And no apology?' he retorted.

She glared with her nostrils flared and her jaw clenched tightly. 'If I discover that you are involved, I will ensure that you suffer, Brodie Deacon.'

CHAPTER TWENTY-FIVE

Raj was about to put the mug of coffee to his lips to listen more to Shields's story about Elspeth and her dead son when his phone vibrated in his pocket. He placed his mug on the coffee table and retrieved his phone.

Petra Holland was calling him. For a moment, he thought of cutting her off, but then he decided he was being childish. 'Excuse me, Georgie, I have to take this call.'

Georgie nodded and watched Raj leave the living room and wander into the kitchen. However, she could hear him; the wall between the living room and kitchen was a stud wall.

'Petra.'

'Raj, you'd better come back to the office.'

'Oh yeah, have Uniform managed to track down this bogus cleaner?'

'Er, sorry, no.'

'Right, okay. Thanks for the update.'

'Raj.' She hesitated. 'Why are you avoiding me? We work together, partners and all that. What have I done wrong?'

'Nothing, Petra. I've just been swamped, and we've had two different jobs to do. We've needed to work separately, so there's not a problem with us.'

'Yeah, Raj, I understand that, but you haven't spoken to me. Are we over?'

Raj swallowed and tried to clear his throat. 'Er, Petra, I think it's for the best, and besides, it's not a good idea to be colleagues, and whatever it is we were.'

'Fuck buddies, Raj. We were fuck buddies.' Her voice cracked, and he knew she was hurt.

'Anyway, I called to tell you that Drake, the sly fox, has forced your private drawer open.'

'You *what*? How dare he?'

'Raj, they are all investigating something more than Dixie's murder. I don't get it. And they won't bring me in. They're like a separate cackle of hyenas – actually more like a den of snakes – sneaking around fucking whispering to each other.'

Raj felt his heart sink. He had wrongly assumed she was in with them, but now he realised she wasn't. She was trying to get information and doing it the best way she could.

'Are you still there, Raj?'

'Yeah, er, what else have you discovered about Drake and his mob?'

'Well, listen to this.' She sounded excited. 'I was at the custody desk looking through my notes when I heard Drake and Evans talking. And from what I could gather, Drake was expecting the Deacon brothers back in custody. Drake said there was no point in trying to make the charges stick. That someone called James had finished with them.'

'*Finished with them?* Oh my God, have they murdered them?'

'I don't know, Raj. What shall I do? They were bloody shocked to see me there, and Drake demanded to know what I'd heard. I said I didn't know what he was talking about and scooted off before he got nasty. I don't trust them, Raj. Drake, Evans, and that cow Lardon are as dodgy as fuck, mate.'

'Dodgy as fuck?'

'Yep, I did a little bit of research on them myself, and I have to be honest. At first, I couldn't find Carol Lardon. That was because she was listed under her maiden name. Anyway, she had a few complaints against her and – *get this* – she was under investigation. But her own sergeant investigated the issue and found the complaints unfounded, so they were never taken to a higher level. And that's the same with Drake. I tell you, Raj, someone above Fitz is holding their puppet strings, believe you me.'

'I hope to God they are not connected to a paedophile ring.'

'Raj, they are all involved in something, believe me.'

With every claim coming out of Petra's mouth, Raj felt guiltier by the second. He had assumed that Petra was getting in with them, when, all the while, she was acting like a double agent. 'Petra, I'm sorry. Can we go for a coffee, drink, or steak even, when you're free, of course?'

'Er, yeah, sure, but you said you didn't want—'

She didn't get a chance to finish. 'I was wrong! I'm so sorry. We *are* good together, Petra. Can we have that coffee and a chat?'

'Er, no, Raj, you mentioned steak, you tight bastard.'

He chuckled. 'Steak it is, then.'

'Shit, Raj, there's a black van pulling into the yard. I think it's MI5. It looks like the same van that took Brodie and Mac Deacon away.'

'Keep watching. Clock every move. I'm on my way.'

'Sh-it,' she said, in a drawn-out fashion. 'Raj, they are helping the men out of the back of the van. One of them – I think it's Mac – is in a bad way. They are holding him up. Oh my God, he can't walk. Raj, he looks like someone's put him through a fucking mincer. His face is black and blue.'

'I'm on my way. Please, Petra, watch everything, and if you get a chance, go in and see him. Take photos, and please try to keep him safe.'

Raj rushed back into the living room. 'Hugh, come with me. Mac and Brodie are back at the station, but Petra reckons Mac is in a bad way.'

Georgie gasped, her hands flying to her mouth. 'What on earth is going on, Raj? None of this makes any fucking sense.'

'I'm sorry, Georgie. I need to get to the station before, God forbid, they disappear.'

As he flew out of the front door, he noticed that the young officer, Matthew Level had gone and there was no police car outside. It raised his anger to another pitch. He clicked his key fob and nodded for Shields to get in the car while he hurried back and banged on Georgie's door.

She opened it in a second.

'Georgie you have no protection. There is no one, so go somewhere else, but stay safe, until we can sort this mess out.'

'Don't worry about me, Raj. Go and get the lads,' she said, before closing the door behind him.

Her mind wasn't on her safety, it was focused on Raj's words. She was sure she'd heard him say 'paedophile ring'. Her mind went back to the box in Dixie's wardrobe where she'd found the baby teeth and the small trainers. She shuddered. Was Dixie a wrong 'un? Her hands shook, thinking that his secretive ways had been about his sick obsession. With kids. Possibly boys. If it was true, it would destroy her daughter. She prayed it was something innocent; however, the more she tried to think of a reason for what she had seen, the more she drew a blank. The trainers weren't from his own childhood because they were a recent design, and they were too boyish to have been for Dixie-Lee.

***

It was pitch-black as Raj and Shields drove through Bromley to the police station. And there was barely a soul around except for those hurrying to catch the last train.

'I appreciate this, Raj.'

'No worries, Hugh. I joined the force for many reasons, but the main one was to see justice done. There are too many injustices in this world, and I think we are walking into one right now. Petra said Mac was badly beaten. Fucking MI5. As if Mac and Brodie are caught up in anything that serious.'

'No, Raj, they definitely aren't, but let's get in there. I want to see my clients right away.'

'Me too,' said Raj, as he swerved his car, barely missing the black van, before screeching to a stop in his designated parking space. They hurried to the back door, where Raj entered his passcode before pushing his way in and going straight into the corridor. By the time they reached the custody suite, Evans was already scribing notes in the custody records log.

Out of character, Raj grabbed the logbook from his hands. 'Oh no, you don't, mate. I want to be present when you fill out anything. Now, where is the custody sergeant?' He looked up at the camera, noticing the red light was off. 'And why isn't the fucking camera on?'

'Whoa, what the fuck are you doing, Raj?'

'No, mate, what the fuck are *you* doing?' He pointed to the camera and then read the newly added information on the custody records log. 'Mac *fell*? Fucking fell down the concrete steps? Are you serious?'

Evans looked at Raj, in astonishment.

'I know what your game is, Evans, and believe me, this ain't over. Fell down the stairs? That old 1970s stunt. You're having a laugh, ain't ya?'

Shields suddenly stepped forwards. 'Evans, take me to my clients right away. If that note says my client has been injured – because I understand you would have to make a note of that – then

I want to see him right this minute, and if his injuries warrant a hospital visit then you'd better have an ambulance on its way.'

Evans was stumped, and his gaping mouth spoke volumes.

'Detective Evans, I'm not waiting. Now, I insist that you take me to my client now and also have everything you have on my client to charge him, or I will be walking out of here with both Brodie and Mac Deacon, and I will make sure the press has every tiny little detail. You know they love a good saga because, Evans, that is what this is.'

'I . . . er, I need to, er . . .'

'You need to take me to the holding cells this minute.'

Raj wanted to laugh at Evans because he could see the man was desperate to hold himself together.

Evans could see that the situation was slipping out of his hands. So much was happening and so quickly, his brain couldn't keep up with the pace of events.

'What are you waiting for!' Shields bellowed, in such a harsh deep Irish accent that even Raj was shocked.

He established at that point that Shields had reached his boiling point. He had seen him annoyed before, but this level of anger was new to him.

Raj hurried to the key safe, helped himself to the keys, and literally pushed Evans out of the way. 'I don't need this prick to take me to the cells. I am a rank above him, anyway.'

'Raj, you can't just go in there.'

'Fuck off, dog's breath. And, yes, I fucking *can*. I am human as well as a copper.'

Two uniformed officers were outside the holding cells. One was older, a large rotund man. Raj knew him as Stan Watkins. He was known to be a bit of a soft touch. The other officer he realised was Matthew Level, whom he'd reprimanded over the phone business.

'Which cell is Mac Deacon in?' Raj demanded.

Officer Level didn't hesitate to point to cell number three.

Raj unlocked the door and gasped at the sight. 'Jesus Christ.'

Shields pushed Raj aside to look at Mac. Instantly, his blood ran cold.

Mac was lying on his side. Thick dark blood was dripping from his nose. His grey tracksuit, issued by the police, was covered in claret.

When Raj looked at Mac's vastly swollen feet, which were hideously black and blue, he knew then he had been tortured. His face was so swollen to the point that he was unrecognisable. The sight would bring any grown man to tears.

As Shields kneeled by Mac's side, Raj glared at the two officers. 'I take it, an ambulance is on its way?'

Watkins looked at Level, before looking back at Raj. 'No, I don't think so. Detective Inspector Drake is fetching some clean clothes and Mr Deacon's shoes.'

'I see. Is that to fucking hide the claret all over his tracksuit? Have you two seen the state of that man?' He stepped forwards. 'Well, have you?'

'Sorry, we have only just arrived. I don't know anything about this man,' said Watkins.

'Go and fetch some water. Now!' Raj yelled.

As soon as the older officer hurried off, Raj turned to Level and shook his head. 'I was hoping you'd make a good officer.'

Level glanced up the corridor and then produced his phone. 'I have footage and audible. Look, they turned the fucking cameras off.' He pointed to the camera in the cell. 'I might be new and all that, but this is worse than a gangsters' feud.'

Raj saw a small part of the footage where Mac was bound and dragged into the cell. 'How did you manage that?'

'I am discreet with my filming.'

'Good lad. Send it to me, will you.'

'Raj, I mean, Detective, I know my dad was a bit of a wrong 'un, but I promise you, I'm not.'

Patting the lad's arm, Raj nodded. 'I know you're not. I reckon you would make a good detective. It seems to me you prefer to be on the right side of the law.'

'Yeah, I want to work with you, Raj.'

'Okay, you can start right now by getting that footage across to me. And call an ambulance.'

Level smiled. 'I've already done that.'

Raj tilted his head. 'Have ya?'

Level nodded. 'Mr Deacon is in a bad way.'

'And Brodie Deacon?'

'He is doing his bollocks in cell one.'

'I bet he is.'

While Shields was talking to Mac in cell three, Raj opened cell one to find Brodie pacing the floor.

'What's happened to Mac?'

'I am going to make sure he goes to the hospital,' Raj assured him.

'That fecking bitch James said he'd be taken there. That's rubbish. I saw the state of him. Hospital? My fecking arse. He didn't even get a plaster. The lying whore. I will hunt her down, woman or not. I will find that bitch and kill her!'

Raj was shocked to hear Brodie losing his temper. He always appeared to be in control.

'And can you please tell me what's happening to my niece? Have you found her yet? Only, that poxy MI5 bird reckons Dixie-Lee's disappearance has nothing to do with her.'

Raj waved his hands to calm Brodie down.

'And will someone take these restraints off me? I can barely feel my fecking hands.'

Just at that moment, Level entered the room. He instantly went to work by removing the cable ties.

Brodie flexed his fingers, rolled his huge shoulders, and then ran his hands through his hair, moving it away from his face.

Raj placed a finger over his lips, indicating that Brodie should be quiet. Then he whispered in his ear. 'Dixie-Lee is safe, but say nothing. Let's just get you out of here.'

'Take me to Mac.'

Raj didn't argue. He was past caring about protocol and procedure. As far as he was concerned, this was a terrible miscarriage of justice, and a medieval act that to him seemed so barbaric. And as for Evans trying to cover it up, it was the final nail in the coffin. As he escorted Brodie to Mac's cell, Raj heard the noisy boots belonging to Drake, and he spun around to confront the man.

Drake was holding a clear plastic sack containing another police issue grey tracksuit and some white trainers. Behind him was the older officer with a bottle of water. Also lurking like a predator at the end of the corridor was Evans.

'What the hell is going on here, Raj? You can't—'

'Stand back, Drake. Don't you dare come anywhere near me. I have just found Evans falsifying records a few minutes ago. And Mac Deacon has been without medical care. And as for you coming here to change his clothes, do you think that giving him a clean set will miraculously make him appear as though nothing has happened, you fucking cruel bastard.'

'If you have an issue, take it up with the IOPC. You write your report, and I'll write mine.'

'You really believe that you are invincible, don't you? Well, I have a reliable witness who will state that Mac walked into the building via the back door and straight into the holding cells. But Mac didn't walk up or down any stairs, so when your detective wrote in the custody notes that Mac's injuries were from a fall, then, believe me, I have enough on you and him to make a complaint. It will be so damaging that you will find yourself behind bars, the whole damn fucking lot of you.'

Drake smirked, looking Raj up and down. 'You are never part of us, Raj. We stick together, but you—'

With his face burning in anger, Raj leaped forwards. 'I would never be part of your lawless fucking mob backed by a toff and knobs to protect their own fucking illegal acts. Now, back off, Drake. I can hear an ambulance, and if you dare try to stop me, I will go to the press.'

Drake laughed. 'And what the fuck do you have that makes your story so interesting that the *Kent Messenger* will want to publish it?'

Raj pulled out his phone and smiled when he saw that Level had forwarded the footage. He held up his phone and watched the recording. 'I think the tabloids will be rubbing their hands together. Now move, Drake. And you had better have a good reason to have these two men in custody.'

Drake's eyes widened, and his shoulders slumped. He dropped the plastic sack as the older officer rushed past him and into Mac's cell. 'I am waiting for—'

Raj cut him off again. 'Ballistics? Yeah, sure you are. The report's already back. Evans has already told me. So stop stalling, Drake. And tell me this. The gun planted in Mac's car. Was that gun used to kill Dixie? Was there residue on Mac's clothes, and were there any of his prints on the gun?'

Drake slowly shook his head in defeat. There seemed to be a noisy commotion at the end of the corridor, and as he glanced back, he saw Detective Constable Petra Holland running towards them with two paramedics behind her.

Drake realised then that it was Holland who had witnessed the arrival of Mac and Brodie. He looked back at Raj. 'How did you get that footage?'

Relieved that paramedics were on their way, Raj smiled. 'Not everyone in this nick is on your payroll. Some of us do the job to protect the public, not to line our pockets with dirty money.'

'You don't know what you are talking about.'

As the paramedics squeezed past, Holland stood by Raj's side. She had just caught the gist of the conversation. 'He may not have all the facts, Detective Inspector Drake, but I have been doing my homework, and your sidekick Detective Constable Lardon has a big mouth when she's had a few vodkas. She wanted me onside, she did. She said I could earn a few quid, by losing some paperwork and turning a blind eye. The silly cow even showed me a photo of her new Beamer. Like any good detective, I recorded the conversation. Oh, and I can trace the money. I'm good at that, aren't I, Raj?'

Drake's face turned deathly white. A sudden rash of sweat beads peppered his brow, and white phlegm coated the corners of his mouth. 'I don't think Chief Superintendent Fitzgerald would appreciate you trying to bring down Bromley Police Station, do you?'

'I'm not. You see, I believe there are still a few coppers in here who aren't being bought by you, so no, I don't want to bring the station down. What I want to do is to remove the cancer. And trust me, Drake, I will do that, regardless.'

As Drake stormed off, Holland slid her hand into Raj's. 'I think we make a good team, Raj.'

He glanced behind him before he kissed her cheek. 'We do, Petra. I'm sorry for before. Really, I am.'

CHAPTER TWENTY-SIX

Georgie used a loft pole to push open the loft hatch before she hooked the ladder and pulled it down. A few cobwebs and specks of dust floated in the air, but no spiders fell down. As much as she wasn't afraid of people, she could easily scream and shake at the sight of a spider. Still, with her torch and her claw hammer in her hand, she shimmied up the rungs and shone the light, initially to carry out a brief sweep for unwanted insects. She thought for a moment that she could see two eyes staring back and assumed she might have rats inside the house. However, when her eyes adjusted to the dark and the torchlight, she realised it was the glass eyes of Dixie-Lee's ancient teddy bear. She smiled, contemplating bringing it down with her and giving it a good wash and placing it next to her daughter's pillow, once she had cleaned all the sheets, of course.

Standing up straight in the loft was difficult, but the pitch was high enough to move freely. She shone the torch on the small light switch partially hidden by the overfilled cement pointing around the exposed brickwork. After flicking the switch, the loft illuminated. Once again, she had a quick glance to check for creepy-crawlies. The false panelled wall was thick with dust, and it was just how she wanted it to look. No one would ever have guessed that behind the wood was a small compartment for her secret belongings. Having created the false wall using cement to fill the gaps in the planks of wood to match the overfilling of the exposed brickwork, she had been thrilled with the results. Even though it was fake, it was not too obvious because the space behind it was very small. So no one snooping around would have thought that the dimensions didn't add up.

Lowering her head, she walked towards it. But then she stopped in front of an old trunk which was adjacent to a cot and buggy. Her eyes roamed the clear thick plastic bags that were coated in a layer of dust. The tag on the bag read 'age five'. Brushing away the dust, she saw one of her daughter's dresses. It was a pretty strawberry print. She remembered that dress. It was the one that had a rip in the hem where Dixie-Lee had rolled down a bank into the river and screamed her head off because she'd torn the dress – the one she'd insisted on wearing before her birthday.

Her daughter's birthdays, thought Georgie, sighing. There were so many she'd spent alone with her daughter. There would be a cake for breakfast and a small gift that she'd saved hard for. When Dixie-Lee went to school and was invited to her classmates' parties, Georgie would save even harder. And it became a tradition that Dixie-Lee's special day included jelly and ice cream and all kinds of fun and games. Pass-the-parcel and musical statues came to mind.

Suddenly, Georgie fell to her knees and let the built-up tears roll down her face. Wiping them away, she looked from one bag of memories to another. All Dixie-Lee's old clothes were here along with many of her drawings from a very young age. She looked at one of them. It was a drawing of the two of them and in the sky was a stickman with a halo around his head. 'And that's Daddy,' she would say, with her sweet lisp. 'He is watching over us, Mummy.'

Every bag, folder, and suitcase held her daughter's memories, and Dixie-Lee's father had missed each one. Her first school play, being awarded her swimming badges, getting chicken pox and meningitis. The list was endless. She'd been the parent always by her daughter's side, not Dixie. Another tear dropped onto the dusty bag. And her tears of sadness turned to burning tears of anger.

'You were alive all that time, and we were alone. Why?' she cried, as if he was in the room with her. She pounded her fists on the wooden panels she had used to board the loft. Of course, she had learned how to do everything. She'd had no choice. Dixie had taken that away from her. And she'd had to teach her daughter things she shouldn't have had to do. Survival had been the number-one priority. Having seen the best and the worst in people, she'd prepared her daughter for both. Knowing how cruel this world could be had worried her. If she'd died, then Dixie-Lee would have been alone, until six months ago, when Dixie had returned. Biting down on her bottom lip, she wished he'd never come back.

As far as she was concerned, he wasn't the same man, and as much she'd tried to love him, that deep-seated sense of frustration from grieving for years and years and crying night after night – giving birth alone and always being alone – had held her back.

‘Why, Dixie, fucking why?’ She assumed his reasons weren’t genuine, but she’d also assumed he would never tell her the truth. Maybe she didn’t want to know because it would change her feelings for him. Perhaps, deep down, she preferred to resent him now because she hadn’t really loved him. And now this nagging thought that he was mixed up in something so dark made her insides burn. She didn’t know what was worse: him getting shot dead or him being involved with kiddies.

Wiping another tear, she saw some movement out of the corner of her eye. She looked to the left to see the old mirror that had cracked when she’d tried to fix it to the wall. She had never thought she was anything to look at. In fact, for years, there had been no one to tell her she was.

But there was another thought going through her mind. It was sometime after Dixie had returned to the family home. She and Dixie had made love. But, in retrospect, it had all seemed so cold and emotionless. Somehow, it had felt like a duty. Her mind had switched to Rohan. When he had eyed her, she had felt special, even beautiful. A sob stuck in her throat, and then she coughed, feeling angry again. ‘Why did you have to come back and ruin everything, Dixie?’

She had never wished him dead, but now he was, he’d brought even more grief, and her Dixie-Lee was devastated. Wiping her nose with the back of her hand, she grabbed the claw hammer before getting to her feet. It was time to put all thoughts of Dixie to the back of her mind. Her priority was to ensure Dixie-Lee and herself were safe.

She embedded the claw end of the hammer into the lowest plank of wood and eased it open. Once one plank was free, she could tug the others away from the frame. As soon as there was enough room, she reached in and felt for her canvas bag in which she had stored guns, some wire, and a knife.

She knew one thing: if any of those Olivers came to her house again, they would get hurt – very badly hurt. Dropping the canvas bag out of the loft onto a soft pillow she had put there for this purpose to break its fall, she turned the light off and clambered down before brushing off the dust, pushing the ladder back up, and closing the loft hatch.

She scooped up her weapons from her ex-Army days and dashed into her bedroom, where she laid everything out on the bed and then went through her checks as if she was still in the service. Confirming that the gun worked, and the bullets were in place, she forced the magazine back into the handle, grabbed the other pieces, and made her way downstairs. Her sofa with the valance was a great place to hide her weapons unless the police did a raid, but for now, she needed to ensure her home was safe. She slid the knife behind the large photo of her daughter and Dixie, which Dixie-Lee had insisted on having done to replace the photograph she'd kissed frequently growing up. *Where should I hide the wire attached to two handles?* she wondered. It was her favoured weapon. After a few moments of thought, she eventually decided that the best place was in the kitchen. It seemed to blend in with her cheesecutter, but, of course, it was so much more robust. And she knew that: she had made it herself.

She looked at the back door, deciding what to do about that. It was still unlocked, and she didn't have the key. She could only assume that one of the Olivers had stolen it. All she could think of doing was to remove the handle from the exterior so no one could open it unless she did by using the handle inside the house.

Once she had everything she could think of in place, she went back into the kitchen to make a sandwich. She was absolutely starving. Buttering two slices of bread and checking that it hadn't grown a fur coat, she then sliced some cheese. She wasn't a fan of cheese, but there was little else. Then she made a coffee.

Henry jumped into her thoughts, and she suddenly had the urge to call him. *Poor Henry*, she thought. She called the ward to check he was okay, and to her surprise, the nurse asked her to wait a moment while he came to the phone.

'Hello, Georgie, how are you, love?'

She felt her shoulders relax as she listened to his soft voice. 'Yeah, all good, Henry. And what about you? You're up and about already, I hear.'

'Yeah, gal, you know me, and listen, while I have been lying here bored, I had an idea. I was thinking if, of course, the insurance covers it, perhaps we could go into business together and open a trendy bakery-cum-coffee shop. Maybe it will help to take your mind off things.'

'Henry, it sounds perfect, mate. I'm up for that.'

'Oh, and Billy and Kirby were up here chatting up the nurses. They made me laugh so much I popped me stitches, the fuckers. Listen, my gal, I've gotta go. Speak soon, yeah? The nurse wants the phone. Give my love to Dixie-Lee.'

'Bye, Henry.'

She was about to finish her sandwich when she heard a tapping at the back door. The sound was gentle; no one was bashing the door down. After wiping her mouth with the tea towel, she stepped into the hallway and looked directly through the glass pane in the back door. To her surprise, she saw an oldish woman. With grey hair and wearing a mauve overcoat, the woman waved a walking stick to grab her attention.

Georgie knew that the man who lived at the end of the terrace was nursing his mother, who had dementia, and she assumed this person was her. Not even contemplating this woman could be dangerous, she headed towards the door.

As she opened it, she greeted the woman. 'Hi, can I help you?' she said, in a low caring voice.

'I'm a little lost, you see, and I am so cold. Please may I come in until I work out where I am?'

Assuming the woman was the person she thought she was, Georgie said, 'Yes, of course. Is your son Paul?'

A deep frown creased her forehead. '*Who?*'

'Your son, Paul.'

The woman smiled. 'Yes, he has gone to work.'

'Come in, and I'll make you a warm drink. You look frozen.'

The stranger entered the living room and sat in the armchair. She had put her brown leather handbag on her lap and the walking stick by her side.

'Would you like a tea with sugar?' Georgie asked, with a smile.

'Yes, please, two sugars.'

Georgie smiled again and noticed how the woman gazed around the room, momentarily pausing at each photo.

'That's my husband and my daughter.'

'Beautiful. You must love her very much.'

'Yes, she's my world. I'll make that tea, and then I'll go and find your son.'

While filling the kettle, Georgie stared out of the window and spotted a taxi pulling up outside. It was dark, and it didn't help that the streetlamp wasn't working, so she couldn't see who was getting out. However, from the silhouette, she thought it could be Rohan. So engrossed was she in watching him that she jumped when she felt the water on her hands. She'd overfilled the kettle. After emptying some of the water, she turned it on and hurried to the door. Her heart was beating so fast, she thought she would get giddy, and so, taking a deep breath, she pulled open the door.

For just a second or two, their eyes met, and at that moment, it felt as though they were the only two on the planet. She knew then he felt the same way. Giving him a coy smile, she lowered her gaze, only to hear a voice behind him say, 'It's bloody freeing.' *So, Finella had come here as well!*

'Quick, Rohan, get inside. I'm as cold as a frozen Christmas turkey.'

Georgie hurriedly stepped aside as Rohan, dressed in an expensive black leather jacket, a cashmere sweater, and faded jeans – who somehow appeared even more handsome than she remembered – hustled in with his mother in tow. Rohan's cheeks were pink, and his eyes had a captivating sparkle that sucked her right in.

'Georgie, me mam wants to stay here with you. Shall I run her bag up to Dixie-Lee's room?' He raised his brow as if to say, 'It's nothing to do with me.'

'Yes, yes, of course,' she replied, still excited that Rohan was in the room. As he stepped out of the way, Georgie was suddenly embraced by her mother-in-law.

'What a fecking shitty state of affairs. I had to come, my darling. There was no way, I was staying in Ireland when all me family are here. Now, are you okay, me sweetness?' She didn't give her daughter-in-law a chance to answer before she carried on. 'It must have been a terrible shock. And our poor Dixie-Lee only just getting to know her father. And now he's gone.' Her chin trembled and tears filled her eyes.

Georgie, who hugged no one, put her arms around Finella and gently patted her back. As she did so, she breathed in the strong scent of her mother-in-law's expensive perfume. 'And for you,

Finella. I am so sorry for you. I know how excited you were to see him again.'

'Yes,' she snivelled, as she pulled away and looked at Georgie. 'We have a lot to catch up on, and I am parched. The fecking taxi driver, I am sure he was in cahoots with the petrol station. He drove all around the fecking country to get here.'

Georgie wanted to laugh. Finella could be so funny, but when it came to her boys, she ruled them with a rod of iron, like a sergeant major on the parade ground.

For someone who was quite petite, Finella still had a profound presence. This was accentuated by her dress sense, which was impeccable. As she unbuttoned her fitted coat, Georgie noticed the beautiful emerald-green suit and the gold chains around her neck. Even her hair was in perfect waves, which was pulled back to show off her face. And for an older woman, Finella oozed grace and confidence, comfortable in her own skin.

Georgie suddenly remembered the neighbour who was still in the living room, but as she was about to enter it, she heard the back door bang shut. Looking outside, she could see the woman hurrying away. *Strange*, she thought. She would check on the neighbour to make sure his mother got home okay.

Turning to Finella, she decided to make her and Rohan a hot drink.

'Take a seat and get warmed up. You can turn the fire on and boost the heat in the room,' she said, watching Finella rubbing her hands together.

As Finella limped into the living room, Rohan came down the stairs. 'Are you okay?'

Georgie could see the puzzled expression on his face. 'Yeah, well, sort of.'

He nodded for Georgie to go back into the kitchen and then he followed her. 'Why are there bloodstains on Dixie-Lee's bed?'

Georgie sighed. 'Rohan, so much has gone on. Rest assured that's not Dixie-Lee's blood. She is quite safe.'

Rohan nodded. 'Hugh filled me in. Mac's in the hospital. I'm taking Ma there in the morning. Brodie is not the same Brodie. I have never known him to be so angry, and he is the calm one. He is absolutely raging. God help anyone who steps out of line.'

When Rohan stopped and looked at her again in that gentle way, his eyes longing for her, she glanced away and made the tea for Finella, her heart almost breaking. Now he was back in England and in her kitchen. All she wanted was to hold him, to kiss him, but how could she? Her husband wasn't even in the ground. Still, what hadn't changed – though she would never admit this to anyone – was how she felt about Rohan. She loved him. As she opened the biscuit tin and placed a few digestives on a plate, she suddenly felt his hand on the small of her neck. She froze and instantly wanted to cry. Life was so unfair. Apart from her daughter, the one person who made her happy – despite the short time she had known him – was Rohan. Not a day had gone by when she hadn't thought about him.

'I had to stay away from you. You do realise why, don't you?'

Georgie couldn't stop the tears. They rolled down her nose and dripped onto the plate.

'I know.' She turned her head away, so he couldn't see her crying.

But Rohan had already spotted the tear on the plate. Unexpectedly, he put his arms around her and kissed the top of her head. 'I missed you so much. I know it was wrong. I know you loved my brother. But I just wanted you to know how I felt about you. God, why am I telling you this now?' He coughed to hide the lump in his throat.

'I didn't love him, Rohan. I tried, but after a few weeks with Dixie, I knew that the love I had for him was long gone. It took me a while to realise that I was in love with a ghost because the part of him I loved died that day he was blown up, and it never came back.'

'I can't turn this fire on,' Finella called out.

Rohan instantly let go of Georgie, took the two mugs of tea, and went into the living room, leaving Georgie to wipe her eyes and sort out the biscuits.

'I have to go to my neighbour's for a second. I just want to check on his mother.'

'What do you mean?' asked Finella, relieving Georgie of the tray of biscuits and pre-packed cakes.

‘His mother has dementia, and she came knocking at my back door. She looked so lost. She just left when you arrived, so I want to make sure she got home safe.’

Finella smiled. ‘You’re a good girl.’

‘There you go, Ma,’ said Rohan. ‘The fire is on. Now, don’t sit on top of it, or you’ll get corned beef legs, just like Granny had.’

‘Your granny didn’t get her mottled skin from the fire. It was the two bottles of whiskey a day that messed *her* up.’

‘I’ll be back in a few minutes,’ said Georgie, as she grabbed her thick chunky cardigan from the back of the sofa.

‘I’ll come with you,’ said Rohan, taking a quick gulp of his tea.

Finella frowned and then looked away. But that look didn’t go unnoticed by Georgie. She suddenly felt ashamed. *How complicated life is*, she thought. *When Dixie reappeared, her life turned full circle. And to complicate things even more, everyone assumed she would naturally take up where they had left off over eighteen years ago.*

But that was then and this was now. She knew she loved Rohan – even though the situation was awkward to say the least – but she wanted him to return the feeling. However, he had not expressed his feelings clearly enough to her. And they had never even slept together or even been out on a date. She liked to think there was something between them on some deeper unspoken level; either that or it was all in her head.

‘I will go out the back door. She may be hovering around the back alley. I’m sorry, Finella, but the back door won’t lock. I’ll only be a few minutes.’

Finella rubbed her hands in front of the fire. ‘Never mind me. I’m fine. I’ve got a mug of tea, a cake, and a warm backside. The poor woman. Was she dressed for the cold?’

‘Yes, she was, but I’m sure she was unsteady on her feet. I’ll go and check. I’m sure she’s back home.’

‘Okay, I’ll unpack my things. And when Dixie-Lee comes home and all this business is sorted, I’ll check into the hotel. The one we used six months ago.’

Georgie nodded before she opened the back door and headed outside. The wind instantly bit her face. And it was difficult to see her footing because the alley was so dark. To make things worse, none of the neighbours’ lights at the back of their terrace were on.

Her next door neighbour and friend, Lucy Bean, was in Wales with family for a month and she had taken her children with her, so it had been peaceful.

'I want to talk to you, Georgie,' said Rohan.

Georgie pulled her cardigan tighter around her and shivered. 'What about?' She hoped it was about them. She wanted him to say he would make a plan for them to be together or to announce he loved her or that he wanted to be with her.

'So you know about the Olivers and the feud years ago. Right?'

Georgie nodded. 'Yes and Elspeth.'

'What? No, not that load of rubbish. I am talking about when Eamonn Oliver shot the car off the road and into the lake where Mac escaped.'

'Yes, I know about that, and Hugh mentioned it was dealt with and put to bed.'

'Well, we thought so too. When it happened, forensic divers went down to search for a body. The problem was the lake. It is so deep, and so it would have taken a lot of effort and money to bring a vehicle up from those depths. They found a car, but what they didn't find was a body, even though the doors were shut and the windows were up. Now, without finding a body, it was classed as a car crime or a TDA. So, the police believed the car was pushed over the edge. And considering they had warrants out for Eamonn's arrest prior to the incident, the police concluded that he had ditched the car he'd stolen into the lake and done a runner to evade prison.'

Georgie listened as she took careful steps since it was so dark.

'Now, that lake has a lot of sediment, and it can get pretty murky when it's been disturbed. So, initially, the forensic divers who were looking for a body didn't take any real details of the car, only that it was a BMW. Now, remember this all happened a long time ago, and so, at the time, the police naturally assumed that the car they found was the *only* car. What they failed to take into account was that in that lake there are strong undercurrents that would probably have moved the car some considerable distance from the spot where the car plunged into the water.'

'I get that, Rohan, but what are you really saying?'

'It's this, Georgie. Two weeks ago, there was a scientific boat on the lake with a marine biologist, who believed there was a huge fish in that lake, a Lock Ness type of fish. So, he got a grant and was able to investigate.'

Georgie gasped. 'Ah, now I get you. So did this marine biologist find *another car* with a body inside?'

'Yeah, and so it was announced in the local paper.'

'I see, so the Olivers now have proof that their brother was in that car. The story I heard was they had forced Mac into the boot of the car, and Eamonn, who was supposedly drunk, drove off the road and into the lake.'

'And that is why the feud was ended. It was a tragic accident, and we are lucky that Mac didn't drown in the car's boot.'

'I sense a but coming.'

'There is. When the car was brought to the surface, the police discovered that the seat belt was wrapped around Eamonn's neck, so it is now potentially a crime scene.'

'Oh shit. So the Olivers believe Mac murdered him, do they?'

'I haven't had a conversation with the Olivers, but I can take a wild guess that's what they believe.'

Georgie stopped dead. 'And did he?'

'No, he didn't. There is to be a coroner's inquest because there is the possibility that Eamonn tried to get the belt off himself before the car hit the water, but, somehow, he got tangled up, and he broke his neck. So, a friend of mine, a copper back in Ireland, told me.'

'Fuck, so this is about revenge, is it?'

'It looks like it, so I have hired a villa for Ma, you, and Dixie-Lee in Portugal.'

She smiled gently in hope. 'Will you join us?'

He shook his head, and she felt her heart ache. The external cold was nothing compared to the ice she felt running through her veins. It was as if he was saying goodbye. Maybe it was the dark casting shadows on his face. She decided not to push the subject any further.

CHAPTER TWENTY-SEVEN

Finella jolted when she saw the bloodstains on her granddaughter's bed. 'God, that girl must be at her wits' end. All this worry,' she said to herself, as she stripped the bed of the covers and pulled the pillow from its sleeve. Just as she gathered everything up in her arms, she heard the back door either opening or closing and naturally assumed it was Georgie and Rohan returning.

'I hope you don't mind, Georgie. I've stripped Dixie-Lee's bed and I'm about to put these bedclothes in the washing machine. Have you got plenty of salt? I reckon it will need quite a bit,' she said, as she descended the steep staircase, careful not to trip. However, she was surprised when Georgie didn't answer. Nevertheless, she could hear footsteps. When she reached the bottom step, she turned to walk towards the kitchen, but someone caught her eye as she glanced to her left, straight into the living room.

For a moment, Finella didn't recognise the woman, and she assumed that the neighbour with dementia had returned. 'Oh, love, my daughter-in-law has gone looking for you. I believe she has also gone to see your son. Take a seat, lovey. I'll put this washing in the machine, and then I'll help you to find your house. How about that?'

As Finella shoved the bedding into the washing machine, she heard the woman laugh. It was not the cackle you'd expect from a frail old lady with dementia, but from a younger woman with a nasty streak in her.

Finella paused and blinked a few times before she closed the washing machine door and limped into the living room. At that point, she felt her stomach turn over. The realisation that this woman was actually Nancy Oliver hit her hard.

Nancy was an old archenemy, the only woman she despised, the woman who had laughed when her sons had pushed her out of their house and who'd kicked the shingle into her eyes and spat at her. And now the bitch was standing in her daughter-in-law's house with brass balls and pure loathing in her eyes.

She had been quite a looker in her day, but her prettiest features had dulled to the point where she now looked resentful and spiteful.

They had grown up in the same village. Nancy had wanted to marry Michael Deacon, but he'd only had eyes for Finella, so their discontent began in their early teens.

Finella had unintentionally outshone Nancy at everything, from coming top in her lessons to winning cups at sports day, to making the best Holy Communion dress. And if Nancy hadn't been so horrible to everyone, she would have had the friends, the pats on the back, and the encouragement. Instead, she was cruel. She was the school bully. And when she left school, she turned to a life of crime. She married a villain and then raised more villains, including her daughter Elspeth, who ran wild, like her brothers.

'What do you want, Nancy?' asked Finella, lifting her chin as if she was daring the woman on. Because as much as Nancy and her sons had terrified her the day they threw her out of their house, she herself had changed a lot since then, and Nancy Oliver wasn't someone she would be shaking in her boots over.

Nancy glared, and her thin humourless lips slowly parted into an evil grin. She tilted her face down and peered up through her eyelashes. A ghoulish chuckle came out of her mouth.

But Finella sighed. 'Nancy, trying to scare me won't work because monsters who look like monsters don't bother me, but monsters who look like teddy bears do. Now you, Nancy, I'm afraid to say, look like a monster.'

'You were always that way with your quick wit and bullshit. Still, it never changed the fact that your youngest fecked off because you were such a bitch, Finella.'

If Finella hadn't known the truth as to why her youngest had left and heard it from his own mouth, then that remark would have cut her deeply, but she took great pleasure in smiling and watching Nancy's lips return to a thin-lipped pout.

'Ha, you see, Nancy Know It All – who really only knows feck all – you thought I'd be in floods of tears, but you bullied me once and never again. Now, what is it you want? Apart from a new personality and a serious makeover.'

'Your family ruined mine, Finella. Your son killed my youngest son, and we both know that to be true.'

'Aw, feck off, Nancy. He never did. But you never ever see wrong in your kids, do you? Elspeth shagging all and sundry, Jonas burning me boy's cars and garage, and your youngest on his way to murdering my Mac.' She paused and took a deep angry breath, believing that one of the Olivers killed her Dixie. 'I swear to God, Nancy, when I find out which of your lads killed my Dixie, I'll cut his bollocks off and shove 'em down his throat. I swear I will, and then I'll hang him up and watch the fecker die a gruesome wicked death.' Her words became louder and louder until she was red in the face and foaming at the mouth. 'Your lot are fecking evil, and that grandson of yours took his own life because he didn't want to be part of an evil family known as the nutty Olivers.'

The smirk on Nancy's face instantly diminished, and her eyes narrowed. 'You nasty bitch, Finella, how dare you mention my grandson's name – in fact *our* grandson's name in that way?'

'Grow the feck up and get a grip, Nancy. That kid was not my grandson, no more than fecking King Kong is. Look at me, Nancy. Fecking look at me. I'm hardly dressed in rags, am I now? Do you think for one minute, if I believed that boy was Rohan's child, I would have let him be and not be a part of his life? No, you stupid fecking woman. Your Elspeth was dark-haired like my Rohan, and that kid was platinum blond, and my Rohan never slept with her, so leave it be. But you fecking won't, will yer? One of yours killed my boy. Admit it. Go on, Nancy, admit it.'

Nancy grinned like a psychopath. 'Yeah, and when I get my hands on your granddaughter, she will suffer. Oh, believe me' – she shook her head – 'she will suffer.'

The thought that Nancy was in the same room as her and making threats against her granddaughter sent Finella over the edge. 'You fecking won't!' she screamed, before she launched herself at Nancy.

Not expecting Finella's attack on her, Nancy lost her footing. With both hands already in her coat pockets, one hand gripping a gun, she felt the full force of Finella as the woman dived at her. The impact compelled her to pull her hands from her pockets and put them out to grab something to stop herself from falling. However, all she grabbed was Finella's suit jacket, and, to her horror, she found herself underneath Finella. It wasn't the best position to be in.

Finella was raging. Even now, in her sixties, she was ready to poleaxe Nancy. All the grief of losing her son and hearing that her granddaughter had been kidnapped at the hands of this family compelled her to fight like a cage fighter on speed. Her skirt was up by her waist as she straddled Nancy.

There was no stopping Finella now. She clawed at Nancy's eyes, enjoying every moment, as the screams became louder and louder. Then she pulled her fist back and punched Nancy across the nose. The popping sound, followed by a mist of blood spraying across her cheeks, gave her the confidence to go in even harder. Another punch caught Nancy's right eye, and immediately, it began to swell.

But what Finella did not expect to see was the state of Nancy's natural hair. She was in fact wearing a wig, and in the fight, it had turned sideways covering part of her face.

Unperturbed by the movement of her hairpiece, Nancy was more determined than ever to free herself before Finella left her blind or unconscious. She squirmed about until she managed to get her hand back inside her pocket and grip the gun. With her free hand, she grabbed Finella around the throat before pulling the gun from her pocket and sticking it into Finella's face.

Instantly, Finella stopped what she was doing, knowing that Nancy would shoot her. She knew only too well the woman was slightly deranged and unpredictable, so calling her bluff was not an option.

'Now, bitch, get the feck off of me.'

Finella's mouth gaped like a fish out of water. With her eyes on the gun, she slowly got up and staggered backwards. Her injured leg was throbbing, and her heart was pumping so fast, she thought she would go into cardiac arrest at any moment.

Glancing at the back door, hoping fervently Georgie and Rohan would not return, she sensed that Nancy, now in the ascendancy, would have no qualms in blasting them to kingdom come. She couldn't lose another family member: it was hard enough to hear that Dixie had been murdered, let alone face another death.

'See, you're not so cocky now, are ya,' said Nancy, as she straightened her wig and got to her feet. 'You look like you've just shit a live fecking goose.'

Ever the optimist, Finella felt that if she could keep Nancy talking, she might talk sense into the woman. 'Nancy, my Rohan spoke with the copper in charge of Eamonn's case, and he said that Eamonn most likely got caught up in his seat belt as he tried to escape before the car hit the water. My Mac never killed him. Why can't you just accept it was a night when things went wrong for Eamonn?'

'Your Mac killed him. That's a fact. He had the seat belt wrapped around his throat because your Mac was trying to strangle him, the fecker. I will *not* have my son buried with a stain on his name. We will bury him as a victim, not a lad who stole a car and drove off the road into the lake.'

Finella nodded. 'Oh, I see. So it's all about reputation now, is it?'

'Shut up. It's about revenge, you fecking imbecile.'

Finella shook her head. 'No, it's not, Nancy. It's about bitterness and jealousy. It's about how the village dislikes your family and likes mine because my boys do the right thing and yours don't. Kidnapping a young woman? What in God's name were you thinking?'

Nancy's face suddenly darkened. Her eyes were like two black beads. 'Your granddaughter killed *two* of my boys. Fecking murdered them.' She poked herself in the chest. 'My boys!' she bellowed. 'She fecking *killed* them, Finella.'

Finella's mouth went suddenly dry. She couldn't imagine Dixie-Lee hurting anyone. 'You must have it all wrong, Nancy. Dixie-Lee is a child. She wouldn't—'

'A child? She's fecking eighteen. I bore my son at the same age, and so did you. And she did kill my Chubs *and* my Jerry. My sweet fecking boys.'

Finella knew exactly who Nancy was referring to and she also knew damn well they were anything but sweet. Chubs had been accused of rape and indecent assault and served a few years for domestic violence. Jerry was also similar in nature, considering his criminal record, and he served five years for attacking a local schoolgirl he'd been stalking for a year.

Finella decided not to bring up the woman's family's past, but she couldn't just leave things like this. 'If Dixie-Lee killed them, then, knowing her, she must have had a very good reason. She's not a hardened criminal. You know, she's studying law at college.'

'Shut up bragging about your kids.'

'That's what grandmothers and mothers do.'

'And where the feck are you going with this, Finella?'

'I was just saying that Dixie-Lee wouldn't hurt anyone for no reason, and I think you know that.'

Finella could see that Nancy had suddenly felt the chill of those words. 'Be honest with yourself, Nancy, for fecking once in your life.'

'My lads are good lads.' Her words petered off as if she hardly believed them herself.

'Listen, you know what it's like back in our country. We give birth to a handful of lads. But we never know if they will stay on this side of the law or not. When they fall on the wrong side, right away, we blame ourselves, but saying it out loud is something we never do. But, Nancy, it's not *our* fault. We have them home at teatime, maybe at breakfast, but they are making a name for themselves in the big wide fecking world the rest of the time. Whether that be a good name or a bad one, it's still a fecking name.'

Just when Finella thought she was getting through to the woman, a sudden change in her expression confirmed otherwise. Her lips returned to that bitter thin line, and her eyes clouded with anger right before she morphed into a demonic puppet with a shrill voice.

'You have no idea what I will do to you and your family, but believe me' – she screamed – 'I will make it so nasty you will be vomiting through your fecking arsehole.'

With no warning, Nancy engaged the gun and pulled the trigger. But she completely missed her target. The bullet hit a mirror, which smashed into a million pieces. The blast showered them both, and the noise was so loud, the shock had Finella almost wetting herself.

Finella screamed. If the explosion didn't make Nancy jump, the scream certainly did. The sound of the gunshot and the exploding mirror compelled Finella to crouch down and try to shield her head. The echo rang in her ears and vibrated along her jaw. She didn't look up, in fear that she would see the second bullet coming. Instead, she just closed her eyes and hoped.

Finally, when she got her senses together, she realised Nancy had left the house.

CHAPTER TWENTY-EIGHT

Ten minutes earlier

Georgie stumbled and lost her footing, but Rohan managed to catch her before she fell. Simply feeling his hand to steady her gave her butterflies, just like a lovesick teenager.

'I should have brought the torch.'

'I could use my phone, but the battery is almost dead,' he replied.

'It's okay. We're almost there. It's that house second from the end of the terrace.'

'I am not surprised that this alleyway is never used. It's completely overgrown,' said Rohan, as he removed a bramble from his jeans.

'Yes, except our garage.'

'Do you use it?'

'No, but . . .' She paused. 'Dixie used it.'

'I know he slept in there before, well, before, you know what I mean.'

'No, Rohan, he used it afterwards as well, but clearly for a different purpose. But you're right about the alleyway. It is so overgrown. I rarely come down here. But here's the thing. I noticed there was something different about the garage. Dixie put a new door with a huge padlock on it. And another thing: the frame has been reinforced. But what I don't know is why.'

'I'll take a look at it tomorrow.'

'I think he held on to a few secrets.'

'He was probably trying to settle in by slowly easing back into family life. You know how these things are, Georgie. You were in the Army. He would have told you everything once he felt safe and secure.'

Georgie stopped walking. 'He had fucking *six months*, Rohan. You don't understand, do you? No one does, except maybe Dixie-Lee. But he wasn't the same man. He was so quiet. And he'd go off and come back when he wanted to. Then, he would stare at the TV. He hardly bloody spoke to me.'

'I want to ask you something, Georgie, and I know it's really personal to you and Dixie, but . . .'

She laughed. 'I know what you want to know. Did I sleep with him?'

Rohan tutted. 'Sorry, it's not my business. You were husband and wife.'

She turned to face him, clutching his arms. 'Rohan, we were *not* husband and wife! Christ, I thought I was a widow for all those years, and then, when he came back, it was as if I was supposed to carry on like he was my husband, but, Rohan, he was a *stranger*. Sure we had sex a couple of times.' She looked down at her feet. 'Now it's my turn to be open and honest. When we did, I imagined it was you.'

Rohan lifted his hands and clutched both sides of her face. 'I wish, with all my heart, it had been.' Before he kissed her forehead, he said, 'Look, Georgie, we both like each other and yet this is wrong. Dixie isn't even cold, and I have this urge to kiss you.'

She nodded. A lump wedged in her throat and tears sprang into her eyes. Whether it was from feeling guilty of how she truly felt about Rohan or because the time she'd had with Dixie since he re-entered her life had been so woefully inadequate, she wasn't sure. But she was determined now that she was going to go after the man she truly wanted. She'd had years of heartache. Surely, she was allowed to have a man in her life, someone she loved.

'Rohan, I want you, and I understand if it might look as though it is too soon. But I want to ask if you would wait for me. I am too old to play coy and dance around the question. I just need to know.'

He leaned in and gently kissed her lips. As he pulled away, he nodded. 'I think Dixie knew.'

'What? How?'

'He probably saw us together that day in the kitchen. And a week ago, he asked me to come to London and meet him for a talk. He needed to discuss something with me.'

'Really? Do you have any idea what it was?'

Rohan shook his head and dropped his hands by his side. 'I don't know, but in answer to your question, I *will* wait for you. I want to tell Ma before we do anything, because any cloak-and-dagger stuff is not what I'm about, and I don't think you are into that, either.'

'Do you think she will understand?'

'Our Ma is the most understanding woman on the planet, and she loves us both, so, yes, she will. Let her grieve first for Dixie, as we all need to, until this mess is sorted out.'

They walked to the end of the alleyway and onto the side street, turned left, and walked back past two houses before they arrived outside the neighbour's house.

Georgie knocked. It was so late, she wondered if the neighbour even knew his mother was missing.

However, when the door opened abruptly, there in a dressing gown and with a five o'clock shadow stood Peter Loveridge. 'Mrs Deacon, what brings you here at this late hour?'

Georgie had always loved Peter's well-to-do accent and his beaming smile. 'I think your mother came to see me.'

Peter frowned. 'Is that a joke, or are you a medium?'

It took Georgie a few seconds before she realised what Peter was saying. 'Oh no, I am so sorry. Has your mother passed away?'

'Yes, yes, a few months ago now, so whoever paid you a visit, it certainly wasn't my mother.'

The sudden realisation hit Georgie. Her eyes widened, and she stared at Rohan. 'Oh no. Your mother is in the house. The door won't lock. We have to get back.'

As they ran back along the road and turned into the alleyway, they heard a bang.

'No!' screamed Georgie, as she ran towards her house.

Rohan was at her heels, and in the distance, they could just about see a woman running in the opposite direction. However, the figure wasn't at all fit, and he could see the person was no match for Georgie.

'Rohan, see to your mum.'

Before Rohan could argue, Georgie was off running through the overgrown weeds and brambles like a cheetah chasing a gutless poacher.

Georgie knew she could outrun the woman. The bang she recognised as a gunshot, and the explosion was, she suspected, the sound of a bullet hitting glass. As she tore along the alleyway, she felt her adrenaline spiking, along with her rage; it evoked her primal instinct to hunt down her prey and fight to the death. She could only guess that the woman was Jesse Oliver's mother. Hugh had informed her of how deranged this family was. But although her daughter was now safe, no one was more enraged than a mother whose daughter had been kidnapped by these monsters. As soon as she was almost within reach, she had to stop dead.

The woman spun around and pointed a gun at her. However, she was so breathless, she could hardly keep the gun straight. Her hands shook so rigorously that she couldn't release the safety mechanism, and Georgie knew how hard that was to do. Assessing her risk, she had to act quickly. It was dark, so the woman wouldn't have a complete vision; she was also out of breath and shaking.

Georgie didn't stand with her hands up; she made a sudden sideways move and rolled into the long grass before Mother Oliver could shoot her.

Before the woman could pivot and aim the gun, Georgie fly-kicked her in the hip. And as she went down, Georgie leaped on top of her, grabbed her wrist, and smashed it violently against the hard ground, forcing her to let go of the gun.

With rage still flowing through her veins, Georgie pulled her fist back and viciously punched her in the head. It was then she noticed how the woman was already bruised, with a swollen right eye. *So Finella had put the woman through her paces*, she thought.

Holding her on the ground, Georgie glared into the eye that wasn't swollen. 'You fucked with the wrong family. I would never hurt an elderly lady, but when fucking needs must, I'm all action. Now, where is your son Noel, or is he really called Jesse?'

The woman coughed and spat the blood from her mouth. She then tried to inhale. 'I . . . I . . . will die before . . . I tell you.'

Georgie jumped up, kicked the gun into the bushes, reached down, and grabbed the woman by her arm, yanking her to her feet.

'You are coming with me, and I swear to God, if my mother-in-law has so much as a hair out of place, I'll put your head through my fucking window.'

She pushed Jesse's mother in the back, forcing her to walk towards her house. 'Go on, keep walking.'

By the time they reached Georgie's back garden, Nancy was ready to collapse. She'd torn the muscles in her legs thinking she could run like a twenty-year-old, and then when she fell to her side from the harsh fly kick, she felt her rib crack and her hip almost dislocate.

***

Understanding that her sons were on their way, Nancy Oliver was still confident that this wouldn't end well for the Deacons. They had warned her to stay low until they arrived, but she wasn't going to take orders from them. She wanted to do things her way. And as the matriarchal head of the family, she was the one in charge. She wanted to show her boys how it should be done since they had already messed it up. Her plan had been to get inside Georgie's house and hold a gun to her head, to force her to call Dixie-Lee. And when her boys finally arrived, they would cart Dixie-Lee away as well as Georgie and make her watch as they killed her precious kid.

She had forced herself to hold it together and suck up the grief even while she held Chubs, her dying son, and stared at Jerry, who was lying in a pool of blood – dead – as she devised her plan.

Sudden shocking grief had been a part of her life. She had never got over her grandson's suicide or her Eamonn's death, which was now almost confirmed as a case of murder. She believed Mac had killed him. She had to think that because she had to be angry with someone. Her bitterness also stretched to Rohan for not being a father to her grandson. If he had, then as far as she was concerned, her grandson would still be alive, and now, she wanted to end the lives of every Deacon, including the girl.

Jesse had already messed the plan up by leaving Chubs and Jerry in charge of Dixie-Lee. His only job was to get Georgie to coax Rohan to a place where he would be wide open with no weapon because they knew that tackling a Deacon who had forewarning would never end well. However, ambushing a Deacon when they least expected it would guarantee a capture.

Dixie's slaughter had been a piece of cake, and that was all her genius idea. And the police believed she was a credible witness to the murder of Dixie because they would never have thought that an old lady who arranged flowers at the church and worked for Cats Protection would be in any way responsible for the man's execution. The plan had worked perfectly, so much so that it had secured the temporary incarceration of Mac and Brodie, leaving Rohan wide open and with no protection from the other two.

Collectively, they had slowly put the plan together by eagerly watching the moves of all the Deacons. They had quickly established that the Deacons, apart from Dixie, were never alone or in a position where they could take out either one of them. However, they'd managed to plant a gun in Mac's car; it happened to be Mac's old gun that they had stolen from him the night of the lake incident. It was a shame that it wasn't the gun used to murder Dixie, but they couldn't be in two places at once, so they'd planted it in Mac's boot before shooting Dixie. Stupidly, Jesse had assumed that Mac had used the gun in the past and the police would have Mac and possibly Brodie charged with their previous crimes also. Jesse never dreamed the gun was clean, but there was, in fact, no history with the weapon. So their scheme hadn't worked because they had made crucial mistakes. What they hadn't indeed factored in was the strength of Georgie, but their second mistake was underestimating Georgie's daughter.

Her own daughter Elspeth, who was still utterly obsessed with Rohan, especially since her son had taken his own life, had followed everything he was involved in, including collecting the reports of Dixie-Lee being in a coma and the arrest of Georgie Deacon. Elspeth had sourced every newspaper and trawled every website for any report, photograph, and follow-up. It was because it became Elspeth's daily job to know where Georgie worked, her hours, where Dixie-Lee went to college, and what she was studying. She had even sat in Henry's café and listened to the men who worked with Dixie, so she knew where he worked and what he was doing.

However, it didn't end there. Elspeth became increasingly angry with Georgie because one reporter's photograph showed Rohan and Georgie together. They were looking at each other, and from that image, Elspeth had concluded that he was in love with Georgie, and so she hated the woman with a passion.

Nancy had tried to justify it, but she couldn't. What she had learned from Elspeth was everything about the Deacon family. As much as she wanted revenge for her son and her grandson's death, she wanted revenge for her daughter more. She hated seeing her daughter becoming the soulless shadow of the person she once was. Elspeth barely washed, she took drugs, and Nancy knew that if she didn't get this right, she would also lose her daughter. The death of

Georgie Deacon may well bring Elspeth back from the hell she was living in.

***

Nancy felt Georgie's firm grip on her arm as she was dragged along the garden path and into the house.

Rohan was consoling Finella.

Nancy didn't bother acting unperturbed. She wasn't in a position to act hard and shout her mouth off, but when her boys turned up, there would be a war. She had no doubt about that.

'Nancy Oliver,' said Rohan, as he stood by the side of the sofa, resting his hand on his mother's shoulder, who was seated and picking a piece of glass out of her hair. 'The bane of my fecking life.' He shook his head. 'What is this really all about?' He didn't shout, but his words were firm and threatening.

'You know what it's about. I am going to even the odds. Mac killed my son—'

'You are insane. All of you are fecking mental. I will tell you about that night, shall I? And what led up to it.'

Nancy suddenly felt lightheaded. Her initial adrenaline spike was wearing off, and she could feel the pain in her face, ribs, and hip. Unexpectedly, she staggered backwards, but Georgie pushed her into an armchair before she fell and cracked anything else.

'I'll make some sweet tea.'

Beads of sweat coated Nancy's top lip, and although her eyes were red and purple, the rest of her face was a deathly grey colour. 'Thank you, Finella,' she said, as Finella headed to the kitchen.

'Oh, I am not making tea to be kind. I want you awake to listen to what Rohan has to say, and I want you to understand and then feel shame and guilt and go to your grave knowing you have made an unforgivable mistake which left you a bitter, spiteful woman,' Finella replied, with a caustic tone in her voice.

Rohan stood dead opposite Nancy. 'Sixteen years ago, a young woman – let's just call her Jane – was raped by your son Chubs.'

Nancy stared with no reaction as if this was old hat.

'And when she went to the police, they wanted to know the ins and outs. They made her feel dirty and when they asked if she could be examined, she ran out of the station and told her father everything. He went to the police and demanded they do something. When the police interviewed your bastard son Chubs, he took umbrage.' He pointed a finger in her face. 'And so your son, ol' Billy Big Bollocks, Chubs, took revenge. He broke into Jane's house and stole everything of value, including a gold watch which he placed in a pawn shop in the next town.'

Nancy shook her head. 'I don't believe you.'

'Ah, see, Nancy, you do believe me because you know what your sons are like. Anyway, Jane's father asked if we could do anything.' Rohan bit his lip and flared his nostrils. 'Now, little Jane, the sweet kid, was destroyed. It bothered me, but it bothered Mac the most because he liked her, and he liked her a lot. That's probably why Chubs raped her.' He stepped forward, placing his hands on his hips. 'We found Chubs in a pub pestering another young lady, so we took him outside, and he told us where he had put the stolen goods.'

'What, just like that? He told you?'

Rohan nodded. 'With a little coaxing.'

'You're all fucking bullies!'

'No, no, no, Nancy, bullies we are not. Anyway, please don't interrupt. We returned all the items to Jane, and Chubs agreed to stay away. However, he went back on his agreement. He stalked that girl and followed her to a club that Mac was in where he was having a quiet drink with Jane. Your fat fucker of a son called all the brothers for backup because he couldn't take Mac down alone.' Taking a deep breath, Rohan's lip tightened as his jaw clenched tight. 'They planned to kill my brother. Elspeth, your deranged daughter, called Mac outside the club. And then they beat him, took his gun, and your Eamonn, who, by the way, was in the club getting pissed, decided to act the big man. They forced Mac into . . . now, this is the crunch. They forced Mac into the boot of a BMW, a stolen BMW. There is no fecking access from the boot to the back seat. It wasn't a fecking SUV. Your son drove like a lunatic, fuelled by booze and arrogance to prove his worth to your other sons. In a state of recklessness, he took a corner way too sharp and ended up in the lake. The boot opened on impact, and, apparently, it can do that. Mac swam out. In fact, he swam to the top, gulped air, and then he swam back down to rescue your son, but the silt and muck made it so murky, he couldn't see Eamonn, and so he assumed he'd escaped. The fact that we now know they have found your son with the seat belt around his neck is more than likely from him trying to escape. But you, Nancy Oliver, must think the worst. You had to take your grief out on us. You need help, or prison, or a noose around your neck.'

Nancy stared, listening to every word, knowing in her mind that Rohan's explanation was probably true. She loved her boys, but she also knew that Chubs had issues. They all did, even her daughter, with her obsessions.

She lowered her eyes and suddenly felt the sting of a tear. Exhaustion had taken hold of her, and her emotions were coming to the forefront. Whether it was grief, a moment of sanity, or simply a time to be truthful to herself, either way, she felt the tears roll down her cheeks. Once they began, it was as if the floodgates had opened. But there was no arm around her shoulders and no kind words. Instead, she had to accept a cup of tea shoved in her hand and Finella's harsh words.

'I said earlier that our lads are mainly the result of their own doing, not us mothers, but I lied, Nancy. I fecking lied because your sons and your daughter are fecked up, bitter, twisted younger versions of you, and, of course, not forgetting your pervert of a father, a schoolteacher, who preyed on young lads. But not my lads, though, because he knew my husband would have beaten the fecking shite right out of him. You came from shite, and you raised shite. You made your kids angry and jealous. You raised monsters, and I will see you either all dead or all behind bars, so they can never hurt another person again.'

Nancy didn't argue; she was sobbing.

'If you want to put all of this right, then you need to tell the truth to the police because God will send you to hell for this, Nancy Oliver.'

CHAPTER TWENTY-NINE

Raj was in a deep sleep, having hardly slept at all in the last couple of days. Petra's hair was tickling his nose, and when he turned over in the bed, he realised it wasn't her hair that had woken him but his phone buzzing. 'Damn,' he muttered, annoyed he had somehow switched the phone to silent mode. He sat up straight and swooned in an instant; his eyes were blurry, so he struggled to make out the phone number. Once he could focus fully, he knew he didn't recognise it. However, who would call him at five in the morning? Pushing himself up and off the bed, he grasped he was naked and then had a flashback from last night. Turning around, he saw Petra's bare backside poking out from the sheets. He smiled for a second before he answered the call. 'Raj speaking.'

'Detective, it's me, Matthew, er, Matthew—'

'Yeah, mate, I know who you are. Why are you calling me at this hour? I was asleep.'

'I listened to what you said. You know, about doing my job properly, and you were right. I know they pulled the protection from Georgie Deacon. I don't know why but, anyway, I thought, on my way home, I'd pass her house and make sure everything was okay. There's a car parked at the end of the road with three men in it. I phoned the station to run the plates, and it's registered as stolen.'

Raj hopped around looking for his pants. 'Are you in uniform, Matt?'

'No, Raj, I'm off duty. I'm in my mum's car, but I'm parked just along from Mrs Deacon's house. What shall I do?'

'Right, now, listen and listen good. No fucking heroics. You stay in the car, and if they approach you, pretend to be on your phone. Don't engage. Do nothing. But if you can see their movements, keep me updated. Oh yeah, you didn't notice if one of them had a scar running the length of his jaw, did you?'

'No, it's too dark. The streetlamps are terrible on this estate.'

'Okay, I think I know who they are, so don't interact with them. They are dangerous men and could well be armed. I'll have backup on the way. What's their number plate?'

Level reeled off the registration plate and the description of the car.

'Good lad,' said Raj, as he scribbled it down on a notepad, which he always kept by the side of his bed.

'What if they go into Mrs Deacon's house?'

'I am going to call her now. Prewarn her.'

'But, Gov, she's just a—'

'If you say woman, Matthew, I will have your guts for garters. And, by the way, she ain't *any* woman. She's ex-military and can fuck up a man better than most men can. Don't be blinded by her feminine features. You would want her on your side in a fight. I promise you that.'

As Raj put on his trousers, his mind went back to the two Marx murders. Even though Georgie had been charged with their deaths and then exonerated, he knew she had committed a double murder and probably more. However, even knowing what he knew about it, he had already decided not to get involved. Besides, his idea of the good and the bad had changed lately. The force which people depended on had some of the dregs of society thrown in among the good coppers.

He called Georgie's mobile, and he was surprised she picked up so soon.

'Georgie, it's Raj. Listen, a car with three men inside is parked at the end of your road.'

'So the Olivers are here, then?'

'How do you know that?'

Georgie glanced at Nancy. 'Because the mother, who is pathetically in disguise with her matted wig and old lady croaky voice, is in my living room.'

'*What?* Are you okay?'

'Yeah, I am, but she sure frightened the hell out of Finella.'

'Frightened her?'

'She had a shooter, Raj. She tried to kill Finella but missed and smashed my mirror. Finella is picking glass out of her hair, even now.'

Raj quietly gasped. 'Is Finella okay?'

'Yes, she's fine, so what's the plan?'

'I am calling for backup. I'll have the roads secured. Don't open the doors. We will capture these bastards, Georgie. Now, what about the mother?' asked Raj, having suspected the woman would be held prisoner.

'She is sitting here having a cup of tea. I think she also had a bit of a shock.'

Raj smiled to himself, knowing that the mother would, without a doubt, have a shock trying to mess with Georgie Deacon.

Petra stirred and turned over, so Raj decided to leave her to sleep; she couldn't do much anyway.

'I'll call you in a few minutes. I need to secure the area because they are probably armed, and we know they are dangerous.'

'Okay, Raj, then I will have to keep Nancy Oliver intact. Oh, and if they do get in, I can use reasonable force to protect my home, myself, and my family. That's right, yeah?'

'You know you can.' Raj nervously laughed before he ended the call, wondering if she was joking. He guessed she probably wasn't, and if he hadn't called her, she might have taken the woman's head off – literally. He wondered if what she deemed as reasonable force was an excuse to annihilate them.

'Raj, what are you doing? It's only fucking five o'clock,' said Petra, as she pulled the sheet up around her naked body.

'The Olivers are outside Georgie's place. I'm going over there with backup. I wanna nail these bastards.'

'You know how the armed unit can get a bit trigger-happy? Make sure they don't kill them before we know where Dixie-Lee is.'

Raj blushed slightly and then nervously smiled. 'Dixie-Lee has escaped their capture, but she is in hiding for now.'

Petra didn't return the smile; instead, she frowned. 'And why didn't you tell me? I'm supposed to be your partner.'

'I was so tired and—'

'Not too tired to rewrite the Kama Sutra. Anyway, you'd better be off. I'll go to the station. Fitz is back, and he will want a brief.'

'Fitz has returned from his holiday?'

'Yeah, I saw him pull up just before I left the station.'

Raj looked at his phone and decided he would dial Fitzgerald's number, as this was the time he definitely needed the boss's help, especially in calling out the armed response team. There was no way he would engage with Drake, and he wondered if Drake was writing his resignation over a bottle of cheap whisky.

The phone rang only twice before a sober voice answered. 'Fitzgerald here.'

'Gov, it's Raj. I need an armed response team and serious backup at Georgie Deacon's house. I believe three men sitting in a car at the end of her road are the Olivers. They are more than likely planning to cause harm, and I believe they are armed, and I know they are dangerous.'

'Raj, I'm not fully up to date with the case. I understand there has been a right royal fuck-up at the station with the Deacons. Damn those Tonbridge guttersnipes. Anyway, I trust you, and I'll authorise it right away. Where will you be?'

'I'm on my way now to Mrs Deacon's house. I'll be there in fifteen. As I said, the Olivers are parked at the end of the road, and young Matthew Level, a PC, is parked at the other end keeping a look out.'

'Raj, I will organise it from my end. Keep me posted.'

***

Georgie grinned as she stared at Nancy. 'Give me your phone.'

Nancy's eyes widened. 'What?'

'I said, give me your phone. I don't want to have to search your person for it.'

'You might catch something, Georgie, the dirty minger,' spat Finella.

Georgie wanted to laugh at the old-fashioned terminology.

Nancy didn't protest. She slid her hand in her pocket, removed her mobile, and handed it to Georgie. 'Passcode is all sixes,' she said, in defeat. However, she hadn't anticipated for a second what Georgie would do next.

With no one flying off the handle, the room was calm. However, that was Georgie's way when she wanted to do damage, and she could be the most premeditated person on earth. A master at planning.

After tapping in the passcode, she saw a text from Jesse. It read

Mum, if you have Georgie secured, open the front door. I'll go in the front, and Jared will go in the back.

Georgie looked at Nancy and smiled. This was gonna be a walk in the fucking park. She checked previous text messages from Nancy to Jesse, and it seemed they weren't too hot on spelling, so she wrote a misspelled message back telling him to come in through the front door and for the others to remain in the car. The front door would be open.

Once done and she could see the text was read, she deleted the message, wiped her prints from the phone, and handed it back.

Rohan didn't say a word. He watched Georgie leave the living room and enter the kitchen. He knew she could handle this situation, and whatever happened, he would be by her side.

Once Georgie was in the kitchen, she stared at the wires, and for a second, she contemplated using them; however, she thought about Dixie-Lee and knew she had to do damage to Jesse Oliver but not get herself a lengthy prison sentence at the same time. Grabbing a few potatoes, she quickly peeled one, leaving the bag on the kitchen side, and then held the knife, which was now coated in starch. The blade wasn't large but it was long enough to cause an injury but not necessarily large enough to kill someone. Reasonable force. 'Rohan, can you and Finella move to the fireplace.' She then opened the front door, but not wide open, and waited. *No one kidnaps my daughter without feeling the consequences.*

***

Raj drove as though he had just stolen the car through the streets from Bromley towards St Mary Cray. His phone rang, and he'd already saved Matthew Level's number under 'Good lad'.

'What's happening, Matthew?'

'Raj, one of the men from the car is heading towards Mrs Deacon's place. He's walking like a fucking Ninja Turtle. Shit, Raj, I think he's got a gun.'

'Matthew, can he see you?'

'No, Raj.'

'Listen, sink down now in your seat. Don't let him know you are there.'

'But—'

'Do as I say.'

As he ended the call, he could feel his back wet with sweat, even though the early morning chill was enough to freeze the balls off a brass monkey.

He called Georgie, but all he got was voicemail. 'Pick up, Georgie, pick up.'

He tried again before it dawned on him. She was obviously up to something. 'Oh fuck! Don't kill him, Georgie. Killing – that's not reasonable force. Shit!' he muttered, under his breath, willing her to be level-headed now that he suspected Jesse Oliver had nearly killed Henry and kidnapped Dixie-Lee. Georgie would never spare an ounce of empathy or compassion for the man.

***

Georgie retained her composure. She had to be sure that it was Jesse who was about to enter her house and not a neighbour or any of the drippy police. She held her breath and watched the door open. First, she saw two hands clutching a gun before she saw the side of his face. There was a long scar that ran the length of the man's chin. It was Jesse. At that moment, she wanted to kill him, but she had to be in control. In a flash, she lunged the knife in his face scraping his eye, knowing he would be blinded and in pain and disoriented before she stabbed his rib and then his side. The movement was so fast that he barely had time to get a round off before he dropped the gun and clutched his face, now screaming like a child. The bullet shot through the hallway and straight through the back door.

Georgie briefly congratulated herself for ensuring Rohan and Finella were out of harm's way before she kicked the gun up the hallway out of his reach.

Rohan flew into the hallway to check Georgie was okay. He knew she'd had a plan, but he had no idea what it was.

Jesse Oliver, the man he'd hated all his life, was bent over yelping. 'My eye, my fecking eye.'

As Jesse doubled over, gripping his side, and knowing he was bleeding pretty badly, he believed he was dying.

Georgie searched his pockets, but he was too alarmed to stop her.

'Passcode?'

Jesse didn't answer until Georgie pointed the knife at him. 'Wanna another dig?'

'It's . . . it's . . . all the fours.'

She opened the text message and deleted the one from Nancy's phone before she gave it back to him.

In all the carnage, Nancy didn't move. She stared at her son with no emotion.

It was Finella who clocked it. She walked over to Nancy, who was casually taking another sip of her tea, and said to her in a compassionate voice, 'You don't love him, Nancy, do you? Why?'

Nancy thought for a moment, took another sip of tea, and then looked up at Finella. A sad smile tugged at her cheeks. 'Because deep down, I know the truth about that boy.'

'Mum, help me, help me!' Jesse screamed, in a baby voice.

Finella looked back at the man sitting in the hallway with one hand holding his eye and the other holding his side. There was something extraordinary about him. He seemed to have reverted to a little child, and even his babyish voice was so pathetic that she had to stare at him because surely she wasn't hearing the hardman Jesse Oliver.

'Mum, I'm dying. Help me, please, someone.'

'You're not dying, ya prick,' said Georgie. 'I'm not allowed to kill you, but I can hurt you really, really bad, so stay in pain and shut the fuck up. You are giving me a headache. And, oh yeah, that was for kidnapping and terrifying my girl and for the nightmares that she will probably endure in the future. Oh, and before you do shut up, why did you carve a cross into my husband's head, eh? You sick bastard.'

The moment he smirked, she pushed the knife into his neck. 'Why?'

'All right, all right, please. Look I . . . I wanted to confuse everyone. I knew the story about the cross from the news. Carving a cross . . . the filth would think it was one of those Marxes. It would throw the filth off our scent. We needed options, in case . . . in case . . .'

'In case what?' Georgie hissed.

'In case, Mac found the stuff in his boot and guessed it was . . . was . . . us.'

‘So you carved the cross as a back-up plan?’ she hissed, before she kicked him hard in the leg.

Jesse nodded.

Finella looked at Nancy before she kneeled beside the armchair, making herself lower than Nancy. ‘What is the truth, Nancy? Please tell me.’

Finella could see a tear trickle down Nancy’s nose.

‘I saw Rohan. It was the first time I have seen him close up. When he helped to pick the glass out of your hair, he had his arm around you. I watched his mannerisms.’

Finella was lost. ‘And?’

‘He is nothing like my grandson, nothing at all. I was a fool to believe Elspeth and Jesse when they said he was. I think it was more Elspeth’s wishful thinking and Jesse’s detest for Rohan and your other boys.’ She stopped for a moment when she heard the police sirens and lowered her eyes.

‘Go on.’

But she didn’t have a chance because Jesse, in his bitterness, glared at Georgie. ‘Your precious daughter will be going to prison for killing me two brothers, so feck you, Georgie Deacon.’

‘No, she won’t, Jesse, no, she won’t,’ said Nancy.

Everyone was stunned into silence, listening to what else Nancy had to say.

‘The family have been through enough. My two sons, Chubs and Jerry, had a fight, and they both managed to hurt each other and they bled to death.’

‘No, Mum, no, that’s not what happened.’

Nancy wiped the tear away. ‘Jesse, I was the last person to speak with Chubs, and that’s what I will be telling the police.’

‘No, no, that’s not right. Mum, that’s not right. And Rohan, Mum? What about him? He is responsible for our little Rohan’s death. He should have stepped up and been the father.’ He stopped when he saw his mother get up from the armchair and walk towards him, her battered face a ball of fury.

‘That scream of yours, Jesse, that childish voice, is our little Rohan’s. His blond hair was like yours when you were a child. You were my only blond-haired child, just like young Rohan, Jesse.’ She stepped closer. ‘You and Elspeth were inseparable. I knew it wasn’t right, what you both did. And your hatred of the Deacons –

because Elspeth was obsessed with Rohan – fuelled that hate. So much so that you brainwashed me, making me believe that Mac killed Eamonn. And all the time you knew the truth. He was in the boot of the car, not in the back. And Eamonn was a little shit, God rest his soul. But you planned to murder Mac. You were going to kill him, and now this. No, Jesse, enough is enough. I would have died for each of you, but seeing how Rohan loves his mother, I know that none of you love me like that, so when the police question me, I will be telling them that Dixie-Lee escaped and my two sons killed each other.' She paused and shook her head. 'Jesse, you are on the run for a list of offences that include shooting down Dixie Deacon in cold blood. You will be going to prison for a long time, and know this, Son. I won't be visiting you.'

'Mum, please help me . . . I'm . . . dying! Look!' He showed her his hand that was covered in blood.

Nancy didn't say a word. She watched the police enter through the front door and then she stepped back, holding her hands together, awaiting the handcuffs.

It was Raj, who followed in behind the armed police. He looked at Georgie, relieved to see her, and then he glanced down at Jesse, who was very much alive, although seriously injured. Then he looked back at Georgie, who pointed to the small kitchen knife on the worktop. 'Reasonable force.'

Raj rolled his eyes and noticed the smashed glass in the back door. 'He fired a weapon. But no one got shot, I guess.'

Georgie smiled. 'They were all by the fireplace when he came in. I was peeling spuds, and I saw the gun and had to protect my family.'

Raj looked around and saw the police arresting Rohan. 'No, no, he is not a suspect. This guy on the floor is. Someone call the paramedics and arrest that woman.' He pointed to Nancy.

Nancy didn't put up a fight; she looked at Georgie and mouthed the words 'I'm sorry.'

CHAPTER THIRTY

As soon as the team of police and the armed response unit had gone, having taken the Olivers with them, Georgie felt her shoulders relax.

Raj remained behind, confident that Fitzgerald had the situation well under control. He had left earlier to escort the Olivers personally to the station.

'Reasonable force? Or was it a fragment of revenge? Like last time, perhaps?' he said, followed by a wink.

'Revenge, I guess. My girl has been through enough, and the thought of that man kidnapping her. Well, I couldn't let it go. Anyway, you have a few notches on your belt now, Raj.'

The sudden evaporation of his smile was confirmation enough that he was still sensitive to the actions of the police as a whole. They were at one about that. Neither particularly cared for them.

'Sorry, Raj, that wasn't supposed to come out that way. I guess I still have a bitter taste in my mouth, and I must make a conscious effort not to lump all the police together.' She smiled. 'You're a good one, Raj, and I mean it. You have been a godsend to me.'

'Oh yeah, really?'

'Come on, Raj, who do I let in my home? Yeah, mate, you, because you are the copper I can trust. You are one of the good guys.'

'Why don't you stay for a coffee? You look like you could do with one,' said Finella, with her hands on her hips.

'I could do with a good sleep and a shower, and I don't care in what order, but thank you, Finella. I also have a ton of paperwork to fill out. Not just the Oliver arrests, but what happened to Mac and Brodie. I'll not let it go.'

He looked at all three pairs of eyes and returned his gaze to Finella. 'I promise you, Finella, that I will make sure those coppers get done for their behaviour. I thought the station was overrun with these new recruits, but, as it turns out, I do have a lot of support. Even the big boss Fitzgerald will be formalising the complaint.'

'They should be shot for what they did to my Mac. I haven't seen him yet, but from what Hugh told me, he was pretty badly hurt, and I won't rest until heads roll.'

‘I don’t know about shooting them.’ He laughed. ‘We don’t tend to use that type of punishment in this country, but I want them out of the police force, and I will push for criminal action to be brought against them.’

He smiled when he saw Finella’s face light up; it was just a shame that it was in retaliation for the actions of a few bad coppers.

‘Do you think you have enough on the Olivers to keep them behind bars?’ asked Rohan, who hadn’t said too much, until now.

‘Jesse Oliver is wanted for a string of offences and is known to be on the run. As for Jared, he is wanted for questioning regarding aiding and abetting a murder, and Jonas will be tried alongside them for kidnapping.’

‘And what about this Elspeth? I bet she was the one who helped Jesse burn down the café,’ said Georgie.

‘Quite possibly, but we haven’t found her yet. We will, though. Yes, in time, we will track her down.’

‘Raj, will you be travelling anywhere near the hospital? I want to see my son.’

‘I can drive you there. That’s no problem, Finella. I’d love to. I’ll start the car and warm it up for you.’

As the door closed behind him, Finella turned to her son. ‘Rohan, my boy.’ She stroked his cheek as though he was five years old. ‘You’re a good man. You were always a good kid, and you were the one who strived to do the right thing. But listen to me, love. There are times in our lives when our hearts overrule that, and quite rightly so. I loved Dixie. He was my baby, but I lost him. I grieved for years believing he was dead, and when he came back, he was a stranger, even to me, Rohan.’

With a sudden flush to his cheeks, Rohan looked away, embarrassed.

‘It’s all right, Son. I know you love Georgie. I’m your mammy, and I know about these things.’

Georgie looked to the floor like a schoolgirl in the headmaster’s office awaiting her punishment.

‘You can’t help who you love, and you two were in love before Dixie came back into our lives. And I know you, Rohan. You will be eaten up with guilt. But understand this. You will be feeling guilty because you think you are doing something bad behind Dixie’s back. But Dixie didn’t love Georgie like you do.’ Then, she turned to Georgie. 'And you, darling, love Rohan. Having stayed single for so long living in the past when you and Dixie had only been married for such a short time and with the world as you knew it full of champagne and roses, who knows if it would have ever worked out. You were both children yourselves. And I have to give you credit. You took a stranger into your home and tried to make a marriage that died many years ago and inject love and life back into it. You did your best, love.'

Georgie looked up, her eyes filled with tears. 'I did try. I gave it everything I had, but I couldn't. And to be honest, I don't think it's what he wanted either. There was no chemistry, no passion, and I'm not sure we were even friends. Dixie-Lee kind of got it as well. I think she could see we weren't happy. I don't know if it was the PTSD or something more, but it was as if he was going through the motions of life. Maybe that's what PTSD does to a person.' She decided not to mention her recent thoughts regarding Dixie, after finding kids toys, a baseball cap, and trainers.

Finella shook her head. 'No, it wasn't anything as complicated as that. I believe he had a life somewhere in between your marriage and his return.'

Georgie nodded. 'You could be right. There was so much we never spoke about. Actually, he wouldn't speak about the past at all, only the future, and to be frank, it was dull and mundane. There were no exciting times ahead of us. He was going through the motions, like I was.' Her bottom lip quivered as she tried to hold everything together.

Seeing Georgie tormented, Rohan put his arms around her. 'It's okay,' he whispered, as he kissed the top of her head.

Finella rubbed Georgie's arm. 'We only really get one good go at love. I was lucky. My husband loved the bones of me. You two deserve to find happiness. Don't let guilt ruin it.'

Finella left the house to the car waiting outside.

'Did your mother just give us her approval?' asked Georgie, gazing up into Rohan's hypnotic eyes.

'Yes, she did, and what she said makes so much sense, but she is just saying what she thinks, if she was you or me. But it really doesn't just depend on what *she* thinks. We have to talk to Dixie-Lee about it because my brother was her father, and it would devastate me if our relationship ever affected yours with your daughter.'

'No, it wouldn't because we are close, and I think she knows about us anyway.'

As if Dixie-Lee had just read her mother's mind, the landline phone rang. It was a private number, and she knew then it was her daughter checking in.

'Dixie-Lee, it's Mum. Everything is fine. The Olivers have been arrested.'

There was silence for a moment. 'Password.'

Georgie smiled. Her daughter had remembered the code they used. 'Bunny.'

'Oh, Mum, seriously, have they been arrested? What shall I do, Mum? I . . . ?'

'Don't speak on the phone. Come home. You're safe and all is well. I understand that the two men who held you captive ended up fighting each other, and, apparently, they are now dead.' She had to let Dixie-Lee know that she wouldn't be arrested by the police for a double murder.

There was a long pause. 'Oh, okay. I'm on my way. See you soon, Mum. Oh, and I love you.'

'I love you too, my girl.'

***

Feeling utterly exhausted, Georgie lay on the sofa as Rohan went to the kitchen to make coffee. However, when he returned, she was asleep. He placed the two cups of coffee on the small table and kneeled beside her, staring at every inch of her face and hearing her gently purring as she slept. He carefully ran his hands over her thick auburn waves, and when her hair suddenly parted, he noticed a deep scar on her head. He moved her lock to cover it and sat back wondering what kind of life Georgie had led. It seemed to him that she had been fighting the world. He wanted nothing more than to make her life as comfortable as possible. He wanted to fill it with romantic meals for two, or three, if Dixie-Lee wished to join them, and tropical beach holidays with cocktails. He gazed around the elementary tired-looking living room and wondered if Georgie would like a new home equipped with everything she ever desired. He could do that for her; he had the money and more. They were all reasonably well off, and although she had turned down offers of financial help from his mother, he wondered if they decided to get married, she would accept it from him then.

Glancing at the photos of Dixie-Lee and the seaside knick-knacks, he wondered if familiarity was her way of coping with her past. Having the things she shared in her little house with her daughter was her sanctuary. It was evident that it was a home she'd built for them alone, where she didn't need a man or anyone else. So he recognised that if she wanted him, she must love him. He glanced around again and had to ask himself this question: would she ever enter his life, or would he have to live in hers? Either way, he wanted her and would do whatever worked for her.

***

Ignoring the visiting hour, Finella marched along the corridor to the ward. A nurse opened the door and was about to tell her something when she was stopped in her tracks. 'Listen, my son was brutally attacked and is on your ward. I have flown in from Ireland. I've had no sleep and no fecking food. I am reserving my last bit of energy to see my son. Now, please show me to Mac Deacon's bed before I collapse, or you'll have me here on a bed beside him.'

The fast yet sharp Irish tone of a short woman with an air of authority took aback the young nurse. 'Yes, sorry, we don't normally—'

'I know, sweetheart, and I understand that kind nurses like yourself are worth their weight in gold. I much appreciate it.'

'Oh, er . . . okay, thank you. What I was going to say is he already has a visitor. His brother came in with him and has refused to leave his side. He said he is his protection in case whoever did this comes back to attack his brother again. I understand they are the two uncles of Dixie-Lee Deacon, so you must be her grandmother.'

'Yes, that's me, so you know about the incident with Dixie-Lee?' She tilted her head to the side, now very surprised.

'Yes, of course. We followed the case daily at the time. How is she now?'

Finella nodded. 'She's okay, thank you very much.' She was not eager to divulge any information to the nurse.

‘That’s good. I’ll take you to Mac and his brother, who looks like he needs a strong cup of coffee. Shall I make you one as well, Mrs Deacon?’

‘Well, that would be lovely, thank you.’

As soon as Finella saw her two sons, she gasped and threw her hands to her face. A sense of fury shot through her body with the force of a Boeing 747. ‘Oh, dear Mother of God,’ she said, as she hurried to her youngest son, who was sitting propped up on his pillows, his face bandaged and his exposed feet resembling purple balloons.

Brodie was asleep in a comfy chair. His usually immaculately clean-shaven face was sprouting a beard, and his complexion appeared almost sallow and grey. He instantly opened his eyes when he heard his mother’s shrill voice and jumped up.

‘Ma, what are you doing here?’

She embraced her son, ignored his question, and leaned over the bed to whisper in Mac’s ear, although, technically, there was no point.

‘Mac, Mammy’s here. Can you hear me?’

‘Ma, the whole building can hear you.’

‘How are you feeling, Son.’

Mac’s eyes flickered until they finally opened. He blinked a few times. ‘A little under the weather, Ma.’

‘For feck’s sake, you boys and your sarcasm. So what does the doctor say?’

‘He said I have a head injury, so they are waiting for my results to come back. They want to keep me in a for a few days until some of the swelling goes down, but, apart from that, I’m fine for light exercise.’

‘Light exercise?’ She looked at his feet. ‘You won’t squeeze those into a pair of ballet shoes anytime soon.’ She smiled, trying to make light of the situation. ‘Seriously, Son, are you okay?’

‘Yes, Ma, I am badly bruised and I feel like shite, but I’m okay.’ He closed his eyes again.

‘I’ll let you rest, love, and I’ll be back tonight.’

Brodie escorted his mother from the ward, and once they were outside, she turned to him. ‘And you look like shite, boy, as well. You need to get some rest yerself.’

He nodded, his eyes bloodshot. 'He will be okay, Ma. How is everything else?'

'They have arrested all the Olivers, well, apart from drippy knickers Elspeth. So tell me, Son,' she said, quickly changing the subject, 'what is this MI5 business all about?'

Brodie shrugged. 'I really have no idea, but I am going to find out, and that bitch who had those thugs do that to Mac will pay.'

Finella's eyes opened wide. 'No, leave it be, Brodie. You cannot afford to upset the fecking likes of MI5.'

'I guess you're right, Ma. I'm exhausted, that's all, but I will rest. Anyway, you get off home and rest yourself.'

As Finella bustled back along the corridor to the entrance, she saw the nurse holding two steaming cups of coffee. 'I'm sorry, love, I can't stay, but I am sure Brodie will love a coffee.'

The nurse smiled prettily. 'I was going to fetch him a sandwich as well. I'm not sure what he would like.'

'Ah, you are a love. He likes all food. They both do. I brought them up with two choices for dinner: take it or leave it.'

The nurse giggled. 'But does he have a favourite?'

Finella smiled when she clocked the sparkle in the young nurse's eye. 'Yes, he does. He likes ham and cheese. He also likes redheads.'

The nurse gently touched her fringe and then blushed. 'Thank you.'

Suddenly Finella felt like a matchmaker. She would love to see her boys with wives, especially her Rohan, and she didn't mind at all if Georgie was the woman he married. With her thoughts on her sons when she exited the hospital, she almost bumped into the paramedics pushing a sickly-looking woman on a stretcher. She glanced briefly at her deathly white pallor before continuing. Then, suddenly, her heart was in her mouth. That woman was Elspeth. She turned and hurried to catch up with the paramedics. 'What happened to her?' she said, almost bringing the stretcher on wheels to a standstill.

'Sorry, madam, please step aside. We must get her to A&E. She's taken an overdose. Do you know her?'

Finella stared at the woman for a moment. 'Er . . .'

'Sorry, madam, if you do, follow us. We don't know exactly what she has taken, but she may not make it, so if there is anything you know about her, please inform the nurses.'

Finella didn't know anything about Elspeth, apart from the grief she had caused her family. 'No, sorry, I'm mistaken.'

'I don't really think it matters so much now,' said one of the paramedics. 'She's gone, this time.'

'Shit, I'll let the doctor know so he can announce the time of death,' said the other paramedic.

Feeling suddenly overwhelmed, she hurried to the exit door and gulped in as much cold air as possible to stop herself from fainting; it had all been too much. Once she was feeling herself again, she walked to where the cab drivers waited for a cheeky fare and hopped into the first one in the queue. After instructing the driver to take her to the Bromley Court Hotel, she sat back and bit her lip to stop it from quivering. She couldn't cry. Everyone was safe, and all was well.

'D'ya mind if I put the news on, love?'

'No, not at all.'

Finella sat back and rubbed her stiff hands together. As the heat in the car began warming her bones, she fell into a state of relaxation, accentuated by the movement of the car, until the newsreader mentioned a name she recognised. The name was Marston-Smith. She sat bolt upright and asked the cab driver to turn the radio up.

'HM Revenue and Customs have towed a boat back to shore from off the coast of Margate. The vessel is believed to belong to a former Army lieutenant, Gordon Marston-Smith, who was recently found dead on Margate beach. Detective Inspector Hinton from Margate Police Station, who is in charge of the investigation, has confirmed that Marston-Smith's death is not being treated as suspicious. Dr James Fergus, the medical examiner, suggests it was a freak accident that caused his fatal injuries. The boat was carrying a large quantity of class A drugs secured underneath his vessel in watertight containers. Dr Fergus informed us that his injuries resulted from him being caught up in the boat's propeller while underwater. We will have more on the situation as we receive it.'

CHAPTER THIRTY-ONE

Having slept for five hours, Georgie awoke at midday to see her daughter dozing in the armchair. Sitting up straight, she looked around and assumed Rohan must have gone to the hotel. Relieved to see her daughter, she desperately wanted to hug her, but she decided it was probably best to allow her to sleep. The poor kid had been through enough, and, judging by the bruise on the side of her face, probably more so than anyone. If her daughter had killed two men, then knowing how sensitive she was and how she'd had to fight Ashby to his death only six months ago, she wondered if her daughter would need therapy. Although, she conceded, since having to kill Ashby in self-defence, she had handled the trauma of it all well and maybe her therapy had been to get on with her studies.

Dixie-Lee's eyelids flickered open. She smiled and got up from the chair, holding out her arms to embrace her mother.

Georgie hugged her tightly, careful not to crush her. 'You had me turning myself inside out with worry. I can't tell you how glad I am that you're home. Jesus, it frightened me.'

'Not as much as it scared the hell out of me, Mum. Anyway, it's behind us now.'

Dixie-Lee pulled away to look her mother in the eye. 'Mum, you have lived your life for me, this house, this area, this life. We have to change that, Mum. We have to move.'

Georgie smiled. The truth was she wanted nothing more, but she had chosen this basic life of working in the café and making every penny count. Glancing around the room, she said, 'A move for us would be great, love, but it's not that simple.'

Dixie-Lee rolled her eyes. 'But it is, Mum. I've already spoken with Uncle Rohan.'

Georgie held her breath. She needed to sit down.

'Mum, it's all right,' Dixie-Lee said, as she returned to her seat. 'Look, I know you tried to make it work with Dad, for my sake. But I'm not stupid, Mum. And I am grateful for my life and everything you've done for me and how you were mum and dad for all but six months of my life. I have to be honest with you. It was a strain for me, too, when Dad came back. I had imagined him to be some kind of hero. I idolised him, but he wasn't who I'd imagined him to be. Don't misunderstand me: I am devastated he's gone, but, Mum, I live in the real world. My relationship with my father was separate from yours. You didn't have to have a relationship with Dad for me too. You had already moved on before Dad came back. I know I may be your child, but I'm not a kid. I am a woman now, Mum.'

'I don't understand what you're saying, love.'

'Rohan, Mum.'

'What about him?'

'I knew you liked him before Dad came back.'

Georgie shrugged and looked away.

'Mum, start a life with him. I love Uncle Rohan. He is a good man, and it's not like having a stepdad, is it? He is my blood, and he loves me and you.' She looked around the room. 'Mum, this house holds lots of beautiful memories for me, but it also holds a terrible one. I killed Ashby in this very room. Mum, it's time to move on. I know I want to.'

Their intimate conversation was stopped short when the front door opened and in came Rohan holding a huge McDonald's bag and a cardboard cup holder with milkshakes. 'Bloody queue.' He laughed as he settled the bag and drinks on the coffee table.

Dixie-Lee winked at Rohan and then smiled at her mother. 'Think about it, Mum, please.'

Georgie took the milkshakes handed to her by Rohan. 'Thank you,' she said. 'Have you heard how Mac is doing?'

Rohan nodded. 'The doctor is discharging him now with a ton of medication. Ma has booked him and Brodie into the Bromley Court Hotel so she can fuss over them. She said she would pop over to see you and Dixie-Lee once Raj has taken a full statement. And Brodie is on his way over, hence the large bag of burgers. Apparently, he is starving. All he has had to eat is a ham and cheese sandwich.'

Georgie looked at her daughter, who was sucking the thick milkshake through a straw. 'How is Riley?'

'Still sore and badly bruised, but, Mum, he was so good to me. I can't tell you how kind he was. Anyway, we stayed in a hotel – twin beds – nothing improper, Mum. And he has decided if he doesn't make it in the art world, he wants to be a paramedic. He said I can blame you for that.' She chuckled.

'Paramedic, yeah?'

'Something about gluing him back together.'

When a loud bang at the door made Georgie jump, she knew at that point, she and her daughter really must move from this place.

As Dixie-Lee rose from her seat and headed towards the door, Georgie noticed she wasn't limping. She thought perhaps she was seeing things. But when she walked back into the room with Brodie behind her, Georgie could see more clearly that her daughter's leg was fine now.

Brodie still looked shattered; dark half-moons sagged beneath his eyes, and his skin was a deathly shade of grey, just like a defeated man. He looked a far cry from who he really was.

'Christ, mate,' said Rohan. 'You look terrible.'

'Cheers, Ro. I just need some beauty sleep.'

'Beauty sleep? You need to fecking hibernate.'

'I need to fatten up first. Pass us a burger. My stomach thinks my throat has been cut.'

As soon as Rohan handed Brodie a burger, he demolished it in seconds; after he had devoured another three, with an audience watching him, the colour returned to his cheeks, and he sat back in the armchair.

'So, listen, Rohan, be honest with me, mate, as I know you will be, but did you ever visit a man serving time inside for murdering his daughter and grandson?'

Rohan frowned. 'No, never. Why?'

'I'll tell you why. MI5 believed that one of us had. Nonetheless, an MI5 officer called James, who, by the way, is a woman and the daughter of some big shot in MI5, was convinced it was one of us who had visited this guy a couple of weeks ago.'

Rohan sat next to Georgie, sensing that this would be a long story and he would have to be all ears.

'This bitch claims her father is missing, and she believes it is to do with one of us. Well, she did believe it, until I convinced her we weren't involved. However, I'm not happy with that.' He suddenly stopped talking. Tears in his eyes welled up and he coughed and rubbed his face.

Rohan knew that his brother was getting emotional.

'That bitch – that cold-blooded evil bitch – was more brutal than any woman I've ever met.'

Georgie bit her bottom lip, thinking that Brodie didn't know *her* very well, then, but she kept quiet and listened.

'She ordered the men to fecking hang our Mac in front of me so I would give her answers to what she wanted to know. Jesus.' He stopped again, and this time, a tear escaped. He shook his head. 'I have never been so terrified in all my life. I mean, they had him on tiptoes. They fecking smashed seven bells of shit out of him and held me at gunpoint.'

Dixie-Lee began to cry, which stopped Brodie. 'Oh my God, I'm sorry, Dixie-Lee, and look at you with that mark on yer face. Come here and give me a cuddle.'

Dixie-Lee got up and threw her arms around Brodie. 'Haven't our family been through enough? Poor Uncle Mac. He is so kind and sweet. I would love to get my hands on . . . shit, I mean, I would love it if she got her comeuppance.'

After Dixie-Lee retook her seat, she smiled. 'Please carry on, Uncle Brodie. I'm not a kid.'

'No, you're not that, that's for sure. And when or even if those Olivers do get released from prison, I will make sure their lives are hell.'

'It's okay, Uncle Brodie,' said Dixie-Lee, sensing her uncle was getting irate. 'Tell us about this MI5 business.'

Brodie took a mouthful of his milkshake and relaxed his shoulders. 'So, anyway, the bitch was adamant that it was one of us. Long story short, I talked her round to facing facts and managed to convince her it was nothing to do with us. Then Mac collapsed. I had to beg her to allow Mac to go to the hospital. She finally said he could go there, but when I got to the police station and saw Mac, he didn't even have a plaster on him. So she lied. He could have died, and I won't rest until I see her in pain and in whatever form that takes.'

'Who was this guy? Did she give you a name?'

Brodie nodded. 'It was someone called Rodney Potter, but I'm fecked if I know any Rodney Potter.'

'Me, neither,' replied Rohan.

All eyes were on Dixie-Lee, the moment she threw her hands to her mouth and gasped.

'What is it?'

'Dad! It was *Dad*. He knew Rodney. I heard him talking on the phone. It was the day I left college early, and Dad was in the back garden smoking, but he had the back door open, so I heard him, but I thought little of it. Why would I? I mean, I assumed he was a customer or something.' Suddenly, she dipped her hands down the inside of the armchair and then tried the other side.

'What are you doing, love?' asked Georgie. 'I thought I'd checked the armchair. Oh, hang on. No, I didn't, in the end.' She recalled being interrupted by a phone call.

'Mum, this is where Dad always kept his phone. He tucked it down here,' she said, before she pulled it out. 'I forgot, what with all that was going on, but look. It's his phone.'

Georgie frowned. "That's not his phone. I bought him an iPhone. That looks like an old pay-as-you-go burner.'

Dixie-Lee shrugged before handing it to her mother.

'I think there was more to Dixie than he let on,' said Georgie, gripping the phone with both hands.

Brodie's face seemed to sport an angry wolf's stare. 'If he was involved in this business with Rodney Potter, then he should have warned us. Our Mac nearly died.' His anger suddenly halted, and his face softened. 'I forgot for a moment that he is dead. I'm so sorry, Georgie. Christ, I'm sorry, Dixie-Lee.' He ran his hands through his hair and shook his head. 'I really need to get a grip.'

'You've obviously visited hell, so stop worrying. We'll get to the bottom of all of this, and, maybe, I'll get to know who my husband really was and what he was all about. It seems to me there are some deep secrets that he kept from us all. Any idea what the passcode would be?'

In unison, both Brodie and Rohan reeled off a number.

'Blimey, that was quick. Why that number?'

'It was our father's safe combination, and it became a family joke, so we all use it,' said Rohan.

As soon as she turned the phone on and entered the passcode, the phone sprang to life, with missed calls and messages. She swallowed hard, and her hands shook. 'Am I going to discover who my husband really was?'

Rohan put his arm around her shoulders. 'We all need to know, Georgie.'

She smiled and put the phone on loudspeaker so they could all hear the messages. The first message began with no sound. Then they heard a man's voice. He sounded old and croaky. 'Hello, son, I am getting worried, mate, that you are not answering your calls. Book another visit, please. My prison number, in case you forgot, is MT2482C. They've not moved me. I am still in Rochester. Please, lad, I need to know what's going on.'

There was silence as everyone started processing the words.

'Turn the phone off, in case that bitch is trying to track the phone.'

'I don't think she can because she would have by now, surely, and if MI5 suspected you guys, wouldn't they have suspected Dixie as well?'

'No, because he didn't work for us. She just put two and two together and came up with five, but if you want to know about Dixie, then write to the man and request a visit,' said Brodie, still annoyed with his brother Dixie.

'Or wait until this man calls back because I bet he will,' suggested Dixie-Lee.

Georgie looked at the dozens of missed calls. 'Actually, I think you're right. This guy called so many times, and his voice sounded desperate.'

Rohan sighed. 'You know what? I heard in that man's tone a familiarity to the point he knew Dixie well. He called him *son* in a gentle manner.'

'He did, didn't he. Well, there's nothing I can do except wait.'

'What about your garage?' asked Rohan, as he stood up and looked down to the end of the garden.

Georgie jumped up. 'Yeah, yeah, you see, Brodie, that's another odd thing. He reinforced the garage and put a new door on and a padlock that weighs a ton. And he went to all that effort when the house needs doing up. It made little sense, and to be honest, I rarely go down to the garden, so I've only recently noticed it.'

'Dad used to go out late at night sometimes and I'd see him down in the garage. I just assumed it was his way of dealing with his old life, somehow making the garage a shrine to his past.'

'No, sorry, Dixie-Lee. Although that sounds very romantic, it glosses over the fact that there was something he was hiding.'

Dixie-Lee smiled sadly. 'And, yes, of course, maybe that too.'

'Right, we need a heavy-duty hacksaw to get through that padlock, and by the way, there is a camera above the garage.'

'Mum, why must you be so GI Jane about it? Why don't you simply use the key?'

Georgie looked at her daughter. 'Where is the key, Miss Clever Clogs?' she asked.

'I should think it's in the same place where he hid the phone.'

She slid her hand between the cushion and the hard sides of the armchair and rooted around before she smiled and produced a key. 'D'ya think this is it?'

Georgie rolled her eyes and snatched the key. 'So let's find out what's in the garage-cum-Fort Knox that he wanted to keep so secret.'

Rohan looked at Brodie, both hearing the bitter undertone in Georgie's face, and they nodded in agreement. Georgie had every right to be just a bit peeved with the situation.

They all made their way down the garden, stopped in front of the garage, and stared.

'It appears as though he has done some updating,' said Brodie, scratching his head. 'Well, let's get this door open.'

Georgie once again trembled. She wasn't sure she was ready for any more surprises, yet she knew she wouldn't sleep if she didn't open that garage door. The key slid easily into the padlock, and with a gentle turn, the lock pinged open. She removed the padlock, gripped the bottom of the garage door, and lifted it up, surprised at how quiet it was. As soon as it was up and the light shone into the square room, Georgie stepped back.

'What the fuck?' said Brodie.

'So it seems to me, Brodie, that our Dixie was just like you. Fecking heck. That Aston Martin must be vintage, is it not?'

Brodie was staggered. 'That, Rohan, is a gem of a car. Wow, the sly old fox, keeping that a secret. What an absolute beauty of a machine.'

Georgie stared in disbelief. Her husband had been keeping a car worth more than their house, if she'd owned it. Feeling utterly blindsided, she stormed back to the house with Dixie-Lee hot on her heels.

Rohan was about to run his hands across the perfectly polished bonnet when Brodie suddenly had a thought.

'Don't touch the car. Close the garage.'

'But look, there's a box over at the back. Hadn't we better take a look?'

'No, not yet, Rohan. Listen, I need to rest. I must sleep before I fall over. Can we come back to this another time? I need to think straight.'

Rohan didn't argue. He closed the garage and secured the lock. 'Georgie is going to be pissed off.'

'Yeah, I know, but, Rohan, stay with her. She needs you right now, mate.'

Rohan stopped in his tracks and turned to his brother to face him. 'What do you mean?'

'Oh, come on, Ro, I know when you returned to Ireland, you were in bits for a while, and I see how you are with her. You both love each other. Anyway, like I said, I am fecked, mate. I'm going back to the hotel. Call us a cab, will you?'

Rohan pulled out his phone and arranged a cab for his brother and braced himself to face Georgie, knowing she was completely confused and angry by recent events. Nevertheless, to his surprise, she was in the kitchen making drinks and carrying on as if nothing was wrong.

When the cab arrived, Georgie hugged Brodie goodbye and returned to the kitchen. She stared at the butter melting on the bread and tried to control her temper, but it pained her. How could he own a car of that much value and yet act as though he was a vagrant? Nothing made sense. She took a few deep breaths before carrying the tray full of mugs of tea and toast into the living room, where Rohan and Dixie-Lee looked as if they were studying her.

'It's okay. I'm angry, yes, but I guess I am more curious than anything. I just want answers, that's all.' She looked at Rohan. 'And I also want to move on and have a life, I . . . we' – she pointed to Dixie-Lee – 'deserve.'

The burner phone rang just as she was about to sit down and drink her tea. All three stared for a moment. The caller was from Rochester Prison. Georgie answered the call and waited for the formal pre-call prison spiel, after which a croaky voice said, 'Thank God, son. I was so worried.'

'This isn't Dixie.'

There was silence.

'I need to talk to you. I need a visit,' Georgie replied, her words tumbling out before he had a chance to end the call.

'Who is this?'

'I'm Georgie Deacon. I understand you knew my husband.'

'*What?*' The man's voice had a slight shriek to it as if he was shocked. 'Your husband? You said *knew*. Please tell me he's not dead, is he?'

Georgie sensed the man was some old sweet guy.

'I'm sorry, but, yes, he was shot dead in the street.'

'Fucking MI5, the bastards, the fucking bastards. I'm sorry, love. Who did you say you are again?'

'I am, I mean I *was* his wife. Please, can I visit you? I think I need answers, and you, Mr Potter, are the only man who may well have them.'

'Love, I'm not sure if it's even safe, even though they've got to him.'

'They didn't, Mr Potter. It was someone else who, believe me, will be behind bars soon enough.'

'Really? Okay. Look, I need to add your name to my list. I've got a pen and paper, but I need your name, address, and date of birth. Then I will add them to my list, and then you have to book a visit online, apparently. Do you have my prison number?'

'Yes.' She then gave all her details and waited for his.

'My date of birth is 12th October 1947.'

Suddenly, she frowned. 'If Dixie visited you in prison, he must have given you his real name to book the visit. So, MI5 would have known who he was.'

'No, he gave his real surname but a fake first name. He was clever, that lad. He also had fake papers.'

'Oh, I see. Okay, I'll book it now if you can add me to your list, Mr Potter, and by the way, I know what it's like being in prison. Is there anything you need?'

'Well, if you don't mind, I need some shoes. Dixie was going to send me some in.'

'Size?'

'I'm an eight. Anything comfortable – trainers – not those expensive ones but anything cheap and cheerful.'

'Okay, I'll do that. All I ask is that you be honest with me. I don't want to be spared any details.'

‘I understand. Although I am baffled. Please, come and visit me. I have to know exactly what happened to him. He was all I had left of the family.’

The call ended, and Georgie stared at the phone. Her forehead creased, and her eyes narrowed. ‘Oh my God, that tells me that Dixie had another life he never shared with me.’

CHAPTER THIRTY-TWO

Two weeks later

Georgie drove alone to HM Prison Rochester. It surprised her that it didn't take long to drive there. She parked her car in the large car park, which visitors and prison wardens used. She looked around for directions to the prison entrance. It wasn't signposted very well, but she noticed two women clutching designer bags who seemed to know where they were going.

Even in the depths of winter, the women were showing off their fake tan. Their jeans were tight, and their hairstyles were a mix of extensions and their own bleached hair.

Having taken an educated guess that they were visitors rather than officers, she followed them to a large hut which resembled a Portakabin. As soon as they pulled open the door, the warm air hit her. It was such a welcome relief from the bitter cold outside.

Since she had no idea how the visiting process worked, she joined the two women and watched. Behind a partial glass screen, which could only be described as a kiosk, was an officer who could easily have passed as a schoolboy in a prison officer's uniform. When it was her turn to reach the kiosk, she stood in front of him. He asked her who she was here to visit, checked her passport, ticked her off the list, and stuck an aluminous pink strip of paper around her wrist.

That was straightforward, she said to herself, before joining the ten people inside the cabin who were all seated around low plastic tables. *Surely this wasn't where the prisoners joined them?* Deciding to go with the flow, she sat down. There was nothing to do except gaze around.

A few minutes later, a tall woman in jeans and a jumper announced with a beaming smile that the visitors could make their way down to the main gate. Again, Georgie had no idea where that was, so she followed the others and queued for about five minutes outside until the door was opened, and an officer checked their names off the list again. She queued again to go through the security detector before being gently rubbed down by a female officer. It surprised her how friendly the staff were. She was then taken down a short corridor, past a sniffer dog, and escorted to the main visiting room. Yet another officer checked their names off the list, checked their paper wristbands, and gave them the allocated table number. It worried Georgie because she had no idea what Rodney looked like, except she knew he was old.

She walked along the first row, counting the tables, until she came to table ten. There were three chairs on one side and one on the other side of the table. She tried to move one closer to the table, but it was cumbersome, and that told her they weren't to be moved.

Relieved it was warm inside, she gazed around, taking in her surroundings. Over on the far side was a tuck shop. Deciding it would be polite to buy a few goodies and a hot drink, she joined the queue but she kept an eye out at her table to see if Rodney had arrived.

She tried not to overthink anything. She was there to get to the truth. The lady in front of her had piled her tray full of crisps and sweets and was faffing over a packet of Jelly Tots.

Soon, it was Georgie's turn at the front of the queue. The tall extremely handsome Asian man smiled at her, and for a moment, she was sucked into his kind eyes. Wearing his armband, it was evident that he was an inmate, but he didn't seem as though he should be there. His voice was gentle and educated.

Georgie suddenly felt that life was merely a time we spend trying to understand everything – a life of curiosity. If she was feeling bold, she would have asked him why he was in there, but today, she would save her questions for Rodney.

Unsure what Rodney would like, she ordered tea, a coffee, a hot chocolate, and just like the lady in front of her, she dithered over what treats to buy.

The tall handsome man smiled again. 'Who are you here to visit? I might know them.'

'Rodney Potter.'

The man gave a cheeky wink. 'He likes chocolate, digestive biscuits, and cakes. Anything sweet. I'm glad he has a visitor today.'

Those words made Georgie believe that Rodney Potter, who supposedly killed his daughter and grandson, was not guilty. She would confirm her thoughts once he arrived. She filled her tray, headed back to her seat, placed the tray on the table, and nursed a hot coffee while she waited.

Finally, he came through the door, and the man behind him patted him on the back. The inmate seated at the table next to them nodded politely to him.

Georgie looked across and decided that these men, who were built like brick shithouses, were hardened criminals, which strengthened the notion that Rodney wasn't the monster this bitch James had decided he was.

Potter walked over to her and stood for a second, leaving Georgie to wonder if she was supposed to embrace him. But she didn't know him. He bowed as if she were royalty, and then, as she straightened up, he held out his hand for her to shake. At that point, she stood and gently shook his hand.

'Thank you for seeing me, Mr Potter.'

'My dear, please call me Rodney. Everyone in here does.' He pointed to his trainers. 'Thank you so much. It means a lot to me. My feet are as old as I am, and these feel as though I am wearing gloves. Oh, and thank you for the jumpers. You have no idea how bloody cold it gets in here. Even the mice climb under the blankets.'

He took a seat and smiled, pointing to the drinks. 'Hot chocolate for me?'

She nodded. 'Please help yourself. I wasn't sure what you'd like.'

He looked over at the tuck shop and waved to the tall handsome man. 'Thank you, Bal.'

'Rodney, I hope I can be blunt with you, and I want you to be honest with me, no matter how brutal it is.'

Potter sipped his hot chocolate, opened the small packet of biscuits, and dunked them in the drink before he wolfed them down.

She studied his face and concluded there wasn't a smidgeon of evil there. He was an open book, as far as she was concerned, and as for his cloudy eyes, they were wide and friendly, and that smile of his was the genuine article.

'How did you know my husband?' There, straight out with it. She knew she had no time to waste.

Suddenly his sunny disposition dulled, his eyes dragged down at the sides, and he clutched his hands as if praying. 'Dixie was one of my daughter's patients. She worked in a rehabilitation unit with the military.' He sighed. 'When Dixie arrived with serious injuries – physical and mental and with severe amnesia – the authorities wrongly identified him as someone else. It was due to a mix-up over the dog tags. The other guy hadn't made it. His body and face weren't recognisable.' He paused and looked up. 'Sorry, it all sounds a bit graphic, doesn't it.'

Georgie put her hand up. 'Please, I was in the military, so be as graphic as you like. I just need to know the truth.'

'He was on the ward for months. He couldn't walk, talk, or even function without assistance. My daughter . . . my daughter.'

When he stopped to compose himself, Georgie had an instinctive urge to hug him. She recognised that pain on his face, but she remained seated and waited patiently. 'It's okay, Rodney. Please, take your time, love.'

'She was his primary carer. She more or less brought him back to life, and then, once he could walk and talk, they threw him out on the streets. Just like that. Bang. Out on the streets.'

'I have to ask, did he know who he really was when they released him?'

Potter shrugged. 'Maybe. It's possible, certainly. We weren't too sure when exactly he realised his name was Dixie. My daughter assumed he was in denial, but the medical staff dismissed his mad notions. Anyway, when the doctors released him, they assumed he had family. But he had nowhere to go and that was that.'

Georgie tried to put the pieces together. 'Do you know when they released him?'

Potter looked up to the ceiling. She could tell he was working it out.

'I would say around sixteen years ago.'

Georgie nodded. It made sense. Her daughter was almost three then. That was when who she thought was just a random homeless guy made an appearance. It was the same time that someone had thrown stones at her window to catch her attention because Dixie-Lee had fallen off her swing. She later found out it was her husband – the vagrant.

'Anyway, a few years after that, we had a very cold winter, like this one, and my daughter was at work when Dixie was rushed back in. He had caught pneumonia and almost died. The staff nursed him back to health, and that's when my daughter decided to bring him home – to our home. We lived together, you see. Her mother died in childbirth, so I raised my Janey by myself. God, she had the patience of a saint.'

Georgie knew he was reminiscing, and so she waited.

'He wasn't easy to look after, either. Such a troubled man. Anyway, my Janey, God love her, she nursed that man. She held him when he had his night terrors, she fed him when he had the shakes. But something was missing. I knew there was, I could see it, but my Janey said it was this PTSD, and it was something that only sufferers would understand. He would go off for weeks at a time and then return. I suppose he hated who he was in some ways. His face all scarred up like that. But it never bothered my daughter. She loved him with all her heart.'

A tear unexpectedly escaped and ran down his cheek, and he swiftly wiped it away. 'I'm sorry, love. I keep forgetting that you are his. I mean, you were his wife. It must be like finding out that your husband has cheated.' He moved his hand along the table towards her to make a comforting gesture.

She didn't pull it away; instead; she reached out and rubbed his mottled fingers.

'Ya know what, Rodney? I kinda feel comfort in your story. I'm not bitter. I know I should be, but you are giving me an explanation that works for me, and that's all I need. Please, carry on.'

'Anyway, he would go off and come back looking like a vagabond. Janey never imagined he was having an affair because he looked like a scruffy homeless guy. Still, as I say, she worshipped the ground he walked on. She wasn't one of these dolly birds. My daughter was a plain girl with a big heart. And then, one day, she came down the stairs, her face as white as a sheet, it was. "What is it, love?", I said to her, and she burst into tears. It was the time that Dixie had gone again. And that was the thing. He'd go. Without so much as a by-your-leave, just poof, gone, and we never knew where he went or how long he'd be gone for. But, that morning, she needed him more than ever.' Tears filled his eyes.

‘She fell into my arms, breaking her heart, she was, because she found out she was expecting.’

Georgie could feel her nose tingling. She knew she was about to tear up, so she sniffed the air and changed the subject. ‘Would you like another hot chocolate?’

He shook his head. ‘I want you to know the story before you leave, and I think you need to know it as well.’

She smiled. ‘Yes, sorry, please carry on.’

‘So he was away this time for nine months. I wondered if he knew she was expecting. I mean, she wasn’t hiding it. She had a big baby bump. I often wondered if he watched from a distance, you see.’

Georgie gave him an understanding smile. ‘Yes, I do know exactly what you mean.’

‘Anyway, he was a big and beautiful baby. She gave birth alone. I waited outside the room. For a man of my age, it wasn’t the done thing to be inside the room with a woman giving birth. However, as soon as he was born, I went inside to make sure my Janey was okay, and then she let me hold him. He was bonny. I fell in love with that boy, there and then. He was his father’s child, all right, with those huge green eyes and that mop of black curls. He was the apple of my eye. A funny sweet little baby. Then Dixie returned, but as much as he held Joseph – that’s what she called him by the way – Dixie never seemed to look him in the eye. I don’t know, it was hard to explain. But over time – in between his weeks away – he slowly built a bond with Joseph, and Joseph, as he got older, accepted that his father would disappear. He also accepted that his father had a dark past and he was not to push him for answers.’

‘Did he look like Dixie when he was a teenager?’

Potter frowned. ‘Yes, the spitting image of him. Why?’

‘My daughter does, too. She looks nothing like me. She’s all Dixie.’

‘I bet she’s a beauty.’

Georgie nodded.

‘I loved Dixie as if he was my own son, but his toing and froing affected our Joseph. He began going off himself, sometimes for a night, only to return the next morning. He would have us all frantic. You see, in the main, he was a sweet lad. There was not a nasty bone in his body, but he had that look in his eyes, like Dixie's – a faraway look. He wouldn't say what was wrong. I knew something had happened to him, though. It was something he couldn't tell us about.'

He paused and looked away, trying to compose himself, which made Georgie hold her breath. Whatever he was about to tell her, it was sure to be heartbreaking.

'My Janey went to his room one night when, like Dixie, he was having night terrors. He'd been bullied at school, ya see. Anyway, on that particular night, he awoke screaming, and when she pulled back the bedclothes to get in with him to calm him down, she saw the blood. It was all over his pyjamas.' He paused and took a few deep breaths. 'Janey screamed for me to come to the room. What I saw turned me over. He was only fifteen. Not a worldly fifteen-year-old, but an innocent kid. We rushed him to the hospital where they managed to fix him. He'd got infections and was hospitalised for a week. He had to be fitted with a colostomy bag because the infection had caused horrific injuries.'

'Oh my God. Did someone do this to him?'

'Yes. But it wasn't just one man. A few men did but there was one man in charge, one man who *really* hurt him.'

Cutting to the chase, Georgie asked, 'Was he a rent boy?'

'No, no, not at all. He was going off and meeting a few older boys who would drink and smoke dope and just be a nuisance, but unbeknown to our Joseph, they were also part of a group who identified troubled kids like our Joseph – easy pickings. They would get paid for taking them to this secret house.'

Georgie put her hand to her mouth in disbelief.

'My daughter managed to put together everything about the incident and reported it to the police.'

'And which police station would that be?'

'Tonbridge.'

Georgie nodded.

'She gave them names and places because he knew where they had taken him and he knew the head guy's name because someone had slipped up and called him by his real name. And so before my Janey went to the police, they googled the man. He was high up in MI5. Joseph was prolific on the computer. Anyway, when the police investigated the situation, they accused my Joseph of fabricating the whole story because he had managed to get into files kept by MI5, and so they sent my grandson packing with a threatening message. My Janey was livid. She said she wouldn't stand back and let it go. She would start a campaign and bring this Lord Hockenberry to justice.'

He stopped and ran his hands through his thinning hair. 'I was mad, so mad, but, see, Dixie, he was gone at the time when she needed him the most. He wasn't there, and she was dealing with the police all by herself. I couldn't do much to help, and I knew she would need money, so I asked for overtime at the garage. I worked such long hours that by the time I got home, I assumed they were both in bed. In the mornings, I was out before they were up. After a few nights, I noticed nothing in the kitchen had been moved, and there was a smell in the spare room when I opened the door.' He stopped and covered his face.

Georgie could see his shoulders trembling as he sobbed. She hurried from her seat and crouched beside him, her arms around his shoulders, her eyes streaming with tears. This poor man had suffered unimaginable cruelty. She could feel his bony spine and realised that underneath the thick jumper she had also bought for him was a frail old man who was stuck inside a prison for a crime he didn't commit, all to hide the fact that one if not more of MI5 were part of this paedophile gang.

He stopped crying and wiped his eyes with the back of his hand. 'I'm sorry. You came here for answers, and here I am, crying like a baby.' He took a deep breath. 'So when I opened the door, I stared and stared, trying to snap out of what I thought was a nightmare. This wasn't happening, not to us, a simple family. My sweet Janey was propped up in a sitting position. Part of her face was missing.' He coughed, to stop the tears. 'And my grandson . . . my beautiful Joseph had been shot in the chest. I . . . was in shock. I could barely speak once I'd called the police . . . I don't even remember giving them a statement.'

Georgie retook her seat. 'Dear God, I just can't imagine what you went through. Please take your time.'

He looked up at the clock. 'I must finish because they will end the visits soon.'

'Okay.' She nodded.

'Dixie had no idea what had gone on until he returned to our home. One of the neighbours told him. You see, there was no press coverage. Anyway, he went to the court case, which was over in a day, and then he got a burner phone, and we stayed in contact being careful what we said on it.'

'So Dixie came to visit you. Did you give him all the details of this MI5 guy?'

Potter nodded. 'I told him everything I knew.' He looked up at the ceiling. 'One of the inmates who cleared the visiting room managed to mess with the camera, so Dixie's face was never seen.' His eyes widened and he looked directly at Georgie. 'I am worried they will question you now.'

Georgie tilted her head. 'Don't worry about me. I can handle myself all right. So, did Dixie plan to kill this Lord Hockenberry?'

'He felt so guilty for not being there for Joseph, it was eating him up alive. He said he had been torn. He wouldn't explain why, but he was now racked with guilt and wouldn't sit back and do nothing, so when you answered the call, I assumed MI5 had got to him. You see, they don't like me having visitors. They want me silenced, and I am an old man now. I'm mentally weak and not physically strong. I just want that man punished for what he did. He took my whole family from me to save his reputation. And now, even Dixie, who I did love, is gone.'

'It was a family called the Olivers. It was a family feud. They shot him while he was at work.'

'So you are sure it wasn't MI5?'

'Positive. According to Brodie, MI5 actually dismissed any involvement by Dixie. They thought your visitor was either Mac or Brodie Deacon, one of Dixie's brothers. Anyway, MI5 has pissed me off. I'm disgusted with what they've done. This Lord Hockenberry has taken away the chance of my daughter having a brother. She never even got to know him.'

The pain residing in Potter's face would break the heart of anyone seeing it. 'He would have loved to have known he had a sister.'

'My Dixie-Lee is eighteen and a lovely, kind girl. She will get to know about Joseph.'

'So you will you tell her, then, will you?'

'I will, and I bet she will want to come and visit you to get to know who he was. She's like that.'

'I would love that so much, Georgie. I am surprised you are not bitter that your husband had this double life you obviously knew nothing about.'

She shrugged her shoulders. 'I lost my husband, or I thought I had, in 2003. Dixie had hovered around in the background on and off for years, but I think he came back to me and Dixie-Lee when your grandson was murdered. I don't know why. Maybe he needed to be present to stop anything from happening to his daughter. I guess he thought he needed to protect her because he hadn't managed to keep his son safe. Who knows, Rodney? But I now know the truth, and that's all I needed to know.'

'I guess that bastard is still out there. He's probably raping other young lads.'

Georgie slowly shook her head. 'No, he isn't. That's why MI5 questioned Mac and Brodie. They assumed one of them came to visit you because now this top guy is missing.'

Potter's eyes nearly popped out of his head. 'He is missing, then? Not dead?'

'I have no idea, but if he is missing and Dixie was responsible, then, since Dixie has been lying in the mortuary for over two weeks now, wherever this man is, he is either dead or at death's door.'

An officer called out 'Please end your visits and make your way to the far door.'

Georgie rose from her chair and put her arms out to embrace the old man.

He hugged her tightly. 'I'm so sorry for everything. I hope you got what you came for, love.'

'Oh, it's not over yet, Rodney. I promise I will bring Dixie-Lee here to see you, and I am a woman of my word. Stay in touch. I have an excellent lawyer who can play dirty too.'

'What, you would do that for me?'

Georgie smiled. 'You are my daughter's brother's grandfather, so why not.'

Potter beamed at her.

'Oh, one quick question. In my garage is an Aston Martin worth a hundred grand, at least. How did Dixie acquire such a valuable car? Did you leave it to him?'

'Oh my God. Is it blue?'

Georgie frowned. 'Yes, why?'

Potter looked around him before he whispered, 'Bloody hell's bells. That's Lord Hockenberry's car. So Dixie found him, then.'

'Looks that way.'

She hugged him again before following the other visitors out of the room and back to the main gate.

CHAPTER THIRTY-THREE

In a daze and still reeling from hearing about Dixie's life, Georgie somehow made her way out of the prison. Feeling completely devastated, she took a few deep breaths as she leaned against the stone walled perimeter. The thought that her daughter's brother had been subjected to such a heinous crime by the people who were supposed to protect the country and keep its citizens safe was beyond comprehension. She managed to shake off the feeling of unjustness and head towards her car, although bitterness and rage still lingered like a bad smell.

As she clicked her key fob, she clocked a tall woman. She was dressed in a long black coat and black leather gloves. But what really struck her was the nasty sneer on the woman's face.

Georgie looked away. She didn't know the woman, yet she could sense she was staring her way. As she opened her car door, the woman walked over. 'So you must be Georgie Deacon.'

Georgie didn't like the cocky sound of the woman's voice. Looking up at her, she guessed who this woman was, and instantly, it unleashed her anger.

'Yes, I am Georgie Deacon. Who wants to know?'

'Oh, I should imagine you know who I am. I would assume your two brothers-in-law told you.'

Looking around, Georgie soon established that the woman was alone. She smiled and remained silent.

'Why are you smiling like that?'

Georgie decided not to answer. She wanted to see how easily James would get wound up.

'Why were you visiting Rodney Potter today? Oh, and before you ask how I know, I have access to those records. So what was the purpose of your visit?'

Georgie slammed her car door shut and watched as James's left eye nervously twitched.

'You're rather nosey, aren't you? I mean, what's it to you? That poor old man is going to be spending the rest of his life behind bars. And you made sure of that, but James, James, James.' She chuckled. 'What a stupid name for a woman, by the way. Was your father hoping for a boy he could wank over, but, disappointedly, he ended up with a girl instead? He must have been gutted.'

James stared; her eyes held a fight-or-flight gaze.

'Ya know what, *Ms James Hockenberry*? Brodie told me how you treated him and Mac, and he said you had to be the cruellest woman he'd ever met.'

Georgie stepped closer and grinned. 'But the thing is this, James. I bet *I am* the cruellest woman Brodie ever met.'

'Are you threatening me, Georgie?'

'Mrs Deacon to you. And threatening you? Ha! What's wrong, sour tits? Feeling a little on edge, considering you don't have your muscle with you, are you? What is it, James? Did you assume I would crumble – fear *you* – and suddenly blubber like a frightened child? No, love. You see, someone like you, you don't fucking scare me, but I know I could have you begging. Yes, James, begging for mercy.'

James stepped back. She could feel the rage coming off Georgie Deacon and the fearless look in her eyes; she'd not seen that in the hardest of men.

'So it was your husband who visited Rodney, was it?'

'Late husband, James. Late husband. Dixie is dead, but you already know that.'

'What did Potter tell you?'

Georgie suddenly realised that James's tone wasn't one of a hard bitch, as Brodie portrayed her to be, although she would never suspect him of lying. There was more to it. Registering that James was without her protection officers, which spoke volumes as far as she was concerned, she wanted to rile her up because she already knew James was not here on official business. It must be personal business.

'I want to see your identification. I want proof you are actually part of MI5, before I speak to you.'

Georgie folded her hands and smiled. It always paid to know your enemy, and so two weeks ago, she had spent some time with Raj getting him up to speed with what she and her family had found out after discovering Dixie's burner phone. He, in turn, had told her he would look into what she'd told him.

A week later, he had phoned her to tell her that James had been 'let go', although a whistleblower within MI5 was ready to spill the beans about her brutal methods to *The Times*. It wasn't the only reason for her getting fired. It appeared that her father, who had once held a high position, had been replaced by James's boss, Lord Fairly, who had only employed James because her father was his boss. Now Hockenberry was missing and presumed dead, he could get rid of parasites paid for throwing their weight around, and she was top of the list.

Clearly uncomfortable, James glanced down and then back at Georgie, both her eyes twitching as she chewed the inside of her lip.

Georgie laughed. 'So, James, it's clear you're not here on official business, or you would be flashing your ID card. They fired your arse, didn't they?'

'No!'

'Oh, don't go down that road, James, or you could be charged with impersonating an MI5 employee, and, as it stands, you probably have already done that by requesting information from the prison.'

James suddenly flared her nostrils. 'All I want to know is where my father is.'

Georgie nodded slowly. 'Probably in the same place as the Devil. Down in the fires of hell for what he did to that kid and no doubt many more. Before you totter off, James, I want you to know that I won't stop until your paedophile of a father and his cronies are brought to justice. I want that, whether he is alive or dead. I will have his name blackened and called out for the damage he caused.'

'Shut up. My father never did anything like that. It was all lies. That boy made it up, and Rodney Potter killed his own grandson and his daughter.'

'Bollocks. If that is true, why was it all hushed up, eh? Not a slither of it in the press, was there? James, you are not just deluded. You are also hell-bent on saving your father's name for your own selfish reasons. But listen and listen good. Brodie once said to me he wants you punished, whatever that looks like. And as for me, I will make fucking sure it happens.'

The harsh words resided on James's face and compelled her to back off and hurry to her car.

Georgie smiled to herself; she loved the fact that she had just managed to put the wind up the woman.

As Georgie drove back to St Mary Cray, she planned her next move and started by calling Hugh and Raj to meet her at her house.

***

By the time Georgie reached her home, both men were there waiting for her.

She first turned to Raj. 'Would you believe it. James turned up at the prison! She wanted to know why I was there. Well, to cut a long story short, I scared the shit out of her. Told her Brodie was on the warpath! So watch out!'

Raj grinned and nodded enthusiastically, thinking how fortunate he had been to be involved with the Deacon family saga. First the attack on Dixie-Lee, then the arrest of Georgie and all that business with the Marx family and the Army, and finally more drama, with a family feud and issues surrounding Dixie's life. His thoughts were cut short when Georgie spoke again.

'Anyway, a couple of weeks ago, I managed to open the garage only to find a valuable car inside. I was fuming because I believed it was Dixie's. However, having visited a chap called Rodney Potter in Rochester Prison today, I now understand this valuable car belongs to Lord Hockenberry, the MI5 guy, whose daughter interrogated Brodie and Mac. So, anyway, I think it was in fact Dixie who was responsible for this Hockenberry's disappearance, and the answer to the man's whereabouts lies probably in the garage.'

Raj was so struck dumb, his mouth fell open. 'What! Seriously?'

She nodded. 'I'll explain everything later, but, trust me, Lord Hockenberry is the owner of the car inside my garage. None of us have touched the car, so it won't have our prints on it. I think you'd better be the first to take a look. I don't want to be charged with any kidnapping, murder, or anything like that.'

Raj laughed. 'Georgie, you won't be.'

As they approached the garage, Raj put his finger under his nose. 'There is a nasty smell around here.'

'Cor, not half,' said Georgie, as she pinched her nose. 'I bet it's the drains.'

'No, that's a death stench.'

Georgie stopped in her tracks. 'Fuck, do you think Hockenberry is in the garage? We opened the garage two weeks ago, and there was no smell then and no bodies . . . just the car.'

'Maybe the body was in the car and because of the cold spell, it hadn't decomposed when you opened the garage, but the weather has warmed up a few degrees since. Shit! That smell is strong. I'm afraid the sight won't be pretty.'

Georgie handed Raj a key. Hesitantly, he took it and unlocked the padlock before he swung the door up. Instantly, he was surrounded by a swarm of bluebottles, thousands of them, buzzing around his head. 'Shit,' he said again, as he frantically waved his hands before pulling out a pair of disposable gloves from his pocket and putting them on.

Georgie stepped back. The smell made her gag, and the relentless flies were buzzing like a summer's day.

Holding his hand over his mouth, Shields peered into the garage to see Raj open the car boot. As he did, another swarm of flies flew out.

Raj glanced inside the boot briefly before tearing back outside and waving his hands in front of his face. 'Fuck that,' he said, as he gulped the air.

'Well?' said Shields, impatiently.

'Hugh, clearly, mate, you may rest assured that in the boot of that car is a dead body.' Gasping for air, Raj put his hands on his knees, trying to get his breath.

'Is it a man? Do you think it is that Lord Hockenberry?' asked Georgie, who was feeling like death warmed up herself.

'Georgie, listen to me. I will have to call this in. It's now a murder investigation. See that body, that decomposing body.' He shuddered. 'It was bound and gagged. So, get ready because this place will once again be buzzing with police, just like those poxy flies.' He swatted a few away from his face.

'Come back to the house, Raj. I'll get you a drink.'

'I can't, Georgie. I can't leave the scene unattended.'

'No, sure. Okay, I'll fetch a drink for you.'

Raj was still flustered when he nodded.

Shields accompanied Georgie back to the house. 'Luckily, Dixie-Lee is on a plane with Finella to Ireland. She would be freaking out, seeing this.'

'Why do you think I didn't open that garage door before she left?'

Shields frowned. 'I don't know.'

'I thought I got a whiff the other day when I opened the bathroom window, but I thought it best to get Dixie-Lee away. So that's why I bought a ticket for her to travel to Ireland with Finella. She's experienced way too much drama and I wanted to give myself time to visit Rodney and get some answers before I opened that garage door. He told me the car belonged to Hockenberry, so I knew then it was time to unveil the truth.'

'Dixie, although he is no longer with us, will be charged with murder if there is enough evidence.'

'I know, but this will also open up a can of worms and hopefully uncover the truth behind this Lord Hockenberry and his cronies, the rapist paedophiles.'

'What?'

'Hugh, let's get a drink, and I will explain everything. By the way, you have a new client, Rodney Potter.'

***

After a few minutes, the madness of the flies died down and most had left the garage. Raj called Fitzgerald and explained the situation, and before he ended the conversation, he said, 'Gov, don't send anyone apart from my team.'

'Absolutely, Raj. I don't want any outside interference. This case is all yours, buddy. And, by the way, I should tell you that Drake and his team are suspended pending an investigation.'

Before the garage would be an official crime scene, Raj walked back inside and had a chance to look around. He noticed a small open box like a letter rack. In it were some letters and prominently placed on the top was one for Rohan.

Being super careful, Raj took them all out and photographed them. He knew forensics would bag them up and take them away, but he wanted to be sure they would be returned. There was a letter for each member of the family. The last letter was for himself, which utterly shocked him. Underneath his name, it said: **The Truth**. He would rush the letters through forensics to be able to read them and make a case – a case against Lord Hockenberry.

Raj was cringing, knowing he should look at the body and make some notes, but it was so grotesque. The face was eyeless and crawling with maggots, and the skin was a multitude of colours. Rats had chewed away at the lips; he thought he had seen one scurrying under one of the wheel arches of the car. He gagged and momentarily turned away. When he looked back, he noticed something he recognised. A Marilyn Monroe wig and a pink bikini. They looked to be the same as those in the photograph that Matias had sent him. Matias must have uncovered something: however, he was on annual leave for three weeks. He would chase it up as soon as he could get away from this stinking garage. After taking one last photo, he looked away to face the letters again.

The letter for Rohan was not sealed, so he slid the single piece of paper from the envelope and read three simple lines.

If I don't manage to see you, know this, brother. I give you and Georgie my blessing. Please love her and Dixie-Lee and be the man I couldn't be. Make a life for them. Make up for what I put them through – I love you, Ro.

Those three lines almost had Raj in tears, but he quickly composed himself when he saw Georgie approaching with a tall glass of iced water. 'Are you okay, Raj?'

He smiled, came out of the garage, and gratefully accepted the drink. 'Yes, I am. Dixie was a good man. I think he did what he had to do. And I do believe that man in the boot of the car is most likely Lord Hockenberry.'

'Raj, will you call his daughter and have her identify him?'

Raj screwed up his face. 'Aw, I don't know. That ghoulish-looking corpse in the boot of that car is probably more for forensics to identify.'

'*Raj*, will you have *James*, the fucking woman who had Mac and Brodie tortured, identify *her father*?'

After a second or two, Raj realised what Georgie was actually asking of him. 'Sure, yes, you are quite right. She should.'

'Brodie said he wanted her punished, whatever that looked like. If that corpse is as bad as you say it is, then her identifying it may well be the punishment she deserves. I guarantee it will leave her with night terrors for the rest of her life. I think the trauma Brodie and Mac went through will haunt them forever. And no one should be allowed to get away with that.'

Raj stared into Georgie's cold unmoved eyes, 'And you, Georgie, won't let anyone get away with a wrongdoing, will you? But you will make it right in your own way.'

She smiled, uneasily, not sure what that comment was supposed to mean.

'Oh, and, Georgie, the police will want to go over your house because Dixie lived there too, so I would remove the wire tools. I saw them in the kitchen. Very nice tools they are too. And I suggest you remove whatever else you may have lying about that you wouldn't want questioned.'

It was at that moment Georgie was reminded of the fact that the only person who knew the truth about her was Raj. And yet, the one thing she didn't know about him was why he had never pursued an arrest. 'So, you know what I did? Why didn't you, er . . .?'

'Because I joined the police to get the bad guys. We don't always do that. We sometimes get the good ones instead and let the bad guys go free, and that's not who I am, Georgie. So your secret will always be safe with me.'

Once he had finished the cold drink, he watched her return to the house. He was alone, with curiosity reaching its peak. His trust in the force had dwindled so much he couldn't trust anyone. So, he had to take a quick look in the box before forensics carted everything away and the contents went missing.

Inside the box, there was a pile of office binders. He opened the top one to find cellophane sleeves, and as he turned over each one, he realised that the photos were telling a story.

The first set were of Hockenberry meeting other suited men; most were over sixty. There were photographs of the men collectively and singularly, and each photo was labelled **Paedophile**. Then, he saw images of a house and a gated drive; this one was labelled **The Sick Den**. The next set of photos were of young lads, which had been marked **The Victims**. He shuddered when he saw the extent of the sickening pictures of young lads tied up; some were as young as ten. Raj noticed the images of the kids were taken through a window, no doubt using a telephoto lens. But more damaging for the powerful men involved was that they were also in the photos – even naked – with the young lads.

Raj's heart raced as he uncovered the work of a top-class detective, Dixie Deacon. Then, as he got near the end of the file, there was a crystal-clear image of a man he knew well, but not for a good reason; it was Martin Drake who was drinking with Hockenberry and Carol Lardon. He turned to the next sleeve and discovered a disturbing picture of Drake with a lad who was clearly not of age. He stared for a moment in utter shock and hoped Dixie had more than just photos. In anxious anticipation, he hurriedly opened the next file. Bingo! There were names, dates, descriptions, maps, times, and even phone numbers. And on the last few pages were statements from boys and their ages, who ranged from eleven to fifteen.

However, more importantly, there was an iPad tucked at the very bottom. Raj made an educated guess that it was used to watch anyone trying to break into the garage by using the camera above the garage door. He also assumed that there was stuff contained in the iPad that hopefully would give them more evidence. Possibly videos.

Raj photographed as much as he could, including many of the photos. What he had just looked at was evidence of a case against several influential men and a woman. He stared at the box. Once he had closed it, he realised that Dixie had tried single-handedly to bring a paedophile ring to its knees. He sighed, wondering how much of this would be eligible in court, since Dixie was no longer alive to give a statement. Or even present to explain the contents of the box.

His mind suddenly returned to the photos that Matias had left in the drawer for him. It dawned on him that those were taken by West. Matias had alluded to the fact that West was being paid his wages by these influential men and he wanted to leave. So as much as Dixie was uncovering a paedophile ring, West was probably doing the same, and no doubt between the contents of the box and West's accounts, they would be able to crush the ring and bring these monsters to justice, even if they were supposed to have been part of the justice system. It made sense now why Drake broke into his private drawer. Maybe he suspected Matias was on to him. Perhaps he recognised Matias as West's boyfriend.

Raj stood there in further thought. He had said to himself a while ago now that he wanted to remove the cancer from the police force. So, come what may, he would finish what Dixie had started.

A year later

Georgie, dressed in a blue suit, could smell the white rose pinned to her lapel; in fact, everyone in the courtroom could smell the white roses because everyone was wearing one apart from the judge, the prosecution, and the usher, including her daughter, who was there among the defence barristers. Georgie was in awe. Dixie-Lee was the youngest person in the legal team and had been permitted to sit in as a pupil. She obviously didn't wear the magpie suit and wig. However, she did wear a fitted navy-blue suit and a white blouse. Her hair was pulled back in a French bun. And as she walked with grace around the courtroom, she filled Georgie with pride. Unexpectedly, tears welled up in her eyes, knowing that Dixie would have no doubt been crying with his chest puffed out and a broad smile on his face, if he were alive. He had been murdered in the middle of collecting evidence that would screw the likes of Hockenberry – even though he was dead – and the rest of the paedophile ring to the wall. And now, watching Dixie's daughter helping to finish what he started was just so endearing to witness.

It seemed to Georgie that she had spent so much time inside a courtroom. The Olivers' case had finished a few months ago now. She'd enjoyed watching Jesse, Jared, and Jonas get their just desserts, but, somehow, she felt saddened when Nancy Oliver was sentenced to ten years in prison. She would be a very old woman when she was released, *but would she come out all the better for it?*

And now this case, which for the first part was all centred around the conviction of this prolific set of paedophiles who were supposed to be in a position to protect the public – not abuse their powers. Naturally, with such well-known figures came colossal press attention, so the world could see the likes of men in power brought to justice, and there, like a little bird in the middle, was her daughter. The trial had gone on for months. Carol Lardon and her brother Paul Lardon had received a lot of attention because she was a woman involved in this ring, and that had infuriated and sickened the public; she was sentenced to fifteen years, and so was her brother, for luring young lads to the members of the ring.

God help her, thought Georgie, *when she ends up inside. The inmates will eat her alive.* She felt no empathy for Carol, though. It was as if she had sensed Lardon was a wrong 'un from day one.

Mac had been present when they sentenced the bully boy who had battered him outside Georgie's house, before taking him to the station. He had been one of the 'Tonbridge Lot', and now they were treated as guilty by association. The guy got four years. It was a long sentence, but Hugh Shields had been told that the judge would not be lenient because the likes of these men in this ring had managed to shatter the public's belief that the judiciary was there to protect them. So high-powered members of the MI5, the police, and the judiciary were losing the respect they had once earned from the community.

She remembered the look of a frightened child on Martin Drake's face as he stood in the dock awaiting the jury's verdict, and when they found him guilty, he fell to his knees screaming like a baby before the judge announced he was sentencing him to life in prison.

Raj had forgotten himself and whooped so loudly that everyone glanced his way.

Petra, like a naughty schoolgirl, sniggered and gripped his hand. 'You did it, Raj, mate.'

'No, Petra, it was a joint effort.' He smiled, thinking about the letter Dixie had left for him. *That was a revelation and then some*, he thought. He tapped the letter that was folded up in his pocket. **The Truth**, it read on the envelope. Inside on a single piece of paper, Dixie had written the following:

Dear Raj, I don't know you well, but I think I'm a good judge of character. If you should find this, then it's because I'm probably dead, murdered by MI5, but check the files inside the cardboard boxes and you'll know what I'm talking about. I felt you needed the truth before my wife, Georgie, gets arrested. I killed Marston-Smith. I was on his boat, and when he went underneath to retrieve a container of drugs, I started the engine, knowing he was next to the propeller. I wanted to turn him to mush for what he had done to my wife, but, sadly, I only

partially decapitated him. I understand you are one of the good guys, so Georgie told me, so I hope you believe me. I wish you well capturing the scumbag connected to the paedophile ring. Everything you need is in the box, and hidden in my wardrobe is a pair of trainers that will have DNA evidence on them. I managed to retrieve them from that mansion house. You have all the details. If the other items in the box concern you, they are my son's baby teeth and his favourite toy. I only wished I had got the chance to buy the trainers Joseph wanted instead of saving his old ones as evidence. Thanks in advance, Raj.

Dixie Deacon

Giving Petra's hand a squeeze, he focused on the case in front of them. Because today was the final day of Rodney Potter's retrial, based on the overwhelming evidence proving his innocence. Of course, even though everyone knew the outcome, there were still the formalities to be concluded and everyone who could be there was there.

Georgie looked across at Raj. He was standing at the back with Matias and West. She had got to know them well during the trials.

West had spent hours giving evidence. He confirmed everything Dixie had documented and photographed. And he, too, had followed Hockenberry and managed to photograph a little lad, but he could not help the boy for fear of being caught before collecting enough evidence to bring Hockenberry to justice. Little did he know the boy was Joseph Deacon, Dixie's son.

Everyone stood up when the jury came in and they held their breath waiting for the result. The foreperson of the jury read the unanimous verdict: NOT GUILTY. The people in the gallery leaped up from their seats in a rapture of claps, whoops, and screeches.

Shields and the rest of the legal team hugged and patted Rodney Potter. Everyone loved him; he was a sweet man, living with the worst heartache anyone could bear.

Georgie watched as the usher came forward and handed Rodney the trainers that Dixie had kept in his wardrobe – the trainers he had snuck into the evil den and retrieved before he hid them, knowing they would be used in evidence.

Rubbing her tingling nose, Georgie sniffed back the tears as Rohan slid his arm around her shoulders. 'Dixie did good, eh? Without him, those monsters would still be carrying on raping and destroying people's lives.'

***

The next day

Georgie looked at the three white roses in her hand and then peered across at Finella, who was in tears as she also clutched her three roses.

Finella glanced back at Georgie, and a sad smile swept across her face. This was a hard day. This would be the day she would go to her son's grave, knowing they buried him beside his son Joseph, the grandson she'd never got to meet, and his second love Janey.

As far as the eye could see, the graveyard was packed with people; from reporters to well-wishers, and even some of the prison staff were there. And every one of them was holding white roses. All except Rodney Potter. He'd only just been released from prison, and so he hadn't got to see where his daughter and grandson were buried. Brodie's friend, a stonemason, had made three matching gravestones, hoping Rodney would approve. And today, all the Deacons were at the graveyard ready to fill the graves with white roses that would symbolise – among other things – innocence, spirituality, and hope.

With three enormous bouquets almost camouflaging herself, Dixie-Lee weaved through the people surrounding Rodney and stopped dead before him with a beaming smile. 'Rodney, you can lay these now.'

His face lit up when he cupped her cheeks and kissed her forehead. 'I can't thank you enough. My Joseph would have loved you so much.'

'I wished I'd got to meet him, Rodney, but all I can say is I am blessed to have you in my life.'

Georgie watched the interaction between Rodney and her daughter, and tears fell down her cheeks before she could stop them. Wiping her eyes, she smiled at Rohan. 'I am so glad we moved, Ro. I think my girl has flourished since. Look at her. She has done such a good job.'

Riley nudged her arm. 'She has, hasn't she, Mrs Deacon.'

'Riley, seriously, you make me feel old. Please call me Georgie.'

'One day, I will. I might even call you my mother-in-law, eh?'

'Don't push it, Riley.'

'Nuffin wrong with my boy, Georgie. At least he stuck around, not like that little pussy boy Marley. I mean, who calls their kid Marley? Ain't it a dog's name? Nah, he missed a trick there with Dixie-Lee. Still, you can't beat my boy.'

'All right, Sheila,' said Georgie, rolling her eyes. 'Marley and Dixie-Lee only went out on one date, and that was a year ago now.'

'Yeah, well, I'm just saying.'

'Come on, let's lay our flowers and get to Henry's café.'

'You will have to stop calling it that,' said Rohan, kissing Georgie's cheek. 'Firstly, it's also yours, and secondly, darling, it's a high-end bakery. No sausage and mash served there.' He laughed. 'But you're right. Let's get over there after we lay the roses. Everyone will be waiting, and after laying the flowers, we have a lot to celebrate.' He kissed her lips and stroked her hand as his fingers ran over the large diamond on her third finger.

'Get a flaming room,' said Sheila, before she squeezed past.

As they started to walk back up the path to their cars, Georgie stopped. 'Sorry, Rohan, I just need a moment.'

Rohan knew she needed to say goodbye to Dixie and so he gave her an understanding nod and continued heading to the car, only looking back briefly to see her walk towards his brother's grave.

Georgie couldn't get too close because the grave was surrounded with roses. As she stared at her husband's gravestone, a tear rolled down the side of her nose. Quickly wiping it away, she felt her daughter's arm slide around her shoulders.

'Are you okay, Mum?'

'Yeah.' She sighed. 'I wanted to tell your dad I loved him so much for so long, and I wanted to thank him for giving me you.' She rubbed her daughter's cheek. 'I just feel a little guilty, I guess.'

'Guilty? Why?'

Georgie wiped away another tear. 'Because of Rohan and because I misjudged your dad. I thought . . . Well, I suppose I was angry with him because I knew he had secrets. I only wished I'd known what they were before he died. Not only that but I wanted him to be the same man he was when we were first married. I had never stopped loving him in eighteen years . . . until your Uncle Rohan.' She paused and bit her lip to stop herself from crying. 'When your dad returned, he shattered my illusion of him and left me bitter, I suppose. I never understood that he was being the man he was meant to be.'

She turned back to her daughter and smiled. 'Outside of the military, he was the country's hero, and I only wished I'd known that. But still' – she sighed again – 'at least we get to lay him to rest with Janey, his one true love, and Joseph, his son.'

'Mum, he wanted you to be with Rohan. I *know* because Uncle Rohan showed me the letter. So don't feel guilty. Please, he wouldn't want that. Me, I'm going to work hard, and if he is watching over us, I'll make him proud.'

As they walked away from the grave, Georgie suddenly felt an alien presence. It must have been a sixth sense because she knew something was not quite right. Glancing back towards the gravestones, she thought she saw someone crouching behind one of them. A cold shiver shot through her body as her finger traced the deep scar hidden under her hair.

Other works by Kerry Barnes

Ruthless

Ruby's Palace

Raw Justice

The Hunted

The Rules

The Choice

Deceit

Cruel Secrets

Wicked Lies

Ugly Truth

Raising A Gangster

Outcast

Voice of Reason

Voice of Rage

Trusted

Taboo

Torment

Nemesis

Printed in Great Britain
by Amazon

55276117R00176